TEA, CAKE & MURDER!

A VERY BRITISH COSY MYSTERY

K.J.HERITAGE

SYGASM

Copyright © K.J.Heritage 2024

Tea, Cake & Murder

Published 2024 by *Sygasm Publishing*

All rights reserved.

Cover design: *K.J.Heritage*

This is a human book. Artificial Intelligence (AI) was not used in any way in the writing or plotting of this novel, nor in its cover design, or in any other aspect of its production. They are far too busy trying to take over the world.

No parts of this publication may be reproduced, stored in retrieval systems, beamed via black hole to other dimensions, copied in any form or by any means, electronic, mechanical, photocopying, recording or otherwise transmitted without written permission from the publisher except for the use of brief quotations in a book review. You must not circulate this book in any format.

Travelling back in time to publish this book before its official publication date is strictly prohibited.

All characters in this publication are fictitious and any resemblance to persons, living, dead, undead, existing in parallel dimensions or those having reached a higher plane to exist as intelligent corporeal gases, smells, or colours, is purely coincidental.

Sygasm Publishing
http://sygasm.com
ISBN: 978-1-915927-26-2

I say!

Contents

Prologue: A Place to Hide

I've been waiting for an eternity, my back propped up against the stolen Land Rover Discovery. The dark wood that stands around me is quiet and eerily still, with only the occasional rustle of leaves to break the silence. I hug my arms to my chest, trying to ward off both the chill in the air and my fear, feeling like someone, or something, is watching me. But that is nothing new for me… I've been watched all my life.

"Why on earth did I come here?" I whisper into the dense foliage. But I know the answer. A desperate plea from my sister, Andromeda. Or at least a desperate message, sent from inside our preferred cell phone gambling game. The way we had learnt to contact each other after the war began and they started rounding up the witchweavers.

Her message simply said:

We need to meet!

Just that, followed by twelve seemingly unrelated words, three of which I put into a popular geocode location app that links unique word combinations to exact geographic coordinates anywhere on earth. Which is what brought me to this precise location. A cold, bleak wood in the middle of bloody nowhere.

Technology and the knowledge of how to use it is what made me and my sister different. It gave us an edge. A way to work against the enemy. Unlike the rest of our kind. But then again, Andromeda and I were always creative. It is why we were so damn good.

Solely relying on majiks made the other witches lazy. They fostered an arrogance against the modern world. Who needs a cell phone when witches have been able to converse majikally with one another for hundreds of years? But we saw their potential. No eavesdropping spells will ever work on a smartphone, that's for sure.

A breath of wind somewhere high up in the boughs above, the leaves whispering and hissing. Places like this freak me out. I'm a townie, like all my kind. The countryside holds no allure. Then again, where else could me and Andromeda meet? It had to be out of the way in the middle of nowhere and in the middle of the night, simply because the cities were too dangerous these days. Too many eyes to seek me out. And they're looking for me. Needing my skills to fulfil their vile plans. But I know how to hide… And it's that ability they want. My skill at weaving concealing spells. I'm the best witchweaver of my generation. Even Andromeda has to admit that.

My phone buzzes. A quick glance at the screen and I freeze…

It's a trap! Get out now! They know where you—

I jump back into the Land Rover and gun the engine, reversing down the muddy track and out upon a small country road, my eyes glancing up at the night, whilst simultaneously casting a See-all spell. A quick flash and the sky becomes bright purple—for me anyway. And there it is, a black thing crawling through the sky, its many snake-like limbs pulling itself along, writhing and searching. My heart sinks. It won't notice the Land Rover, but once it finds me gone, that thing will have my scent. And once a bloodseeker has your scent…

I have no choice but to use my talents to hide myself and soon. But where? The bloodseeker is only minutes away from finding me. I see a large cottage sitting back from the road and slam the brakes, sliding the Rover into the driveway, flooring the accelerator, and glimpsing a 'For Sale' sign.

In seconds, I'm out of the Rover and blasting open the front *doors with a swipe of my wand. The place is uninhabited. No furniture. No books or paintings, nothing.*

No place to hide!

I run through the cottage, doors flying open. The place appears to be empty until I find a study with packed bookshelves on every wall, a series of filing cabinets and a desk with an old computer. Taped up boxes fill the floor space.

I hear the screeching wail of the bloodseeker. It will be on me in moments. I quickly bind the door with another flick of my wand and make a choice. I ignore the banging and clattering of the frustrated bloodseeker outside and centre myself. Slipping down inside my mind, my wand now dancing in the air before me, like a sped-up spider creating its web, weaving, and knitting at a frantic pace.

New spells are difficult, they can take months to master, and I only have moments. I need to be as accurate as possible, but that's just not going to happen. The spell, if I can finish it, will be unpredictable.

A blast from outside and the door rattles, majiks spitting and fizzling around the hinges.

Just a few moments more…

Another explosion and another. Dammit!

My spell isn't finished, but I have no choice. I knit the threads together and ignite them with the blazing torch of my mind, just as the door blows inward, consuming me in blue and purple flame…

Death & Cake

"**M**ISS! I'm sorry to wake you, but it's a note from the vicar! …Miss!"

I open my eyes to find a flustered-looking woman in a badly fitting bonnet staring down at me with an insistent look plastered across her wide, red face. Who on earth is she and what is she blathering on about? I'm groggy and dull-headed as if I've awoken on the wrong side of a bottle or two of Shiraz, but instinctively knowing that isn't the case. No matter, I fully expect things will come back to me soon. "A note from who?" I mutter, my voice oddly posh-sounding and high-handed with a hint of an accent.

"A note from the vicar!" the woman repeats, waving a square of folded paper covered in spidery writing at me like it is some kind of improvised fan.

I sit up and find myself in a quaint, chintzy-like bedroom with far too many hanging patterned sheets and flowery bits for my liking. It's a rather old-fashioned, country-style room with white walls and a wooden floor. The furniture is mostly antique pieces, including an old mahogany dresser that stands against one wall, flanked by two wingback chairs and a tall wardrobe. A dressing table sits close to an open window, next to an ancient looking radiator. I'm lying in a four-poster bed, covered with a patchwork quilt and an array of colourful pillows. An open door leads to what looks like a bathroom and another to a landing outside. A fire roars in a fireplace on the far wall facing me whilst a draft of air blows inside from flung open windows. The quality of the light is summery, but the air has a morning chill to it.

"You need warmin' and airin', miss," the woman says in explanation, her voice a mix of hard to place, generic rustic tones. "A roarin' fire to keep you warm, and fresh air to improve your humours. Somethin' I swear by."

I eye the woman again, hoping for my recollection to return, but she's a complete stranger to me. "Who… who are you?"

"I'm Molly, miss, your new maid." She performs a half-curtsy.

I give her the once-over. Molly is a short, thickset woman of indeterminate age, dressed in an old-fashioned maid's uniform. A mad array of russet-blonde curls sprout from underneath her bonnet, seemingly with no real idea about what they are doing there, other than adding to her general sense of agitation. "Have we met before?" I ask with the startling tone of an interrogator.

"Yes, miss, the day you arrived."

I stare at her again. Nothing. This isn't an early morning brain freeze, but something more serious. "Then, my dear, it appears we have somewhat of a situation." My voice sounds odd to me, the words precise and well-formed, like I'm giving a lecture rather than having a conversation. And I sound so dreadfully condescending, even though that isn't my intention.

Molly doesn't appear to notice or care—she's far more fixated upon the note she's holding. "That's right, miss… the vicar's comin'!"

"The situation I'm referring to doesn't actually involve the vicar—whoever he may be, not yet at least—but it does very much involve the fact that I have no idea what this place is, who you are, and, most importantly of all, *who I am*. Unless my thumping headache is anything to do with it. Have I been in an accident?"

She gives me a wide, inane smile. "You were taken all peculiar after your long trip from Africa, miss. You've been asleep for nearly two days, no wonder you're all discombobulated."

Africa? Could that be the reason for my odd sounding voice?

Molly waves the note insistently at me and I feel obliged to take it off her.

Miss Emily Crookshanks
Woodside Cottage

The penmanship is excellent and practised. Lots of cursive sweeps, loops and self-important twiddly bits. The name meant nothing. "And that's me is it… this Emily Crookshanks woman?"

"Yes, of course, miss."

"And this reverend fellow?"

"He's comin' here for tea," Molly says, carefully pronouncing her aitches. "This morning!"

"How do you know that? I haven't opened the note yet?"

Molly flushed. "It were young Billy, miss. It were 'im who delivered it. Does a lot of work for folk around the village. Mostly deliveries and whatnot. Said the reverend was plannin' to visit you. And I'm sorry for speakin' so plainly, miss, but you 'ave to finally get out of that bed, get dressed, and come down to meet 'im."

Something isn't right. I'm anxious, but I'm not sure what about. "I don't think I'm up to meeting more people. Not at the moment."

"But you can't say no to a vicar…"

"Write him a note back at once and apologise," I bark, again unintentionally, my voice ricocheting off the walls."

"Me write a note, miss? Me? A maid? To the vicar! I couldn't. I just couldn't. That'd be such an insult, miss. The Rev'rend 'as it in for me as it is. And besides…" Molly's voice dries.

"What is it, Molly?"

"You can't say no to a man of God. You just can't." She crosses herself dramatically. "And Mrs Willoughby won't be 'appy with me. Not at all. She's a big lady with quite a lip on her. I sure don't want to get on her wrong side."

"She sounds like an ogre."

"It's not for the likes of me to say one way or t'other, especially as she does so much work for the church, havin' taken over the duties of the vicar's poor wife."

"What's wrong with the wife?" I ask, a strange euphoria enveloping me. Asking questions is giving me quite the thrill.

"Now you mention it, I'm not sure. She's not well enough to help the vicar like a vicar's wife ought to. That's all I know. She spends a lot of time in her rooms and even misses the Sunday sermon. And no one dares to miss 'is sermon. So it must be somethin' serious. But here I am blatherin' away when the vicar 'as sent you an important note...."

I take the hint, opening the envelope and unfolding the paper.

The Reverend Wilson-Smallsey
The Vicarage
Little Pucklewick

Monday, June 5th 1922

Dear Miss Crookshanks,

Let me first welcome you to the enchanting village of Little Pucklewick. It is a quiet place, with everything fitting perfectly in its place. I'm sure you will also fit in perfectly.

I would have invited you to the vicarage, but I am informed that you are presently indisposed which is the reason you missed my church service yesterday. No doubt due to a malaise associated with your travels from that awful continent upon which you previously resided. No matter, God's representative on earth will find a way for all of his flock to hear his word!

Please be expecting me today at eleven o'clock this morning, prompt.

Yours faithfully,

The Reverend Wilson-Smallsey

The man's signature is as wide as the page. "He sounds rather pompous."

"The Reverend Wilson-Smallsey knows everythin' that goes on in Little Pucklewick, miss. And he takes 'is duties seriously. Very seriously. Like I said, you can't say no to 'im. You just can't."

The woman is on the verge of tears. "I see." The letter intrigues me as does the man and I realise that I want to meet this Wilson-Smallsey. I take a deep breath. "The last thing I desire is to cause an international incident. I suppose I could meet the fellow."

Molly squeals in delight.

"Apparently, he's coming here at eleven o'clock prompt."

"The reverend is comin' at eleven?" Her excitable green eyes glance nervously at an impressive clock perching heavily on the mantle above the fire. "That's only an 'our and a 'alf! Right! I'll get downstairs and get started on me bakin'. And after that I'll make a fire in the sittin' room and be back up here to dress you."

Before I can tell her that I am more than capable of

dressing myself, she's gone, thumping out of the room like an elephant on a mission to snaffle all the buns.

I get out of bed, noticing something drop to the floor. An antique fountain pen made from polished and rolled tortoiseshell. I pick it up noticing how nicely it fits in my hand. Perhaps I'm a writer of some kind? Shrugging, I make it to the window on unsteady feet and stare outside, unexpectedly feeling vulnerable and stepping back to peek from behind the curtains. This house sits on a small hill with a gnarly, old wood to one side and a picturesque village on the other, both nestling within an impressive, sweeping, velvety green valley. Little Pucklewick—what an odd name—looks like a picture postcard created by an artist who possessed a romantic love of the past. It's almost too perfect. A beautiful church sits across the lane at the bottom of my garden. Beyond is a village green circled by shops and cottages. The village itself is surrounded by greener-than-green fields, criss-crossed with hand-built stone walls and crammed with sheep and black-and-white cows.

I enter the bathroom and wash myself, pipes rattling as the water struggles to warm up, aware of my reflection in a large mirror, and frightened of it. I steel myself and take a look. But it's just me. Emily Crookshanks, I guess. A rather good-looking woman, in her thirties with long, unruly hair and intense green eyes.

There's another door in the bathroom that leads to a walk-in wardrobe where I find an array of similar-styled black jackets, trousers and skirts, and a rack of black boots. However, the chief feature of this room are the shelves of brightly coloured hats festooned with costume jewellery, bows, feathers, and other adornments. The hats look out of place against the drab black clothing. Flamboyant and ostentatious maybe, but beautiful. I find myself mesmerised by them.

I put on a grey blouse and a skirt. But the skirt doesn't

look right on me. Instead, I choose black trousers. They are loose around the legs but tight-fitting around my bottom. I look in the angled mirrors and I'm impressed. Next, I pull on a pair of boots and find that they fit me with the intimacy of long use. The jackets are long, and all have multiple pockets. Both inside and out. I marvel at how functional they are. I slip one on and check myself in the mirror. My bottom is hidden by the long jacket, which is probably for the best. But something is missing. What I need to complete the ensemble is some decent headgear. And I have a vast choice. I try on the different hats, which are all agreeable but just not quite right. I spot some hatboxes and accidentally knock them over. One of them opens and spills out newspaper cuttings from a series of South African newspapers, cut-outs that feature a rather fetching woman wearing a long jacket with many pockets, trousers, and boots. *Myself!* And perched on my head, a series of fantastic hats, some that I recognise from my collection. I scan the headlines.

The Headmistress solves the mystery of the disappearing Pretoria Pearl

The Cape Town Cutthroat caught by amateur sleuth, Emily Crookshanks, the Headmistress

The curious incident of the body in the locked attic – another triumph for Emily Crookshanks

I read some of the stories, marvelling at myself. I've solved a lot of high-profile mysteries and made quite the name for myself as a sleuth. So what am I doing in England with amnesia? I notice one more cutting.

Emily Crookshanks—the scandal that shook South Africa

Before I can read further, Molly shouts from downstairs.

"I lost all track of time, miss! The vicar, he's comin' up the path now!"

I drop the newspaper cut-out, grab a magnifying glass from the dresser top, and the nearest hat—bright red with a large purple bejewelled bow and a single magnificent peacock feather—and quickly head downstairs just as the doorbell tinkles.

"The Rev, he's here!" Molly appears from what I'm guessing is the kitchen. "You're not meeting the vicar looking like that... are you?"

"What's wrong with the way I'm dressed?" I reply, taken aback.

"I'm sorry miss, there's no time to change now." She quickly points me towards the sitting room, and I slip inside and sit down, noticing that the windows are wide open, letting in rain from an early summer shower, the sun shining beautifully from behind heavy droplets. I experience an urge to slam them shut and to quickly draw the curtains—but I'm not sure why. The room is warm from another of Molly's roaring fires. My maid is, I'm guessing, rather peculiar.

I hear the flustered tones of Molly as she ushers the Reverend Wilson-Smallsey inside and, seconds later, the sitting room door opens to reveal a rather imposing but charismatic-looking gentleman in his late fifties. Handsome and then some, with an unexpectedly rugged jawline and impressive cheekbones. His full head of thick white hair gives him an unkempt appearance, and yet it doesn't detract from his good looks. If anything, his hair, unlike Molly's curls, knew exactly what it was doing upon his head—being weirdly sexy for a start. He stands a good six-foot and strides into the room with a sense of grandiose purpose that comes with all self-important men.

"Ah, Miss Crookshanks, so very pleased to meet you." His voice is a loud drone with more than a whiff of pomposity.

His eyes widen at the sight of my hat, and even wider when he sees my trousers.

I notice raindrops and freshly cut grass on his boots. "I hope you didn't get caught in the shower?" I stand up to welcome him, but he ushers me back to my seat with a condescending wave of a long-fingered hand.

"I always carry a brolly. As I say to my flock, *to pray is to ask God for rain*."

"It is?"

"Indeed so, Miss Crookshanks, and faith... *faith is carrying an umbrella*."

Molly gives me a supportive nod and disappears.

The reverend's collar is expertly starched, unlike the skin of his face which is pleasingly tanned. His cassock is tailored, made slightly tighter than necessary to emphasise his broad shoulders. A conscious decision to make him appear more imposing, and more attractive. I notice the brown stained fingers on his left hand—the man is a lefty as well as a chain smoker. Despite the application of a mint, I can still smell the tell-tale aroma of smoke on his breath. And he's been drinking, evidenced by a slight slur to his words and the clear outline of a hip flask in his cassock pocket. The details flood into my mind in a most peculiar and satisfying way. But then again, I suppose I'm *the Headmistress*, amateur detective and sleuth extraordinaire.

"Now my dear, I hope you realise that the village women are all in a tiz about your arrival? They are desperate to discover who you are. Your maid has been chit-chatting to all and sundry, of course, the curse of her gender and her class, but she has been unusually short on details. So I'm here to put wagging tongues to rest."

The reverend sits down, smiling to reveal a spectacular array of Stonehenge-esque teeth—if the monument was still standing, that is—his eyes sparkling underneath overgrown black eyebrows that contrast sharply with his whiter than white hair. Occasionally jumping and twitching like two warring caterpillars when he speaks. I'm mesmerised by them.

"It's not just Molly who likes a bit of gossip, regardless of her class. Admit it, vicar, you're just as interested in who I am as are all those village ladies." Again, I notice how the tone of my voice is more acerbic than intended, but, like my boots and trousers, it fits me well. And besides, I like it.

The smile, plastered upon the Reverend Wilson-Smallsey's face, disappears as abruptly as it had arrived. "Quite. I can see that your life living abroad has made you bolder than is normally expected of a respectable country lady, even in these so-called modern days." He pauses, as if to let the rebuke sink in, before his smile returns, this time, even wider. "But that will not put me off, my dear. It will only encourage me. It's why men like myself are put on earth. Why God put me here. To help those lost sheep find their way back home."

He places a hand on mine. Can it be possible? Is the Reverend of Little Pucklewick something of a lech?

"I do so love new blood."

I pull my hand away, although this doesn't seem to deter the vicar.

"I want you to know that I'm here for you, Emily—may I call you that? It's more informal and I'm all for encouraging informality, especially with my lady parishioners."

The sound of my name sounds weird on his lips, and I don't like him using it.

"I will do my best to make your introduction into Little Pucklewick a smooth one. I will arrange with Mrs Willoughby for you to join her regular Monday morning get-togethers."

"Will you now?"

"Of course." He pats my arm. "She provides scripture and tea, but mainly the gossip that you ladies enjoy so much. She will also help you learn how to… erm… dress in a manner more becoming of an English country lady. Those trousers are most distracting my dear, most distracting. And I'll get Mr Simmons, my curate, to add you to the church rolls. He's new, and rather disagreeable, I'm afraid. But he will soon learn to toe the line."

Before I can protest, Molly bursts into the room proudly carrying a rattling tray of teacups, a teapot, and a rather uneven looking cake. She bustles over, banging it heavily onto the table, giving the reverend a shock. She curtsies, reddens, and quickly leaves.

The reverend looks at the cake with disdain. "Like I said, your housemaid is a terrible cook. It's why she has been unable to get work elsewhere. I will find you a replacement forthwith."

"Molly may have the curls of a rather manic medusa, and the grace of an elephant on heat, but she will do me just fine, vicar."

"Quite… I will nevertheless find you a replacement anyway. I think you will discover that, in this village, I am seen as someone who knows what's best." He smiles with benevolent threat. "With that in mind it would be a dereliction of my duties if I didn't warn you about a certain gentleman. A Mr Eriksen. An explorer recently returned from one of those dreadful foreign lands. And, if I may say so, full of many peculiar and dangerous ideas. If he calls, I would strongly advise you to not answer. Eriksen and his manservant, Sheng, are heathens, and as such I cannot have them preying on the good ladies of this village. I've already had one confrontation with him and I'm afraid it won't be the last. I've forbidden everyone to talk to him."

"And now you're forbidding me?"

The vicar nods, eyes sparkling.

This Mr Eriksen has gotten under the vicar's skin, that's for sure. I make a mental note to seek him out at the first available opportunity.

He takes a sip of tea and a small bite from the cake, grimacing. "Molly will simply have to go. This is unacceptable. I made sure that she knew I was coming this morning, and she serves me this piece of dried-up stodge? No, no, no, no." He slams down his saucer on the table.

"Oh dear, that is a shame, Vicar.

"A shame? It's a disgrace."

"I think you misunderstand me. I'm not referring to Molly's cake, but to you."

"What?"

"Yes, I'm afraid I have quite a strict rule about ungracious behaviour."

"I don't understand…"

"Then let me make it crystal clear. You have come to my house uninvited, you have insulted my maid, my clothing choices, and now my cake. You may be a reverend, but that does not give the excuse to be so rude." My voice is calm but there can be no mistaking that I want the vicar to go and to go now.

"I beg your pardon?"

The vicar must be more sozzled than I realised. I stand up and hold my hand out to him. "I've a busy schedule this morning. Lots and lots to do. Cut-outs to read, hats to try on, very tight trousers to squeeze into. That kind of thing. The list is quite endless."

"You want me to leave? I've only just gotten here?"

"Ah, the penny has finally dropped. That is the thrust of my gist, yes. And the sooner the better."

"Well, I never!" The vicar stands, his face red and full of anger. And I glimpse the real man under the facade. "You're making a serious mistake, my dear, a very serious mistake indeed."

"May I ask if there's any reason why you're still here?"

The Reverend Wilson-Smallsey draws breath to speak, a

peculiar look upon his face, before he pitches forward onto the table, sending cups, plates and cake flying everywhere.

Bamboo & Smudges

I **JUMP** out of my seat, somewhat startled, and notice a wooden shaft sticking out of the middle of the vicar's back. I know instinctively that the man is deceased—his eyes are open and staring—but I check his pulse anyway.

Molly puts her head around the door. "Did I hear somethin' smash, miss?" Her face turns to one of shock. "What's 'appened to the reverend?"

"A very apt question, Molly." My voice sounds matter of fact. I suppose this is not out of the ordinary for me. "There's every possibility that the man has been, well, murdered. In fact, I may be going out on a limb somewhat, but I'd say that's exactly what's happened. And in my sitting room."

"What, miss? The vicar? Killed!" Molly's voice is almost a scream. "What will Mrs Willoughby say? And 'is poor wife. Oh my! Oh my, oh my, oh my!"

I stride over to the open window and look outside, aware of a quick movement in the old wood to the left of the cottage's front garden. My instinct is to climb out and give chase, but I don't know the terrain and, whoever was in the woods, for good or for evil, will be long gone before I can get there.

"But who could've done such a thing?" Molly wails, bouncing up and down like she is on a trampoline. "And why, miss? Who would want to kill the reverend?"

I go back to the vicar and examine the bolt sticking out of his back, marvelling at the accuracy of the shooter, shutting out Molly's hysterics and feeling very much in my element, especially as my pounding headache has disappeared. There's little blood, the shaft pierced the heart, meaning death was almost instantaneous. As for the arrow? It looks like bamboo. But Little Pucklewick is in the heart of England. Bamboo is an exotic wood in these parts.

The tinkle of the doorbell and loud knocking, followed by the sound of the door opening and a posh, sing song voice saying, "What-ho in there! Everything alright? Molly?"

"Thank the saviour! It's Doctor Roberts, miss! In here, sir!"

The door to the sitting room opens and a tall, wide-shouldered, dark-haired man enters. He's in his early thirties, wears a ridiculously thick black moustache, and carries a large medical leather bag.

"Hello," I say, impressed by this quite wonderful specimen of manliness. He's attractive, even with that hairy slug perched above his lip. I notice smudged black ink on his fingers and that the bottoms of his trousers are wet.

"I'm so sorry for barging in like this but I heard Molly screaming and… I say, is that Wilson-Smallsey?" He strides over to the prone vicar and checks his pulse, frowning at the shaft of wood sticking out of his back.

"I've already done that, doctor. I'm afraid he's as dead as the proverbial doornail."

"He is that… the man has bought it alright. Crikey! Molly, be a good girl and go and call Inspector Troughton at the new station, will you?"

Molly says nothing, her mouth open, staring at the corpse.

"Snap out of it, girl! I'm rather afraid the vicar has passed away, and it certainly wasn't from a heart attack. Go and get the inspector on the horn now!" Molly stops her nervous bobbing and takes a few steadying breaths. "Yes, doctor."

"And for God's sake don't mention what happened, otherwise it will be all over the village, you know what Ethel at the call centre is like. Just tell Inspector Troughton that the doctor says he must come over straightaway."

Molly wipes at her tears, nods determinedly, and leaves.

The doctor sticks out an awkward hand. "I'm Cecil Roberts. But everyone calls me Ceddars. We have sort of met already, the day of your arrival when you were taken ill. I'm dreadfully sorry that we're meeting again under such awful circumstances."

I shake his hand, my slim fingers looking almost childlike within his large powerful palm. It's also rough like all doctors. I have no recollection of the fellow and I'm sure I would've remembered his absurd moustache and those wide shoulders.

"And what an interesting hat."

I go back to the vicar and bend over.

"By Jove!"

I twist around to see the doctor staring at my trousers. His face reddens and he quickly looks away. "What's the matter, you never seen a pair of trousers on a woman before? Although, admittedly, they fit me better than most."

"Of course, but that fit is so bally unusual," he splutters,

I smile to myself and turn back to the vicar, rifling through the pockets of his cassock.

Ceddars crouches down next to me and frowns. "I say, what the devil are you doing?"

"Looking for clues."

"Now listen here, what? I think you should stop that right away. You're obviously in shock. I suggest that you go upstairs and have a lie down. The inspector and I will take care of this awful business."

I ignore him, pulling out the vicar's hip flask.

"I must insist that you put that back."

I unscrew the cap and give it a sniff.

"Miss Crookshanks, please!"

"Brandy."

"What?" He takes the flask off me and gives it a swig. "I say, the old sneak. The reverend is always warning us about the evils of drink. Seems like the hypocrite enjoyed a secret snifter. And that's expensive hooch."

I continue to rifle through the rest of the vicar's pockets, much to the consternation of the doctor, finding nothing else except cigarette papers and rolling tobacco. I turn my attention back to Ceddars. "You arrived here quickly. One could say, suspiciously quickly. Did you see or hear anything unusual?"

"I beg your pardon?"

"Do you now? I don't give out pardons, unless you want to be let off for ogling me so unashamedly?"

Ceddars jaw flexes. "I was not ogling," he protests, reddening again. "It's just that the cut of your trousers is—"

"Please answer the question."

He looks at me for long moments before replying. "I was next door making my regular morning visit to poor Mrs Bates, of course. The old dear is quite bedridden, but a jolly old soul all the same. I can't really do anything for her, except offer a friendly face and a smile or two, what?" He smiles, seemingly to show me how it is done, and I warm to the odd fellow, despite the hairy caterpillar squatting on his top lip. "I heard quite the ballyhoo coming from your open windows and… well here I am. Sadly too late to help the vicar." His smile creases into a frown. "You can't possibly imagine I had anything to do with this dreadful business?"

"At the beginning of an investigation it is wise to suspect everyone."

"Oh, hang on! I see it now! You're one of those detective chappies… I mean, chappesses."

"Guilty as charged, doctor."

"How bally wonderful. I love a good murder mystery. I say, what can you deduce from me. I must be swathed in clues and whatnot!"

We both stand up, and I'm aware that he's a good head and a half taller than I am. I let my eyes rove over him, removing my attention from the dead vicar. "Your trouser bottoms are damp, which means you have recently walked through long wet grass. The modern tailored cut of your suit tells me it's from Chadwick's Gentleman's tailors on Jermyn Street, London SW1. That's one of the most expensive gentleman's outfitters in London, which means you have money, more money than you can earn as a country doctor, money that came from an inheritance. My guess is that it was inherited from an older sibling who probably died during the Great War. Your shoes, by contrast, are functional and worn. The left heel slightly more than the right because you walk with a slight limp, which I assume was an injury acquired in the same war. Not as an infantryman though. Your speech tells me you were in the RAF, probably a pilot. A manner of speaking that also makes you sound jovial and approachable—useful in your role as a country doctor. But it hides something deeper. You've seen your share of action and have suffered loss."

"Crikey, that's astounding!"

I smile inside. It appears I have quite the skill for deduction. It's intoxicating, although I can't help but think I've missed a an obvious clue.

"I was nicknamed *The Flying Doc'* in the RAF, as I'd not yet finished my medical training when I earned my wings. And yes, poor Johnnie, my older brother—and quite the bees' knees and all that—bought it early on, poor bugger. He was the real wise head of the fam'. He received the bulk of the inheritance after daddy died—and the reason why I, as the younger brother, trained as a doctor. After Johnny passed away, well, his money came to me, but I'd rather have him back. I miss him so bally much… but how could you possibly know my tailor?"

"I glimpsed the label inside your jacket and guessed the rest."

"Hey, isn't that cheating?"

I shrug. "Observation is the mark of a good detective. For instance, those black smudges on your fingers. I did wonder if they came from your morning paper, but I cannot imagine a doctor would leave the house without first washing his hands, especially if he is supposed to be touching and examining patients—and shaking hands with devilishly attractive women."

"Golly! In all the commotion, I'd forgotten about that."

"Forgotten about what?"

"Nothing important."

I hold out my hand. "Give it to me, doctor."

"I say, what?"

"You unconsciously touched your right trouser pocket where there is a bulge."

He looks down and frowns.

I'm almost intoxicated by my powers of deduction. It gives me a confidence I've never felt before. "You will come to learn that it's impossible to hide anything from me, doctor. Now hand it over."

He reluctantly pulls out a screwed-up piece of paper and gives it to me. "I found it pinned to the garden gate of the vicarage on my way to Mrs Bates' earlier."

I carefully unravel it, making sure to get no ink on my fingers, and reveal an alarming poster:

> **Do you know the real Reverend Wilson-Smallsey? Would it shock you to discover that he:**
>
> *Has lied about the true feelings of his heart to trusting souls?*
>
> *Has hounded an innocent girl to an untimely death?*
>
> *Is an adulterer and a bigamist?*
>
> *Has fathered many bastards?*
>
> *Has embezzled church funds?*

Is a drunk and a gambler?

He is all these things and more!

"My, my! That's quite a full list of accusations. Have you heard any of them before?"

"Of course not! I say, this couldn't be related to the murder, could it?"

He's deflecting. My guess is that one or more of the rumours are true, or at least he thinks they are. "Was this the only poster you saw?"

He nods.

"But if there's one, it's likely there will be others." The crumpled paper has given me another clue. One that I decide not to share with the doctor. "You decided to keep this, any reason why?"

He shrugs. "No reason, other than I was in a rush. I could've easily thrown the bally thing away."

"I see. From my own limited experience of the vicar, from what I saw of him this morning, I'd say he was somewhat of an unsavoury fellow."

"You would? But the ladies of the village all loved the chap. Doted on him in fact."

"He was very much in love with the sound of his own voice and came across as pompous and domineering. And one other thing… he was far too touchy-feelie for my liking."

"*Touchy-feelie?* Oh, I see. Touchy-feelie! Haha. I'll have to remember that one." Ceddars says, his warm, green eyes sparkling above a quick smile, a smile that abruptly disappears. "You're saying the vicar tried to… to interfere with you?" A flash of anger and his face darkens.

I shake my head. "Let's just say that he was used to women being far more compliant around him." I fold up the poster and place it into one of my jacket's many inner pockets. "I was actually kicking the annoying fellow out of my house when he unexpectedly performed a fatal face-dive into Molly's cake."

"You have a very peculiar vernacular, Miss Crookshanks. And you're so very direct. It's bally refreshing, what?"

I smile at the compliment, although I'm not sure Ceddars meant it that way. One thing is for sure though, both of us are very comfortable being this close to death. But then again, he is a doctor and survived the most awful war in human history.

"I say, you don't think someone possibly saw this poster, got angry, and decided to take a quick pot-shot at the old vicar? Blimey! Or maybe it was the person who put them up that did it?"

"Possibly. I saw movement in the wood next to the house soon after the shooting. I'm sure someone was in there."

"You did? Golly. That's why you were interested in my damp trousers. Mrs Bates' garden is somewhat overgrown. I really must get my gardener to come over. And with the recent shower…"

"Apart from the posters, is there anyone you know of who had a gripe with the vicar? I heard that he had a recent confrontation with a Mr Eriksen?"

"You know about that?"

"You will discover that I know an awful lot of things, doctor."

"But how?"

"The vicar mentioned him just before popping his clogs."

"Let's not forget this is a man of the cloth we're talking about, Miss Crookshanks."

"Tell me about the confrontation."

He gives me another frown and takes a deep breath. "William Eriksen was giving a talk at the village hall about his recent travels to the Far East and China yesterday evening when it was interrupted by the vicar and Mrs Willoughby. The vicar was quite miffed. That manservant of Eriksen's,

Sheng, I believe he is called, has been hosting spiritual get-togethers with some members of the village and the vicar had his nose put out of joint. Banned everyone in the village from attending. There was quite the verbal dogfight. And Sheng, well you know what they say about Chinese chappies, what? Inscrutable and such and such. Well, Sheng was just about the least inscrutable fellow I've ever met. He had a rather murderous expression on his face... or so I thought. Eriksen had to abandon his talk, which I found particularly dull as it happens. He'd even brought in some of his finds from foreign lands."

"I'm guessing one such find was a crossbow of some kind, am I correct?"

The doctor nods, a surprised look on his face. "How can you possibly know that? Unless..." he examines the bolt closely. "Golly, this is bamboo, isn't it? Gosh, you don't think Eriksen or Sheng are responsible, do you?"

I give him a hard stare. "I thought you said you were a fan of mystery novels."

"I am. Why are you looking at me like that?"

"Because the murderer is unlikely to use a weapon that ties him or herself to the victim. What is likely, however, is that whoever killed the vicar witnessed the argument last night, saw what you saw and took the opportunity to steal the crossbow and implicate Sheng or Eriksen in the murder. Obviously."

"Yes. Right. Of course. I rather got ahead of myself there. Unless, you know, this was a crime of the moment? Sheng did appear murderous. And from what I've heard, the fellow is rather dangerous. A weapons' man by all accounts."

"You do seem overly convinced of your theory, doctor. If you are indeed a fan of mysteries, you must always be surprised when you get to the denouement."

"I am rather. But I'm sure I'm right about Sheng. Would put the family silver on it, what?"

A knock at the door and the flustered sounds of Molly talking to someone. A few moments later, a rat-faced, short man enters the room. He wears an ill-fitting blue suit that has seen better days and carries a raincoat folded over his arm. A portly and red-faced police constable follows him. The man takes off a worn homburg and places it down with his coat. "Good morning, doctor, and I believe you are Miss Crookshanks? I'm Inspector Troughton and this is Constable Jakes… now, what is all this about?"

Scribbles & Threat

"**WHAT** all this is about, inspector, is that the local vicar has been murdered in my sitting room by a person or persons no doubt hiding in the wood next to my cottage. Murdered in the 'very much dead' sense of the word if that helps?"

"Yes, Molly did inform me of what had occurred." His voice is condescending, containing an irritating nasal twang. His thin, dark hair is greased back onto his skull, and like the doctor, he too possesses a moustache, but it is a thin, emaciated-looking thing. Less of a hairy slug and more of a squashed fly.

Ceddars gasps with exasperation. "And I bally well told Molly to keep quiet about it."

Inspector Troughton stands at an officious distance away from the body, as if its presence is offensive to him. "Take a look at the vicar, constable."

"Me, sir?"

"Yes, constable, and be sharp about it."

Constable Jakes, who appears to be mightily flustered by the situation, makes a big show of removing his helmet and placing it under the crook of his arm before bending over the body, the rounded pate of his bald head wobbling unsteadily. "He's dead, sir."

The inspector takes out a black leather-bound notebook and a small pencil. He opens the notebook, licks the end of the pencil, and begins to write painfully slowly. "Are you sure?"

The constable puts his helmet down and struggles his

immense weight onto one leg, placing his ear to the vicar's mouth. "'He's not breathing, sir, his eyes are open an' glazed. His face is covered in cake, sir. An' what looks like raspberry jam."

Ceddars frowns. "I say, inspector. Didn't you hear Miss Crookshanks? The fellow has passed on."

"That may well be, doctor, but I have to follow procedure. Especially in an extraordinary case such as this one. Any visible wounds, constable?"

Jakes pushes himself back up, his face reddened and somewhat guilty looking. "There's somethin' sticking out of his back, sir. A thick wooden arrow."

The inspector scribbles into his book. I notice that he is left-handed, his hand struggling to push the pencil across the page. The words are small and precise, and I get the impression that he is more interested in how they look than any evidence they may contain. "I see. Now Doctor Roberts, can you certify, in your role of general practitioner for Little Pucklewick, that the body found in the sitting room of Woodside Cottage, Little Pucklewick, is the Reverend Wilson-Smallsey, vicar of Little Pucklewick?"

I lift my eyes away from the annoying detective's notebook. "But wait a minute, aren't *you* going to examine the body?"

"The constable has identified that the vicar is deceased, and that he was most likely murdered. And I particularly wanted Constable Jakes to do so." He gives Jakes a cold stare and the man lowers his eyes, the guilty look returning to his already flustered face. Troughton turns back to Ceddars. "If you could answer the question, doctor?"

"Yes, inspector, the body is that of the vicar."

More scribbling. "And may I assume that you have examined the body?"

"Yes, yes I did."

"And in your expert opinion, is the Reverend Wilson-

Smallsey deceased?"

Ceddars flicks me an exasperated look. "The vicar is most certainly dead. The wooden bolt observed by your constable is in my opinion the cause of death. It entered in the upper back and most likely punctured the heart or aortic artery. Death would've been almost instantaneous."

The inspector turns to me, after spending more long moments scribbling in his notebook. "Now Miss Crookshanks, in your own time, tell me exactly what happened this morning?"

I go through the events while the inspector writes everything down, line by slow line.

"You say he was shot through the window?"

I nod impatiently. "Most likely from the woods."

Ceddars points, somewhat excitedly. "And that's a bamboo bolt."

"I will be the judge of that, sir."

"Shot by a crossbow very likely taken from the village hall last night during William Eriksen's lecture on the Far East."

"I'm fully aware of what happened last night, doctor."

"You are?"

The inspector turns back a few pages of his notebook and reads, his nasal twang becoming more pronounced and even more annoying. "On the evening of Sunday the fifth of June, in the year of our lord, nineteen twenty-two, the Reverend Wilson-Smallsey, vicar of Little Pucklewick, made a complaint to the local police officer, Constable Jakes. He reported that a threat upon his life had been made by a foreign gentleman in the employ of a Mr William Eriksen who also lives in Little Pucklewick."

Ceddars gives me a triumphant look. "By Jove! That's Sheng alright."

The inspector ignores him and carries on reading. "The name of this gentleman was reported as a *Mr Sheng*. He made the threat to the vicar in front of multiple witnesses as he was leaving a meeting at the village hall. A threat that was verified by a *Mrs Gladys Willoughby*. Isn't that correct, constable?"

"Yes sir. I was policin' the event last night at the behest of Mr William Eriksen, when the lecture he was givin' was interrupted by the vicar an' Mrs Willoughby. I didn't see or hear the threat, but tempers were high, sir, an' things did get out of hand. But I have to admit, I didn't take the threat seriously, sir. I thought it so much hot air, so to speak. I never once considered that…" His voice dries.

"Constable Jakes didn't think it was advisable to go and interview this Mr Sheng, which appears to have resulted in the most terrible of consequences."

"I jus' didn't think there was anythin' to it, sir. I—"

Inspector Troughton holds up his pencil. "Thank you, constable, that will be all. If you could go and stand guard at the gate. A death like this will cause a certain amount of interest and more than the normal share of unwanted prying eyes and wagging tongues."

The constable salutes and leaves.

"And there you see what not following the correct procedure can lead to. Murder most foul. The constable will lose his job over this."

"I say, go easy on him. Poor Jakes is a good fellow, what?"

"Not good enough, I'm afraid." The inspector snaps his notebook shut. "I think I've seen and heard enough to make an arrest. Doctor, I will leave it to you to inform the widow and to get the body removed."

Ceddars nods. "Of course."

I'm incensed. "That can't be it… can it? Any number of people could have heard the argument and the death threat and used that as an excuse to murder the vicar."

Troughton smiles at me as if I'm an errant child. "But where's the evidence?"

I take out the folded poster from my inside jacket pocket and hand it over to the inspector. He makes a big show of unfolding the paper before reading it with feigned disinterest before shaking his head and smiling. "This is a step up from the usual poison pen letters that are common fare in small villages such as this one. And as such, I can't see how it has any bearing on the murder." He scrunches up the poster and throws it into the open fire.

I can't believe that the inspector can dismiss and destroy such an important piece of evidence and I'm quite unable to disguise my anger. "What on earth are you doing, inspector? If any of those accusations are true, it's more than possible that there could be one or more suspects. And besides… only a moron burns evidence!"

A long pause, only punctuated by the slow flexing of Ceddars' astounded jaw and the aghast expression creasing his face.

"You may be new to the village," Troughton says, his pencil pointing threateningly, "and you may have had quite a shock, but I am an inspector of his majesty's police force, and you will treat me with the respect I deserve. Do you understand me?"

"Please forgive the old girl," Ceddars says, trying to calm the visibly annoyed detective. "Miss Crookshanks is something of an amateur sleuth."

A look of dawning realisation crosses Troughton's face. "Oh, I see. Let me assure you, Miss Crookshanks, that unlike all those pompous fictional detectives that no doubt takes up the majority of your bedtime reading, I work in the real world, where motives and murders are so much more straightforward and, dare I say, rather ugly." His eyes flick over to the dead vicar for the first time since he arrived, and he grimaces.

"Miss Crookshanks is far more than a reader, inspector," Ceddars says, coming to my defence. "She is one of those lady detectives, what? She has already deduced that the murder weapon was a crossbow, and the likely suspect was Eriksen's manservant, Sheng."

"I did no such thing?" I protest, realising that's exactly what I'd done.

"But come on, old girl, it's cut and dried. Just look at the evidence."

I grip my hands into twin fists, my knuckles turning white. "Something is off. Something doesn't add up. It's too obvious."

Ceddars smiles encouragingly. "The famous detective gut feeling, what?"

Exasperated, I say nothing.

Inspector Troughton snaps his notebook shut again. "I will contact the superintendent who will need to know about such a high-profile murder, and arrest Mr Sheng immediately, although I suspect he may have already made a run for it. Still, a Chinese gentleman will find it hard to stay hidden for very long in England."

"Sheng won't run, Inspector," I say.

"And why, pray, is that?" Troughton asks, the squashed fly on his upper lip twitching in annoyance.

"Because the man is obviously innocent. An innocence I will prove forthwith."

Troughton gives me a condescending smile, whilst flicking an equally condescending version of the same smile at Ceddars. "You may be wearing trousers, Miss Crookshanks, but murder is a man's business," he says triumphantly, chuckling as if he's just won an intense bout of verbal jousting.

"What if you're wrong? What if Sheng doesn't go on the run? Will you let me speak to him?"

"He will run, Miss Crookshanks, be assured of it. But if he doesn't, you will be more than welcome at the police station. I'll even get Constable Jakes to make you a cup of tea—at least he can be trusted with that. Now, I must be on my way." He replaces his Homburg, nods to us both, and leaves.

I sit down heavily. "He didn't even examine the body. He talked about correct procedure, but he had already made his mind up. That doesn't mean we have to do the same. There's more to investigate here. And you will help me."

"Will I now?"

"Yes, you will."

"I think you see me as the rather well-meaning but dim sidekick, what? But either way, I agree with the irritating detective. Sheng must be the murderer. And with respect, you were not there last night, you didn't see the man. If you had done so, I think you would change your tune. Now, if you don't mind, I need to telephone Mr Shufflebottom, the undertaker."

"I think we should also go and visit the vicar's wife as soon as possible. The news of the vicar's demise will be spreading like wildfire and it's probably best she hears the news from you. I hear she's bedridden which means you must know her quite well. The constable will be able to deal with the undertaker on his own when he arrives."

"We? You mean you're coming with me?"

"Of course."

"You're incorrigible."

"I think you'll find I'm very corrigible, given the right circumstances and a large glass of wine. You do have wine at your place, I hope?"

"I beg your pardon?"

I let the moment linger. Ceddars is quite the figure of a man and just the right amount of dim to keep me interested. "I'm afraid you've already used up all my pardons. Now get a move on."

Ceddars gives me a sideways smile. "I'll phone Shufflebottom."

Outside, a few minutes later, we find a very upset-looking Constable Jakes. Ceddars claps the man on the shoulder. "There, there old chap. I'm sure they'll go lenient on you."

"Thank you, sir. But I think my goose is cooked."

I ask, "Do you know of any reason why the vicar might've been killed other than last night's argument?"

The portly constable shakes his head.

"Has anyone recently seen or heard anything suspicious?"

"Now that you ask, there has been a stranger seen hanging around."

"Whereabouts?"

"The vicarage, miss. An' one sighting on the edge o' town. Oh, an' I glimpsed the fellow at Mr Eriksen's talk last night. I was gonna have a word with 'im, but then all hell broke loose."

"What's his description?"

"Just a short, bearded fella in a brown leather coat, a large cap and glasses, miss. You think he might have anythin' to do with it?"

"I don't know but pass that information onto the inspector."

"Troughton don't like me. He never has."

"If this stranger is somehow involved, and not Sheng, it might be the information to get you off the hook."

"I'll write that down in my notebook, miss, but I don't think it will do any good." He fumbles inside his jacket trying to locate what I'm guessing is a missing pencil.

Ceddars gives me a wink. "A stranger, eh? Methinks you may be hoping too much."

"Maybe, but as I like to say, a clue is always a clue."

"How terribly trite."

Leg-ups & Genders

WE make our way towards the still open sitting room window. I see the prone form of the vicar lying where he fell inside, and, following the trajectory of where the bolt was likely fired, head towards the thickly overgrown wood that overhangs the roughly built shale wall to the left side of my front garden. "The shooter was hiding there. That's a good thirty feet. He or she must be a crack marksman to hit the vicar in the heart from such a distance."

"Rather."

"You must've also fired a few guns in your time in the RAF, Ceddars."

"I see where you're going with this, but what-ho, turns out I'm a bit of a non-starter when it comes to letting off the odd pot-shot. In a kite though, I was rather ding-dong during a dogfight. I mostly shot the Hun's planes rather than our own chaps, mostly, haha. But back on the deck, the closest I got to a fire stick was my service revolver and I only ever took the bally thing out to clean it. Not my bag at all."

I peer over the wall and notice the wet grass and ferns have been trampled. "Footprints. They could've been possibly made by a man with smallish feet or a large woman. I'll know when I take a closer look."

"A woman? You think the murderer could've been a member of the fairer sex?"

"Why not? I take it you're a man of the world. You must know that women share the same shades of light and dark, the same desires and needs as their male counterparts."

Ceddars flushes red. "I'm not sure I should be talking

about such things with a woman I'm barely acquainted with."

I chuckle. "I'm sure you've been acquainted barely with quite a few women."

"I say, now that's enough of that kind of talk."

"But you get my point? Polite society likes to think women are these delicate creatures, but on a personal level, people know the opposite is true. They are, and can be, just as earthy as the next man. Which means they can have the same motives and are just as capable of murder."

"Yes, if you put it like that, I suppose you're right."

"I am right. A detective should suspect everybody. And if we are to spend any time together, you need to know that I'm first and foremost a detective. Secondly, you also need to know that I'm an adult woman of the world, with all those shades of light and dark I mentioned, and of course, all the same desires and needs as my male counterparts."

"By Jove, old girl, you are terribly forward. Are all women from South Africa like you?"

"No one is like me, Ceddars. I'm what you call a one-off." Our eyes meet for a few moments and Ceddars is the first to look away.

"And stop calling me 'old girl'. My name is Emily."

"Right-ho, Em'." He winks. "So, you want me to go along with your idea that Sheng isn't our man. Happy to help, but I'm warning you, I will be playing Devil's Advocate."

"Good. Having a soundboard for my theories will be useful."

"And you think a woman may have done it?"

"Possibly, it would be silly to rule out suspects just because of their gender."

"It's not unheard of, of course, but isn't poison more your gender's game? Arsenic in the ale pie and all that, what? A crossbow is more a fellow's weapon."

"You make an interesting point. But you're wrong. Crossbows have been used by women throughout the ages.

They do not need the upper body strength to pull a bow, and the later crossbows are easy to prime and load."

"You certainly seem to know your stuff, Em'. I am impressed."

I'm also impressed. My breadth of knowledge is not only intoxicating but highly satisfying.

Ceddars shrugs his shoulders. "But I can't help but think that Sheng is somewhat of a diminutive fellow. He's still fitting the bill in my book."

"I'll need to get over the wall for a closer look. Give me a leg up."

"I beg your pardon?"

"Help me over the wall."

"Have you gone quite mad? What if someone sees? What will they think? Me touching a lady's leg and not in my official capacity? That would give quite the wrong idea to the gossips of this village and tongues are already wagging about me and Eriksen's secretary, don't you know?"

"Eriksen has a secretary?"

"Francesca Feltham. She's another of you modern women. Eriksen bought her in to take care of admin' and to help him collate his collection. Smashing young vixen. Very much in control of her red head. But of course, in a village like this, a gal like that… well…"

"Well… what?"

"They assume she's up to no good. Has designs on either Eriksen or myself. They see her as rather shameless to be honest."

"She turned you down, did she?"

Ceddars reddens for seemingly the hundredth time since I've met him. "Is it impossible to hide anything from you?"

I shrug. "Apparently not."

"I see. Well, I did sort of show interest in the gal. In a perfectly honourable fashion of course. Slung my fishing line into the pond so to speak. But the old pike didn't want to bite. It appears the gal is more interested in her career than settling down with a flat tyre like me. Even a rather rich one."

"And Eriksen?"

"If something is going on between them, he is very good at making it look the opposite. He spends all his time on his collection and writing his memoirs. Has his head firmly in the clouds. I doubt he even notices her. Besides, the rumour is that he has interests elsewhere."

"Go on?"

"Another village lady. A widower by the name of Dorothy Knight. A looker, and a rum cookie despite being in her middle years and carrying a few extra pounds. A lady, Mrs Willoughby disapproves of."

"Why, what has she done?"

"Done? The woman has the dreadful impertinence to be new to the village. And that just won't do."

"How long as she lived here?"

Ceddars smiles. "Four or so years—since the end of the Great War. She worked in munitions by all accounts. Part of the home front effort, what? She came into a little money and bought a shop in the village."

"I wonder what the village will say about me?"

"With the vicar dying in your sitting room? Tongues will surely drop off. With that in mind, being seen cavorting with you, just won't do, don't you see?"

"Well, doctor, I don't want to ruin your reputation. The village would go into meltdown." I find purchase on the rough slate wall and heave myself over in what I guess would be described by the doctor as 'a non-lady-like fashion'. I land heavily at the other side. "I hope you didn't glimpse my bloomers."

"Don't be silly. I turned away of course. I am a gentleman." He then realises I'm wearing trousers and chuckles. "You modern women! I blame the war you know. Gave you all ideas above your station, what?" He places his heavy medical bag on the wall and expertly vaults over, his injured leg not inhibiting him in the slightest, and lands ahead of me, right in the middle of the footprints I saw earlier.

"Ceddars!"

"What is it, Em'?" He looks down at his feet in alarm. "Bally hell, I'm stepping all over the evidence." He backs away, taking long strides and I notice the doctor's feet are smaller that I would've thought for a large man such as himself.

"It's no use, you tramped over everything."

"I'm sorry Em', I just didn't think. I hoofed over the wall without a second bally thought. What must you think of me?"

He is genuinely upset. "Forget it." I take a closer look at the small clearing. "Despite your clumsiness, I'm sure this is where the murderer was standing. You say Sheng is a diminutive man, you think he could see over this wall?"

"It is a little high, but then again there's nothing stopping him getting a foothold and levering himself up into position."

"You're right," I'm forced to admit. The crack of a twig being broken, and I whirl around to see a tall, skinny young man with longish white-blond hair standing about twenty feet away. He realises he's been seen and makes a run for it."

Sweat & Roses

"I SAY! That's Eugene Knight, Dorothy Knight's son."

"William Eriksen's love interest has a grown-up son?"

"Yes, she does. He's just turned seventeen. But he's a young seventeen if you get my drift. A bit of an oddball by all accounts. Typical angry young man and all that. I wonder what he was doing here?" I see the wheels whirring in the doctor's mind. "You don't think…?"

"That he might be involved in the vicar's death somehow? Possibly. He may also be a witness."

"A bit suspicious, running off like that, what?"

"Indeed. We will need to ask him what he was doing here later—if we can find him. But first we have more pressing concerns." I walk around the area, trying to disturb as little of the scene as possible, finding it hard to believe that the inspector didn't think it necessary to examine out here, meaning I will have to do his job for him. How he became an inspector is beyond me.

"You see anything?"

I shake my head. "I was hoping to find a cigarette butt or a discarded button, or any number of clues, but the area appears to be empty. It looks like—"

The sound of crashing and squawking birds from above, and Ceddars lurches at me, pushing me over. We both land in an ungainly heap in the fern, the doctor's heavy frame atop mine. There's a resounding thud barely inches away from us. A heavy branch has fallen where I was just standing, my red hat crumpled underneath, the fabric looking like blood.

"I say, that was a bally close one. You alright, Em'?"

I nod, although I'm shaken. "I wonder what the village gossips would say now," I say, aware that Ceddars is lying between my legs.

He jumps up very quickly and retrieves my battered hat and passes it to me. "Crikey, that could have been your noggin."

I push myself up to my feet, straightening my clothing and brushing away bits of fern and bark, before retrieving my hat and placing it back on my head.

Ceddars gives me a nervous once-over. "As good as new, what?" He examines the fallen branch while I peer up into the tree. I can see nothing, except thick foliage and dappled sunlight.

Ceddars whistles. "The thing was bally rotten. Just bad luck that we happened to be standing underneath the thing when it fell."

I realise that Ceddars has saved me from serious injury and possible death. A shiver passes down my spine. This was just an accident… *wasn't it?* I look at the fallen branch myself. It is indeed rotten. But I can't help wondering if there is more to the incident, regardless of the evidence.

"If I hadn't acted bally quickly, well, we would've both bought it, what?"

I track back to the road, followed by Ceddars, remembering the weight of his body atop mine and feeling a trifle hot. I have no idea about my life before waking up in Little Pucklewick—apart from those newspaper cut-outs. Nothing at all about romance. One thing is for sure though, I like the doctor. And a sure way for a man to get into a woman's affections is to save her life.

We trace the route that the killer most likely took to get into the wood. I can see that someone has brushed past and flattened the odd fern, but that's all. It could be the killer, or it could be Eugene Knight, or one and the same. Although

I'm sure the person who murdered the vicar wouldn't hang around. My guess is that they are long gone. We exit the wood a short time later and find ourselves on a small country road that also runs past my front garden. On the other side is a large but rather quaint building standing opposite the church.

Ceddars nods in the building's direction. "The vicarage. I must go and talk to Mary, to the now widowed Mrs Wilson-Smallsey. It's the part of my job that I dread the most. Having to tell loved ones the bad news. I always tried to do the same in the war, you know. Better having someone who knew the deceased to pass on the awful news, what? Face to face and all that. But you never get used to it."

The doctor points to a gate under a brick archway in a high wall. "This is where I found that awful poster."

I examine the wood. A new brass drawing pin tells me how the poster had been attached. I prise it free with a fingernail and take it as evidence.

Looking impressed, Ceddars opens the gate, and we enter the north side of a large garden, in the centre of which is the vicarage, surrounded by an impressive grass lawn bordered with summer flowers and punctuated by the odd clump of well-tended roses in bloom. The building itself is swathed in a bright green, leafy vine that has recently come into bloom—a facade of white flowers hangs beautifully, although an occasional black drainpipe and window peek through this display to remind us that this is a building of bricks and mortar.

"Behold, the vicarage, what?" Ceddars says. "It's not up to much but I've always envied Mary's garden."

Another door on the eastern wall, leads to the small, picturesque church on the other side. From this angle I notice the roof is part-covered in scaffolding that appears to have been there for a long time. "How long has the church roof been like that?"

"A few years. The Rev has been raising cash to get it fixed."

"He has?"

"Fundraisers and all that. I even put in a chunk of money myself."

The door in the eastern wall opens to reveal a peculiarly tall, stressed looking, middle-aged, stick of a man with a pot belly wearing an ill-fitting cassock and white collar.

"That's the new church curate, Mr Simmons," Ceddars explains as he stalks quickly towards us, his head thrust forward as if on a mission.

"Is it true, doctor? Has the vicar been… *murdered?*" Simmons ululates, clamping his hand over his mouth, worried that he might've been overheard. He comes closer.

"You've heard, old man? Crikey! Yes, I'm afraid that the vicar has somewhat passed on."

"Oh my! God rest his immortal soul." He closes his eyes and drops his head, prayers whispering upon his thin lips.

Curate Simmons is a bald man with a circle of bright red hair giving him a religious aspect that is not shared by any other part of him. He's taller than Ceddars, slightly overweight, and wears gold-rimmed glasses that seem too small for his face. Twin rings of sweat encircle his armpits, while fresh droplets festoon his face and neck. His thin hands are clamped together, the fingers wringing stressfully—with no black smudges. An impressive set of keys hang from a tight belt that emphasises his pot belly. I'm surprised to see him wearing the *Military Medal*—a war decoration established in 1916 and awarded for bravery in battle. The man, despite his somewhat unfortunate appearance, has earned an impressive award in the Great War. To me it meant only one thing. Simmons was no stranger to killing, despite his curate robes.

"How did you find out, old man?" Ceddars asks.

The curate's head jerks upwards, his eyes flicking backwards and forwards from the church spire. "Ethel at the telephone exchange. I'm pretty sure that the whole village knows by now. I can't believe it…"

"Ah, Ethel, the village blather-wire."

Simmons wipes sweaty hands on his cassock. "But who would want to murder the vicar and why? This is the most, terrible, terrible news. And poor Mary, the vicar's wife! That's where I'm heading now—to let her know before she hears about it."

"I'm Emily Crookshanks," I say, forcefully intersecting into their conversation. "I heard you and Vicar Wilson-Smallsey didn't see eye to eye?"

"I… I beg your pardon?"

Ceddars raises his palms. "Please excuse Miss Crookshanks, Mr Simmons, she's had somewhat of a trying morning."

"Yes, I was there when the vicar unfortunately passed away."

Mr Simmons takes my hand in his and I try not to wince at his still sweaty, clammy palms. "I'm so sorry to meet you in such dreadful circumstances, it must have been a terrible shock." He closes his eyes. "May God cleanse you of your ghastly experience. It is in him we trust. In him who we place our immortal soul." The man speaks in short bursts, the words hissing from his wet lips in quick succession. His eyes open again, the look in them manic. "And the victim is the poor vicar! There's evil afoot here, there must be."

I extract my hand, wiping it on my trousers and press on with my questioning. "It *is* awful, and that's why I want to know about your relationship with the vicar. I believe there was some friction between the two of you."

"I beg your pardon?" Mr Simmons is shocked or wants me to think so.

Ceddars gives me a warning look. "Please don't misunderstand Miss Crookshanks' intentions old chap, she is just keen to get to the bottom of what happened to the reverend. Perhaps a little too keen."

Mr Simmons points his hollow eyes at me. "But who would say such a thing?"

"The vicar himself."

"What? I don't understand."

"He told me shortly before he died. He said, *Mr Simmons is new, and rather disagreeable. But he will soon learn to toe the line.* I wondered what he meant by that?"

"The vicar spoke those words?"

I nod, pleased at my perfect recall.

He crosses himself and makes a silent prayer, his eyes flicking upwards towards the church spire again. "I suppose he wasn't fully happy with me. I'm rather new you see. Maybe I was trying too hard to impress. The old curate, Mr Jones, had let things slip somewhat. And I am very much the new broom. And he wasn't in favour of me helping out by giving the odd sermon. He was particularly against it, as it happens. And I've yet to conduct a wedding or a funeral. He didn't think I was ready. But I am used to being tested by God."

"I see." I remember the rumour from the poster that accused the vicar of embezzling church funds. "And was one of your duties to help with the church finances?"

"The finances?" He crosses himself again.

I'm wondering if the man is slightly unhinged. Then again, the vicar's murder could have hit him hard. I nod for him to continue.

"I wanted to help him, but the vicar liked to control the purse-strings himself. He was very strict about the matter."

"And where were you this morning at just after eleven o'clock?"

"What? You can't possibly think I'm a suspect in this dreadful business?"

"Do you want the murderer to be found?"

"Of course, I do."

"Then it is important that we do not waste time on the

wrong people. Isn't it better to rule yourself out?"

"But I heard the culprit was that Sheng fellow, manservant to Mr Eriksen. Which doesn't surprise me. He's from one of those godforsaken foreign countries. And men living without God are capable of the most heinous crimes." His eyes flick to the church spire again. He appears to be obsessed with it.

I follow his gaze, but see nothing special, just an old wind vane with an arrow pointing to the four points of the compass. "That must be why there is never any crime in England."

"I beg your pardon. How very rude."

Ceddars grimaces. "Again, I'm very sorry, old chap. Like I said, Miss Crookshanks is—"

"Mr Sheng isn't the murderer," I say, speaking over the doctor. "As I will soon prove. Now tell me, where were you this morning at eleven?"

Curate Simmons prominent Adam's Apple, bobs. "Sheng not the murderer? The man is a heathen. Him and Eriksen alike. Ungodly… the pair of them together. Ethel said that Inspector Troughton was on his way to arrest the man?"

Ceddars smiles awkwardly. "Now there's a story, what? Miss Crookshanks doesn't believe he is the guilty party, but, as yet, does not have a theory about who else could've done such a thing."

Curate Simmon's eyebrows raise into the bald pate of his head. "I don't understand. What difference does it make what Miss Crookshanks thinks?"

"Ah, well, erm, Em', Miss Crookshanks, is somewhat of an amateur sleuth, isn't that right?"

"I'm more than just an amateur," I reply proudly, remembering the newspaper cut-outs. "It's how I made my living in South Africa, solving a series of complex cases." My memory may not have returned but I know this is what I was created for. To solve mysteries and to catch the bad guys.

"You didn't tell me that," Ceddars says, surprised. "I

thought it was a hobby and all that. Of course, I bigged you up to Troughton, mainly to get a rise out of the annoying fellow, but I never once thought that… Crikey!"

This news appears to have a profound effect on Simmons who takes a nervous step backwards. "Oh, I see. You're a professional. And of course, I will want to assist in any way I can. But I follow God's will and God's will alone."

"Then, tell me where you were this morning at around eleven o'clock."

His hand fumbles unconsciously with his set of keys, the other wiping sweat from his brow. "I was going about my regular morning church duties, as I always do."

"And those duties were what exactly?"

He purses his lips, staring at me worriedly. "I opened the church doors at nine and found Old Jack sleeping in his favourite corner."

"Old Jack?"

"Yes, vagrants are mercifully not a problem in this parish, but Old Jack often ends up sleeping there on a Sunday evening. He comes for the sermon, you see? Very concerned about his mortal soul." He crosses himself for the umpteenth time. "But he does like to drink somewhat. Not his fault, although my prayers have so far failed to turn him away from the evils of hard liquor. He lost his entire family some time back in a nasty house fire. I've told him many times that God's will is not for us to question. We all must suffer it and if we are lucky, be asked to carry it out."

"And what happened with this Jack?"

I brought him sandwiches and a flask of coffee to get him back on his feet and sent him on his way. I then unlocked the inner rooms—we keep them locked these days. A sign of these ungodly times we are forced to live in."

"Go on."

"Afterwards, I checked the candles, replacing them where needed and did a few other minor chores before the cleaning lady arrived at roughly nine-thirty, who I always supervise, liking to keep her company while she works. Mondays are always a little busier with more to do than other days. When she was finished at roughly ten and was leaving, Mrs Knight arrived."

I glance at Ceddars. "You mean, Mrs Dorothy Knight? Mother to Eugene?"

"Yes, she's the village florist who takes care of the church's flower arrangements. Normally, the flowers are replaced on Sunday morning before the reverend's service, but she was out of the village yesterday. I think she was visiting a relative. A rather striking woman if I may be allowed to say such things. Always impeccably dressed. However, she can be very particular, which I put down to an artistic soul."

"Why would you say that?"

"She seemed a little agitated. Hardly wanted to talk to me at all. And when the vicar arrived unexpectedly a short time later, they both went into the vestry where I heard them… well… having an argument."

"You were not expecting to see the vicar this morning?"

"No, but now that I think about it, maybe Mrs Knight was waiting for him. There's been some friction between her and Mrs Willoughby of late."

"Friction you say?"

He nodded. "It's poor Mary, the vicar's wife. Her being bedridden has left somewhat of a void and the ladies of the village have been in constant competition with one another to help out in her absence. Mrs Willoughby has ruled the roost for some time, but Mrs Knight has been trying to edge her out. And the vicar was stuck in the middle." He crosses himself again.

"Did you hear what their disagreement was about?"

A quick shake of his head. "But afterwards, Mrs Knight left in a hurry and the vicar came to speak to me. He was in a bad mood. The last time we ever spoke to one another, how very sad."

"What did you talk about?"

"Nothing much," he answers quickly. Too quickly for my liking. "Just church business. After which, and in the absence of Mrs Knight, I was forced to replace the flowers myself. I'm afraid my arranging isn't up to her high standards, but again she did leave me in the lurch. After that I made my way back to my cottage for elevenses."

"And what time was this?"

"I heard the village clock chime half-past ten."

"And that's it?"

"On the way I checked the church vault. We've had some vandalism in the past and as such, we keep it locked." He rattles his keys. "I don't normally check the door, if someone was to break in, they'd hardly use a key, but I depressed the handle and found it to be unlocked. I don't know how long it had been like that. I must've left it unlocked at some time in the past."

"And what is in the church vaults, may I ask?"

"Nothing in particular. The rooms down there are mainly used for storage. Bit of a maze by all accounts. I don't go inside."

"Why not?"

The curate shuffles uncomfortably. "The war. Ever since I left the trenches, I don't like enclosed spaces."

"I'm sorry old chap," Ceddars says, "I didn't know. "We all have a cross to bear from that nasty conflict."

I can't help thinking it's odd that the doctor didn't know of Simmons' condition when everyone else did. He is the village physician after all.

Simmons grabs his medal, seemingly getting strength from touching the metal. "Thank you, Doctor. God gives us trials, but God also gives us enlightenment and purpose."

"You say the door was open?" I ask, getting him back to the subject I'm interested in.

He nods. "After locking the door, I went home."

"And where do you live, exactly?"

"The role of curate comes with a very modest income, and a small cottage at the end of the terrace on the other side of the church."

"Did you see anyone on your way back to your cottage?"

"No. It's only a short walk from the church."

"Can anyone verify you went home and nowhere else?"

"I'm afraid I'm finding your constant questions quite tiresome, Miss Crookshanks. I was, as I always am, under the sight of God. He is my witness, and my defender."

"I see. And Mr Eriksen's lecture? Were you there last night?"

Mr Simmons becomes quite agitated. "No. Of course not. As I said, Eriksen and that heathen of his are ungodly creatures. I believe it is their presence in the village, their evil, that has directly led to such dire events. But more than that, the vicar instructed me to not attend. And why would I disobey him?"

"One more thing. Are you aware of any rumours about the vicar?"

"I don't understand?"

"I'm afraid rather nasty posters about the vicar were pinned around the village this morning."

The news stuns the curate. "If you can excuse me, I must go and give the awful news to Mary. I've dallied enough."

Ceddars shakes his head. "Sorry to pull rank, old man, but I'm afraid the inspector has requested that I talk to Mary Wilson-Smallsey on his behalf in my official capacity as village doctor."

"Then perhaps I should accompany you. I maybe new here, but I have become her firm friend. And I also have a bigger responsibility to protect her immortal soul."

"'Fraid not old chap. I've known Mary for many years and, unfortunately, I have a lot of experience of giving similar news to bereaved relatives. So forgive me, but I think it best to decline your offer. But please feel free to drop in on her after we have left to give your support and condolences. I fear she will need all the support she can get."

He brightens. "Yes, I can certainly do that. But may I ask… you are both going to see Mary? You *and* Miss Crookshanks?"

"Yes, as I mentioned, Miss Crookshanks was with the vicar in his final moments."

I can see that Simmons is upset by this development, but he nods in submission.

I give him a tight smile. "I suppose you will have a very busy few days ahead of you, and a few sermons to write. The parishioners will be looking to you now for spiritual support."

Simmons claps his hands to his mouth. "Oh my! I suppose I'd better get off to the church. The village will require true guidance in this terrible time of need."

I may be wrong, but I have the impression that the curate is looking forward to his new responsibilities. Mr Simmons says his goodbyes and heads back to the church. "What a strange fellow. And did you notice how much he was sweating?"

"I say, you won't question the poor widow in the same way you did Simmons, will you?"

"Of course not. You will hardly notice I'm there at all."

Ceddars is not convinced.

Gossip & Grief

THE Vicarage door is answered by a middle-aged maid, who has not yet heard today's shocking news. She smiles at Ceddars, who she obviously knows very well, and gives me a suspicious once over. "Morning Charlotte," Ceddars says in greeting.

"Anything up, Doctor? It isn't like you to be so formal."

He pulls a tight smile. "We need to see Mary, it's important."

"It must be," Charlotte replies, her thick eyebrows furrowing, before ushering us upstairs to an impressive sitting room. Inside, we find a pale-looking Mary Wilson-Smallsey, perched on a chair in front of a large set of corner windows giving views of the church and the village to the south. The room is well-lived in and is very much her domain—I can see no influence of the vicar in its decor. I notice a cabinet containing a series of small trophies across a variety of disciplines… javelin, discus, archery, and gymnastics. And a few acting medals adorned with the head and shoulders of England's greatest dramatist, William Shakespeare. All no doubt won as a youngster. Another smaller window, in shadow from a large tree outside, sits on the west side of the room in the corner. There is also a writing desk covered in papers, and two walls devoted to shelving and many books.

She turns to face us. Mary Wilson-Smallsey wears a light summery lace smock and lace gloves, through which I can see her long, elegantly manicured fingernails. Her blonde hair is short and loose in the modern fashion, framing an attractive, slightly lined, high-cheekboned face. She appears to be a lot younger than her husband and possesses looks that I am jealous of. A real beauty only gently touched by age. "Oh Ceddars, what a terrible day." Her voice is deep and more earthy than I would've expected from a vicar's wife.

The doctor rushes over and takes Mary's hand, a look on his face that tells me he is rather taken with her, as was Curate Simmons. She has the power to turn men's heads, that's for sure.

"I'm bally sorry, Mary, but it appears you have already heard the awful news…"

"Yes, Mr Shufflebottom phoned." She glances towards a telephone stand in the corner, a distraught look on her face. "He was under the assumption that I knew my husband had… The poor man was beside himself when he found out what he'd done."

"The blower would be the Devil's own work if it wasn't so bally useful, what?"

Mary gives Ceddars a sad smile. "I made him tell me everything. Is it true? Was Albert murdered?"

He takes a deep breath. "Yes, I'm afraid so, old dear. What a terrible business."

She removes a hanky from her dress sleeve and buries her face in it. Ceddars stands and puts his arm around her shaking shoulders.

"Was it quick?" Mary asks between sobs.

"He didn't suffer," Ceddars replies. "Let me introduce Miss Crookshanks. She was with the reverend when it happened." His eyes make contact with mine, warning me to go easy. I find his gallant demeanour most attractive.

Mary wipes away her tears and fixes me with red-rimmed green eyes. "How… how did it happen?"

I offer her my hand, which she takes, squeezing it with a firm grip. "I'm afraid he was shot in the back."

Ceddars makes an exasperated sound. "I say, Miss Crookshanks, that's a little harsh."

Mary turns to him. "Is it true?"

"I'm afraid it is, old dear."

A long pause, where I fully expect the newly formed widow to burst into tears, but she composes herself. "Did you see who did it?"

I shake my head. "He was shot from a distance, through my open windows."

"They're arresting a man called Sheng," Ceddars says. "The manservant to Mr Eriksen."

"Yes, I've heard of him. He was attempting to steal the vicar's flock, if my husband was to be believed. From what I heard, the man was more of a spiritualist than a hothead. Then again, who can ever know what is truly inside a man's heart?" She turns her attention away from us to stare out of the windows.

I sit down on a small, well-used couch, Ceddars sitting beside me. "May I ask what is the nature of your illness?"

"Mrs Wilson-Smallsey is suffering from a long-standing lethargy," Ceddars explains. "Making it bally impossible for her to do very much at all, isn't that the case, old dear?"

"I'm afraid so. I must take things very easily. I have good and bad days. On the good days, I like to go outside and tend to my garden, especially the roses. Have you seen them? They have bloomed early this year."

The forced small talk isn't surprising, the woman has had a terrible shock. "Yes, I remarked the same to the curate," I say, interested in her reaction.

Mary's face darkens at the mention of the man.

"Have you known him long?"

"Mr Simmons? Not really, but he does so like to visit and pray with me. If I want to or not."

"He is rather fond of you."

"I dare say the curate urgently needs a wife." She gives me a knowing look and I realise Mary Wilson-Smallsey is also a woman of the world. "It was that awful war, so many fine young men were cut down in their prime. I'm afraid the curate is the best Little Pucklewick could get."

I'm surprised and pleased by her candour. She is erudite and intelligent. Both qualities I admire. Having talked to the vicar just for a short while, I can't imagine that they were a good match. Then again, marriage is a lottery in this age. I point to the cabinet containing the trophies I spotted earlier. "You were quite the athlete in your youth."

Mary glances over to them, her face coming suddenly alive, her lips parting to reveal a fine array of perfect teeth, and again, I'm struck by her effortless beauty. "I won those at my French finishing school where they encourage the gals to take part in sports and other activities. Those days seem like a different world to me now."

"I wonder, Mrs Wilson-Smallsey, do you sit by this window often during the day?"

Ceddars squeezes my arm, unhappy with my question.

Mary turns back and smiles at us. "I'm afraid I have little else to do. I spend most of my time in this room."

"Meaning you have a good idea of the regular comings and goings?"

"Little Pucklewick runs on clockwork, especially in the mornings. The village hall clock is visible from here, which means I can predict where nearly anyone will be at a certain time."

"Did you see anything unusual this morning? Anybody out of place? Anybody running early or late?"

"Funny you should ask, but I did. There was a man I didn't recognise. A stranger who I've seen once or twice before."

My interest is piqued. "Constable Jakes mentioned that a stranger had been seen in the village, it's possible that's the same man. Can you describe him?"

"He was wearing brown trousers, a heavy leather coat and boots. I couldn't see his face due to a large cap, but I glimpsed a pair of spectacles and a small beard."

The same description given to me by Constable Jakes. "Was he carrying anything?"

"He had a leather satchel hung over his shoulder."

"And his stature? Was he a big or a small man?"

"Average, I'd say."

"Was he acting suspiciously?"

"A stranger in Little Pucklewick is always suspicious, but he did seem to be heading somewhere, if you know what I mean?"

"Where did you see him and in what direction was he walking?"

"Along Church Street, the road that runs parallel to the south of the road your cottage sits on, Miss Crookshanks."

I'm surprised she knows about me, but then again, my arrival must've been the prime source of gossip before the murder of the Reverend Wilson-Smallsey.

"It runs past the vicarage, the church and along the edge of the village green towards the village hall."

"And what time was this?"

"About ten-thirty."

"Did you see anyone else who might have got a closer look at the man?"

"I'm afraid not. The village is a flurry of bodies on a Monday morning. People going hither and thither, but there is a lull between ten-fifteen and ten-forty-five. I think you'll be lucky to find another witness."

"Was there anything else that was unusual?"

Mary shakes her head. "I'm afraid not. If only I had a window looking to the north. I may have spotted Sheng outside your cottage, although I'm not sure I would've wanted to see him, especially after we know what he did."

"Quite. May I also ask you about Mrs Willoughby?"

"Now look here, Miss Crookshanks," Ceddars says, playing the gallant knight again. "Mary has had quite the shock. The last thing she wants to do is answer your many questions."

Mary puts her hand on the doctor's arm. "Stand down, Ceddars. I really don't mind. Please continue, Miss Crookshanks."

"I gather Mrs Willoughby has taken over most of your duties while you are infirm?"

"Yes, she has. I don't much like the woman. Can I say that? She is an officious, bossy, gossip-obsessed person, but I cannot fault her dedication to the vicar and to the vicarage. I don't know what *he* would have done without her."

The way she stresses 'he' indicates a certain resentment. "You bear her no ill feelings for taking your position, so to speak?"

"Oh no. Not at all. Tea and cake mornings were never my thing. If I were healthy or not. I suppose the vicar's death will put quite the crimp on her social life." Her eyes well up with tears again. "Mrs Willoughby does so like to be the centre of things."

"Do you also know Mrs Knight, the florist?"

A slight pause. "I am aware of her, although we've barely spoken. Why do you ask?" The tone of Mary's voice is slightly higher.

"It's just that the vicar had an argument with her earlier this morning."

"He did? What about?"

"I was hoping you could tell me."

Mary shakes her head. "Albert and I live mostly separate lives."

"One more thing," I say to a warning look from Ceddars, "were you and your husband happy?"

Ceddars jumps to his feet. "Now, I say, Miss Crookshanks, that's enough! I'm sorry Mary, I shouldn't have brought her with me."

Mary waves away his concerns with a single gloved hand. "It's very splendid of you to come to my defence again,

Ceddars, but Miss Crookshanks is quite right. You see…" She pauses to compose her thoughts, "Albert and I have not been close for many years. He wanted a vicar's wife and instead got an invalid. I'm afraid any affection he had for me disappeared years ago." She dabs her handkerchief at her eyes, her eyelashes fluttering.

Ceddars grabs her hand. "Oh Mary, I'm so sorry, I didn't know. Why didn't you say before?"

Mary visibly sags in her chair. "I'm feeling tired. Do you mind…?"

"Of course, of course. We will leave you to your grief."

After saying our goodbyes, we descend the stairs to the entrance hall. A door is flung open to reveal a rather larger than life woman wearing an imposing costume of purples and silver, giving her the aspect of a Roman empress. She is tall, thick-limbed, and stout of stature. Behind her, in what appears to be the vicarage sitting room, are more ladies in similar but less impressive get-up.

"Doctor Roberts? I hope Mrs Wilson-Smallsey is alright?" she says, glancing upstairs.

"Ah… well… um…" Ceddars tries to answer, unable to frame a coherent reply.

"The vicar's wife is fine," I reply for him.

The woman rounds on me, as if she's shocked that I answered on the doctor's behalf. "And you are?"

"I'm Miss Emily Crookshanks."

"Oh. The newest addition to our village." Her eyes assess me, and she doesn't like what she sees, that much is for sure, her eyebrows creasing at first my hat, then my jacket and finally my trousers. "Pleased to meet you," she says in a tone that suggests the opposite. She coughs, a dry, hacking sound, covering her mouth with a folded handkerchief. "And what a lovely hat. I am Mrs Gladys Willoughby. I am sure you must have heard of me?" Her voice is full of authority, her words precise and deliberate, with every vowel and syllable emphasised. Like an overblown teacher of the theatrical arts.

"Yes, I'm afraid I have."

"And what do you mean by that?"

"Mrs Willoughby, ladies," Ceddars says, cutting in. "I have some rather terrible news, what?"

"You do? Then get on with it, man." The offhand way Mrs Willoughby talks to Ceddars, indicates that she doesn't lend him the respect normally expected of a doctor. I suppose Ceddars isn't exactly a typical country village physician, especially in the way he dresses or talks, but it's still rude.

"Perhaps you ought to sit down?"

"Oh dear, it *is* Mary, isn't it?"

"I really think you ought to sit down, what?"

"Just tell me, doctor. What has happened?"

Ceddars takes a deep breath, his face creasing with discomfort. "I'm sorry to inform you all that the vicar, that the Reverend Wilson-Smallsey, died this morning. I'm afraid he was murdered."

"Murdered!" Mrs Willoughby flops to the floor in what I can only describe as an 'affected swoon', giving Ceddars enough time to run over to catch her, taking the supposedly semi-conscious woman over to a hallway bench and sitting her down. The other ladies in the room gasp and wail in surprise. Some visibly sobbing while others are white-faced in shock.

An attractive woman in her late thirties but slightly overweight, well-dressed, and smelling heavily of lavender, walks towards me. Her hair is dark blond, worn long enough to emphasise her high cheekbones, and to frame a pair of mesmerising bluer than blue eyes. A look only marred by a sizable double chin. To find one beauty in the vicarage was unusual, but to discover another may be more than a coincidence.

"I'm Mrs Dorothy Knight, village florist and senior member of the village inner coterie," she says in a rather overblown and put-on posh accent.

I remember what Mr Simmons said about her and the vicar having an argument, and my interest in her is immediately piqued. This close to the woman, I notice that she has gone to seed somewhat, her eyes are bulbous and watery, and she wears too much makeup, but she is still very attractive, even if those good looks are on the turn. Looks that are very reminiscent of her son, Eugene.

"Is it true? Has the vicar passed on?"

"I'm afraid so."

Tears appear in the corners of her eyes. She dabs at them with a tiny embroidered and frilly handkerchief that becomes smudged with makeup. "Oh my, oh my. Such terrible news." She crosses herself dramatically and looks up to heaven. "God rest his immortal soul." She takes a deep breath and composes herself. "But life must go on… What an awful phrase, don't you think? Of course, life goes on and we can do nothing but grieve and suffer." She speaks loudly, making sure the other ladies in the room can hear her.

She looks back at me, her wet eyes taking me in properly for the first time, her eyebrows rising. "You must be the new Miss Crookshanks? I'm correct, am I not?"

I nod. "Pleased to meet you Mrs Knight. I was with the vicar when he…" I look at the grief-stricken faces and carry on, "when he passed away."

The news brings a chorus of wails and more sobbing. The ladies of the village appear to be more upset at the vicar's death than his own wife. I'm rather taken aback.

"May I ask what you all are doing here?"

"It's our weekly Monday meeting, of course," Dorothy Knight replies, like this information is known by all.

The late vicar's words pop into my head… *I will arrange with Mrs Willoughby for you to join her regular Monday morning get-togethers.*

"And you said the reverend was… *murdered?*"

"I'm afraid so."

"How very ghastly." Her eyes fill with more tears, dripping down her face to land upon her ample bosom. She takes out the hanky again and delicately dabs at them. "Do forgive me, Miss Crookshanks."

"The news is as dreadful as it is shocking, it would be unusual not to shed a few tears."

"You don't understand. How could you, but…" She lowers her voice to a whisper, her head coming close to my ear. "… the last time myself and the vicar spoke together, we had a horrible argument. It was a silly thing, but…"

"Yes, Mr Simmons mentioned that to me. He said he overheard heated words."

Her face pinches like that of an angry child. "That horrible man is always eavesdropping."

"You don't like the curate?"

She lowers her voice to a whisper. "I'm a widow, Miss Crookshanks, and some men, even curates, see that as an opportunity, if you know what I mean?"

"What was the argument about?"

"That commotion last night at William's, at Mr Eriksen's talk at the village hall. The vicar and Mrs Willoughby quite ruined it, so they did. The vicar and Mr Eriksen don't get on you know? At loggerheads. I was annoyed at him for what he did. He doesn't know Mr Eriksen like I do. I wanted the vicar to leave him alone, but he was set on more confrontation."

"You didn't talk about anything else?"

"No. And if that awful man says otherwise, he's lying. You can't trust anything that comes out of Simmons' mouth."

"Why, what has he been saying?"

"This and that. You know the kind of thing? Nasty gossip. I suggest you talk to him and ask him yourself, if you can get a straight answer that is."

I also lower my voice. "Do you have any idea of who may have murdered the vicar?"

Another shake of her head. Her blue eyes widen for a moment. "Although, now I think about it, Mrs Willoughby and the vicar have not been getting on as they usually do."

I remember that Simmons said the two women didn't like each other, which means I need to take what she says with a pinch of salt. "You're suggesting that Mrs Willoughby might be involved in the vicar's murder?"

She gives me an irritable shake of her head, her double chin wobbling. "I can't stand the old busybody, but I do not believe she is capable of murder. Nevertheless, I have noticed that things have changed between them recently."

"There was a falling out?"

"I'm not sure, you'd have to ask her about that. But I think so." She looks around, conspiratorially, her voice becoming almost inaudible. "Mrs Willoughby was late this morning which is unheard of. And, quite flustered, I'd say. Quite flustered indeed."

"How late was she?"

"I heard Charlotte let her in and poked my head out of the sitting room door." She points to a small timepiece sitting on a hallway table. "I noticed the clock. It was twenty past the hour."

"Did she give an explanation for her tardiness?"

Dorothy Knight's makeup encrusted eyebrows furrow. "May I ask why you are asking so many questions?"

"I'm helping Inspector Troughton. I'm a detective by trade."

She says nothing for a few moments as she digests my lie. "Then that must be why you're dressed like that." Her eyes glance up at my hat, and she frowns. "You detectives always feel the need to be so very eccentric, don't you think?"

"You don't like my outfit?"

Mrs Knight ignores my question. "Let me wish you the very best in your endeavours. Now, I must have time to grieve. You understand?" More tears appear in her eyes, and

I can tell that the woman is genuinely upset.

I make my excuses and go back to Ceddars to see how he is getting on with Mrs Willoughby. I let my eye rove over the large woman, who fans herself with an over-ornate, over-sized purple fan covered in amethysts and tiny pearls. Even sitting down, she has an imposing presence. Her dress is expensive, and I notice tell-tale inky smudges on the cuffs, although they are harder to spot on the purple material. Mrs Willoughby has been in touch with the same posters that stained Ceddars' fingers. I'm certain of it. I find this detail too hard to resist.

"Mrs Willoughby," I begin, interrupting Ceddars' rather ineffectual administrations. "May I ask you a few questions?"

She peers at me from over the top of her fan. "No, you most certainly cannot!" Her tone is aggressive but descends into a series of coughs.

"I say," Ceddars says with concern, "you really ought to let me take a look at you, that cough is quite nasty. How long have you had it now?"

She waves his concern aside with a flabby hand. "I've told you before, doctor. I prefer my own man, in Harley Street."

"And what does he say?"

"It is nothing but a summer cold. Now away with you."

I step closer. "Please, my questions are about the vicar and who murdered him."

Ceddars raises his hand. "Can't you see the poor woman is grief-stricken?"

"But I have—"

"I'm putting my foot down this time. No more silly questions. We know who did the murder, for bally's sake!"

"It was that vile Sheng!" Mrs Willoughby shouts from a strained, croaky throat. "He did it! I was there when he threatened the reverend! And besides, he works for that godforsaken heathen, Eriksen. Who knows what kind of things go on at his place? Especially with that young redhead who works for him. One can only guess at the nature of their relationship."

"Now, now, Mrs W," Ceddars says. "I know Franny. She's a stand-up gal. I won't have a word spoken against her."

She scoffs. "You may be a doctor, but you are still a man. It is all so very sordid. And look what has come of it. A man of God murdered!"

Fran Feltham is the career girl who rejected Ceddars' advances, or so he told me. Perhaps she was involved with Eriksen in the way Mrs Willoughby suggested. I will know more when I talk to her. I decide to do that as soon as possible, and hopefully chat to the mysterious William Eriksen at the same time. I would also love to meet his manservant, Sheng. I'm pretty sure Inspector Troughton has arrested him already, which means I can go and visit him. If the inspector keeps his word that is.

There is nothing more I can do here. But I need to find out about those ink-stains from Mrs Willoughby sometime soon. Her reaction to the vicar's murder was more theatrical than I liked. I leave the hysterical women behind and head toward the back of the house. There's someone else I'm eager to meet.

Ash & Dragons

I OPEN a large door to the kitchen area and find a modest but functional cooking space. Charlotte jumps up when she sees me, her face a mess of tears. "Have you bin callin' miss? It's just that with the poor vicar passin' on, I've quite lost myself."

"No, no. I was just wondering if you could help me with a few things related to the vicar's death."

She wipes away her tears. "Of course, Miss Crookshanks. Anythin' to help."

"I was with the vicar when he sadly passed away. Inspector Troughton wanted me to find out about his movements this morning."

"I see. Although there's not much to tell. The vicar is an early riser and likes his breakfast in bed. Which I took to him like I do most mornin's." Tears well up in her eyes as she speaks and slowly drip down her cheeks. "Afterwards, he gets dressed and goes straight to his study to take care of his correspondence. And that's when I go attend to Mrs Wilson-Smallsey."

When mentioning the vicar's wife, her tone fosters a certain amount of uncertainty. "Is there something you want to tell me?"

"Of course not, miss," she replies defensively. "I've been with the Wilson-Smallseys since the day they arrived. And I won't have a word spoken against them."

"If you could please answer the question. It could be very important. The inspector wanted me to find out everything about this household. And you never know what may be important to him. We need to be thorough, for the vicar's sake."

"I have nothin' against her, the vicar's wife, so to speak, but…" she lowers her voice to a whisper, "I can't help think she wasn't as supportive of her husband as she could've been."

"But surely, the woman is ill and unable to help him."

She tries to form a reply but ends up shaking her head and shrugging—whatever she was about to tell me, she's decided against it.

"Did anything out of the ordinary happen this morning?"

"No, nothin', other than Mrs Willoughby was late for her ladies. Which is so unlike her."

"Yes, I've heard that. Did she tell you why?"

She shrugs. "No, but she wasn't herself that much were for sure. She looked like she'd had a scare. She's normally so punctual. Arrivin' exactly ten minutes early to check on me cakes and tables. She's a stickler for that kind of thing and can't abide it if any of my settin's are out of place."

"I see. Mr Simmons said the vicar turned up at the church unexpectedly, do you know anything about that?"

"Oh, now you mention it, he did go out at about ten. He were only gone about twenty minutes though."

"Do you know why?"

"A note arrived for him. Maybe it was sumfin to do with that?"

"A note? Who delivered it?"

Charlotte shrugs. "It just arrived on the mat."

"Where is that note now?"

"It will be in his study."

"Can you take me there? This note might be very important."

The maid frowns. "Ain't nobody allowed to go in the vicar's study unless he's already inside. Them's his rules."

"But in the circumstances…"

"I don't think you understand. The vicar keeps the room

locked at all times."

"And that was it? Nothing else out of the ordinary?"

No, miss. Although, come to think of it, Mrs Knight was also late today. She arrived a few minutes before Mrs Willoughby."

A bell rings making the maid jump. "That's Mrs Smallsey. I've got to go." She opens the door for me, and I walk back into the hallway, before she hurries away.

I stand by the kitchen for a few moments, taking my bearings inside the house, remembering the windows I observed from outside, and then head down a short corridor to a locked door, which I'm guessing is the reverend's study. I remove two pins from my hair, kneel, and insert them into the old lock before I know what I'm doing.

What am I doing?

The mechanism clicks satisfyingly. I open the door and steal inside, amazed at what I've just done. It appears that along with my investigating skills, I'm also a competent lock-pick. To use Ceddars' charming lingo… *by Jove!*

The room is compact, the walls covered with shelving containing various books, knickknacks, and small busts of very important looking men. A desk sits in pride of place in the centre of the room looking out of a small window to the back of the vicarage. I see the path where we met Curate Simmons. The desk is covered in a few opened letters, nothing of importance. The drawers are all locked. I look around for a key but can't see anything obvious. My eye falls on the empty fireplace and onto the fresh ashes that lie there. A quick sniff reveals that something has been recently burned. I take out my fountain pen and dig around, discovering a small piece of burned paper that had resisted the flames. Only a single word is left…

…marriage…

The door to the study flings open to reveal Mrs Willoughby looking at me with a face of thunder. "How dare you!" she says in a loud, but controlled voice, although I can see the woman's anger burning under the surface. "Charlotte told me you were snooping around and here you are, standing like a thief in the vicar's private sanctum. How very dare you!"

I walk over to her as nonchalantly as I can muster. "Tell me, Gladys, exactly why were you over twenty minutes late for your weekly Monday morning women's get-together?"

"I beg your pardon?" She coughs, dabbing at her mouth with her handkerchief.

Everyone is begging my pardon this morning and the phrase is beginning to grate. "It's a simple question. Where were you? Putting up nasty posters about the vicar?"

All her bluster leaves her, and I'm pleased to see the pompous woman visibly deflate. "You… you know about those?"

"Ceddars, Doctor Roberts, came across one pinned on the vicarage gate."

"He did? I thought I had found all the vile things. That is why I was late. I was on my way to the vicarage as is normal on a Monday morning when I saw this strange fellow standing by the big oak on the common, pinning up a poster of some kind. I waited until he had moved on and went to have a look. I could not believe my eyes. I did the only thing I could do. I went around the village and pulled them all down."

"Let's say I believe you, what did you do with them?"

Mrs Willoughby opens her voluminous purple leather handbag to reveal a sheaf of folded, inky pages. "See?"

I snatch one out before she can stop me and unfold it. It's the same as the one Inspector Troughton burned. I can also see the holes where it was pinned up and ripped off. Her story rings true, but it could also be a part of her alibi. If she murdered the vicar, then she could say that's what she was doing. Her being late puts her in the frame for murder though, that's for sure. "What did this stranger look like?"

"A small man with a beard in a thick leather coat, wearing a flat cap and glasses."

"I see." At least that part of her story corroborates with what Mary Wilson-Smallsey saw, although the vicar's wife described him as average, not small in stature. "And these allegations," I say, showing her the poster. "Is there any truth to them?"

"You think that vile nonsense is anything other than vile nonsense?"

"I've heard you were close to the vicar, very close. Did you know about any of these alleged dalliances?"

"Dalliances! Just who do you think you are? Coming here on a day like this and insulting such a great man!"

"Don't you want to find out who murdered the reverend?"

"But we know who did it. Sheng! I was there when Albert, I mean, when the reverend was threatened by him."

"Exactly. Anyone who was at the village hall last night could've heard the same and used that as a perfect opportunity to murder him."

"But why? What is the motive?"

"That's what I will find out. And these accusations of impropriety may be behind it. Now, is there anything more you want to tell me? I've heard you and the vicar were not on the best of terms."

"No doubt from that dreadful Mrs Knight."

"What was the disagreement about?"

"The vicar took it into his head to give her more responsibility in the parish. Mrs Knight had a hold on him. I'm sure of it."

"What kind of hold?"

She scoffs, dabbing her mouth with her handkerchief. "Why don't you ask her? Not that the awful woman ever speaks the truth."

"I intend to."

"Good. I've let you talk to me in this unbecoming way for too long. It is girls like you that will be the ruin of this country. You and that awful Francesca Feltham girl. Women should know their place and stay in it. Now, what in tarnation are you doing, breaking into the vicar's study? It's a violation, that's what it is. I'm of a mind to report you to the constable!"

"You don't know where the reverend kept the keys for his desk, do you? I thought that if anyone knew, it would be you."

"Get out! Get out now!"

"Bally hell, ladies!" Ceddars expostulates, appearing in the doorway, his absurd moustache flexing rather amusingly. "What is going on in here?"

"It is this so-called young lady," Mrs Willoughby says, pointing at me in accusation. "She broke into the vicar's study."

"I did no such thing—the door was open."

"Never! Albert always keeps it locked. I want her out of here, Doctor Roberts. I want her out of here now!"

Ceddars waltzes into the room, grabs me not too roughly by the arm and drags me outside. "What the bally hell are you doing?" His voice is a harsh whisper. "You've gone too far this time. Too far."

"I need to talk to William Eriksen."

"Are you not listening to me, Emily Crookshanks?"

We are both startled by the use of my full name, but I don't let it put me off. "There's too much that doesn't add up about the vicar's death. And shouldn't a good investigator follow up on all clues?"

"I admire your sleuth spirit, what? Of course I do, but you can't run riot around a village like Little Pucklewick, flinging accusations left, right and centre. You will never recover from it. Especially if you have someone like Mrs W on your case."

"Will you take me to Eriksen's place or not?" I sound angrier than I intend and hope I'm not pushing Ceddars too far. He's been a great help to me this morning, and besides, I like him. And I think he likes me.

He sighs. "I suppose I have to. Someone needs to stop you getting into even more trouble, although Eriksen is a bit of a pariah. A heretic and all that, what?"

I experience a sense of relief as we leave the vicarage, getting back out into the summery air. A sense of relief that abruptly disappears as a cloud crosses over the sun, followed by a gust of cold wind.

"June is such a changeable month in this part of the world," Ceddars says, but it doesn't stop the shiver that jackhammers down my spine.

I walk around the vicarage to stand under Mary's windows. The ones that look out across the village and the other smaller window sitting on the corner, hidden by a large oak growing on this side of the building and almost covered in ivy. "Did you see that window when we were talking to Mary?" I ask Ceddars. But he just shrugs.

We trace our steps northwards to the gate we entered the vicarage garden through earlier and arrive on the country road that travels from east to west in front of my beautiful, quaint cottage—like what you'd find on a tin of biscuits, marred only by the large black funerary van parked outside and a few onlookers. An equally beautiful but older cottage sits next door to mine, which, according to Ceddars, belongs to the infirm Mrs Bates. I must go and pay her a visit when I get a chance. Infirm people spend a lot of their time looking out of windows and she may have seen something of interest. For now, I have bigger fish to fry.

We turn eastwards, walking past Dooleys Wood that stretches all the way along the opposite side of the road. I let my eye rove over the thickly wooded boughs, choked with ivy and brambles noticing how bent and twisted they are. The forest has a threat to it. I remember the heavy falling branch that almost killed me and Ceddars, and shudder. The wood appears watchful and alive with eyes. I'm dreadfully exposed out here, at the mercy of… I don't know what exactly… but instinctively sense that I'm in terrible danger.

"I say, Em', are you alright?"

The sun once again emerges from behind the clouds, bathing Dooleys Wood in dappled, flickering sunlight. The trees momentarily blur, and their threat disappears.

"You're looking very queer. Have you found another clue, what?"

I shake my head. "I'm fine. But the wood is a trifle unnerving, don't you think?"

"Dooleys Wood? This place has quite the history. It's where they took the witches to be hanged or burnt back in the 1600s. It's also where a hundred or so years later a group of roundheads were hiding during the civil war. They were found and surrounded by the king's men, and half-starved to death before the wood was set afire, and the roundheads were burned alive. And that's just the beginning of it. You should find out more about Little Pucklewick, it has quite a rummy history, and Dooleys Wood is at the centre of it."

"Witches?" I ask, not sure exactly why.

"Little Pucklewick was famous for its witch trials. Bunkum of course unless you believe in that sort of claptrap."

Ignoring Ceddars' babbling, I take a steadying breath and feel more like myself again, and carry on walking, coming to an impressive two-storey house, its bricks painted yellow, with a well-tended forecourt. "That's my abode," Ceddars chirps. "A bit too large for a single gentleman, but you never know, one day not too far away, there may be a Mrs Ceddars."

"I didn't realise you lived so close to me and also next to the wood."

"I have an office above the bakery in the village centre, but this is the old HQ, what?"

Ceddars' house is only minutes away from my cottage, from the scene of the murder, and I'm forced to remind myself that everyone is a suspect, even the eccentric and charming doctor. As to his motive for murder, who knows?

"You will have to invite me round when this business is done and dusted. I believe you promised me a glass of wine."

"I don't think I did…"

"No, you didn't, but now's your chance."

He chuckles, putting his arm in mine. We come to a junction and turn right onto a new road that drops down a small hill to the south. Here we find a pair of impressive if not rather odd gates, the posts of which are two stacks of bricks capped with twin oriental dragons. The dragons are a more recent addition.

"How gauche," I exclaim.

"Can't agree more, but if you like gauche, you're in for a treat."

We walk past the entrance gate and up a gravel driveway that turns through a clump of beautiful trees, Lebanese Cedars by the look of them, and emerge to face a rundown, Gothic mansion, tall windows dominating the frontage. The place is old and rather imposing—consisting of two floors built with lichen-stained grey stone, topped with crenellated pseudo-battlements. These surround a centrepiece of twin towers between which, the building rises to a third central floor, also topped with battlements. An empty flagpole completes the vista. Below, a grand central doorway is framed by two identical wings of the mansion.

The gravel drive widens out to create a vast forecourt. The mansion would have been quite majestic in its heyday, but despite being occupied, it has an abandoned air. The surrounding gardens are overgrown and the gravel full of weeds.

"It looks a bit uncared for. You sure Eriksen lives here? Or anyone for that matter?"

"Despite appearances, Eriksen is rolling in it."

"He's rich?"

"A bit like me in that department, except on an entirely different scale. Was left the entire family fortune. Apparently, he sold the family's country pile and used his money to fund his adventures." His tone is dismissive. Ceddars doesn't like him, that much is obvious.

"He sold his country house? Then what's this place?"

"He picked it up after his return from the Far East. Not sure why he chose Little Pucklewick to settle down, or this ostentatious ruin, but the man is a trifle eccentric."

A roar of an engine and a white and chrome open-top motor car speeds past us. It's driven by a man in his forties with blonde hair that blows out behind him in the breeze, his face is rugged and unshaven. The car, a beautiful Mercedes lined with red leather, its fenders and wheels streaked with mud, slides to an abrupt stop.

"That's the man himself," Ceddars says, "and he appears to be in a bally bad mood."

William Eriksen jumps out of the car. He is a tall man in his forties with shoulders *carved from granite*, as any number of romantic novels would describe them. His face lined and pitted, his ice-blue eyes are almost hidden within his eye-sockets, but they are intelligent and piercing, yet, the man, like his car, has seen better days. His hands are large spatulas, and for the third time today, I notice ink-stained fingers. He strides up to us on sturdy, muscled legs, his white, pearly teeth flashing. "What the hell are you doing here, doctor?"

"And what-ho to you, as well old man," Ceddars replies, purposely ignoring the man's bad attitude. "And about why we are here… I'm sure you've heard already, but Wilson-Smallsey has been murdered and—"

"Yes, that idiot Inspector has arrested Sheng! He had nothing to do with it. Nothing at all. That policeman is a buffoon, like most people in this nasty little village. I should never have come here. I suppose you're here to gloat?"

While Ceddars tries to put a sentence together in reply,

I step forward and offer Eriksen my hand. "I'm Emily Crookshanks, a detective. I also do not believe Sheng is guilty of the crime he has been accused of. Pleased to meet you."

Ceddars & Snakes

ERIKSEN ushers us both inside his mansion, striding through the entrance hall and into the west-wing, entering what would have been a majestic and imposing room, if it had not been left untended for so long. The cornices are elegantly sculptured, but in places they're chipped and falling apart. A giant ornate fireplace is full of wooden boxes, its cracked mantle stacked with books and other whatnot. The rest of the room is filled with more wooden boxes, some of them opened, others nailed shut. I glimpse exotic statues, weird looking vases, and sculptures as well as strange musical instruments and jewellery. Indeed, the mansion appears to be more of a warehouse than a place of residence. Eriksen breezes through, taking us to a pair of double doors at the far end leading to another room that has an office feel about it, evidenced by a desk, a typewriter and an attractive, young red-headed woman sitting at the desk and typing.

"Any more news about poor Sheng?" she asks with concern as Eriksen throws himself down onto a chair?

Eriksen says nothing. He opens a drawer in his desk, takes out a half full bottle of whisky, pours himself more than two fingers, and knocks it back.

Fran Feltham is pretty. Prettier than I was expecting, which must be a disadvantage for a girl wanting to make a career for herself and not catch a husband—if Ceddars' description was anything to go by. She has strikingly red, thick hair held by a plain hair band. Her grey eyes are wide, intelligent, and cold, sitting behind a pair of functional and deliberately unattractive glasses. They do little to hide the beauty of her pixie-like face, the skin of which is pure alabaster without blemish. Her twin-piece is beige tweed and formal, but, like her glasses, it too is unable to hide her considerable female charms. I now understand what has put Mrs Willoughby in such a tizzy over the girl. My eyes are drawn to Fran's earrings. I almost missed them. Pearl drops mounted in silver. They are understated, but I notice them for what they are—the real deal. Significantly more expensive than anything she could afford.

Ceddars gives her a wide smile. "What-ho, Franny." He still is rather taken with William Eriksen's secretary, that much is for sure.

Fran flicks her long eyelashes in the direction of Ceddars, but only for a moment. "Hello doctor," she says dismissively. "And… this is?"

"Emily Crookshanks," Eriksen replies, as the smile on Ceddars' face disappears.

"Pleased to meet you, Miss Crookshanks." Her cold eyes are not quite able to hide a look of disdain as they glance over me. "I hear you are new to the village."

"She's somewhat of a professional sleuth," Ceddars adds, but Fran's eyes don't move away from me. She stands and we shake hands. Her fingernails are smooth and well-manicured, her shoes, functional but new and well-polished. The way she moves tells me she is confident and in control of herself. Already I can see that she is a formidable character. She must be, I realise, to work for William Eriksen.

"You're a detective?"

I nod.

"You certainly look the part."

Eriksen bashes his fist on his desktop. "You're too late, Miss Crookshanks. Troughton has already got his man and that's that!"

"I know that you're upset. But as I said outside, I believe Sheng is innocent. A convenient patsy. That's why I'm here…

to prove that innocence."

Eriksen sighs, his body deflating in the chair. "Truth is, it's looking very bleak for him."

"Bleak? Has more evidence come to light?"

The explorer gives me a grim nod of his head. "Sheng was seen having an argument with the vicar moments before visiting your house."

"Who was the witness?"

"Eugene Knight. He's a high-strung blond kid who I'm always seeing hanging around."

Fran Feltham nods. "He's an odd one that's for sure. I've caught him a few times spying on me. That mother of his, Mrs Knight, lets him run riot."

"Spying on you?"

"An adolescent boy, a very attractive young woman? You can guess the rest," Erikson replies drily.

I remember Eugene lurking around in Dooleys Wood after the murder and remind myself I need to talk to the boy.

Ceddars shrugs. "I say, that puts the nail squarely in the coffin, what?"

I give him a stern look. "The doctor here is convinced of Sheng's guilt, isn't that right?"

"You know what they say? If the shoe fits and all that whatnot."

Eriksen scowls at the doctor and they stare at each other tensely. "Sheng has been acting off for a few days now. It was so unlike him to threaten the vicar as he did last night. Very much out of character." Eriksen sighs again. "And this morning... he also wasn't himself. The evidence may point towards him being the culprit, but I do know one thing, doctor. He is honourable. If he were to kill, and God forbid if he did so—the man is an accomplished weapons master—he would never, ever, shoot a man in the back."

"Weapons master?"

He nods. "Sheng is from a noble Chinese family and, as

such, was warrior-trained from birth. He's a fine swordsman, a master of throwing knives and," he sighs, "an excellent shot with gun or bow."

I remember the crossbow bolt lodged dead centre in the Reverend Wilson-Smallsey's back and must concede that it was the shot of a master marksman.

"It may be hard for you to imagine," Eriksen continues, "but in Chinese culture, such men as Sheng are akin to the English knights of old. Their honour is a badge. That is why I'm convinced of his innocence."

"May I ask, if Sheng is a Chinese nobleman, why is he here working as your manservant?"

Eriksen laughs darkly. "That is what the village-folk believe. They can't imagine Sheng is an equal, a man akin to my brother. As a friend and companion. I have never stated he was my manservant. That is an assumption made by small minds. To some of them, he is seen as a heathen, and nothing more. But as I have told you, he is noble above measure."

I see tears forming in the corners of the man's eyes. "The way to prove Sheng's innocence is to find out as much information as we can."

Eriksen stands up and offers me his hand and we shake. "We'll do everything in our power, won't we Fran?"

The girl nods.

"May I ask what it is you are doing here, Miss Feltham? I heard you were Mr Eriksen's secretary, but—"

"Fran is helping me with all this," Eriksen replies for Fran with a sweep of his arm, indicating more boxes and exotic paraphernalia. "My collection. When we're done here, I will present to the Royal Society."

Fran sits up. "I'm collating and indexing everything that Mr Eriksen has brought back from his expeditions in the Far East. It's turning out to be quite a job."

"Do you work here every day?"

"Weekdays. I start at around nine-thirty in the morning

and finish at around four."

"And where are your lodgings?"

"I'm in a room above the local public house on the outskirts of the village. The Green Dragon. I left just after nine to cycle here."

"Did you see anything unusual on the way?"

A shake of her head.

"And you arrived here at roughly nine-thirty?"

"Yes." She gives Eriksen a nervous look.

I touch her arm, and she focuses her attention back onto me. "Is there something that you want to tell me?"

"I don't know."

Eriksen takes out a cigarette from a beat-up old silver-case and puts it to his lips, offering one to me.

I decline, again noticing the black ink stains on his fingers.

He doesn't offer one to Ceddars, but Fran takes one. Eriksen lights Fran and the pair make eye contact. "You might as well tell Miss Crookshanks, Fran," Eriksen says. "She witnessed an argument. Me and Sheng going at it about the vicar. He wanted to go and see Wilson-Smallsey and have it out with him. I managed to calm him down."

"I heard loud voices talking in Chinese," Fran says, nodding, "but I didn't know what they were arguing about, although I heard the vicar's name mentioned."

"They were talking in Mandarin?"

"I'm fluent," Eriksen explains, "Sheng taught me. He is an excellent and patient teacher."

"Things calmed down after that," Fran continues. "I prepared myself for today's delivery. The morning was a busy one as we were expecting the arrival of more items from Mr Eriksen's collection. You've seen all the boxes and crates outside? Just as they arrived, the phone rang. It was a gentleman asking for Sheng. He's never gotten a phone call, as far as I know. I gave him the receiver and before I left, I heard him speaking in Chinese again."

"He got a phone call?" Eriksen says in surprise. "Why the hell didn't you tell me? Who from? He knows no one in England apart from me."

Fran shrugs. "You were busy with the delivery. I left him on the phone to come and help."

"What time was that?" I ask.

"Just after ten. I was helping with the boxes until around ten-thirty when… when I realised I'd left my spectacles back in my lodgings. I absolutely needed them if I was to type up everything. I was just about to leave to go get them when I overheard Mr Eriksen and Sheng having another heated exchange." She glances over to Eriksen and gives him an apologetic look. "I'm sorry, William, I didn't mean to eavesdrop, but I couldn't understand what you were saying anyway."

I turn my attention back to the explorer. "What was this second argument about?"

Eriksen shrugs. "It wasn't exactly an argument. Sheng seemed so dreadfully off, if you know what I mean? Something was bothering the man, and he wouldn't tell me what. No matter how much I badgered him. And he usually tells me everything. I wanted him to sit down and talk to me, but he said he had to go out and, of course, I couldn't stop him."

"Did it cross your mind that he might've been planning to do the vicar harm?"

A quick shake of his head. "That was behind us. This was different, I'm sure of it."

"And you told all of this to Inspector Troughton?"

He nods. "Sheng is innocent. We have nothing to hide."

"I see. May I ask you about last night? I believe you had some items from your collection on display, including weapons?"

"A crossbow was stolen during that nonsense caused by

the vicar and that awful woman, Mrs Willoughby. I told that to Troughton. I told him that any one of the people there could've taken it during the commotion. Or hidden it to pick up later. But he wouldn't listen."

I nod in agreement. "That was also my thought. Now Fran, you said you headed out to retrieve your spectacles?"

Eriksen's pretty secretary nods, delicately placing the cigarette into the side of her mouth, her full lips pressing together as she inhales, before parting again to release a gentle trail of smoke. "I cycled back to my lodgings."

"And when did you return here?"

Fran looks a little uncomfortable and takes a few moments longer to reply. "At around quarter past eleven."

"That's forty-five minutes, when it took you only thirty minutes to cycle here in the morning."

"I say!" Ceddars intervenes. "Leave the poor girl alone. She's got nothing to do with this. I can vouch for that, she's a stand-up gal."

Ceddars' outburst appears to annoy Fran. "I was late because I couldn't find my spectacles. I searched everywhere. Twice. Got in quite a panic as it happens. They are my only pair."

"Did anyone see you?"

"I must protest!" Ceddars' voice is high and full of agitation. His penchant for gallantry is becoming annoying.

Fran thinks so as well, judging by the scowl that appears on her pretty young face. "I didn't see anyone. I have my own private door to my lodgings at the back of the pub. I returned here only to find that I'd left my spectacles on my desk. They were hidden under some papers. It had all been a silly mistake."

Fran stresses 'silly mistake' like the phrase means something else. As to what she is implying, I do not know. She's not telling me everything, that's for sure. And arriving back here at eleven-fifteen means she had ample opportunity to murder the vicar.

Fran puts the cigarette between her lips again and inhales. "Sheng returned just after me. He was—I know this isn't helping him—but he was rather agitated. He pushed right past me and into the house. I didn't see him again until the inspector arrived, and he was arrested."

"That means you were on your own at the time of the murder, correct?" I ask Eriksen.

He is a little taken aback. "Yes. I suppose I was."

"So," Ceddars says triumphantly, "you're also a suspect. There was nothing stopping you toddling off to Emily's and taking a pot-shot at the old vicar if you'd wanted to. You had certainly had a motive."

Eriksen and Ceddars are suddenly facing each other, the smell of testosterone strong in the air. I go and stand between them. "Just what is it between you two anyway?"

"The doctor here thinks I'm a coward, isn't that right?" Eriksen says.

"I didn't use that word. But where were you when it counted, eh? What were you doing when bally everyone else was fighting for king and country? Swanning off abroad with Johnny Foreigner, that's what!"

"I was abroad before the thing started."

"So were many other chaps. That didn't stop them coming home."

"You think it was a moral and just war? You think all those young men died for anything? It was a slaughter and nothing more."

"That's no excuse!"

"At least I'm still alive to argue my corner."

"And that's exactly my point. Millions of others are not still alive, including some of the finest men I've ever known. And..." Ceddars chokes. "And many, many good friends."

Eriksen's anger leaves him. "Of course, I didn't mean to sully their sacrifice. I was just saying that—"

"That's bally enough! I'm going outside to get some fresh air!" Ceddars performs a military turn and marches out of the nearest door into a darkened room, his footsteps disappearing into the distance.

"He's still highly strung from the war," Fran says.

Eriksen sucks at his cigarette and frowns. "Quite. But that's not my fault or my concern. You better go after him, Miss Crookshanks. The place is a maze, I'd hate for the doctor to get lost. Or for anything else of mine to go missing."

"What do you mean by that?"

Eriksen smiles darkly, pouring himself another large glass of whisky. "I mean that the doctor is just as likely to be the murderer as anyone else. He thinks me a coward, but that didn't stop him coming to my talk last night. I must admit, I was surprised to see him there. Nevertheless, it gave him the opportunity to steal the murder weapon. Which begs the question, Miss Crookshanks... does the doctor have an alibi?"

"But why would he need one? Do you know of any reason why Ceddars would want to kill the vicar?"

Eriksen nods, somewhat triumphantly. "The doctor may dislike me but had no love for the vicar. Indeed, you could say that he despised him."

"Explain?"

He takes a gulp of whisky and sits back. "Ever since the vicar started sticking his nose into my business, I've been doing the same into his."

"Can you tell me how your feud with Wilson-Smallsey started?"

"This may shock you, Miss Crookshanks, but I am a non-believer, which in the vicar's eyes makes me a heathen and therefore, his opponent. It wasn't my intention or my doing to get into conflict with the man, but he took it upon himself to make me a pariah. Not everyone in the village loves the vicar. Indeed, some despised him. And they saw me as an ally or at least a confidant. And I began to hear things. For instance, I found out that he once forced an innocent girl out of the village."

I'm intrigued. "What girl?"

"It was soon after the doctor returned from the war. He fell for some bright young thing well below his social class—the postmaster's daughter. Loved her by all accounts, and she him. And marriage was mentioned. The doctor went to Wilson-Smallsey for moral guidance. In return, the vicar made sure the girl and her father were hounded out of the village—he would not stand for someone marrying outside their social class. That man had real power in Pucklewick. They treated him like a god. The doctor was devastated but was led to believe it was for the best by the vicar, until he found out that the poor girl had died in poverty. He may seem like a jolly soul, but Doctor Roberts is a man all the same. A wronged man. And those who survived the war all returned damaged. If not on the outside, then very much on the inside."

"That's quite some accusation you're making."

Fran stubs out her cigarette in a large ornate ashtray. "Ceddars may be many things, but he wouldn't hurt a fly. And I'm sorry to speak out of turn, but that is no way to talk about a war hero."

Eriksen pushes back his thick blonde hair with a gnarled, ink-stained hand and shrugs. "I'm just saying that if you wanted a motive for murder, that man is very much in the frame."

I hadn't properly considered that Ceddars could be the murderer. The news that he had both opportunity and motive hits me unexpectedly in the gut. I think back to his appearance only moments after the vicar was shot. That was suspicious... very suspicious. He could've seen the vicar arriving as he visited Mrs Bates next door. And his doctor's bag was big enough to hide a small crossbow. And as an ex-pilot it was very possible he was also an excellent marksman. I have allowed myself to be swayed by his charming manner and his desire to help me. It would make him a cunning murderer and someone I need to be particularly wary of. I then remember the screwed-up poster he had in his possession. Not folded but scrunched up in what I'm guessing was a fit of anger. What had the poster said about the vicar?

He has hounded an innocent girl to an untimely death…

Could that have pushed Ceddars over the edge? No, I realise. This murder was premeditated. The crossbow was stolen to incriminate Eriksen or Sheng the night before. But if the doctor is the murderer, then it may have prompted him to act. Luckily, he doesn't know that I have discovered his possible motive. I decide to tackle Ceddars about it later.

"Did you find out anything else about the vicar?" I ask Eriksen. "He sounds like quite an unsavoury character."

"What if I did? It means nothing now that the man is dead."

"Maybe it does? You have ink on your fingers. Do you mind telling me where it came from?"

Eriksen stares down at them, rubbing at the stains as if noticing them for the first time. "I dabble in *Shufa*. It's a kind of Chinese calligraphy. I find it calming. Why do you ask?"

"It's just that a series of defamatory posters were put up around the village this morning containing accusations about the vicar. People who have touched those posters have ended up with inky fingers. And seeing that you seem to know the vicar's secrets…"

"You think I was responsible for that?" He shakes his head. "Do you have a copy?"

I take the poster out of my pocket and hand it to him.

He reads it quickly. Nodding. "Looks like the man's past had already caught up with him." He scoffs. "What a shame he's not around to enjoy his own impiety and fall from grace. It would've been good to see him destroyed, like he has done to so many others."

"You believe these accusations to be true then?"

He shrugs. "I certainly believe he was a womaniser and a gambler, so I'm not surprised about the rest. I know the man, know what he was capable of. And Wilson-Smallsey was determined to bring me down."

"How?"

His eyes flick apologetically towards Fran. "A young attractive career woman working for a man such as myself— an adventurer and a known heathen? The gossip has been rife. Gossip generated from both the vicar and his awful right-hand woman, Mrs Willoughby. If you were to believe those two, this mansion is a den of sordid iniquity. The things they have been saying about myself and Fran… quite frankly, it was disgusting. Is that not so, Fran?"

Fran removes her spectacles and rubs at the bridge of her nose. "It's nothing I haven't learnt to put up with."

"Even so," Eriksen says, "the things they have accused you of have been vile. Did you know the vicar had been trying to get Fran evicted from The Green Dragon?"

"Is that true?"

Fran gives me a sad smile and nods. "He did his best, but the vicar has been trying to close the establishment for a long time and failed. It sits on the edge of the village and isn't quite part of it. Not that it isn't frequented by many of the locals."

Fran is a capable young woman, but a sustained attack from someone like the vicar is not to be brushed off lightly. "Did you have any personal contact with him?"

"He asked me to have an interview with him after I first came to Little Pucklewick and began working for Mr Eriksen. He told me he was worried about my mortal soul. He'd obviously been drinking as evidenced by his wandering hands. Luckily, I've had experience of such situations before. I suspect other, less worldly girls may not have. I made my excuses and left." Her voice is matter of fact, but her eyes sparkle as she retells me her story.

"I see."

Eriksen stubs out his cigarette in a nearby ashtray. "Now do you get the measure of the man?"

"Yes, I think I do."

"It would be deplorable for Sheng to be convicted of such a despicable person's murder. It would be like he had won. We can't let that happen, Miss Crookshanks. We just can't."

"Just one more thing. Ceddars tells me you have romantic intentions towards a Mrs Dorothy Knight, is that correct?"

Eriksen gazes into his whisky glass. "I have gotten to know Mrs Knight very well over the last few months, much to the vicar's dislike, of course. He saw the women of Little Pucklewick as very much belonging to him and him alone, and he was particularly put out by our friendship. Dorothy has an interesting character. But in regard to romance, I'm afraid I'm a confirmed bachelor."

I nod. "Let me go and find Ceddars and we'll be on our way. I will need to talk to him very carefully about your suspicions. In the meantime, please try and find out who called Sheng this morning. I'm sure it has a bearing on the case. And anything else you can find."

"I'll do my best." He smiles at Fran. "We both will."

I give my goodbyes to Eriksen and his stunning secretary and enter a darkened corridor, heading towards the light of another room. The walls are covered in beautiful Chinese hangings and lined with busts of dragons and otherworldly creatures. I emerge into a large room also full of wonderful Chinese objects. They are arranged with no order in mind, the floor space filled with vases, statues, and a whole host of swords and other weapons lit from above by a wide, but stained skylight. The light throws crazy shadows over the room and abruptly, I feel like I'm no longer alone.

"Hello?" I shout. "Ceddars?"

And then I notice it. A creeping in the shadows. An immensely heavy form, moving through this cramped room without disturbing any of the artefacts. I get the sense it's searching… *searching for me!*

I back away, accidentally knocking over a rack of swords that clatter loudly. The thing rears up and I see it for what it is. A dreadful, black-skinned monster of writhing tentacles, and a wide, gaping, searching mouth. I stop, dead still, aware that the creature has an ethereal quality, its thick scales passing through the vases and statues and other objects as if they are not here. I can see only half of its length, the rest is hidden behind the walls, indeed, it is like the walls don't exist for this monster. But what is it? And what is it doing here? Am I hallucinating? The thing edges closer to me, and I become aware of my fountain pen held tightly in my hand, my hand also making twisting motions and dancing at my waist. Moving and gliding as if controlled by another.

The monster's gaping mouth hole splits open to reveal massive fangs dripping with venom, puffs of smoke coming from where the dreadful ichor drops onto the floor, burning and crackling.

The head gets closer to me, almost touching my face. The movements I'm making with my pen become more frantic and I hear a shout and the exclamation of arcane words, shocked to realise they are coming from my throat. There is an explosion of white and then a blackness descends upon me like a thick, heavy shroud.

Pins & Needling

A WAVE of dizziness and I stumble, almost knocking over a rack of ornate swords. Something dreadful has happened, but I don't know what—like the sense of fear that continues after waking from a barely remembered nightmare, except that I've not been asleep. I'm filled with a sense of foreboding, like I'm being watched, or... *searched for*. But by who or what? I'm Emily Crookshanks, recently returned from South Africa on a mission to find the murderer of the Reverend Wilson-Smallsey—a need that overwhelms and excites me—and yet I'm sure more is going on. Even so, the compulsion to continue in my search for the murderer is stronger than all others. I step forward and...

...the world refocuses around me. My head is abruptly filled with the words of Eriksen. I need to find Ceddars and probe him about what the dashing explorer told me.

I discover the doctor sitting in the garden on an old, ornate cast-iron bench rusting at the seams, smoking a cigarette. His large medical bag resting next to him. He stares into the distance, his thoughts elsewhere. It's a side to him I've not seen before. Serious and harder than the jovial fellow I've come to know.

He notices me, and his demeanour reverts to the Ceddars I recognise—animated and full of gentle airs. "Sorry about going off like a shot just now, but that Eriksen fellow quite gets my goat."

"You really don't like him, do you?"

"If you'd been in the war, and seen what I have seen, then you'd think the same about chaps like Eriksen. As for accusing him of being the murderer… that was a silly outburst. I'm sorry. Heated tempers and all that. But you now must agree that Sheng is the murderer. Especially after what Franny said and Eugene witnessing the vicar arguing with the man."

"The evidence is quite damning, but my intuition says otherwise."

"Maybe I'm shooting wide of the mark, but perhaps you are searching for a mystery where there is none? Sure, you've an impressive noggin and all that, very impressive, some might say, but sometimes there is no deeper mystery to solve."

"Go on."

Well, Em', it's like this. Perhaps, you are, and this is with my Devil's Advocate hat on… a tad deluded."

"That's quite some accusation."

"Bear me out. You arrived in Little Pucklewick only a few days ago and were immediately unwell. I tended to you at the time, but when I met you this morning, you had no recollection of who I was."

I say nothing.

"You're suffering from amnesia… am I right?"

I'm impressed and annoyed by the doctor's astuteness. "What if I am?"

"It's obvious, isn't it? You're not quite yourself, and because of that, how can you possibly trust this intuition of yours?"

The doctor makes a valid point. "I have no memories from before I woke up this morning. Nothing."

Ceddars' eyes narrow with concern. "That's serious Em', very serious. You should've told me."

"Otherwise, I'm not impaired." I decide not to mention the distinct sensation that I'm in danger. "My mind is functioning perfectly well, doctor. My reasoning and powers of deduction have already impressed you. I just don't remember anything else. Like I'm missing a backstory."

Ceddars doesn't say anything for a few moments, his face unusually blank.

"Ceddars? Are you okay?"

I give the doctor a nudge and he jerks back into life. "Of course, I'm okay."

"One thing is bothering me. If you dislike Eriksen so much, why did you go to his talk at the village hall last night?"

Ceddars takes time to answer, his bushy moustache twisting in annoyance. "You caught me out there, what? I have no interest in Eriksen and his damn travels. Quite the opposite as it happens. But I do have an interest in his secretary. I knew Franny would be there and, well, I'm rather smitten as it happens."

"You told me she wasn't interested in you."

He nods. "It's true. She doesn't see herself getting married for a long time."

"I'm not knocking the girl—and god knows she has a lot to contend with if her ambition is to have a career—but don't you think she comes across as overly controlled and a little hard-faced?"

"She is that," he replies animatedly, "I do wonder if there is any emotion lurking underneath that devastatingly pretty exterior, but you can't blame a chap for still hoping, what?"

His reason makes sense, but Ceddars is not off my suspect list yet. And I can't help wondering why Eriksen was so keen to accuse Ceddars like he did. In fact, everything about our recent exchange had a contrived feel about it. One thing was for sure though, the explorer did not like the Reverend Wilson-Smallsey. "Is there anything else you want to tell me?"

"Like what?"

I think back to what Eriksen said about the Postmaster's daughter. Was that enough motive for the doctor to commit murder? My gut instinct tells me no, that Ceddars is innocent. But I'm not sure. I remember the newspaper cuttings in the hatbox back in my dressing room. A string of successes and a single fall from grace. I will need to take a closer look at them.

Ceddars smiles at me and, for the first time since I've met him, his moustache doesn't seem that ridiculous. "It's jolly nice to be able to have a gal to chat to like this, even if she is a wonder sleuth who can see right through me like thin toffee."

He's either the self-effacing and somewhat charming doctor or a cunning and ruthless murderer. I will need to be cautious around him, that much is for sure.

"I say, we don't have to go back inside, do we? Can't we just toddle off without saying our goodbyes, what? It'll be bally awkward. I'm still angry with that cad, Eriksen. I don't think I'd be able to bally control myself."

"I've already told them we were leaving so don't worry about that."

"I suppose Franny thinks I'm quite the idiot."

"It's hard to tell what she thinks. She's the kind of girl who plays her cards close to her sizeable chest."

"Rather." He brightens, and it's like our earlier uncomfortable conversation has been forgotten. "Where to next? To see that Sheng fellow? To sound him out? Grab the bull by the horns so-to-speak, what?"

"Don't you have your medical practice to attend to?"

"That's Wednesday and Friday afternoons. I'm free to help all day and despite the death of the vicar, this is quite the most excitement I've had in a long time. Are we off to the police station?"

"I'm not sure, I think we should chat to Eugene Knight first, and maybe have another word with his mother."

"Dotty Knight? Didn't I see you talking to her already?"

"Yes, but the relationship between her and Eriksen intrigues me. They seem like opposites."

"Their relationship is an odd one, but those two have

been rather close of late. I'd go as far to say that it was one of the things that annoyed the vicar. The gossip is that Eriksen's intentions are to marry the old girl."

"Are you sure about that? Eriksen, told me otherwise."

"Really? It's only rumour and speculation, and Dotty has, well, come to life of late, if you know what I mean?"

"You're suggesting they are having relations?"

"Oh, no, no, no. At least I don't think so. Who knows what goes on behind closed doors, what? It'd be a scandal if it were true. I just meant that she has been enjoying his attention. And for an older gal, she is still bally attractive."

"Have you ever been—?"

"Interested in Dotty Knight? Good gracious no. The woman is a dreamer. Head in the clouds and all that. Dotty by name, dotty by nature, what?"

I disagree with the doctor, from what I gleaned from our earlier conversation, the woman seemed sharp minded—and Eriksen was no fool either. He like Fran, was not the type to suffer fools lightly.

I think back to my exchanges with Eriksen. He was eager to defend his manservant and yet, nearly everything he said added to the evidence against him. Eriksen could have explained away the argument between them as anything he wanted—it was in Mandarin after all—but he chose to tell me it was specifically about Sheng wanting to go and have it out with the vicar. Why do that? Eriksen obviously has a lot of respect for his companion, so why add to the evidence against him? He was either pathologically honest, or he had a reason.

I look at my watch. "Do you know where we can find the Knights at this time of the day?"

"Dotty should be in her shop although I expect the place will be closed as will everywhere else. In light of the vicar's untimely death of course. She lives in the rooms above. I have no idea if Eugene will be there, but we can try."

"Is the police station close by?"

"Nothing is very far away in Little Pucklewick."

"Good, I'm keen to talk to Eugene about what he saw of the argument between Sheng and the vicar."

"Well then, let's toddle off."

We go back up the hill, the gloomy trees of Dooleys Wood silent and watchful. We continue southwards over the brow of the hill onto a road that runs along the west side of Little Pucklewick. As we descend, I notice how the church and the vicarage stand imposingly above the village. I remember that Mary, the vicar's wife, said she liked to watch the comings and goings of its residents, her windows would give her an excellent vantage point. I also wonder why she lied to me about what she had seen this morning. It's been troubling me ever since we left the vicarage. I had been in a mind to discuss my thoughts with Ceddars, but I'm no longer sure he's as trustworthy as I once believed.

We come to the village green, a large rectangle of well-tended grass, bordered with multicoloured summer flowers. An old, vast tree stands majestically at one side. I walk over to examine it.

"That's the Pucklewick Oak," Ceddars says in explanation. Been here hundreds of years is what they say. It's got character, what?"

I walk around the impressive tree noticing how the bark is criss-crossed with ancient looking graffiti, various love hearts, names, and dates. I find what I'm looking for, two drawing pins used to put up the poster that had gotten Mrs Willoughby in such a state. I take out the drawing pin that I found on the vicarage gate and compare it. They are both new and untarnished.

"You seem very interested in those pins, Em', but I can't see how there can be any clues in them. They're ten-a-penny, what? I dare say I've got a box full of the things back in my desk. And so would most people."

"Well, Ceddars, you'd be very much mistaken. There is a clue here."

"There is? Crikey!" He goes up to the tree to take a closer look, his moustache twisting this way and that as he examines the pins from different angles. "I'll be damned if I can see it. If you'll pardon my French."

"It's staring you in the face."

Ceddars shrugs and gives up. "Didn't Mrs W say she saw a stranger chappie putting up a poster on this tree? I'm guessing you've found a clue about the fellow?"

"Two clues."

"Bally hell! I'm impressed, or I would be if I knew what on earth it is you've seen."

"That's why I'm a detective and you're a doctor. Now let's get on."

"You don't need to take these pins as evidence?"

"I've seen as much as I need."

If anything, the doctor is more impressed.

We head across the common towards a row of shops on the far side. A young lad of about sixteen cycles past, zooming along the road on an ancient beat-up bicycle.

"What ho, Bill my lad," Ceddars shouts in greeting.

"Ullo, Doctor Roberts," he replies in a thick accent, inefficiently braking the bike with his boots and stopping some way past us. "What a terrible business with the vicar," he continues, when we catch up to him, saying the words by rote, rather than with any heartfelt emotion. But then again, the boy is just that, a boy. He's lanky for his age, in clothes that he's obviously outgrown. He possesses bright, intelligent eyes and thick black unruly hair, lending him a rakish look. He's an attractive lad, who I'm guessing will be turning many a young girl's head in a few years' time.

"This is Miss Crookshanks."

"You're Miss Crookshanks?"

"I am. You delivered a note to Molly this morning, didn't

you?"

"Yes, ma'am, I did," he says seriously, giving Ceddars a quizzical look.

"It's okay, Billy, Miss Crookshanks here is somewhat of a detective, what? And she's a miss, not a ma'am."

His eyes widen.

I waste no time. "Tell me what happened this morning. What time did the vicar give you my note?"

Billy takes a few moments to order his thoughts. "It were around nine, ma'am… I mean, miss. I was doing a few early morning chores around the vicarage—taking out rubbish and the like, and was just on my way to see Mr Eriksen, who I knew the vicar disapproves of, but he pays so handsomely— when the vicar called me into his study. He gave me a note to deliver to you, miss."

"Mr Eriksen?" I swap a glance with Ceddars. "I've just been to his mansion. No one mentioned you were there."

"Yes, miss, I were helping 'im and… um… Miss Feltham with a big delivery they had this morning. Although I arrived late due to the errand the vicar made me run for him."

"I see. What mood was the vicar in when you saw him? Was he angry about something?"

"He was. How did you know that?"

"Yes, how did you know that?" Ceddars echoes, the impressed look returning to his face.

I ignore both their questions. "And you took the note straight to my cottage."

"I did, miss."

"Molly said you already knew what the note was about."

"That's right. The vicar told me himself, so he did. *Take this to Miss Crookshanks' at once. And tell Molly I'll be dropping in today for tea and cakes.*"

"And this made you late for Mr Eriksen?"

"Not exactly. When I got to your cottage, Molly insisted on sitting me down and feeding me. I knew I shouldn't miss, but I were hungry. I told her the vicar was visiting and she got all in a tiz. Said she had to wake you up and ran off with the note, leaving me on my own in the kitchen. By the time I got to Mr Eriksen's, his delivery had already arrived."

"Mr Eriksen, his manservant Sheng, and his secretary Miss Fran Feltham were all present?"

He nods, looking uncomfortable.

"Did you say why you were late?"

"I did mention to Mr Eriksen that I had to deliver a note for the vicar."

"Now, this is very important Billy, did you tell him the contents of that note?"

Billy squirms. "I didn't see any harm in it," he replies defensively. "Mr Eriksen is always keen to know anything about the vicar, for which he tips me quite handsomely."

"You ventured the information freely?"

Billy shakes his head vehemently. "No, miss, of course not. That's not what happened. I would never have said anything if not for Mr Eriksen asking me directly."

I wonder if Billy is lying to cover his indiscretion. But the kid can't be blamed for making money from Eriksen's feud with the vicar. "And who else overheard?"

"That Sheng fellow was there."

"Sheng heard you?" Ceddars asks, jumping in a little aggressively.

Billy nods, his cheeks flushing. "I didn't know that he was about to…"

I put out a hand to Billy's shoulder. "It wasn't your fault. Indeed, I believe Sheng to be innocent."

Ceddars purses his lips but says nothing.

Billy's downcast face brightens. "You do, miss?"

"Now tell me, did Miss Feltham, his secretary, overhear you?"

"I dunno, miss. Maybe."

"Hey, hang on Em'. You can't think Franny had anything

to do with this?"

I ignore the doctor's outburst. "What time did you leave Mr Eriksen."

"About quarter to eleven."

"Did you see anything out of the ordinary this morning?"

He brightens as if in sudden memory, his right hand brushing his shirt pocket. "Now you come to mention it, I saw Mr Simmons, the new curator, coming out of the church vaults at just after twelve. I was surprised because he told everyone he doesn't like underground spaces. From his time in the trenches, they say."

Ceddars strokes at his moustache with a single hand, his thumb and forefinger rubbing backwards and forwards. "By Jove! He told us about his claustrophobia the last time we met him. Was he lying?"

I shrug. "That's what we will need to ask him. And make a visit to the vaults ourselves."

"Indeed!"

I continue questioning Billy. "Did he see you?"

He shakes his head proudly. "He seemed preoccupied. But I was walking behind tall bushes that grow close to the wall. It's a cut through I use."

"And was the curate carrying anything?"

"As a matter of fact, he was. A satchel. He was clutching it to his chest like he was frightened to drop it."

"And what do you know of the man?"

"He's new, miss. To the village an' the church. He was friendly when I first met him, but this last couple of weeks, he's taken against me."

"Taken against you? How?" Ceddars asks.

"I dunno. But I've caught him staring at me and then crossing himself when I've noticed. He's an odd fellow. Everyone says he needs a wife." He winks at the doctor and flushes when he realises I've seen him. "Sorry, miss."

"Thank you, Billy, you've been very helpful. And if you're

ever hungry again, you can drop in on Molly and she will always give you a meal."

"Why, thank you miss."

"Before you go, I wonder if you could tell me anything about Eugene Knight?"

"Eugene?" Billy's face darkens. "What about him?"

"I just wish to know more about the lad, and you are the same age."

Billy shakes his head. "He's two year older and thinks he's better than me."

"Why would you say that?"

"I don't want to speak out of turn, miss, especially after this morning."

"It's alright, Billy," Ceddars says. "See Miss Crookshanks here as a detective. You can tell her anything and it will remain in the strictest confidence."

"We were best friends, miss. He'd come home from his school for the summer, and we'd always play together. But last year when he came back, well, he wanted nothing to do with me. Seemed angry at me, but I don't know why. He needled me, calling me names. In fact, ever since last summer, he's been acting very oddly. He's always hanging around Dooleys Wood and sneaking about here, there, and everywhere."

"I see. And who are your parents?"

Billy shrugs. "I don't have none. I were an orphan until the Browns took me in. Now I really must go, miss. It's ale delivery day at the Green Dragon and I'm helping out."

We say our goodbyes and Billy cycles away.

"Who are the Browns?"

"A poor retired couple and devout churchgoers. They took Billy in quite a few years ago."

We cross the road to a shop called 'Flowers by Knight'.

"We're here, although I can't see what Eugene can possibly tell you, unless you think he's lying… and speak of the Devil, there he bally is."

I follow Ceddars' pointing finger and see Eugene walking head down towards the florist shop, his longish blond hair covering his face. Before he realises we're there, Ceddars grabs him. "Hey ho, Eugene. We want a word with you, don't we Miss Crookshanks?"

Coppers & Confessions

"**Y**OU?" Eugene sneers, pulling himself easily free of Ceddars and taking a few steps backwards, his face twisting into a scowl. "I know what you did! Shame on you! Shame on you!" He turns and runs away.

"What the bally hell?"

I watch the departing back of Eugene and the startled look on Ceddars' face. The doctor is just as shocked as I am.

"What did he mean by that?"

Ceddars shrugs, the motion exaggerated and jerky, as if to emphasise his confusion. "I don't know. The lad has been off with me for a while now. How bally odd." He turns and raises his eyebrows. "Now, now, don't go reading anything into that."

"And what would that be?"

"That he saw something that implicated me in the vicar's murder, that's what. I've not known you for very long, but I have become more than acquainted with how your mind works. As I bally told you, I had nothing to do with it."

That's not exactly what I was thinking—Eugene was at the police station earlier implicating Sheng in the murder, not the doctor—nevertheless, Ceddars' defensiveness piques my interest. "Did you have any reason to bump off the reverend?"

"I say, what?"

"You know what I'm asking."

"What is this, Em'? What are you saying?" He nervously takes out a cigarette from a silver case and lights it.

"You were at Mrs Bates' cottage next door when the

murder happened, is that correct?"

"Why are you asking me this? I thought we had an understanding—"

"If I was to go and talk to Mrs Bates, would she confirm your alibi?"

He frowns, the irritation returning to his face. "Not exactly. I was on my way there when I heard that dreadful ballyhoo coming from your open windows."

"But you said," I pause to remember his words, "*I was next door making my regular morning visit to Mrs Bates.*"

"I was next door, and just about to knock on Mrs Bates' door as it happens. I certainly wasn't lying to you."

"Meaning you have no alibi at the time of the murder?"

He throws away his cigarette in disgust. "And I thought you and I were rather getting on."

"We do get on, that's true. But if you are lying to me about anything to do with this murder, you must realise that I will find out sooner or later."

Ceddars takes out another cigarette and lights it. "You are very full of yourself, Miss Crookshanks. You may think Fran is hard-faced, but she has nothing on you. I'm not your man. I've seen enough death in my lifetime, too much of it. In the war, and as a doctor. They say you get accustomed to it, but I'm afraid that hasn't quite happened. I've been thinking of giving up the old practice and moving on. But I bally well have no idea where I'd go or what I'd do. I'm pretty dang useless." He takes a deep drag on the cigarette and lets out the smoke in one long sigh.

"It's time we went and talked to Sheng."

Ceddars immediately brightens. "Perhaps the odd fellow will give you a full confession and get me off the hook, what?"

"Unlikely. He isn't the murderer."

"As you keep saying. But if not Sheng, who? Billy perhaps?" he says scoffing. "He knew where the vicar was going to be, didn't he? Or maybe it was that little tick, Eugene? Hell, why not suspect everybody."

"I wouldn't be much of a detective if I didn't. But talking to Billy reminded me that I've been so focused on motive and opportunity, that I forgot one important detail… the murderer must've known the vicar was heading to my house. Billy gave that information to Eriksen, Sheng and Fran. Indeed, everyone in that mansion knew where the vicar would be this morning at eleven, and they all had opportunity to kill him."

"Now steady on! I'm not letting you include Franny in your list. Doesn't it make it more likely that Sheng did it? The evidence is piling up against the fellow, why won't you accept that?"

"The difference between you and I, Ceddars—the same difference between a sleuth and a regular person—is that I force myself to keep all options open, while others are always far too keen to close them down."

"Very eloquent, but I won't have a word spoken against Franny. I just won't."

I can't help but smile at Ceddars' gallant knight act, and if it's just that—an act—he's very good at it. "Right, let's go talk to your prime suspect, Sheng. Where's the local nick?"

"Oh Em', I do so love your vernacular."

As we approach the station, a surly, thickset young man in his late twenties marches out from an abandoned cottage, one of many that are undergoing reconstruction work. The doors and windows mostly boarded up. He almost bumps into us.

"Watch where yers going!" he shouts before lifting his head and noticing the doctor. "Oh it's you. Sorry doc'," he says. He gives me the once over and raises his eyebrows. "And who's this?"

"Good afternoon, Grantham," Ceddars says. "This is Miss Emily Crookshanks."

Grantham stares at me unabashed. "I thought as much.

An' very nice she is too." He winks at Ceddars before turning back to me. "Hey, weren't it your 'ouse that the vicar were murdered in? That was a rum business. That foreign scum they have got locked up forrit should 'ang, for sure. I knew sumfin like this would 'appen when the likes of 'im were allowed to come to Pucklewick. Like I said to me mates… mark my words, nowt good will come out of it… an' I were right."

"I'm sure the police know what they're doing," Ceddars says, grabbing my elbow and walking us both away. "Good day."

"They better know what they're doing!" Grantham shouts at our backs. "Otherwise 'e'll have me and me mates to deal with, for sure!"

"I'm sorry about him," Ceddars says. "He's one of the village thugs."

"Pucklewick has thugs?"

"Doesn't everywhere in this awful day and age? I don't know what happened while I was away. I returned from the war to a country very different from the one I left."

We cross the road from the row of abandoned cottages and arrive at Little Pucklewick police station, a rather quaint single storey building constructed from fresh-looking granite blocks. It seems this whole area of the village is being redeveloped. A new blue lantern hangs above a large black door located at the station's centre. A policeman's bicycle leans against the wall outside.

"The place has just been built," Ceddars says. "It serves the whole district, not just Pucklewick."

"Yes, I did wonder why an inspector was so close on hand this morning. He arrived very quickly—didn't you think?"

"You can't be suspicious of old Troughton, can you? He's a bally copper."

"No one is above the law, Ceddars."

"Crikey, Em'. This all can't be good for you, can it?"

"What can't?"

"All this suspicion that you are living with day to day. Do you ever turn it off?"

I give him an incredulous look, like he's said the most ridiculous thing. "I never turn it off, Ceddars. Where's the fun in that?"

"That doesn't sound very healthy."

"But you like reading mysteries?"

"Who doesn't?"

"Then there is your answer. Now, tell me more about Little Pucklewick. I live here, but know next to nothing about the place."

Ceddars gives me a sideways look but answers all the same. "I've no real idea about the history of the place. It's small, always has been, although there has been some recent development. This place for instance. Indeed, Pucklewick was all set to expand after they built the train station, but the village council had other ideas, what? Rather put the kibosh on it."

"There's a train station?"

"Oh yes. One can travel to London and back in a day."

"Anything else of interest?"

"Pucklewick is like any other village in the south of England. The church sits at the centre of everything, and everyone revolves around it. Very, very boring. Until you arrived that is."

He pushes the police station door and ushers me inside into a small anteroom. It's minimalist—wooden panels and white painted walls. I'm met by an empty desk, behind which is a single closed door.

"Hello?" Ceddars ventures, his voice echoing off empty walls.

I spot a bell on the desk and bash it heavily with my palm. We wait a few moments, and no one appears. I bash the bell a few more times.

Ceddars puts his big palm over my hand. "Steady on, Em'. I'm sure they've heard us by now."

He holds his hand over mine for a moment longer than is necessary, his skin warm and rough, before quickly pulling it away.

Our eyes meet and he draws breath to speak, just as the door opens and Police Constable Jakes waddles in.

"Oh, it's you again, miss… and the doctor."

"What ho, Constable," Ceddars says. "We've come to see the convict, what?"

"I beg your pardon, sir?"

"We've come to chat to Eriksen's manservant, Sheng," Ceddars continues, unabashed. "I believe you have him banged up in here before he faces the local beak."

"Yes sir. Inspector Troughton arrested the fellow in question earlier this morning."

"I'd like to speak to him," I say.

Jakes reddens. "I'm not sure that will be possible, miss."

"And why's that?"

"It being that you're not… um… a police officer, miss."

"But, and the doctor will back me up on this, the inspector said, *Sheng will run, Miss Crookshanks, be assured of it. But if he doesn't, you will be more than welcome at the police station. I'll even get Constable Jakes to make you a cup of tea—at least he can be trusted with that.*"

"Um, are you sure he said that?"

"Of course, he said it, are you calling us liars?"

"No miss, of course not miss."

"Good, I like mine milky no sugar."

"Miss?"

"My tea, that your inspector promised you'd make me."

Constable Jakes shuffles uncomfortably, seemingly rooted to the spot. "I think that maybe I ought to talk to the inspector first. He did say that no one were allowed to see the prisoner. He put me on guard an', well, after what happened this morning, I need to stay in his good books."

I take a step closer to Jakes and fix him with my eyes. "Good books? Oh, it's too late for that constable… although we won't be calling you that for much longer. The inspector was very clear. You're to lose your job over this. He was adamant."

"He said that?" Jakes looks at Ceddars to verify my words.

The doctor nods sadly. "'Fraid so old chap. I tried to talk the fellow out of it, but he's not the type to listen once his mind is made up, what?"

The large man visibly sags, his eyes watering. "But I've been a copper all me life. I don't know how to do anything else. An' what will Mrs Jakes say? There will be hell to pay when she finds out. Oh my."

"Sit down constable. Here…" Ceddars pulls the desk chair over and the big man drops his weight onto it.

"There is one way you might keep your job."

Jakes looks up at me hopefully. "There is, miss?"

"Let me go and talk to the prisoner… to Sheng. I'm convinced he's not guilty of murdering the vicar. If I can prove that, then you will be off the hook. Your failure to take Sheng's threat seriously won't have mattered. And Inspector Troughton won't be able to get rid of you if you were not responsible, will he?"

Jakes' rounded face brightens for a moment then sags. "But that Eugene lad were in here earlier, telling the inspector about the argument he saw between the prisoner an' the poor vicar. It looks like the fellow is very guilty which means…"

"Like I said, I don't believe that. And the way to help me prove that the inspector is wrong is to let me see the prisoner."

"But I can't just let you in against his strict orders. The inspector would sack me on the spot if he found out."

"That's easily sorted," I say.

"It is, miss?"

"What if you were to receive an emergency call? You'd have to leave the station to investigate, isn't that correct?"

He nods. "But emergency calls are few an' far between in Little Pucklewick."

"Not if Ceddars was to make it."

Ceddars' head jerks backwards on his neck. "I say, what?"

"You remember that stranger you saw hanging around the village, well, Ceddars here was just threatened by the man. He was carrying a knife, isn't that correct, Ceddars? And shouting all manner of obscenities. And he absolutely insists that you go and arrest this maniac."

Ceddars' moustache flexes back and forth. "I do?"

Constable Jakes looks confused. "A knife you say?"

"Not really. But, of course, with the village doctor asking for your assistance, you can't say no."

Realisation dawns across the portly constable's face. "I s'ppose I'd have to go. No two ways round it. But we're not supposed to leave the prisoners on their own."

"That's why Ceddars volunteered to man the station why you went to apprehend this awful villain."

"I see, miss. I see."

Jakes stays sat on the chair for a few moments, staring into space.

"Don't you need to be off, constable, investigating the doctor's report?"

"Of course. I'll be on my way now, miss." He stands up, takes out a notebook and a new pencil and turns to Ceddars. "Now where did you say you saw this fellow?"

"What? Oh, I see… Um… well he was running through the village, constable, heading towards Dooleys Wood."

Jakes writes down the information and snaps his book shut. "Right, I'd better be off then. Can you keep an eye on the prisoner for me, doctor? I'm putting him in your care, alright?"

Ceddars nods seriously. "Of course, yes. Absolutely."

"But be forewarned, he's not uttered a single word to anyone since he was brought in. I'd be very surprised if he'd start talking now." He salutes and leaves the police station.

"What if Troughton makes an appearance?" Ceddars says after Jakes has left.

"We tell him what you told the constable."

"But I'm rather against the whole concept of lying, what? Not aux fait with it at all as it happens. Against my personal code and all that, what?"

"That's good to hear, but you'll do the right thing if or when the time comes."

"I'm not sure I will…"

"Do you want to see Constable Jakes sacked?"

"Of course not."

"Good. Now let's go and find the prisoner."

We walk through the police station inner door and enter an office of sorts. A single telephone and three desks. The rest of the room is taken up with cupboards and shelving.

Another door leads to a set of steps leading down to the cells. Three of them. All open-barred. Lying on the bed in one of the cells is a diminutive man in smart-looking Chinese clothing. Eriksen's companion, Sheng.

If Sheng is aware of our presence, he doesn't show it.

A single desk and chair sit outside the cells. I drag the chair to his cell and sit down. "You do not know me, Mr Sheng. My name is Emily Crookshanks and I believe you are innocent."

RAF & Bugattis

"I SAY," Ceddars exclaims in annoyance. "Sit up when a lady is talking to you!"

Sheng makes no movement, he stays as still as a snake, a simile that does not sit well with me.

"As I said, I believe you are innocent of the murder of the Reverend Wilson-Smallsey."

Still no reaction. I'm perplexed, this is not what I was expecting from Eriksen's manservant. He is small, and of slight build. His hair long and fashioned into a ponytail, his features plain, but delicate. He wears a Chinese smock, loose pyjama-like trousers and sandals. In my mind's eye, this 'weapons master' as Eriksen described him to me, was far burlier and more dangerous looking. But then again, looks can be deceptive. "Unless I'm mistaken and you're the kind of killer who shoots another man in the back?"

Sheng's head twitches at these words and, despite his feigned indifference, I notice the pulse of his heart jerking in the arteries of his neck.

"Do you want to die for a crime you did not commit? Do you?" I continue, raising my voice.

Ceddars bangs on the cell bars. "Answer the lady?"

Sheng remains motionless.

"They say that these Chinese fellows are inscrutable, but this chap is downright rude."

I ignore the doctor, keeping my eyes centred on the prisoner. "I can't help you unless you talk to me. I need to know what you were doing outside my house this morning and why you were arguing with the vicar."

Sheng pushes himself up on to one elbow, looks at me with dead-like eyes and turns away to face the cell wall.

"It's quite obvious the man is guilty as hell. Let's get out of here."

"Why won't he speak?" I say, standing up and turning to Ceddars. "It makes no sense."

"It makes perfect sense if he is the killer, Em'. And who knows what goes on in the minds of foreign chaps like him? Give it up, you're barking up the wrong tree."

I'm annoyed and for the first time I wonder if the doctor is right about Sheng's guilt. I drag the chair back to the desk and notice a large brown envelope, and the spidery-like writing of Inspector Troughton. I open it to find what I'm assuming are Sheng's belongings. There's a set of keys, a gold-like coin with a square cut out of the middle—a luck piece of some kind—and a letter addressed to what I'm assuming is Sheng's name in Chinese. Underneath is the address of Eriksen's mansion in English. I open it up, aware of Sheng tensing upon the bed of his cell. I get the sense he doesn't want me reading his mail. But he needn't worry, the letter is written in Mandarin. I have many talents, but reading exotic foreign languages doesn't appear to be one of them. I flip it over to no avail. I can't make head nor tail of it.

"By Jove, these Chinese fellows sure make it hard for themselves, what?" Ceddars says over my shoulder. "All those squiggly lines and whatnot. Must take them an age to write anything."

I fold the letter and slide it back into the envelope, noticing the address of the sender written on the back.

"Where is Upper Cockshoot?"

"That's the next village along and substantially larger in size. Not that far away, but it might as well be a hundred miles. It is frowned upon by the residents of Little Pucklewick. Seen as a writhing den of heathens."

"And why's that?"

"They have a speakeasy, a dance hall, and a racecourse. And, worst of all… the Black Swan public house that allows any and all riff-raff to stay there." He lowers his voice. "And has quite the reputation for *you know what*."

"You mean…"

"Yes, couples signing as Mr and Mrs Smith and no questions asked. Scandalous!" He smiles cheekily and raises his eyebrows.

"Sounds fun."

"Oh Em', you are quite the modern woman."

"Have you ever stayed there?"

"The pub? No, of course not, what are you suggesting?"

"I think you know what I'm suggesting."

"You're wrong. Doctors are too well known to be able to get up to that kind of thing."

"And that's the only reason that stopped you?"

"Now, now. I'm a gentleman, but I have driven out to the village in the old jalopy on the odd evening for a drink or two. There's not much to do in Pucklewick. The vicar saw to that."

"You've got a car?"

"Of course. I'm a modern chap, don't you know? Fell in love with engines during my time in the RAF. It's not a patch on the battered beauty that Eriksen drives, but it still turns heads."

"I'd very much like to take a ride in it."

"You would?"

"Yes, I want to visit the Black Swan."

Ceddars eyebrows rise again. "Do you now?"

"Don't get your hopes up… I want to try and find who sent this letter. Don't you?"

"Oh… You think it's important?"

I sigh. "I don't know, but it's all I've got to go on. Can you take me?"

"I suppose so. It's been a while since I've been out on a

jaunt. And it's a nice day for it. Why not?"

"Do not go!" The voice belongs to Sheng. It is quiet, almost a whisper, but forceful.

I turn back to the cell. Sheng is standing at the bars, his eyes intent on the letter. "Why not?"

He stares at me but says nothing.

"That settles it, we will go over there straightaway."

"I'll go and get the beast and meet you here shortly." Ceddars marches out of the cell block like he is on a mission.

Sheng grasps the iron bars, flexing on his toes and staring at me.

"I don't know why you're being quiet, but I will find out, I assure you. And you will thank me."

The cell darkens, like a cloud has drifted in front of the sun, but we are underground. I'm perplexed for a moment, wondering if there is some problem with the lighting, and take a step back, or try to. I'm rooted to the ground. Sheng stands strangely still, his eyes glassy and full of emptiness. The darkness turns blue-grey and then completely black, punctuated only by twin dots of light that shine from Sheng's eyes like twin spotlights. Lights that dart around the block of cells like they are searching for me! I feel dreadfully exposed, knowing that the lights will find me. I'm terrified.

I come back to myself… I'm not Emily Crookshanks but someone else. I have another name, a name that leaves my lips in a burst of sound—a flurry of words that emanate loudly from the back of my throat. The lights dart towards me, my voice rising to a crescendo, and…

"Miss? You alright?"

I open my eyes to find myself sitting on the single chair in the cell block, my fountain pen held tightly in my fist. My head throbbing. Sheng is back on his bunk, his back to me.

"Miss," the voice continues concernedly.

I turn to see the rotund face of Constable Jakes staring at me with a worried expression. "I thought that fellow had put a spell on you. You were in quite a deep sleep. I couldn't wake you."

I stand up, a little woozy, noticing my red hat lying discarded on the floor. "I'm fine now, constable."

"You sure? You look a little peaky."

"I'm very sure."

Constable Jakes straightens, his eyes flicking to the door leading out of the cells. "Well, if that's the case perhaps you could be… um… leaving? The inspector could be back at any time."

"Yes, of course."

"Did the devil say anything?"

I shake my head, replace the fountain pen in my top pocket, and pick up my hat. What happened just now? Did I fall asleep? Was I dreaming?

"I did tell you that you'd get nothing out of him, but I did hope," he says, like he hasn't heard my question. "I suppose my goose is well and truly cooked."

"Never give up hope, constable."

He indicates to the door, and I step through, heading back up the stairs, where I say my goodbyes and go outside, just as Ceddars arrives in a very smart looking blue Bugatti. The car has an elegant, vintage feel. Its long hood, sleek lines, and low profile perfectly complementing the deep blue of the paintwork, giving it an aura of sophistication and real style. From its signature horseshoe grille to the hand-painted insignia adorning the radiator cap.

Ceddars jumps out, walks around the still chugging car, and opens the door for me like a chauffeur, as if this fantastic machine is just that, a machine, and not a wondrous melding of art, beauty, and engineering. "This way, me lady," he says in a put-on voice, saluting.

I get in and sit back on the plush leather seating, joined a few moments later by Ceddars, his wide shoulders pressed next to mine. He guns the engine and we're off.

The Bugatti's interior is just as impressive. The leather upholstery, walnut-trimmed dash, and intricate gauges work together to give an impression of luxury, but nothing can beat the terrific roar of its powerful engine.

"Did the fellow speak after I was gone?" Ceddars asks, turning the Bugatti onto the village's main road, roaring past the row of businesses including Dorothy Knight's flower shop.

I have a dull memory of something strange happening down in the cells, but my mind just won't latch onto it. "I'm afraid not. But I managed to pilfer this." I take out the envelope addressed to Sheng from one of my many pockets.

"I say, isn't that a felony? Stealing from the bluebottles? If Troughton finds out, he'll go off like a bally top." He smiles at me. "Still, the fellow is such a dreadful flat tyre."

We leave Little Pucklewick via a rather winding country road. "Is this the right way?"

"I may be bad at many things, but navigation is my forte. I can't count the number of times I had to find my way back home in a banged-up kite during the war. And besides, this is the main road and I've travelled it many times. You're in safe hands."

"The main road?"

"Roads were bigger in South Africa?"

"I think roads are bigger everywhere."

We roar up a steep hill, finding a horse and cart piled high with furniture on the other side, blocking the road. Ceddars swerves around it without loss of speed, the back of the car sliding as he pulls the handbrake. "Wahoo! I've often thought I should race the old jalopy. A lot of the old fighter pilots went into racing after the war."

I've not seen Ceddars like this before. Inside the cockpit

of his car, he appears to be a changed man. More alive, and somehow… more real. Even his moustache looks different. More debonair and less silly. I can imagine him in the cockpit of a fighter plane, bravely fighting for king and country and engaging the Hun. The doctor is a man of many parts I realise. And, well, rather dashing. He may still be a suspect, but I can't help liking the amiable fellow.

After a hair-raising but fun drive we crest a hill and spot a village—the peculiarly named Upper Cockshoot—laid out amongst fields of green and yellow. We roar down the hill and screech to stop outside a large pub… the Black Swan Inn.

Like the police station, the pub is made from large granite blocks, but this place has real age behind it. The bricks are eroded, and its thatched roof, sitting atop two stories, is of an older, traditional style. I can also see that it used to be a stagecoach stop as evidenced by an entrance to a back yard. It's wide enough for stagecoaches and horses. The walls on either side striated with hundreds of years of wheel axles that have scraped against them. There is another door to the pub proper, open to the public. I hear the chatter of many voices from within. The doorstep into the pub is eroded into a deep hollow. I wonder how many thousands of footsteps have trod upon it to wear it down. The sign outside, however, is new. A winking black swan with a yellow beak.

The engine dies and Ceddars turns to me, a cheeky look on his face. "We're here… now what shall we call ourselves?"

I get his meaning immediately. "Mr and Mrs Smith would be a little obvious."

"Rather. I've always fancied those double-barrel surnames. What about, Mr and Mrs Barrington-Stewart? But then again, I can't imagine those two getting up to any hanky-panky, can you?"

I'm getting the impression that Ceddars is somewhat of a Lothario on the quiet, he certainly has a way about him.

"Hanky-panky? Is that all you can think about?"

"Well, you know, the war," he says in explanation. "It sort of had an effect on us chaps. Never knew which day would be our last. Living in the moment and all that, what? It sort of washes off on a fellow."

"That's your excuse, is it?"

"Joking aside, Em', I'd be more than happy to find someone to settle down with. But even though there are many ladies who have been very happy to, shall we say, take a trip in my car, none of them have been willing to drive home with me."

"I see. I hope you don't expect me to feel sorry for you?" I scoff. "That doesn't sound like too much of a sad story."

"It is what it is."

I open the small Bugatti door and struggle out, turning to catch Ceddars staring at my posterior again, a faraway look on his face. "Ogling me won't work. Some women find it creepy."

"I say, what?" Ceddars says coming back to himself. "Sorry old girl, I wasn't staring, honest. It was just all this talk of the war. I sometimes drift back there, you understand? All those chaps, my friends, who were lost. It was bally awful. There's no sugar-coating it."

"You're forgiven. Now come on. I want to find out who sent this letter. Hopefully, they will still be here."

We enter the pub, heads turning in our direction, knowing glances and smirks passing amongst the patrons. The doctor said the place had a reputation for hanky-panky and I can see he wasn't mistaken. The bar area is broken into two—a main bar where we are standing and a snug, a smaller enclosed barroom, to one side.

Ceddars guides me inside and we walk to the smaller bar. The landlord, a tall, gaunt looking man with an inert, long face with silly sideburns and whiskers comes to serve us. He drops a large book onto the bar and opens it. "You're lucky.

A room 'as just come available. It's payment upfront and a minimum of one night's stay. Doors close at eleven o'clock sharp. Now if ya could sign your name here."

He turns the book towards us, his dead-looking watery eyes staring right into mine. "I'm assumin' it will be just the one night," he adds without inflexion.

I give the man an indignant look. "You assume wrongly. We are here to ask you a few questions about your patrons."

His inexpressive face creases into a sneer. "Don't tell me you've come here on behalf of that mad vicar from Little Pucklewick? Well, young lady, you can go and tell 'im that how I run my pub is up to me. And 'e should stop interferin' in parishes that are not 'is concern."

"Oh no, old chap," Ceddars says. "We're not here on his behalf. Truth is… the vicar died this morning."

The landlord takes in this news with a nod of his head. "I'm sorry to 'ear that, but ya know what they say… good riddance to bad rubbish."

"I say, that's a bit harsh, what?"

"I've 'ad dealings with the vicar a few times in the past few years and, if I dislike anything, I dislike a hypocrite."

"And what do you mean by that?" I ask.

He shrugs. "Not for me to say. But those that sling stones shouldn't be livin' in glass 'ouses." His tone turns steely, and I realise the landlord is no pushover.

"We're looking for a man who may be staying here. He sent a letter to Pucklewick yesterday. I believe his name is Mr Sheng." I point to the book and to an entry from two days ago. "There he is." The name is written in the same hand that wrote the address on the letter in my pocket.

The landlord nods. "Mr Sheng? Yeah, a curious chap. Put 'im in room eight."

"We would very much like to meet him."

"Well ya can't do that."

"What if we just damn your eyes and go up there anyway?"

Ceddars says, bristling.

"Because, sir, 'e left this morning, not more than half an 'our ago. He took a carriage to the station."

A few minutes later we are back in the Bugatti and charging down country lanes again.

"I don't get it!" Ceddars says over the twin roars of wind and engine. "Why was someone called Sheng stopping at the Black Swan. This is jolly confusing."

"Not if the man was his brother, father, or uncle."

"By Jove! You're saying there are two Chinese chappies!"

"Which means…?"

"You think it was this new chap that did it? That murdered the vicar?"

I shrug. "That's why we need to talk to him."

"What do you know that you're not telling me?"

I give him my best enigmatic smile.

After an even more terrifying drive, we arrive at Little Pucklewick train station. I jump out of the Bugatti, closely followed by Ceddars and rush onto the platform. But we're too late, the train to London has already pulled away.

"Bother it!" Ceddars says. "I knew I should've taken the shortcut."

I give him a confused look. "There was a shortcut?" I'm genuinely disappointed until I spot the back of the head of a familiar figure in the station waiting room.

I push open the heavy door to find Inspector Troughton sitting opposite a Chinese gentleman in a smart business suit.

Ambassadors & Alibis

"**WHAT** in tarnation are you both doing here?" Troughton says, his weaselly voice an annoyed squeak.

I must admit that I'm equally surprised by the inspector's presence. I had him down as a buffoon not interested in the facts or thorough investigation, but here he is, it would seem, following up on the same letter.

"We are here," I reply without hesitation, "to talk to Mr Sheng." I bow to him. "My name is Emily Crookshanks, and this is Doctor Cedric Roberts."

Mr Sheng stands up and bows in return. He is also a diminutive man of similar build to Eriksen's manservant, but he is stockier and older, although the similarity between the two men is striking.

"Am I right in thinking it was you who had an argument with the vicar this morning?"

Inspector Troughton draws an indignant breath to speak, but Mr Sheng raises his hand. "Please, let me answer the lady," he says in perfect English and Troughton reluctantly nods. "You are quite correct, Miss Crookshanks. I was walking to Little Pucklewick from the Swan Inn, located in the next village, to meet with my brother on a private matter. On the way, I met an older gentleman who I believe was the local vicar, and politely asked if this was the road to William Eriksen's mansion. The man became agitated and aggressive. Shouting at me. Perplexed, I left him and carried on with my journey. Now, may I ask why you are asking me the same questions as the inspector?"

"Your brother has been charged with the murder of the Reverend Wilson-Smallsey, the man you argued with. I think him innocent for a number of reasons and have been investigating the case on behalf of his friend, Mr William Eriksen."

"That is very admirable, Miss Crookshanks, but as I have already explained, my former brother cannot have been the murderer because he was with me at the time of the killing."

"Or so he says," Troughton interjects.

"I'm sorry… did you say, he was your *former brother?*"

Mister Sheng nods. "He has brought great disrespect upon our family. I offered him a choice to come home and redeem himself, a choice he refused."

I take a step forward. "Your former brother left Eriksen's house before the murder was committed and returned sometime later in an agitated state. Can you throw any light on why that may be? And why you did not arrive at Eriksen's mansion?"

Mr Sheng shuffles uncomfortably and takes a few moments to frame his answer. "I am not happy with my former brother's choices, Miss Crookshanks. His family also share this sentiment. I sent a letter to inform him that I was coming down from London to help change his mind and to convince him to return to China. And a second letter after I arrived in Upper Cockshoot. When I heard nothing back from him, I decided on a more direct approach and phoned him this morning and told him my intention to visit him and his …companion. He forbade me from coming to the mansion and insisted we met on the road by an old wood that was on the way. We went inside the wood, exchanged words and…" he continues slowly, choosing his words carefully, "we had another falling out. He has no intention of giving up his life here."

Mister Sheng sounds calm, but like his brother, his neck is twitching.

"Which is where I'd gotten before you barged in," Troughton says. He turns his attention back to Sheng's older brother. "Now with respect, how can we believe this is true?"

"He will have the letter I sent him."

"A letter written in Chinese. You could tell me it was anything and how would we know differently?"

"Because I am a man of honour and because I give you my word." Mister Sheng's tone is quiet but threatening. I sense he is no common man.

"Translation services are available in a few agencies in London, if you disbelieve me. You can also talk to the landlord at the Black Swan Inn. I used his telephone to talk to my brother. The call was put through by the telephonist in Little Pucklewick. I suggest you interview them both. And there is one more matter, inspector."

"And what may that be?"

"I do not lie." He reaches inside his waistcoat and pulls out a business card. "I am an attaché with the Chinese Embassy in London. The Ambassador himself can vouch for my veracity, although he knows nothing of the private matter between my family and my estranged brother. He is a close associate of the Commissioner of Police."

"He is, is he?" Troughton says, feigning disinterest although the statement has rocked him.

Mister Sheng pulls a tight smile. "I suggest you release my brother, my *former brother*, straightaway. He may be many things, but he is not your murderer, inspector. I can assure you of that."

"I suppose this does shine a different light on matters," Troughton admits.

"Of course, it does," I say. "Eugene Knight didn't see Sheng arguing with the vicar. Instead, it was this man. His brother. An easy mistake to make as they are both of similar build and looks. It will be simple for you to talk to the landlord of the Black Swan and Ethel at the telephone exchange. And as for the letter…" I remove it from my pocket and hand it to Troughton, "it is straightforward to verify."

"How on earth did you get your hands on that?" Before I can answer, he says, "Constable Jakes! He'll swing for this."

"Jakes has done nothing wrong," I say. "As I see it, he was aiding an investigation that ultimately proved he had not been at fault. If Sheng didn't murder the vicar, then his assessment that the argument between the two men was nothing but hot air, was proven correct. And besides, Jakes was called away out of the police station. I helped him out by staying with the prisoner."

"I see," says Troughton, grabbing the letter and jamming his homburg onto his head. "Good day!" He strides out of the waiting room, slamming the door behind him.

I turn my attention back to Mister Sheng. "I don't suppose you are willing to disclose what the disagreement with your former brother was about?"

He smiles, his lips tight, his eyes cold, and shakes his head.

"I say old chap, seeing as you've been so jolly helpful, can I take you anywhere? I have the old jalopy outside."

Mister Sheng shakes his head again. "I will wait for the next train." He sits down and we are made aware that the conversation is over.

I'm hungry, so we make our way to the station cafe, sitting down and ordering tea and sandwiches.

"You were right about Sheng all along, Em'," Ceddars says as he tucks into his sandwich. "But there's no way you could've known about the brother. No way!"

"It's very simple. The murder of the Reverend Wilson-Smallsey was premeditated. The crossbow was stolen the night before and, importantly, after the very public altercation between Sheng and the vicar. I sense Sheng is intelligent and well-educated, as evidenced by his diplomat brother, but even if he wasn't as intelligent as I surmise, this wasn't a crime of passion. If Sheng had followed the vicar home and murdered him last night, then things would've have looked very different. No. Only a fool would implicate themselves and then murder in cold blood. And Sheng is no fool."

"When you put it like that, it does make sense."

"I've been saying the same thing all day, Ceddars," I reply with exasperation. "You just haven't been listening."

"But if it wasn't Sheng who did the deed, then who?"

"Maybe it was you?"

"W-W-What?"

"It's a simple question, which I think you need to answer."

"Of course, I bally didn't do it! I already told you that!" He lights a cigarette and sucks on it irritably. "You are very full of yourself, Miss Crookshanks."

I take a deep breath. "Did you have any reason to dislike the vicar? Was there any animosity between you two?"

"This is getting quite tedious, Em', quite tedious, actually."

I say nothing, waiting for him to answer, wanting him to tell me what I already know.

"There was another girl. A long time ago now," he begins, and a weight is lifted from my shoulders. "We were to be married but the vicar forbade it. Wrong class and all that bunkum. I never properly forgave him for it. I should've stood up for her, but…" he rubs his forehead. "I did nothing. I was weak and she died."

"And that's it, nothing more?"

He shakes his head. "You are so bally persistent. I quite admired that quality until I found myself on the receiving end of it."

"You didn't blame the vicar for the Postmaster's daughter's death?"

"I tried to. But the blame was all mine… I say! How did you discover she was the daughter of the Postmaster? …Was it Eriksen? It must've been! How the bally hell did he find that out?"

"Apparently, he was collecting rumours about the vicar."

"Was he now? I have a good mind to give the man a good thrashing."

"If you are not the murderer, then you may have been a witness," I say to distract him, an effort that works. "Did you see anything unusual on your way from your house to my cottage?"

He takes a drag on the cigarette and shakes his head, the anger leaving him. "If I had, don't you think I would've told you by now?"

"I suppose so."

"Now I'm off the suspect list, do you have anyone else in mind?"

I look at him knowingly.

"By Jove, you do?"

I say nothing for a few moments, absorbed by my own theory.

"Go on, do tell."

"I won't say just yet. I don't want to be proved wrong."

"My guess is that you're never proved wrong."

Ceddars confidence in me is thrilling. "It is not unheard of, but very unlikely."

We both laugh. After the much-needed meal, we make our way back to the Bugatti. Ceddars jumps into the front seat, and I join him, revelling in the closeness of our two bodies, whilst also reminding myself to not get distracted.

"Where are we off to next, Em'? To go and arrest the guilty party?"

"Not quite. Now Sheng has been proven to be innocent, I'm rather keen to go and talk to Dorothy Knight."

"Dorothy Knight? What has she got to do with anything?"

"That is what I want to find out."

"Righty ho, Em', if that's what you want. Off we go!" He powers the Bugatti engine, and we roar away along the twisty country roads. "Do you like the old beast?" he asks, as he swerves the powerful car around a series of bends. "She sure has an impressive turn of speed. On a good run they say she could make over fifty miles an hour."

"Let's not find out just now," I reply, one hand keeping a hold of my hat as we speed along.

"Have you ever flown?"

I shake my head. We crest a small hill and tear down the other side, racing towards a tight bend.

"Driving is fun, but it's nothing like being up in a kite. I'll take you up one day and you'll—"

Ceddars swerves the Bugatti, missing a bicycle lying in the road by inches, losing control and we spin like a top, ending up with a thump in a thick hedge.

Ceddars glances over to me. "Bally hell! You alright, Em'?"

"Just about."

"I was driving a little too fast. Trying to impress and all that. Bally stupid. But who would leave a bicycle in the middle of the road like that? If we'd hit it, we'd have gone over for sure."

I recover my wits and glance over to the bicycle. The wheels are bent, and the frame twisted. It looks familiar.

Ceddars reverses the Bugatti and parks it safely at the side of the road. We both get out and take a look.

"I say, wasn't that kid, Billy, riding this bike earlier today when we met him?"

"I think so."

"But why leave the bally thing in the middle of the road. Has he lost his senses?"

I take a closer look at the twisted bike and notice a patch of torn material that looks like part of the shirt Billy was wearing and scrapes of white paint.

"He must've had an accident, probably came down the hill too fast," Ceddars ventures. "Leaving the bike here was senseless."

"I agree,"

"You know kids these days. No sense of responsibility, what?" Ceddars grabs the bike and throws it into the hedgerow.

I scan around the road, noticing that part of the hedge is disturbed. I try to look over it, but it's too high. There's a gate to a field a short way further on. I open it and go inside, noticing a body lying in the corn.

Feuds & Fragrance

"**C**EDDARS, come here!" I shout.

I stride through the corn, aware that it has already been trampled and arrive at the body.

Ceddars appears at my side. "Bally hell! That's Billy!" He checks the boy over. "Broken legs and a broken neck. He must've been flying down the hill and failed to take the corner, hitting the hedge. The impact threw him over and he broke his neck on landing. We saw how he had trouble stopping earlier. His bike had no bally brakes."

I'm not convinced. "Wouldn't the bike be in the hedge and not in the road?"

"I suppose… it could've bounced."

"But look at his legs, they're smashed. And his clothes are ripped. No, Ceddars. He was hit by another vehicle travelling at speed, catapulting him into the field."

"Another vehicle?"

"There's white paint from the car or van that hit him scraped onto the bicycle frame. And I'm not the first person to check on him. The corn was trampled."

"By Jove! You're right. You don't miss a trick, do you, Em'?"

"The evidence is obvious to anyone with eyes."

"But who would run the poor kid over and not stop? That's barbaric."

"Someone who wanted him dead, perhaps?"

"But why? Billy wouldn't hurt a soul."

"I wonder…"

I search Billy's pockets to the repeated disdain of Ceddars

and pull out a one-pound note.

"Bally hell! Where did the young oik get that?"

"Billy liked to do jobs for people around the village. It looks like someone paid for his services and paid him very handsomely."

Ceddars closes Billy's eyes and covers his face with his jacket. "Very handsomely indeed. But what was the money for?"

"That, my dear doctor, is what I aim to discover."

"Hey, steady on! I hope you are not thinking that I'm Watson to your Sherlock?"

"There's no danger of that Ceddars, although I do share a similarity with Sherlock Holmes."

"And what's that? Your searing intelligence no doubt. Or your disdain of the normal social conventions?"

"I meant that the great detective and I share an interest in rather fetching head wear."

"Oh, the hats? Right."

"Tell me, doctor, you like your automobiles, don't you? Is white a popular colour?"

Ceddars shrugs. "There are not that many white vehicles in Little Pucklewick. Eriksen's Mercedes of course, which you've seen. That's a mighty beast alright. Dorothy Knight's florist van is also white—and that, I think, is it."

"Does the church have a van?"

He nods. "But it's seen better years. The whole thing is held together mostly by rust."

"Who drives that?"

"Simmons, I would guess. The van is garaged in a lock-up opposite his cottage. He's will be very busy now that he has two funerals to organise."

"No one else?"

"I don't know. I doubt any of the church ladies would drive it."

"What about Mary Smallsey? She went to that European

school. Perhaps they taught their students driving?"

"Mary? No, I told you. She's too infirm to do anything other than potter around her garden, poor dear."

"And Gladys Willoughby?"

Ceddars scoffs. "Mrs W? I don't think so. But even if it was the old battle-axe, the van is dark green, not white."

I shrug. "You mentioned Dorothy Knight's florist van?"

"That isn't driven by Dotty. She has a driver for that sort of thing. Do you think one of these vehicles was involved in this terrible incident?"

"It's possible. They will all need to be examined for damage."

"I suppose they will. How awful. Can you stay with Billy while I go back to the police station and tell them what's happened?"

I have no fear of dead bodies but staying out here on my own feels like a bad idea. I remember the last time Ceddars left me with Sheng in the station cells and… I'm not sure what happened, but it wasn't good. "I think I will come with you. Billy can't be seen from the road and the police will be here soon enough."

"But Em', that's bad form."

"Is it? I can't see there's anything I can do for the boy by staying put. No, I'm far happier coming with you."

"I make you feel safe?"

"Not with the way you've been driving. Come on."

Ten minutes later, after a more relaxed drive—Ceddars has calmed down since finding Billy—we leave the Bugatti on the main village road and walk down a small lane that connects to the street where the police station is located.

We go inside and Constable Jakes bounds over, a beam plastered on his face. "I were sure my number was up, but you were right. That Sheng fellow was innocent if the inspector is to be believed. He just phoned me to tell me the news. An' he's not the type to lie about important stuff."

"Troughton isn't here? I thought he'd be releasing the prisoner."

Jakes shakes his head. "He said I were to do nothing until he got back. Said he had some important business to take care of."

I give Ceddars a sideways look. "He did?"

Jakes nods. "The Superintendent was asking for him earlier on the blower. And when the big boss calls… Now, why are you here? The inspector chewed my ears off for letting you speak to Sheng. I can't let you go down there again."

Ceddars grimaces. "We have some rather sad news, old chap."

"What's happened?"

"I'm afraid it's Billy…"

After we tell him what we found, the large man sags. "First the vicar and now that poor young lad? I'll phone the undertaker and get him to take me up there. Once I've formally identified the body, I'll go and see the Browns. I know them very well. I was Billy's godfather of sorts. They'll be devastated."

After consoling the constable, we make our way outside.

"Poor Billy. I ought to go with the constable to see Mr and Mrs Brown and give the bad news."

"Didn't you do enough of that thing in the war?"

He nods. "But someone needs to tell them. I can't let Constable Jakes go blundering in."

"I think you underestimate the man. He's savvier than you think. He guessed the threat Sheng made was just hot air, remember? You can stand down."

"Can I?"

"I still need to go and chat with Mrs Dorothy Knight."

"You do, even after all that awful business with that poor lad? I thought a stiff drink might be in order."

"We'll have a drink, when we find out who killed the

vicar… and Billy."

The florists is still closed when we arrive, a notice pinned into the window written in a less than extravagant hand. Ceddars bends and reads it out to me. "Due to the untimely death of our beloved vicar, we will be shut for a few days."

I also bend to examine the notice. "A flower shop in Little Pucklewick?"

"What of it?"

"From what I've seen of the place there can't be more than around two-hundred people living here. Is there enough trade to support such a shop?"

"There must be. The place is always full of flowers, what? I believe she operates a delivery service to other villages. Hence the van. And there's always a marriage or a… death."

"That sounds rather organised for someone you described as Dotty by name, dotty by nature."

Ceddars rings the bell, and we stand back. We wait for a few moments, and rings again. A window opens above, and Dorothy Knight sticks her head out. "Can't you read? We're closed… oh it's you doctor and Miss Crookshanks."

The window slams shut and a short while later, Dorothy Knight unlocks the door and ushers us inside. I'm hit by the wonderful smell of flowers, a fragrance fighting with Dorothy's overpowering lavender perfume.

She takes us upstairs to a large sitting room and I realise that the shop is only a small part of a larger house. She rings a bell, and a teary maid arrives to take her order for tea and cakes.

"Now Doctor," she says in a far more dreamy and girly voice than she used when talking to me earlier. "How can I help you on this quite dreadful, dreadful day?"

"Well Dotty, I'm afraid we're here to chat about the vicar."

"Oh, I wish you wouldn't call me that," she says with feigned indignity. "But I do like it." She flutters her eyelashes coquettishly.

I realise Dorothy Knight is one of those annoying women whose demeanour changes when in the presence of a man. It would've been better to talk to her on my own.

"I can't believe Albert has gone," she continues. "It will take a long time for that to sink in."

"It will indeed," Ceddars intones gravely.

"I have no idea how I will sleep tonight. No idea at all. Unless you have a lickle something to help me drift off to Slumberland?"

"Of course, Dotty. I'll pick up a sleeping draft from the dispensary later and drop it off to you."

"You don't have anything in your bag?"

Ceddars pats his bag and frowns. "'Fraid not, Dotty. This is just for show. I'm rather expected to always lug the bally thing around with me, but it's more of a nuisance than anything else. I keep it mostly empty."

I also let my eyes rove over Ceddars' bag and notice how he holds it towards him protectively. I've had a niggling doubt about it for a while now. Despite my gut instinct that he is innocent, I decide to look inside at the earliest opportunity.

Dorothy Knight shrugs. "Oh, I see. I don't want to put you out, but I dare say quite a few people in the village might be suffering from the same malaise tonight."

"Of course, you're quite right."

The teary maid returns with a tray of tea and cakes and departs. Ceddars pours and we all sit back.

"Now what do you need to know about poor Albert? My maid tells me they have arrested that Sheng fellow. I always thought he was a surly looking chap. You can see it in the eyes, they say. And he always looked at me, well, in quite a horrid way. They say he'll hang for sure."

"Indeed," Ceddars replies. "However, it turns out that the fellow is—"

I elbow the doctor in his side, I don't want Dorothy Knight to discover Sheng is innocent just yet. "Is Eugene at home?"

"He went out after he came back from the police station," Dorothy says dismissively. "What a terrible business. Seeing Sheng arguing with the vicar. I think the lad blames himself for not stepping in. He's always out and about. Has been like that since he was a boy. You'll no doubt find him hanging out with that dreadful Billy ruffian."

Ceddars opens his mouth to speak, but I cut him off again.

"You don't like Billy?"

Dorothy shrugs. "The vicar gave him errands and the suchlike, but I never warmed to him."

"Billy told us that Eugene and he have fallen out."

"Have they now? Well, that's all to the good as far as I can see."

"And why's that?"

"Billy is a bad influence. I don't pay those extortionate school fees for my son to hang around with a delivery boy. Eugene is meant for better things."

"Would you have any idea what they might have fallen out about?"

"Boys being boys, I guess. But as I said. It's for the best."

"You must be doing very well if you are able to send Eugene to private school."

Dorothy smiles. "I've always had an entrepreneurial side. I came into a small inheritance and used it to buy this little shop. She turns her attention to the doctor. "What is it Ceddars? Why are you frowning so much?"

"We have some sad news regarding Billy."

"Sad news? I don't know what you mean. Unlike everyone else in this village, I don't listen to that dreadful Ethel woman at the exchange. I despise gossip, doctor. Despise it. And I've told her so on more than one occasion. She knows not to phone me up with her aspersions."

Ceddars pulls a tight smile. "Quite right too, the woman

is a menace. But I doubt she's heard the news yet."

"Heard what?"

"Billy was unfortunately killed in a road accident earlier today."

Dorothy Knight takes in the news with a frown. "Well, I have to say I'm not surprised. The way he rode that bicycle was quite, quite dangerous. I've often seen the lad flying around the village green without a concern for his, or anybody else's safety."

"I didn't mention that he was on his bike, how could you know that?"

"I just assumed, of course. It was an accident waiting to happen. I'm sad for Billy, but these things happen, especially to young boys trying so hard to be men."

Her reaction is not what I expected. "The police don't think it was an accident. It was a hit and run, the poor lad was left for dead. Do you have a car?"

"I do not! How dare you ask me such a thing!"

"But you have a delivery van, isn't that right?" Ceddars interjects.

She gives the doctor a withering look. "Et tu, Brute?"

"These questions need to be asked," I say, "no matter how uncomfortable."

She sighs heavily. "I have a van. But I don't drive it. That would be so unladylike, don't you think? I leave that to my delivery driver."

"And where is this van now?"

She shrugs. "I concern myself with higher things."

"It is a white van?"

"With my name proudly displayed on the side. *Flowers By Knight.*"

I share a look with Ceddars. "You didn't learn to drive in the war?"

Dorothy frowns. "I don't like these questions. You really can't think I had anything to do with Billy's accident, can you?"

"Like I said, it wasn't an accident."

"I suppose everyone with a car must be a suspect, so I will let your rude questions pass. A young boy has been killed, and that is a serious matter. And in answer to your question. No. I didn't learn to drive in the war, or at any other time. I worked in munitions. Sniper rifle manufacture, assembly, and testing. I was proud to muck in with the other girls working for our boys."

"You tested rifles?"

"I didn't fire them—if that's what you're getting at. The parts had to be tested at every part of manufacture. It was life and death if one of our rifles was to malfunction, you understand? Life and death. We prided ourselves on that work."

I remove the poster from one of my pockets and pass it to Dorothy who squints at it, picking up a pair of pince nez and holding them affectedly. "Oh my! What is this dreadful thing you are showing me?"

"They are quite obviously rumours about the Reverend Wilson-Smallsey." Despite the woman's reaction, this information is obviously not new to her. "You have never seen these before? This and others were pinned around the village this morning."

"No, I certainly haven't. And how dare you show it to me! On the day Albert was so brutally murdered. Doctor, how can you let her be so crass?"

"As I mentioned in the vicarage," I continue, talking over her, "I'm working with Inspector Troughton. I'm sure you want to find out the identity of the killer?"

"But it's Sheng!" she warbles. "Everyone knows that! Doctor, please tell her to stop."

Ceddars opens his mouth to speak but I silence him with a raised hand. "We must be sure. A man's life is at stake."

"And a man's life has been lost! Doesn't that count for

anything? And besides, Sheng is one of those horrible foreigners. Men like that are always guilty of something. And you should have seen him last night, the way he threatened the vicar. It will be good for William to be rid of him, that's for sure."

"William Eriksen, the explorer?"

"Yes, what of him?"

"We talked to him earlier today. I believe you two are quite close."

"Well, yes, I'm not ashamed to say we are."

"And you were at his talk last night… at the village hall?"

"Of course. I didn't really follow much of it to be honest, I tend to switch off a little bit when he talks about his travels in those dreadful foreign lands, but I wanted to support him as best I could."

"William Erikson mentioned that the vicar didn't approve of your friendship. Do you have any idea why that was?"

She throws up her hands and shrugs. "Oh, I don't know. Men can be silly creatures, can't they, Miss Crookshanks? Just like little boys. Albert didn't like William and William certainly didn't have any love for Albert. I'd wished that they'd end their feud, but a simple doe's voice is hard to be heard amidst the clash of stags and their antlers. But, as sad as it is, that feud is now over, and William and I are free to unite as one."

"Marriage?"

"I always thought it would be impossible to replace poor Mr Knight, but I have allowed William to enter my affections. We will have to wait a short while until this dreadful business is over, but Little Pucklewick will be delighted by the announcement of our nuptials."

"So, the old bugger Eriksen has proposed, what?"

"Doctor, please! There are ladies present, don't you know? You're not out drinking alcohol with your pilot friends now."

"Bally sorry old girl, I mean… sorry."

"William hasn't proposed yet," Dorothy continues. "But it will only be a matter of time."

I remember Eriksen telling me he was a confirmed bachelor. Dorothy Knight has gotten the wrong end of the stick regarding his intentions, unless he was lying to protect her reputation. Ceddars told me that she had 'come alive' of late, which might mean the two were having secret relations. If he wasn't lying, she will be mightily disappointed, that's for sure.

"May I ask, what… what happened to Mr Knight?" Ceddars says.

"Of course, I'm always happy to talk about him, about Thomas. We were young and in love, and impetuous. We were both under twenty-one and so we eloped to Gretna Green, in Scotland, where the laws are different, and we could marry."

"I say! That quite romantic, what? A lot of the fellows I flew with did the same."

"It was quite the adventure. I didn't realise what little time we would have together. Thomas died from consumption a few months after Eugene was born. It was only my love for my new baby that kept me going through those awful months and years."

"I'm sorry to hear that old gal. Consumption has taken so many. It's the most dreadful disease."

"I'll never forget him, but it is difficult to live one's life alone."

Ceddars is a useful person to have at my side during my questioning, but he does have the habit of wavering off the subject somewhat. "I wondered what you think about Fran Feltham," I say. "Isn't the village rumour that she's making a beeline for William?"

"That's only a rumour," Ceddars says defensively.

Dorothy Knight flicks her eyes knowingly towards

Ceddars. "That little bird has got many a heart aflutter. She only has herself to blame. These career girls cause so much trouble, don't you think? They want far too much. Selfish, I call it. But she is of no concern to me. William assured me that his interests do not lead in that particular direction."

I point at the poster again. "Did you and William Eriksen ever discuss these rumours about the vicar?"

She shrugs. "Well, I feel bad saying it, but Albert did like a drink and... he did like women. But isn't that the failing of all men?"

"You think he was an adulterer?"

Dorothy Knight doesn't like this word, that much is for sure. She shuffles irritably on her chair, the pince nez held loosely in her hands. "I might have told William that that's what I believed. But it was just spitefulness on my part. I had no evidence. Like I said, Albert was a man and an attractive man at that. And well, I'm sorry to say this doctor, but men, even vicars, live their lives by different standards to women."

"About the argument you had with the vicar before his death, I—"

"Please, I do not want to talk about that, it is so upsetting." She starts sobbing but her eyes are dry. Ceddars immediately attends to her.

"Didn't you write a note to the vicar inviting him to meet you at the church this morning?"

The fake sobbing stops suddenly. "What?"

"It's just that, well, I found a note in your handwriting at the vicarage and..."

"You dared to read my private correspondence?"

I shake my head. "No, only one word was left." I take out the burned piece of paper I found in the hearth of Wilson-Smallsey's study. "You can see quite clearly the word 'marriage'. And the writing matches that of the notice on your shop door."

Letters & Lapses

BOTH Ceddars and Dorothy Knight stare at the remnant of the burned note, both surprised.

"I say, Dorothy, that's your handwriting, what?"

"It is."

"Do you have any idea why the vicar would burn your note after reading it?"

Dorothy pushes Ceddars away with an irritated hand. "He burnt it, you say? Well… I suppose he does get rather a lot of notes and general mail, perhaps it was his habit to get rid of them in that way," she ventures without conviction.

"I think, Mrs Knight," I begin, staring at her forcefully, "that you need to explain the full contents of the note and what your argument with the vicar was really about."

"I don't see why. As sad as it is, Albert is now dead. Whatever we argued about is irrelevant now that his murderer has been caught."

"Then you won't mind telling me, will you?"

"You are the most impossible woman, Miss Crookshanks! You know that? Most impossible." She sags and takes a large gulp from her teacup. "But what is done is done. It was Albert," she begins quietly. "He forbade me and William to marry. I… I was very angry with him about it. I wrote him that note and told him to meet me at the church. In hindsight, I suppose my language was a little insulting. Perhaps that's why he burned it? I'm glad he did. It was written in the heat of the moment."

"You were not arguing about what happened last night in the village hall, as you told me, but about the reverend's opposition to the marriage between yourself and William?"

"I say," Ceddars interjects, "maybe I'm a little confused, but I thought you said that Eriksen hadn't proposed?"

Dorothy waves away his question with a chubby hand. "He hasn't. Not yet. But a woman knows. Female intuition and all that. It's only a matter of time before he makes me the happiest woman in Little Pucklewick." Her face lights up and, regardless of Eriksen's statement to me on the matter, I'm convinced she believes this to be true. Perhaps the woman is dotty after all?

"And the Reverend Wilson-Smallsey was dead set against this?"

The smile disappears from her face. "Albert had no right, it's not as if *he* wanted me."

"I beg your pardon?"

Dorothy becomes flustered, her words tripping over themselves. "I'm just saying that the vicar is married. It's not his place to interfere. He had no reason other than spite."

"And did you speak about anything else?"

She shakes her head, her double chin wobbling. "Albert wouldn't change his mind. He was a very stubborn man."

Could that be a reason for murder, I wonder? Could Dorothy Knight have murdered him out of anger? Possibly, but the motive was tenuous at best. And why did she tell me? Besides, I have another suspect in mind. Despite her possible delusion about William Eriksen's intentions, the vicar's opposition to their nuptials wouldn't stand in their way. They could get married anywhere. The motive was too weak, and the murder premeditated—the crossbow stolen the night before. Even so, Dorothy Knight was late for the eleven o'clock meeting at the vicarage. That gave her opportunity unless she had an alibi.

"I was talking to the vicarage maid, and she told me that you arrived at this morning's regular Monday morning eleven o'clock get-together just before Mrs Willoughby, who was twenty minutes late. Why was that?"

It's obvious Dorothy doesn't want to answer.

"Mrs Knight?"

"I'd had the most awful argument with Albert," she replies with irritation. "I went straight home and sobbed my poor little heart out. I knew I couldn't miss the meeting, knew that that would play into Mrs Willoughby's hands. I did what I always do. Touched up my makeup and went out to face the world." Her words are ponderous and overly dramatic.

"Did anyone see you at home? Eugene for instance? Or your maid?"

She shakes her head. "And I'm glad no one did. A lady doesn't like to be observed when she has lost her composure. It can be so unattractive."

"Tell me about Mrs Willoughby. What is she like?"

Mrs Knight is relieved I've changed the subject and immediately brightens. "A dreadful woman, don't you know?"

"You two don't get on?"

"She sees herself as the vicar's right-hand woman and resented me from the start. Especially when Albert told her that she was to relinquish some of her powers."

"Powers?"

"With Mary, the vicar's wife, infirm, there are a lot of responsibilities to fill. Mrs Willoughby took it on herself to fulfil all those responsibilities and I thought it unfair."

"The vicar gave some of those responsibilities to you?"

Dorothy nods. "He said we would share the running of the weekly get-togethers. Mrs Willoughby has not been her normal self of late. Probably to do with that awful cough of hers. Not that I've pried, but it put her nose out of joint, that's for sure. She is a volatile woman, and, dare I say it… she is in love with the vicar."

"I say, what?" Ceddars blurts.

Dorothy shrugs. "Others might not have noticed. But I did. Albert giving into me was quite the betrayal in her eyes."

"Well, I never. Mrs W in love. Now you've said it, I think that's bang on. I should've seen that before. Oh my, yes. Giving you extra responsibilities would certainly upset Mrs W, she lives for the vicar and her duties."

"Then that life is at an end," Dorothy says with a hint of triumph. "With the vicar's demise, someone else will come to Little Pucklewick. A new vicar with a new and more capable wife."

"I'm confused. Why would the vicar risk upsetting Mrs Willoughby by allowing you to share her duties? I thought you and the vicar were at odds with one another?"

"It was all to do with his feud with William. He never liked the man. He gave in to my requests to keep me on his side."

"It all sounds so dreadfully complicated, old girl."

Dorothy takes a sip from her teacup and smiles sadly at Ceddars. "I'm afraid this is what you men do. It was no fun being stuck in the middle. Especially after Albert wrote that letter. William was absolutely livid."

I share a glance with Ceddars. "What letter?"

"The one Albert sent to that group of scientific fellows in London. I don't know the name, except that it's some sort of royal society, detailing the—how did he put it?— the 'ungodly immorality' he believed went on at William's mansion. I've never seen William so angry. He wanted to go to the vicarage to punch Albert in the face, but I managed to calm him down. Men get so upset over the smallest things— don't you think?"

I sip at my tea and digest the import of her words. This feud between the vicar and William Eriksen was more involved than I realised. A lot more. Eriksen had told me about his London ambitions with his scientific society, and now I think about it, I realise the man had a real motive to murder. Ceddars had touched a raw nerve when he had accused him of cowardice, of not coming back to fight in the war. Eriksen was keen to restore his reputation. And the vicar was putting that in real jeopardy.

"As sad as it is," Dorothy continues, "that feud is now over and done with. Sheng will soon hang and that will be the end to the matter."

"Regarding Sheng," I say. "Inspector Troughton has discovered new evidence that clears him of the murder. I suspect he will be released very soon."

Dorothy Knight's head jerks backwards. "Innocent? But Eugene saw the fellow arguing with Albert shortly before he was murdered."

"That wasn't Sheng, but his brother," Ceddars says. "A high-ranking diplomat by all accounts. A well-spoken chap. I was surprised as you are. Gave his brother an alibi."

Dorothy Knight slams her teacup forcefully upon its saucer. "Then who could have possibly done it?"

"You said William Eriksen was very upset about the letter the vicar sent to the royal society?"

I see the thought processes working behind Dorothy's eyes. "You mean you suspect him? No, no, no, no," she ululates. "William is not a violent man. The police can't suspect him… can they? How awful."

"I'm not sure what Troughton is thinking, but he's not the complete buffoon I thought he was."

"You don't need to tell him about that letter, surely? William had nothing to do with it. Plain and simple. It's ridiculous that he should be a suspect. Quite ridiculous. I know him… intimately. He's a good and honourable man."

We chat for a little while longer, but Dorothy Knight has little more to say. We finish our tea, make our excuses, and leave.

"I told you she was dotty," Ceddars says with a twitch of his moustache once we are outside again, standing by the glass front of Dorothy Knight's florist shop. "Although I did wonder why you were interrogating the poor old girl like that?"

"Don't you see? With Sheng proved innocent, everybody is a suspect. Although I now have someone else very much in mind."

"You do?"

"What did you think about that letter?"

"The one Dotty sent to the vicar? That was some fine sleuthing to catch her out like that. I was very impressed."

"No, the letter the vicar sent to London, to Eriksen's royal society."

"What about it?"

"William Eriksen has spent the last ten years in China, he even missed the Great War at some cost to his reputation, and now he is collating his collections, his adventures, and his discoveries. The letter the vicar sent was trying to undermine all that work and time. That would put the vicar squarely in the firing line."

"Crikey! You really believe Eriksen did it! I thought you were winding the old girl up. But you were serious?"

"I have been formulating my theory for some time, but I was missing a good enough motive. That letter and the threats to William Eriksen's reputation is that motive. And don't forget that Billy told him where the vicar would be at eleven this morning. Although he would have no idea that Billy had already spoken to us."

"You think he ran poor Billy over?" He shakes his head. "I don't like Eriksen, but that is a little extreme. Besides, he would never throw Sheng to the wolves. Remember what he told us, Sheng was more his companion than an employee. There's a bond between them. The rumour is that Eriksen's life was saved multiple times by the man."

"I agree that they are close, and it's that closeness which sits at the very heart of the matter—or so I believe. The way I look at it, this was a planned murder of opportunity."

"Go on..."

"Part of Eriksen's scheme was to report the crossbow stolen in circumstances where the thief could be almost anyone. Having met William Eriksen, I don't see him as a person who cares one jot what the village thinks about his travels, and yet, he gave that lecture. I believe his talk was cover to give 'opportunity' for the supposed crossbow theft, and for Sheng to implicate himself."

"This all sounds rather cold-blooded and if I may say, more than a little far-fetched."

"I agree. It would take someone cold-blooded to plan such a thing. Eriksen reported the crossbow missing after his talk, but I believe it was in his possession all along. After that, it was a waiting game until an opportunity arose to kill the vicar. That opportunity arrived this morning when they put the plan into action."

"Golly! If that's true, we should go and speak to the inspector at once!"

We hurry down the pavement towards the police station.

"Hang on… did you say *they*?"

I nod. "Eriksen and Sheng cooked this up together."

"The two of them? So, Sheng is guilty after all? I can't believe it. You've been telling me the man is innocent and nothing else all bally day. And isn't the man supposed to be some kind of Chinese noble? With a code and all that?"

"That's what Eriksen told us, but what do we truly know of Sheng? Nothing. He could've spun us any line he liked."

"But what about the brother? Working at a London Embassy is a high-profile job, a job reserved for those coming from elite and noble families."

"That I don't doubt. But nobility plays by a different set of rules, regardless of which country they are from."

"That's true enough, I suppose."

"My suspicions about Sheng were raised when he failed to talk to me when I visited him in prison. Eriksen had told him to stay tight-lipped and let events unfold, is my guess.

And there was that letter found on him. The one with the address that led directly to his alibi."

"That was rather convenient, granted…"

"It was *very* convenient. Let's look at the chain of events. Sheng receives a letter from his brother, a Chinese diplomat who is coming to stay in the next village. That same morning, Billy tells them both that the vicar will be at my house at eleven. With that in mind, Eriksen and Sheng decide to put the second part of their plot to kill the vicar into action."

"I can see how your theory makes sense, but I think you're putting too much importance on that letter the vicar sent to Eriksen's society. Just because those chaps are members of a royal society, doesn't make them particularly moralistic. They'd probably see the thing as rather admirable. All part of the dashing explorer, what? Not that any of it was true, of course. Franny and Eriksen were never a thing. She told me that he'd shown zero interest in that direction."

"That doesn't surprise me."

"It doesn't?"

"Isn't it obvious? The vicar wasn't writing about Eriksen and Fran Feltham, but about… Eriksen *and Sheng*."

"Eriksen and Sheng? What the devil are you talking about?"

"Remember what Dorothy said about the letter? Wilson-Smallsey accused Eriksen of 'Ungodly immorality', an overblown phrase, granted but it was clear to me what he was implying, even if Dorothy didn't understand the true meaning. The vicar threatened to expose the intimate relationship between Sheng and his supposed companion."

"I say!"

"Don't be surprised. You're a man of the world. You must've known similar fellows during the war?"

"Well, yes, but—Eriksen and Sheng? Really?"

"Everything fell into place for them this morning, don't you see? Mr Sheng phoned his brother at the Eriksen mansion, and they arranged to meet by Dooley's Wood. The reason? Sheng cannot be seen with his brother otherwise their plan will fail. They arrange a time to meet that coincides with the vicar's visit and, before he leaves, Eriksen and Sheng stage an argument in front of Fran Feltham. Eriksen supposedly calms down Sheng who 'wants revenge on the vicar.' But, this was to throw blame onto him, so that he would be arrested. Eriksen knew that Sheng would have an alibi, giving him time and opportunity to sneak over to my house and for him to shoot the vicar. The only other witness was Fran, who conveniently lost her glasses, and was forced to return home to retrieve them. Glasses that mysteriously turned up on her desk when she returned."

Ceddars goes quiet at the mention of Fran. "But what about Dotty?" he asks after a while. She is convinced her and Eriksen are to marry. You saw that yourself."

"Men in Eriksen's position often use relationships with women as cover. Many even get married. Perhaps that was his intention."

Ceddars face creases. "That's bally bad form. Still, after Sheng threatened the vicar last night, there's no way he could've known what would happen today."

"That's right. As I said, it was a murder of planned opportunity. The information from Billy on the whereabouts of the vicar. The letter from the brother and that phone call. It all fell into place. Then, after meeting his brother, Sheng arrives back at Eriksen's mansion out of sorts, witnessed by Fran again. Troughton arrests Sheng who, by coincidence, is carrying the letter that proves his innocence. A letter they gambled Inspector Troughton would follow up on."

"I say, Em', that does make dreadful sense."

"And in the meantime, the true murderer, Eriksen, remains above suspicion."

We arrive at the police station to find a small mob of jeering men, and a few women, led by the thug, Grantham, who we met earlier. Constable Jakes stands in front of them trying to calm things down.

"'E's gonna be let free?" Grantham jeers, "after what 'e's done. It's criminal that is, ain't it lads?" He turns to the angry group. "Well, we'll give 'im our justice if we 'ave to, won't we?"

His words are met with jeers and shouts, and I notice more people joining the crowd.

"Bally hell! What's going on?"

"Looks like news of Sheng's release has reached the ears of the populace."

A small red van arrives, driven by Fran Feltham, with William Eriksen in the passenger seat. They park opposite the police station and get out. We hurry over to them.

"Looks like the morons are out in force," Eriksen says, "but they will not stand in the way of justice. Goodbye Fran," he says before walking past us and pushing his way forcefully through the crowd and entering the station.

"I suppose Mr Eriksen has come to pick up Sheng?" I ask Fran, who's pretty face is creased at the scene before her.

Fran stares at me with those cold grey eyes of hers. "Yes. Sheng was proven innocent. You were right. The inspector called a short while ago. I drove Mr Eriksen over here to pick him up."

"You drove him over?"

She nods. "I learned how to on the farm where I grew up, and once you've driven a tractor, everything else is second nature. Is it correct that you and Ceddars were instrumental in getting him off?"

"It was the inspector who discovered Sheng's alibi, although I was only a step behind. Why did you arrive in the van and not William's car?"

"The Merc? I'm afraid he um… drank a little too much whisky and side-swiped one of the gateposts in his enthusiasm to get here. Not much damage, but one of the tyres was punctured. He managed to drive back to the manor and asked me to give him a lift into the village in his van. He gave me the afternoon off. My bike's in the back."

I swap glances with Ceddars. "His Merc was in a crash you say?"

"Hardly. More of a prang. Now if you excuse me, I need to get back home to eat." We follow her to the van's rear doors where she pulls out her bike. I notice it has a large wicker basket on the front.

"I could give you a lift, what?" Ceddars says hopefully. "Plenty of room in the back of the old jalopy for your bike."

Fran mounts her bike and gives him a tight-lipped smile. "I'm fine, doctor." She cycles away, leaving Ceddars somewhat bemused.

I'm finding Ceddars' obsession with Fran Feltham more than a little irksome. "Did you hear that?"

He nods, his eyes following the back of Fran Feltham. "Eriksen's car was in a fender-bender. It sounds like your theory is proven beyond doubt."

"Let's go and speak with the inspector again."

Accusations & Inaction

INSPECTOR Troughton is not impressed when we enter the police station, that much is for sure, but he has other things on his mind, namely the baying mob outside. The diminutive form of Sheng sits on a chair, quietly chatting to William Erikson in Mandarin.

I walk up to Troughton, forcing his attention upon me. "What is it now, Miss Crookshanks? Can't you see we have a situation? I have no time for your nonsense."

"Don't you want to discover who murdered the vicar?"

The inspector's moustache twitches. "Go on."

I give him my theory about the events of last night and this morning, and he goes very quiet. "You must arrest Eriksen at once," I whisper, making sure that Eriksen and Sheng can't hear.

"You do realise what you're inferring, don't you?" he says in hushed, thin, nasal tones.

"That William Eriksen is guilty of murdering the vicar? I'm sure of it."

Troughton shakes his head slowly and deliberately. "No, not that, Miss Crookshanks. I'm referring to your accusation of an improper and indecent relationship between Mr William Eriksen and his manservant. Such accusations are difficult to prove, and more often than not, it is those that make those accusations who are prosecuted and lose their good name. And I am not about to put my good name in jeopardy. Do I make myself clear?"

"You're not willing to arrest him?"

"Where is the evidence? Where is this letter that the

reverend sent? As far as I can ascertain, it is in London in the possession of a royal society. They indeed may have it to hand, but it could have been discarded, destroyed, or simply misplaced. But let's say that it is found, how can we be sure of the import of the reverend's words? 'Ungodly immorality' can mean any number of things to any number of men. Isn't it more likely that the vicar was alluding to the village rumour about the young woman who works for him? A Miss Francesca Feltham?"

"And that's all that is, rumour," Ceddars interjects forcefully.

Troughton shrugs. "Rumours are rumours, doctor. Their truthfulness is not the issue. But this is a rumour that has not come to my ears. I have heard nothing about any..." he drops his voice to a whisper, "...improper relationship between William Eriksen and his manservant."

"I agree, it is hard to prove," I say reluctantly, "so focus on the evidence instead. I'm sure if you search Eriksen's mansion you will discover the stolen crossbow. But there is also the murder of Billy to consider. His bike had traces of white paint from the vehicle that hit it and Eriksen's Mercedes has been involved in an accident, if what Fran Feltham just told us is true. And she has no reason to lie. Billy told Eriksen and Sheng where the vicar would be that morning. He also had a pound note in his pocket. I surmise that that one-pound note came from Eriksen in payment for the boy's silence. But that Eriksen followed him in his car and made that silence permanent."

Troughton shakes his head. "That's even more supposition, Miss Crookshanks. Still, Billy was a good lad and very much liked around the village. Whoever ran him over will be brought to justice. Be sure of that."

"Then we must go with Eriksen back to his mansion and check out his car."

"Let me remind you that I am an inspector, and you are

not. What I will or won't do, is not up to you."

"Then Ceddars and I will go on our own."

The inspector draws breath to rebuke me but is interrupted by Eriksen. "What are you whispering about, Troughton? There's a mob outside baying for Sheng's blood and you are the root cause. What the hell will you do about it? Because standing around and doing nothing is just not cutting the mustard, you hear me?"

The inspector flushes red. "I'm sorry, sir. But my advice is to stay put until they get bored."

"No, inspector. That just won't do. Not after what you have put us through today. It won't do at all! We're leaving the station and we're leaving now. Sheng has spent too much time here already. Now do your job, man, and tell those ruffians to go home."

"Yes, sir," Troughton says. "I'll go and I'll talk to them right now, sir."

"Good man. Now get to it."

I raise my eyebrows. I can now see the real reason for the inspector's inaction regarding my accusation of William Eriksen. The explorer is of a higher social class. Troughton would've never made the rank of inspector if not for the war, and it's showing. There is no way he will accuse the famed explorer of murder without some damning evidence. Still, I'm eager to see how he deals with the crowd outside. I wonder what he will do… arrest everyone?

Ceddars and I follow Troughton and Constable Jakes out of the station where we're met by the crowd that has grown in size and volume in the short time we were inside. It's off-kilter for what I know of Little Pucklewick so far. I realise that it must be like any other picturesque village or quiet town—whatever it may look like on the outside, there is always a darker element waiting for a chance to show its ugly face.

"Bally hell, Em'! This is a rum do. I'll toddle off and bring the Bugatti round, just in case we need to make a quick getaway, what?"

I nod and Ceddars disappears into the crowd.

Troughton raises a hand, and the crowd drops into silence.

"You are all quite rightly angry at the death of our beloved vicar," he begins, the nasal tone of his voice even more pronounced, "and I know you are as eager as myself and Constable Jakes to find the perpetrator or perpetrators of the heinous crime committed against the Reverend Wilson-Smallsey. But let me assure you, evidence has come to light that proves without any doubt that the Chinese gentleman known as Sheng, who is working under the employ of Mr William Eriksen, is innocent of his murder."

"If you let that bastard go free, he'll have to deal with me an' my mates, you understand copper?" Grantham shouts to a chorus of cheers and growls. The inspector tries to speak but is drowned out.

"Now, now, Johnny Grantham," Constable Jakes says, his voice unexpectedly full of authority and easily heard above the raucous noise. "Why don't you go 'ome and end this nonsense? It'll be better for all concerned."

"You can't tell me what I can and can't bloody do!" He sounds bullish, but his eyes betray him. He's more than a little afraid of the constable.

"Oh, it's like that is it?" Jakes replies. "It's just that there is quite the problem with poachin' on the old estate, and, well, it would be unfortunate if I were to take a personal interest in findin' out which gang of lads were responsible. Very unfortunate."

"You can't prove that were me," Grantham replies, although his voice has lost some of its bluster. "Or any of us." He glances at his mates and pulls a 'so what' face. His friends nod back nervously. They are not as convinced as their erstwhile leader.

"Maybe I can, maybe I can't. But if you want me to look more closely into it, then you're going the right way about it, understand? Now lads, why don't you move along?"

"We're staying put until you bring out that Sheng and he gets what's coming to him."

Jakes calmly walks right up to Grantham so that his face his only inches away. "I'm afraid you 'aven't quite grasped the import of my words, Johnny. I'm issuing you a threat. I want you and your mates to get out of my sight, otherwise I will arrest you forthwith for public disorder. After which, the inspector will put the full force of 'is policing talents on investigatin' every part of your miserable life. The same for your mates. And believe me, that ain't somethin' you want to 'appen anytime soon."

"You can't do that," Grantham says uncertainly, "can you?"

"I have the full authority of 'is Majesty and the law on my side, what do you 'ave?"

Grantham says nothing for a few moments. He may be bullish, but the young man isn't stupid, that's for sure. "C'mon," he says to his mates. "Let's get out of here." They shuffle away. "This ain't over," Grantham shouts half-heartedly, but the ire has left his voice.

"And the same goes for the rest of you," Inspector Troughton says, finding his voice. "Obstructing an officer of the law is a serious offence. And as Constable Jakes says, he will arrest anyone who gets in our way."

The crowd doesn't need telling twice and quickly disperses.

I go over to Jakes. "That was quite impressive, constable," I say, realising that I have may have underestimated the man.

"Jus' doin' my job, miss. Johnny Grantham is a good lad at heart. But you know what young men are like? All mouth and no trousers, as they say. He'll grow out of it. I certainly did."

Once the street is clear of people, Troughton instructs

Jakes to bring out Eriksen and Sheng, who both appear a few moments later.

"I'm sorry about that," Jakes says, as he, Troughton, Eriksen and Sheng cross the road to where Fran Feltham parked their van. And I follow them. "The death of the vicar and poor Billy 'as spooked the more nervous elements of the village and its contingent of drunkards and idiots."

"Thank you, constable," Eriksen says, turning to Troughton with a less than impressed look on his face. "And you, inspector. Although I'm sure Grantham and his mates won't be put off for very long. If they come knocking at my door, which I suspect they will do, I won't be responsible for what happens, indeed, I—"

Eriksen stumbles and collapses onto the pavement, half-caught by Sheng, a wooden shaft of a bamboo crossbow has grazed his leg, ripping through the fabric of his trousers, and drawing blood, before clattering to the pavement. Shot from the row of abandoned cottages.

I glance up and notice that the wood covering one of the boarded windows on the upper floor of the nearest building has been pulled back. I throw my hat to the ground and vault over the low cottage wall and through the open front door into the relative gloom. The upper floor is missing a staircase, the walls greasy with mould. But climbable if you had the intention. I pull myself up and peer inside. As far as I can see, the upstairs is empty, the internal walls all missing. The only light comes from the window where a plank of wood has been pulled aside. I lower myself back down and enter a small, abandoned parlour, the kitchen, and then outside through an open door into an overgrown garden. I can see no evidence that anyone has been through here. No sound of running footsteps, no disturbed foliage.

I go back through the cottage to find the prone form of Eriksen, cradled in the arms of a distraught looking Sheng. A roar of an engine and the Bugatti arrives. The car was parked just around the corner. Why did it take Ceddars so long to get here? He jumps out and comes over.

"Bally hell! What happened? Oh, Eriksen's been shot." He crouches down and inspects the injury. "It's just a flesh wound, you've been bally lucky."

Eriksen wouldn't be beyond staging this shooting to get himself off the hook, I realise. But who could he have employed to do it? My thoughts follow along the same course until I see the ashen colour of Eriksen's face and tears running down Sheng's face.

"I say, are you quite alright, old chap?" Ceddars says.

"Poison," Eriksen grunts in reply. "The stolen bolts were treated with poison." His limbs spasm wildly and he begins to froth at the mouth, before becoming dreadfully limp.

Ceddars checks him over. "He's… he's dead."

Grief & Kisses

THE body of William Eriksen, cradled by his companion, Sheng, is brought back into the station and laid downstairs in one of the cells. Sheng sits next to him, shaking with grief, whilst Ceddars gives him a thorough examination. "There's no other mark on him. The wound is not serious enough to have caused death unless the bally thing was actually poisoned as Eriksen stated."

Troughton produces the bolt taken from the body of the Reverend Wilson-Smallsey and places it side by side with the bolt that struck William Eriksen. They are identical. The tips of each are hardened and finished off with iron, and where the iron tip is joined to the bamboos there are similar stains of green. The inspector turns to Sheng.

"What do you know about this?"

Sheng looks up from the corpse, his face showing naked grief, and I wonder if he will maintain his silence. "The crossbow is Chinese traditional weapon," he says in a thick accented whisper, "made from single piece of mahogany." His voice is shaking, his tone dead, like he's reading out a list of dull facts, but his eyes tell another story. "The one stolen was modern version from Yi tribe region. Smaller. Mostused by women and grown children."

Inspector Troughton nods. "That's what William Eriksen told me. But he mentioned nothing about any poison darts."

Sheng's eyes slide over to the table and the two identical bolts lying there. "Bolts coated with aconite."

The inspector shrugs. "And what is that?"

"Aconite is one of the deadliest and most rapidly acting

poisons," I reply. "A bolt laced with even a small drop can kill in minutes."

"I say," Ceddars says, reacting if he'd also been hit with a dart. "That's exactly what Eriksen said at his rather dull talk last night. I didn't believe it for a minute, of course. I thought it was just for the audience. Got quite an 'ooh' from the assembled ladies when he told them that. I thought he was making it up for effect."

I round on Ceddars unable to hide my anger and frustration. "How can you have kept such vital information to yourself? You told me the vicar died from a shot to the heart."

The doctor raises his hands. "He did bally well die from a shot to the heart. Death was instantaneous. And I had no reason to believe the arrow was anything other than just that, an arrow. As I said, I thought Eriksen was making all that up."

"But that means that whoever shot the vicar knew that the arrows were poisoned!" They were not the marksman as I previously believed them to be, pulling off an almost impossible shot from distance, instead, they were just hoping to graze the vicar, knowing that the poison would do the rest. "Ceddars, you are sometimes quite the buffoon. Didn't it even cross your mind to tell me this?"

"I say, old girl, calm down. It's not my fault. But I get it. You're upset that Eriksen's death has somewhat put the kibosh on your theory, but don't take it out on me. I'm just a bumbling country doctor, remember?"

I was absolutely sure that Eriksen was the murderer, a murderer assisted by Sheng. But his death proves that I was barking up the wrong investigative tree. The knowledge galls me. I was so utterly convinced by my theory that, even now, I find it hard to believe that I got it so wrong. There was motive, opportunity, and even a false suspect to try and throw me off... this whole investigation is far more complicated than I thought.

Ceddars sits down heavily on one of the cell block chairs. "The question," he begins, his jovial tones returning, "is who would want to murder both the reverend and William Eriksen?"

"And Billy Brown," Constable Jakes says. "Don't forget that poor young lad was left fer dead at the side of the road."

I lean back on the desk. "I think we need to focus our investigation on who killed him and why. If we can discover that, we'll unravel the whole mystery."

"I'm afraid you'll be doing nothing of the kind, young lady," Troughton says. "You've interfered quite enough as it is, don't you think? You came here with your high-handed 'better than thou' and rather tiresome attitude, spouting spurious relationships and uncorroborated evidence—all of which was found to be more than a little overblown—and you have been proved to be thoroughly wrong in all of it. I want you to forget about this business and to return home, otherwise I might consider arresting you for impeding my investigation."

The inspector's tone, back to its full nasal twang, is derisive to say the least, although his threat of arresting me is just hyperbole—at least I think it is.

Ceddars gives me a supportive look. "I say, old chap, Em' here was only trying to help. Her theory was pretty plausible," he winks at me, "although the old gal can be a little high-handed."

Troughton shakes his head. "As I told you both before, murder is an ugly business and motives are more straightforward than many people realise. I'll get to the bottom of this without your help." He turns his attention to Ceddars. "I'm looking to you to support me in this, doctor. You'll do Miss Crookshanks no good by indulging her delusions."

Ceddars appears chastened. "Yes. Of course. I'll take Em'

back home now."

I say nothing. Troughton's words have had no effect on me, the man can say and think what he likes. Instead, my mind is still trying to process what's happened. I'm finding it difficult to rearrange my thoughts, to accept that I was wrong. I'm humiliated and embarrassed—*and angry*. Furious at how I could've been so mistaken. I'm always right! Always! I'm the Headmistress, am I not? The darling sleuth of South Africa!

We follow Troughton back upstairs, leaving Sheng with the body of Eriksen. I fume all the way, stamping my feet heavily on the wooden steps. The station front door opens as we get there and in bursts a distraught Dorothy Knight.

"Is it true? Is he dead?" she shouts.

"I'm afraid so," Troughton says.

Dorothy Knight shrieks at the news and collapses to the floor in a mess of wails and tears. "No! It can't be! Not my William! No!"

Compared to Mrs Willoughby's theatrical reaction at the news of the vicar's death, her grief is as real as it is loud.

Ceddars rushes over to attend to her, but there is nothing he can do other than stand and watch uncomfortably.

The woman had pinned all her hopes on a marriage to William Eriksen, that much is obvious. Even though I am sure the man had strung her along to find out what she knew about the vicar, who she was obviously also close to. It's plain to see she was deeply in love with him. I'm desperately sorry for Dorothy, but with the wound of grief, only time will help. There's nothing anyone can do for her now. Indeed, Ceddars tries his best to console her, but the woman wants nothing to do with him.

I open the station door and motion to Ceddars to join me, which he does reluctantly, bowing his goodbyes to the inspector and Constable Jakes.

"Poor old Dotty," Ceddars says as we walk towards the

Bugatti. "She's really taken it hard."

"Best she be disappointed in grief, than by rejection."

"Eriksen had no romantic intentions whatsoever, you think?"

"As I said, his attentions were… elsewhere."

"You still believe that? Even though your theory was proved wrong?"

"I'm a student of human nature. And you doctor, you saw it too, didn't you? Especially in Sheng's reaction."

"I wouldn't know, Em'. That's not my kind of thing at all."

"Don't pretend you've never heard of it."

"Like I said, that's not my kind of thing. Let's leave it at that."

"And I thought you were somewhat of a modern thinker."

"What people get up to with one another is no one's business, except their own. And certainly, no business of mine, or of anybody's for that matter. Live and let live and all that, is my motto. And besides, life is too bally short."

I let the matter drop. I have another bone to pick with the good doctor. "Is there any reason why you didn't tell me that the crossbow darts could've been poisoned? Didn't you think I needed to know that?"

Ceddars sighs. "I only went to the bally talk because Fran was there. I had little interest in Eriksen's adventures. I didn't take him seriously when he mentioned the darts, and now I'm in your bad books."

"Yes, you are."

We climb inside the Bugatti and as Ceddars goes to start the engine, I stop him with my hand on his arm. "I want you to take me to Eriksen's mansion."

"What on earth do you want to go there for? You heard the inspector. He wants me to keep an eye on you."

"You will."

"Don't you think it's time to give this up, Em'? You've already made one serious gaff with your theory about Eriksen and mightily shown yourself up in front of Troughton. I thought that'd be reason enough to stand down, what?"

"It's Billy," I reply. "He's the key to all of this. We must find the vehicle that ran him down. If we can discover who killed him and why, we will also find the person who killed the Reverend Wilson Smallsey and William Eriksen. I'm sure of it."

"But why Eriksen's place?"

"I need to rule out William Eriksen's Mercedes."

"Hang on, it can't be Eriksen because he's dead?"

"Yes, but it might not have been him who was driving it."

"Em', you really have got to give this thing a rest, it's just—"

I put my hand over his mouth and shake my head. "My dear Ceddars, it's pointless for you to argue with me, haven't you realised that yet? I may have been wrong about Eriksen, but I am a bloodhound, and bloodhounds don't stop until they have found their man… or woman."

Ceddars removes my hand and squeezes it. "You will get me into a lot of trouble."

"I think, Ceddars, that you rather enjoy that, so start the car and take me to the mansion."

Shaking his head, Ceddars brings the Bugatti into roaring life, and we shoot up the hill towards Dooleys Wood. Instead of continuing to Eriksen's mansion, Ceddars turns off and parks outside his house. "I need a bally change of clothes, what?" he says in explanation. "I've lost my jacket and I can't go wandering about half-naked like this."

He jumps out and opens the door for me and we both enter his large house.

"I'll just be a jiffy," he says, depositing me in the sitting room. "I gave my maid the day off, so no tea and cakes, sorry."

"We're here alone?"

"I suppose we are."

"I thought you were worried about wagging tongues?

Won't the village gossips have something to say about you bringing me here without a chaperone?"

"I think after Eriksen's and the vicar's murder, the wagging tongues will have a lot more to wag about than just the shenanigans of a country doctor, what? I'll be as quick as I can."

I hear him go upstairs, aware that he has taken his bag with him. Surely, he would leave it at the door, rather than lugging it upstairs? I find myself wishing that Ceddars was not a suspect, and that he would stop doing suspicious things. It annoys me. I hope above hope that he's not involved in these murders, because, regardless of how I may feel about him, it wouldn't stop me. Not in the slightest…

I look out of the window, uncomfortably aware that I'm on my own again. Dooleys Wood, which sits on the opposite side of the road to Ceddars' house, perturbs me, and I don't know why. I quickly turn away and examine the doctor's sitting room. It's quite modest, apart from a large, broken propeller mounted on the wall and a painting of an RAF bi-plane hung above the fireplace, with a younger-looking and rather dashing Ceddars standing next to it. Underneath, on the mantlepiece, is a photograph the painting was based upon, and various other mementos from the war, including an impressive array of medals. There is another photograph of a crashed bi-plane, and I realise the propeller is the same as in the picture. Ceddars has had some adventures, that much is for sure.

I hear footsteps on the stairs and expect Ceddars to arrive soon after, but he doesn't make an appearance. I hear a muffled voice coming from somewhere outside the sitting room. I'm just about to go and investigate when I hear a door open and close and footsteps approaching.

"Righty ho!" Ceddars says, appearing in the doorway, wearing a different suit, and still clutching his large medical bag.

I have the urge to tell him to open it, but it wouldn't prove anything. If he had been hiding the crossbow inside, he's had ample chance to remove it. But it rankles.

"I see you're looking at the old mementos, what? It's all a little showy, but it does impress the ladies. Are you suitably impressed?"

"Very much so… Did I hear you talking to someone?"

"Bally hell! Nothing gets past the old sleuth, what? But yes, I was talking on the blower to an old chum from my war days. Enwright. Another doctor. Done very well for himself. Has a Harley Street practice. I meet him at our annual get-togethers. Likes the brandy."

"Any reason why you were talking to him?"

"Well yes, as it happens. It was about Mrs W and that dreadful cough of hers. She let slip her doctor's name the last time I chatted to her—at the vicarage when you were interrogating Dotty Knight. I thought, well, what's the harm in getting the lowdown on the old gal. I may be the assistant to a sleuth, but I'm also still a doctor."

"What did he say?"

"Wasn't available. The fellow is dreadfully busy. Lots of nobby clients and whatnot. Right, shall we toddle off to Eriksen's? It's just a few minutes away. No need for the motor. Although I still think this is a bally bad idea."

I nod, letting him guide me out of his house.

Minutes later, we are walking again next to Dooleys Wood on our way to Eriksen's mansion. As we approach the gateposts at the start of the driveway, I notice one of the Chinese dragons lying on the ground, scratch marks from a collision on the brickwork, and a smear of white paint.

"I say! It looks like Eriksen did sideswipe the post after all, just as Fran described."

"I don't doubt it."

"You don't?"

"Of course not. If Eriksen had ran Billy over, it makes

sense to have a reason why his car was damaged."

"You still think the poor fellow ran Billy over?"

"I have no idea what to think. I'm just keeping all options open. It may be possible that the collision was manufactured to cover up the true cause of the damage to his car. And we still can't be sure who was driving it."

"You have a very devious mind."

"That is true. Some say that there is very little difference between intelligent and calculating murderers and the sleuths who bring them to justice."

"That's not very reassuring."

I give him a good-natured wink. "I've not planned to kill anyone just yet, but never say never."

"Oh, Em'!"

The afternoon sun abruptly disappears behind a large black, thunderous looking rain cloud, and a blast of cold air blows through the trees.

We rush over to a Lebanese Cedar standing on the side of the driveway, just as the heavens open. A terrific, thundering downpour.

"Bally hell!" Ceddars exclaims as we huddle together.

I become acutely aware of our proximity. Ceddars turns to me as the rainfall intensifies. We are dry under the massive tree, like we are in a private pocket away from the real world. And before I realise what's happening, we are kissing. I'm consumed by the moment, lost to it, and yet a part of me is unable to truly give myself fully. I want to search for my pen but I'm not sure why… yet find both my hands grabbing tightly to Ceddars' back. The moment lingers, time stretching away from me, distending. Until we part and the rains subside. My heart beats fiercely, but as I place my head on Ceddars' chest, the same is not true for him. His heartbeat is a slow thud.

"Crikey!" Ceddars says. "That was rather unexpected, but I suppose you are a modern woman after all." Despite his slow heartbeat, his face is flushed.

"I'm sorry," I whisper, the words stumbling from my trembling lips. "I don't know what came over me."

"Don't apologise, Em', that was, well, rather lovely." He looks around conspiratorially. "I don't think anyone saw us. Saved by the rain, what?"

I pull away. "C'mon." I stomp into the now suddenly clear day and Ceddars follows. I have no idea what just happened. It was like a force outside of my body compelled me to kiss the doctor. Not simple desire, but something else, something equally powerful. There is one other thing… I enjoyed it.

It is a mistake for any investigator to get involved with a possible suspect, but I was simply unable to help myself. And somewhere deep inside, there is a deeper mystery in Little Pucklewick, a mystery that is different from these murders… but what?

We arrive at the mansion and find Eriksen's white Mercedes parked outside.

"He certainly was in a prang!" Ceddars exclaims, examining a bent fender and a twisted wheel with a sad-looking flat tyre. "But it's a sideswipe, just as Franny described it to us.

I agree with the doctor. There is no direct damage to the front or the underneath of the vehicle consistent with hitting a bike at speed and running it over. This was not the car that ran Billy off the road. And even though my theory about Eriksen was proved wrong, it still rankles to see the evidence, or lack of it. I was very much wide of the mark.

I go over to the mansion door and turn the handle. It's not locked. "I guess Eriksen was in a hurry when he left. What do you say? Shall we go inside for a looksee?"

"You mean snoop around inside a dead man's house?"

I don't wait for an answer and push inside.

Swords & Suspects

THE mansion is the same as when we left it, boxes strewn everywhere, some open, others stacked into uneven piles. I stride past them into Eriksen's makeshift office and go over to his desk.

"I say, Em', don't you think this is a bit off? Breaking and entering and all that?"

I ignore Ceddars and rummage inside Eriksen's desk drawers. I find a series of bills and receipts mostly to do with the transport of his collection from overseas, although I do find a letter of recommendation on headed notepaper from *The Lady's Secretarial Agency*, based in Hackney, London, regarding Francesca Feltham, signed by a woman called Mrs Hattersley. I fold the letter and place it in one of my pockets.

"Emily!"

"If we can find out who murdered William, don't you think he would forgive us?"

"Well yes, but—"

"Don't just stand there, search Fran's desk."

"I bally will not!"

I examine a shelf of books and a few open folders containing nothing of interest before rifling through a set of filing cabinets—an inventory of Eriksen's collection. Afterwards, I go over to Fran's desk, pushing Ceddars out of the way.

"This is an invasion of her privacy," he says tersely.

I open Fran's desk drawers to find them all mostly empty. "Odd. And where is her typewriter?"

"She probably took it home with her. Maybe she wanted

to write a letter, or perhaps she's a mystery writer on the quiet, what? That wouldn't surprise me in the least, the damn girl is a mystery all on her own."

"Just what is going on between you two?"

Ceddars shrugs. "You getting jealous?"

"Worried more like. A girl should think twice before becoming involved with a Lothario like you, doctor."

Ceddars laughs at that and is rather too pleased with himself for my liking.

I pull out some of Fran's desk drawers to see if anything has dropped behind them, and I'm rewarded by finding an old photograph featuring a young-looking Reverend Wilson-Smallsey standing next to a very attractive woman. Judging by the appearance of the vicar, and the quality of the photograph, it was taken roughly thirty or so years ago. Wilson-Smallsey was a very handsome young man with striking looks and thick, black hair.

"What on earth is that doing in Franny's desk?" Ceddars asks over my shoulder.

"That's what we will ask her."

"We will?"

I nod. "That can wait for now. While we're here, I think it will be useful to take a poke around Eriksen's private rooms."

"The man is barely cold!"

"What's the phrase, Ceddars? *We must strike while the iron is hot.*"

"But this is quite, quite heinous behaviour!"

"So is murder. Now stop your blathering and come with me."

I go back down the corridor that leads to the garden, pleased to hear Ceddars' footsteps following me. I don't like being on my own and I find the doctor a reassuring presence. I shiver when I again enter the far room stuffed with antiquities, my eyes darting around, looking for... *I'm not sure what.* I hurry through, locating a staircase close to the back garden and ascend two steps at a time, arriving at a wide corridor on the top floor. At the corridor's end sits a pair of double doors. I walk towards them, Ceddars nervously muttering curses at my back. I open the doors to be met by a scene reminiscent of many drawings of the Orient and China. The room is bedecked with Chinese hangings and sculptures, the walls excellently painted in reds, blues, greens, and oranges, behind which, I see the delicate hand of Sheng. It appears the man wasn't just a weapons master but an accomplished student of the arts.

In the centre of the room sits a double bed, its sheets carelessly left awry. As if Eriksen had just gotten up. There is an open door to another room. I peer inside. In comparison, this room is stark. A single, hard-looking wooden bed on the floor and no adornments, the walls a blank dark grey.

"I say, you think this is where Sheng sleeps?"

I nod. "I guess he wanted to be on hand at his master's call."

"It does seem that way."

Back in the master bedroom, my eye is taken by a corner of card sticking out from under the bed. It's part of a folder containing various papers, some scribbled, some typed. A quick glance tells me they are a collection of rumours and allegations against Wilson-Smallsey. Eriksen was building up quite the portfolio on the man.

"C'mon, Em', enough is enough."

"But look at these…"

"I will not, this is verging on sacrilege—"

"Get out!"

We both look up to see Sheng standing in the bedroom doorway, his face twisted in anger and grief. More importantly, he is holding a wicked looking curved sword with a wooden handle.

"I'm so sorry old man," Ceddars blurts, "but…" His voice dries, and I can guess why, we have no excuse for being here.

I, on the other hand, am more than able to find my voice.

"Put down that ridiculous sword," I command, walking over to the diminutive man.

Sheng is not intimidated. "I said, get out!"

I hold up the sheaf of papers. "I think these may hold the clue as to why William and the vicar were murdered. If they match the rumours that have been posted about the village, it is possible that someone was frightened that their secret would be found out. I need to go through these very carefully."

The sword spins in Sheng's hand, the blade blurring, before slicing into the sheaf of papers I'm holding and cutting them asunder, his other hand grabbing what remains of the folder from my outstretched hand and throwing it roughly aside.

"Get out!" he repeats. This time, his voice is a shrill, piercing wail, and I know we must leave. I bend down to scoop up the cleaved papers, but Sheng kicks them away.

"C'mon Em', let's get out of here!" Ceddars grabs my arm and drags me into the corridor.

"We can't leave vital clues behind…"

"Em', come on! We have no idea what Sheng is capable of. And we have broken into his house. We are leaving. Now!"

Ceddars drags me outside the mansion and halfway down the drive before he slows his pace. "That was bally stupid, Em'. Did you not notice his murderous gaze? And when he swung that sword, I thought…"

"I was in no danger. The man is not a killer. Still, it will take him time to calm down, time we don't have."

"What do you mean by that?"

"I mean to return here and take a proper look at those papers."

"You think they're important?"

I shake myself free of Ceddars' arm and straighten my clothing. "Possibly. There has to be a connection between the three murders, and that folder could be it. Perhaps Wilson-Smallsey was killed because he was blackmailing the murderer, or it was done out of malice for something that he'd done. From what we've learnt so far, the vicar was a shady character. Maybe Eriksen was murdered because he knew, or at least suspected who the murderer was."

"Then why didn't Eriksen venture that information after Sheng was arrested?"

I shake my head and sigh. "That's why it's a theory. And that's why... I want to see the curate again."

"Simmons? I'd forgotten about him. Didn't Billy spot him leaving the church vaults after the man told us he never went inside?"

I nod. "And soon after, the lad was found dead."

"Golly! Yes! So you think Simmons is involved somehow?"

"I'm not making any accusations just yet, but his fear of enclosed spaces was perhaps exaggerated. And remember what Billy said? He was clutching a satchel. And the stranger seen around town, the stranger who, according to Mrs Willoughby was putting up the posters, was also carrying a satchel."

"But Simmons is a beanpole of a chap. That couldn't be him."

"That's right."

"So he employed this diminutive chap to smear the vicar with those posters? That would make sense."

"I'm not sure what to think, but it's possible Simmons had an accomplice. And there's one more thing. Do you remember what he told us about working with the vicar. His difficulties?"

Ceddars pulls a confused expression. "Um..."

"He said, "*I decided to help him with the church funds, which he took umbrage at. I found out that he liked to control the purse-strings himself.* Remember?"

"Yes, he did say that. I'd quite forgotten."

"And before Sheng rudely interrupted us, I noticed clues in those papers."

"You did?"

"Yes, and not just rumour. Actual evidence that Wilson-Smallsey was embezzling church funds."

"By Jove!"

"I believe Eriksen was about to expose that, as well as the other things he'd discovered."

"You think he got this information from Simmons?"

"I don't know how Simmons is involved, but I'm sure he found out about the embezzling. But it's more than that. It appears that some members of the village have donated heavily to the church roof fund. I saw a list of names."

"You… you did?"

"A list that included Mrs Gladys Willoughby who has made sizeable donations, very sizeable indeed. There were more names, but Sheng interrupted us before I could read them all."

"Mrs W? I say! Perhaps she found out that Smallsey was spaffing her money away and she decided to knock him off?"

"Possibly. The man was a gambler. The horses apparently. There was a betting ticket for over fifty pounds attached to Eriksen's notes."

"Fifty quid? On the nags? Bally hell!"

"Indeed. Be thankful it wasn't your money?"

Ceddars says nothing for a few moments. "But if Mrs W bumped off the vicar, why would she take a pot-shot at Eriksen? Seems a bit like an overkill to me."

"These are the questions that sleuths like myself deal with every day. The why of it. *The motives*. I'm not familiar with Mrs Willoughby, other than that she's a pompous, overbearing, somewhat proud woman, but maybe Eriksen was blackmailing her?"

"Eriksen, a blackmailer? I just don't see it, Em'. The fellow was more interested in his collection than extortion, don't you think?"

"I agree. It's far more likely that someone like Mrs Willoughby would be worried about her reputation. To be made a fool of by the vicar is one thing, but for it to become widely known… that could push someone like her over the edge. Especially after she saw those posters popping up around town. She was very keen to remove them. I can see how she would think Eriksen was the culprit. And she disliked him as much as the vicar."

"Well I never, Mrs W a murderer. It's quite the mind-jingler."

"I'm not saying it's her, I'm just considering motives and who we should go and see next. And while we're at it, let's not forget your Fran Feltham. She may equally be wrapped up in all of this."

"Franny? You're barking up the wrong tree there, Em', I can vouch for the gal. She's stand-up. And quite above suspicion."

"That coming from the Lothario doctor who was quite happy to slip me the tongue when he had the chance…"

Ceddars shrugs. "Of course, I like the ladies, but which full-blooded chap doesn't, what? And besides, Em', it was your tongue that did most of the slipping as far as I remember."

The doctor is right. I shake my head irritably. "What I'm saying is that this girl has seemingly turned your head. A head that, as far as I can tell, is very easily turned, meaning you can't be one hundred per cent sure she's innocent, can you?"

"I won't have a word spoken against Franny. I'm telling you, Em'… she's not involved in this."

"But why does she have a photograph of Wilson-Smallsey in her desk?"

"Because it's not Franny's desk, that's why. She just works there. It probably belonged to Eriksen."

"A fair point, but she's still a suspect."

Ceddars sighs. "You're barking up the wrong tree, Em'."

I like the doctor, but he can be very exasperating at times, especially concerning Francesca Feltham. "Shall we move on to consider Dorothy Knight and her son, Eugene?"

"That nosy little sprog?" Ceddars moustache wrinkles in anger. "It wouldn't surprise me in the least if he was involved. The lad is a bone-fide creep."

"He could be. The florist was closed today, wasn't it? So no deliveries. Meaning both Dorothy Knight and her son would have access to the van."

"Dotty was beside herself with grief at the death of William Eriksen. It can't be her."

"Never rule anybody out. That's the first rule of sleuthing."

"I suppose so. Unless they have a cast iron alibi."

"Even then. Alibis have a habit of not being so very cast-iron in my experience. Nevertheless, the key to this mystery is Billy and who ran him over. If we can find the vehicle, we will be a lot closer to finding the murderer. According to you, there are only two white vehicles in Little Pucklewick, which puts making another visit to the florist at the top of my list."

"You think Eugene was the driver? Billy told us those two didn't get on. But why would he kill the vicar and Eriksen?"

"Let's not get ahead of ourselves, doctor. Let's first establish if the florist van was involved and go from there."

"Well, one thing is for sure. It wasn't me who ran the lad over. I've been with you all day, remember?"

"You're right. But then again, this is all supposition and possibility. Everyone must still be considered, and, as I've said before, that includes you, kind doctor."

Ceddars scoffs. "You've a funny way of treating me as a suspect, unless your plan is to keep me very, very close."

He gives me a cheesy wink which I ignore. He's right though, I did kiss him. *Wanted him.* Still want him. Which is problematic, seeing that Eriksen's notes also included references to the doctor. From what I glimpsed, Ceddars donated quite a large sum of money to the vicar's fund. I was hoping he would admit that to me, but he said nothing when I gave him the chance. Ceddars is either embarrassed or hiding something. One thing is for sure though, I will get to the bottom of this. And hopefully, when I get there, I won't find the charming doctor waiting for me… "Let's go back to the florist's and see if we can find that van."

"Righty ho! I don't want to hang around here any longer, what?"

Trespass & Insinuation

CEDDARS takes us down a small road that runs behind the high street, heading for Dorothy Knight's florist shop.

"I say, this is rather exciting, isn't it?"

"Shh!"

We enter a small yard at the back of which is a wooden garage. Inside is parked the florist van. It's a new model, the paint light grey rather than white. "There isn't a scratch on it," I say, unable to hide my disappointment.

"Another dead end, what?"

I look inside the cab to find keys hanging in the ignition. "Anyone could've driven the van and returned it."

"But this van didn't knock down poor Billy, I thought that was obvious."

"Are you sure that there are only two white vehicles in Little Pucklewick?"

He shrugs. "As sure as I can be. And both have been ruled out."

"Dammit!"

"What next Em'? Will you finally give it up?"

"The investigation? Of course not. Setbacks and confusions are part of the game." I try to sound upbeat, but I'm not fooling anybody, least of all myself.

A bang at the back of the makeshift garage, and both Ceddars and I are suddenly alert.

"Who's there?" Ceddars grabs a length of piping and brandishes it threateningly.

Eugene Knight emerges from behind the van. "I should

be asking the same of you," he says with a petulant air, pushing his flock of white-blond hair away from his eyes. "It's you two who are trespassing." Despite his bluster, I notice the lad has been crying. I've been wanting to talk to the boy ever since we caught him lurking in Dooleys Wood soon after the murder. We stand between him and the front of the garage. This time, he can't run away.

"You need a good whipping after the way you talked to me earlier, you hear me?"

I remember Eugene's words to Ceddars before he ran off the last time we saw him… *I know what you did! Shame on you! Shame on you!* "Just what is your problem with the doctor?"

Eugene gives me a shrug. Despite his youth, I can see that he will grow up to be a very attractive man. He has a strong facial bone structure, favouring the beauty of his mother, the same good looks transferring well between the sexes. Good looks ruined only by the boy's constant sneer. "I don't have to answer your questions. You should be answering mine! It's you who are trespassing. I should call the police."

"You have heard about Billy?"

Eugene can't hide the look of horror that crosses his face, and a flash of grief. "What about him? He's dead. So what?"

"Weren't you his friend?"

"He was an oik!" His words don't match his tone. His voice is almost breaking.

"I heard you had quite the falling out, isn't that right?"

"I outgrew him. I'm made for better things." The same phrase I heard coming from Dorothy Knight. Was it she who poisoned Eugene against Billy?

"I say old chap. That's a bit harsh, what?"

"Don't you speak to me! Not after what you did!"

"What did Ceddars do?" I keep my voice calm, but it's obvious the boy is carrying a lot of anger inside of him. The majority of it reserved for Ceddars.

"He knows what he bloody well did!"

"You oily little tick!"

"I'd stay away from him!" Eugene shouts, turning towards me.

"And why should I do that?"

"Just stay away, he can't be trusted!"

I can see I'm getting nowhere and try a different tack. "What were you doing in Dooley's Wood this morning?"

"That's none of your business. But I see things, don't I, doctor?"

"What did you see?"

"Ask him! Ask that bastard!" He darts into the cab of the van, shuffles along the seats, jumps out of the other side and runs away.

"What is wrong with that horrible boy!" Ceddars says, throwing down the iron piping in anger. "He needs a father. Someone to give him a bally good whipping. I'd take on the job, but I might not be able to control myself."

"What did Eugene mean when he said he sees things?"

Ceddars shrugs. "The boy is obviously disturbed. I doubt he even knows what the bally hell he's talking about."

"But what could he have possibly seen to make him hate you so much?"

Ceddars lets out an exasperated sigh. "They say spare the rod and ruin the child—an approach that I've never been in favour of, until now."

"But I'm sure he saw something."

"Like what? Me shooting the vicar in the back? Is that what you're getting at?"

I ignore him. I'm stuck. With no leads and nothing to go on except a series of confusing clues. Nothing is adding up. I take a steadying breath, aware that Ceddars is waiting my reply. "We're off to church."

"The church? That dreary place? You want to chat to Simmons again?"

I nod. "Although I'm sure that Mrs Willoughby will also be in attendance."

Leaks & Lies

WE cross the village green in silence. Ceddars was upset by Eugene, that much is for sure, and I'm in no mood for small talk. Not until I can make sense of this mystery.

The church is surrounded by an ancient wall in which stands a wooden entranceway. We pass through, emerging into a well-tended graveyard festooned with beautiful red, white, and pink roses. The result, it would seem, of Mary Wilson-Smallsey's gardening skills. The church sits at its centre, old, rain-stained granite walls rearing up towards heaven. Rusted scaffolding covers one wall. I've never liked churches, I realise, as we approach its open doors. In their heyday, they were bastions of light, magic, and marvels, but today, they are dreary affairs. No wonder attendance has dropped when the populace all now have smartphones and flatscreen televisions…

I catch my thoughts. What on earth are *smartphones* and *flatscreen televisions*? The words sound arcane and otherworldly. I try to repeat them, but they slip from my mind. And moments later, I am unable to remember the phrases at all.

Shaking my head, I follow Ceddars into the gloom of the church to find thirty or so mourners lined up on wooden pews, the sound of their sobbing restrained but no less heartfelt. How very English. Even in grief, they try to hide their feelings.

The church is more rundown than I expected and smells of mould, occasional buckets placed to catch water from where the roof is leaking. But the pews are all polished and flowers adorn the many alcoves. A shudder runs down my spine. I instinctively don't like this place—or at least places like this—and I'm not sure why.

I refocus my mind and try to locate the curate. But the man is conspicuous by his absence. I notice the imposing frame of Mrs Willoughby standing by the dais, her purple clothing replaced with voluminous black, and go over to her.

"Where is Simmons?" I ask her with no preamble.

"Oh, it's you," she replies with disdain. "And you, doctor."

Ceddars gives me a sideways look and raises his eyebrows. "What ho, Mrs W!"

"Please, doctor, show some decorum. This is a church, and its vicar is recently deceased." She coughs, covering her mouth with a black lace handkerchief.

"I'm sorry, Mrs W," Ceddars replies. "We were hoping to have a chat with the curate. We thought the old chap would be here?"

"Well, you thought wrong. He is nowhere to be seen. You would think that after the dreadful events of this morning, he would at least show his face. Then again, according to Albert, the man is a disaster area. He was going to write a stern letter to the bishop about getting a replacement."

I perk up at these words. "The vicar wanted Simmons gone?"

"Oh yes. Very much so. He could not stand the man. Kept sticking his nose in where it was not needed, or so he said. A bothersome individual by all accounts. And the way he idolises Mary… well, it is quite unsavoury. I knew he was not right. The war deranged a lot of men." She looks at Ceddars like she's including him in this description. "Simmons is not even married. A man of his age! If that's not a sign things are not right with him, I do not know what is?"

"I'd happily get married," Ceddars says, his moustache twitching defensively, "but I can't seem to convince any gals into doing the bally thing."

Mrs Willoughby shrugs. "Perhaps you would have more luck if you stopped cavorting with Postmaster's daughters and other unsavoury women like that dreadful Francesca Feltham girl."

"I say, Mrs W, that is a little harsh. Franny has her career to think of and—"

"What is the world is coming to! There was a time when girls like her would be already married. They are ruining the moral fabric of the country." She coughs again, pushing Ceddars away as he tries to administer to her. "And look at the inspector? The man is a commoner! I have no idea what school he went to, or what family he is from, but it's obvious he's not suited to the rank. How could he possibly let that Chinese heathen go free? I couldn't quite believe it! I phoned the superintendent as soon as I heard and told him all about it, but it appears he was already on the case. He has *real* class. Apparently, the bishop had already contacted him. I am sure that between them, they'll sort it out. They both went to Oxford, you know."

Ceddars frowns. "But Sheng was proven to be innocent. We can't go around arresting people just because you don't like them."

"Heathens like him are all guilty of something!" She descends into another coughing fit and Ceddars tries to attend to her again. "Please doctor, it is nothing. I told you… my physician says I'm absolutely fine."

Ceddars doesn't appear convinced but respects her wishes.

"Mrs Willoughby," I say, "despite what you think about Sheng, he is not the murderer. But someone killed the vicar and William Eriksen. Do you have any idea who might want them both dead?"

"You don't think it could be that dreadful curate, do you?" Mrs Willoughby blurts, as if the thought has entered her head for the first time, her chubby hand covering her mouth.

"And why would you think that?"

"As I told you… Albert wanted him gone. And I always said he was deranged in the head. I never thought he could… Oh my, oh my!"

"Simmons is a bit, well, highly strung and a Bible-basher type," Ceddars says. "All fire and brimstone, what?"

Mrs Willoughby nods enthusiastically. "Now that I think about it, Simmons was at that dreadful talk last night in the village hall. He hated Eriksen. And wasn't that when that heathen weapon was stolen? The one that killed poor Albert?"

"You saw Curate Simmons there?"

Mrs Willoughby's massive head bobs up and down, her impressive jowls wobbling. "Oh yes. He was trying to hide at the back, but he was definitely there. I did wonder why, but events got a little out of control and I forgot all about him until now."

"I say, Em', didn't Simmons say he *wasn't* at Eriksen's talk when we questioned him?"

Mrs Willoughby's eyes widen. "He lied to you about it?"

I rub my hand over my chin, feeling a tingle of excitement. "It would appear so."

The large woman's face creases into one of pure malice. "I'm not surprised. Not surprised at all. I need to phone the superintendent again straightaway."

I shake my head. "We shouldn't jump to any conclusions just yet, nor should we engage in idle speculation. But the fact that the vicar wanted Simmons gone, and that he was at the talk last night is interesting. Especially as he lied about both."

"It certainly bally is!"

I ignore Ceddars and keep my attention on Mrs Willoughby. "You said Curate Simmons was sticking his nose in where it wasn't wanted. I wondered if he had found out anything about the church roof fund?"

Mrs Willoughby turns a little grey. "I… I am sure I wouldn't know anything about that." She takes a quick steadying breath, her eyes flicking to the sobbing parishioners. "Now you must excuse me. With the curate away, someone must take charge." She brightens. "And I hear Mrs Knight is somewhat indisposed at the moment."

I'm not about to let her go that quickly. "If you would indulge me, I have a few more questions."

"I am sure you do, young madam. Has anyone ever told you that you are impertinent and far too pushy for a lady?"

"Oh yes, many times."

"Well, I'm very sorry to disappoint you, but I have responsibilities in this time of dreadful woe." Her voice is loud enough for others in the church to hear and a few heads turn in our direction.

"I've found out about your donations to the church fund," I also say loudly.

"You do?" she replies, a visible chink in her certainty, her voice now more of a whisper. "What…what about them?"

"They were substantial and regular. And judging by the scaffolding outside, and all these buckets, it appears none of your money has yet reached the roof."

"The vicar was investing the fund to grow it."

"You mean on the horses?"

A look of horror crosses the statuesque woman's face.

"You don't seem surprised?"

Her jaw flexes, but no words emerge.

"Shall we go somewhere more private to discuss this matter further?"

Mrs Willoughby nods, and leads us off to the vestry, closing the door behind us. She sits down heavily on a chair and removes her large black hat, before falling into another fit of coughing.

"You must know about the vicar's gambling habits?" I ask once the coughing has subsided.

"I knew that he occasionally visited the racetrack in Upper Cockbottom."

"Did you also know that he was betting sums of up to fifty pounds?"

She flashes cold eyes in my direction. "Yes, yes, I did."

"You did?" Ceddars says. "And you did nothing about it?"

"I only found out a few days ago. I confronted him and we had an awful argument."

I sit down opposite her. "But you still accompanied him to the talk given by Eriksen and, as far as I understand it, you didn't tell anyone else."

"I forgave him."

"I say, you did bally what?"

"I forgave him. It is the Christian way, isn't it? And I am first and foremost a Christian woman."

"I see."

"He told me that his gambling was in the past. That he had learnt his lesson. He promised me it wouldn't happen again."

"And you believed him?"

"Albert would never lie to me. We had a special bond." Tears fill her eyes, but I'm not convinced by her performance. It's quite possible for a murderer to experience grief or remorse for what they have done—and to use that grief to hide behind.

"It must've been a very special bond indeed. From the figures I've seen, you gave thousands to the fund. Many thousands. That kind of money is not so easily to forgive."

"Thousands! Bally hell!"

"You don't understand, doctor. I am rich… *very rich*. I made a good marriage to a not so good man. He died unexpectedly at a very young age, and I inherited his full fortune. He had no other relatives and I bore him no children, meaning… I could easily afford those donations. And what I do with my money is my concern, no one else's."

"Are you not interested in how I found out this information?"

"I caught you snooping in Albert's study. You no doubt found things you shouldn't have."

I shake my head. "This information came from William Eriksen."

"That does not surprise me," Mrs Willoughby says without batting an eyelid. "The man was determined to bring Albert down."

"The same man who was murdered this afternoon. May I ask what time you arrived at the church today?"

"You can't possibly be accusing me of having anything to do with this horrid murder business, can you?"

I say nothing and Mrs Willoughby visibly squirms.

"I went home to change after the doctor told me the dreadful news about Albert's death—which is when Ethel phoned, and that woman does love to gossip. I lost track of time. I arrived here about half an hour ago where I heard about William Eriksen."

"Were you anywhere near the vicinity of the police station?"

"Why would you ask such a silly question?"

"Because I need to know your whereabouts at the time of William Eriksen's murder."

Mrs Willoughby glances at Ceddars. "Tell her, doctor."

"Tell me what?"

"Well, Em'," Ceddars explains, "Mrs W's house is practically next door to the new police station."

"Oh..."

"Now, now, Miss Crookshanks, don't you start jumping to conclusions. And besides, what possible reason would a respectable lady like myself have for killing William Eriksen? What would be my motive?"

"You despised him."

"Listen to yourself! Are you actually suggesting I stole that heathen's crossbow and shot poor Albert and then Eriksen? That is quite, quite preposterous. How dare you even consider that I would be involved. Me! An upstanding member of the village." She grabs her hat and stands. "My ladies need me at this awful time, and I will not listen to any more of this nonsense. When I phone the superintendent, I will make sure to mention your interference. You understand me? Good day!" Mrs Willoughby strides outside and slams the vestry door.

"Bally hell! I don't think anyone has ever talked to her like you just did."

"Maybe not, but we are still no closer to getting to the solution of this mystery. Nevertheless, she knew about his gambling, and called him 'Albert', which hints at a greater intimacy than I would've thought."

"Lovers?" Ceddars says, like this is an impossibility.

"I agree, Mrs Willoughby isn't Wilson-Smallsey's type, but something was between them. And more than simple friendship. And remember that Dorothy Knight believes she was in love with him."

"She did give the man thousands. Unless…? You don't think he was blackmailing her, do you?"

"Possibly. The Reverend Wilson-Smallsey had quite a hold on her, that much is for sure. I wonder who else was in the same boat?"

"I bally don't know," Ceddars replies defensively. "But all that stuff about Simmons was revealing, don't you think? He's now squarely in the frame… isn't he?"

"We will see."

Arrests & Resistance

WE leave the church soon after and I find myself thankful to be back out in the daylight. The building was an oppressive place. It felt uncomfortable, like I wasn't wanted.

"I say, Em', this isn't the way to Simmons' cottage. I thought he was next on your list. Especially after what Mrs W told us."

I shake my head. "We're heading for the church vaults."

"Of course we are. May I ask… why?"

"I'd like to check inside before talking to the curate. I have a few ideas about what we might find."

"And just what are these ideas of yours?"

"You'll see," I reply enigmatically.

Ceddars leads me around the church walls until we find the entrance to the underground vaults. We go down a steep flight of worn, lichen-encrusted steps and are met by an iron gate, behind which is a door. I turn to face Ceddars. "Do me a favour and go back up the steps and tell me when I'm out of sight."

He shrugs and jogs back up the steps, giving me a shout a few seconds later.

I hold up an arm. "Now let me know when you can't see my hand."

An equally short time later, Ceddars shouts again. I walk back up the steps to see Ceddars standing a short way away in the graveyard and go up to him. "Don't you think that's odd?"

"That you are making me do strange things? Yes, I bally

well do."

I shake my head. "Remember what Billy told us? *I saw Mr Simmons, the new curator, coming out of the church vaults at just after twelve. I was surprised because he told everyone he doesn't like underground spaces. From his time in the trenches.*"

"What of it?"

"Billy said he observed him exiting the vaults. The only way he could have done that is by standing in the graveyard very close to the top of the steps around where you are standing. But Billy also said, *I was walking behind tall bushes that grow close to the wall. It's a cut through I use.*"

We walk over to the bushes and find a path of sorts.

"Golly!" Ceddars says. "There's no way he could've spotted the bally curate from over here. No way at all. Was he lying?"

"Possibly. But someone had given him a very handsome one-pound note remember?"

"You mean he was paid to follow the curate?"

"Not quite, Ceddars. Remember, he gave us the information freely and with some enthusiasm."

"Because you asked him if he'd seen anything unusual and he wanted to help?"

"Perhaps, but what if the one-pound note was paid to him to spread the rumour about Simmons."

"I've said it before, and I'll say it again. You have a very devious mind."

I smile at the compliment.

"Whatever the reason, the poor lad has passed on, so we'll never know."

"Never say never, Ceddars."

We head back down to the vaults. The gate is latched and opens smoothly without a creak. I examine the hinges. "They've been oiled recently."

"By Jove, yes. You don't miss a sausage, do you?"

I try the door, but it's locked.

"That's that then, I suppose?"

I take out my hairpins and quietly pick the lock. In a matter of seconds, the door swings open. Ceddars says nothing, but the startled shape of his moustache fills me with pride at my own abilities.

An oil-lamp sits inside of the door. I pick it up and Ceddars lights it with one of his cigarette matches, the quick glow revealing a series of impressive granite arches leading into a cobweb covered gloom. The air fusty from damp and mould.

"I hate places like this," Ceddars says. "Always crawling with spiders and whatnot. Urgh."

"You should spend time in South Africa, our spiders are as big as your face."

Ceddars grimaces.

We make our way inside. The place is cluttered with old, rotting furniture—mostly split pews, and abandoned chairs and stools. As well as occasional cracked cartwheels and ancient garden implements.

"Looks like no one has been down here in years."

I lower the lamp to the floor. A clear pathway has been made in the dust by the regular passing of footsteps."

"I really should learn to keep my bally trap shut."

We follow the trail inside, passing alcoves and openings to rooms and corridors. The place is a maze. The trail runs into a dead end at an old empty bookcase. I nod to Ceddars who steps up and slides the bookcase aside revealing a wide, low doorway. "Someone wanted to keep this room hidden, but why?"

I step inside, holding the lamp in front of me. The room has a sharp smell I recognise immediately—printer's ink. And sitting on a rickety table pushed up against the cobwebbed bricks, is a small hand-cranked printing press—or what remains of it. It shines brightly in the light of the lamp as a relatively new addition to this dust-covered labyrinth. But it's in pieces. The oiled machine is half dismantled.

I hand the lamp to Ceddars and go over, finding stacks of paper and a large bottle of black ink. The floor is strewn with discarded posters like the one Ceddars discovered on the vicarage gate, except that these are sub-standard—rejections.

"It's not looking good for Simmons, is it, Em'? It looks like he was the one behind those bally awful posters, what?"

"If it *was* Simmons…"

"You think it could be someone else?"

A movement in the shadows and I'm hit with something heavy that knocks me off my feet. A dark figure hurtles past me, pushing Ceddars off balance so that he also falls. The person jumps through the opening, grabbing the bookcase and throwing it over to block the doorway.

I stagger to my feet, realising I've been hit with nothing more than a thrown ream of paper. I pull Ceddars up and we drag the fallen bookshelf aside before giving chase. Half a minute later we emerge back out into the graveyard, running up the steps of the vault. But there's no sign of our assailant.

"Who the hell was that? I nearly had a bally heart attack," Ceddars says, wheezing. "But it wasn't Simmons. The man was too bally short."

"You got a look at him?"

He nods. "He matched the description of that stranger Mrs W saw. You know the one? That guy putting up all those nasty posters." He scans the graveyard. "Where the bally hell did he disappear to?"

"Maybe Mary saw him? I think we should go and ask her."

"Mary? Are you sure? Why?"

"Look at the grass?"

"Huh? I can't see anything."

"Bent blades of grass, leading towards the door in the wall to the vicarage. Whoever fled, went through Mary's garden. She may have seen where they went next."

We hurry to the vicarage and knock on the door. It's

opened by Charlotte, the maid.

"Were you two knocking earlier?" she says in an accusatory tone.

"I say, what?"

"Someone was knockin' at the door, I went to open it and… there was no one there and now you two turn up."

"I don't know anything about that," I reply. "We're here to see Mrs Wilson-Smallsey."

"Well, she's not to be disturbed," Charlotte says coldly. "She gave me strict instructions not an hour ago. She needs her rest at this terrible time. She's sleeping."

"Well that's put the kibosh on it. Mary will have seen nothing."

I turn my attention to Charlotte. "Can you go and see if she will see us."

"I certainly will not. I'm sorry miss, but you lied to me before when you went sneaking into the poor vicar's office. I won't ever forgive that." She slams the door in our faces.

Ceddars grimaces. "That's you told."

"Indeed."

"I'm afraid to say it, Em,' but with the way you are going about this investigation, I'm worried you'll get yourself irretrievably ostracised from the village."

"If I'm honest, I'm not sure if that would be such a bad thing."

"Now, now. Don't talk like that. Reputation is everything, especially in a place like Little Pucklewick."

"It certainly is, Ceddars. It certainly is."

"So now what? The trail to that fellow we disturbed in the church vaults has gone cold. Shall we inform Inspector Troughton? Get Jakes and the constabulary to keep a look out for him?"

I shake my head. "We go and see Simmons."

Ceddars lets out a sound of exasperation—a gasp of air that turns into an annoyed sigh. "Don't you think we are running around in circles somewhat? Seeing this and that person and getting bally nowhere?"

"You are wrong. I have picked up a lot of clues. Admittedly, they at first led me in the wrong direction. But the thing about clues is that they slowly add up. All I have to do… is make sense of them, meaning… the investigation certainly isn't going nowhere."

Ceddars stamps his foot. "What bally clues?"

"My dear Ceddars, you are a doctor, I, on the other hand, am a professional sleuth. I don't have your medical training, but you do. That's your expertise, even if you did forget to mention the possibility that the Reverend Wilson-Smallsey could've been poisoned by that damn crossbow bolt." Ceddars tries to protest but I silence him with a raised finger. "You don't always notice the clues that I have found because this is my area of speciality, my expertise."

"I suppose that does make a little sense."

"If I can make all the clues connect, you will be the first to know, I promise you that. Just make sure that you're not involved in this, which would be very disappointing."

"You don't believe that Eugene child, do you? The kid is a bad seed, what?"

"As I said. I have picked up a lot of clues. As to which ones are red herrings? That remains to be seen. Now, take me to Simmons' house."

"I think I'm going to regret this." Ceddars lets out another sound of exasperation but complies. "It's this way.

A few minutes later, we find ourselves standing outside Simmons' cottage. A compact end of terrace building with an untended, somewhat overgrown front garden.

"He's got into quite a bit of trouble over his lawn. Bringing down the whole row."

I knock on the old-looking front door, the red paint peeling. No answer.

"Looks like the chap has done a runner."

I'm about to take out my hairpins when a black police car pulls up. Inspector Troughton gets out, followed by a red-faced Constable Jakes.

"What ho, inspector!" Ceddars says jovially. "Come to interrogate Curate Simmons? Well, you're out of luck, it appears the fellow may have done a runner."

"Doctor Cecil Roberts," Inspector Troughton says formally. "I am arresting you for the murder of William Eriksen and the Reverend Wilson-Smallsey."

"I say! Bally hell! What?"

Ethel & Earrings

CEDDARS is flabbergasted and, I must admit, I'm also astounded. "You're arresting Ceddars? On what evidence?"

"We have all the evidence we need," Troughton says, the nasal twang of his voice at its most officious. He produces a pair of handcuffs and Jakes snaps them shut around the wrists of a shocked-looking Ceddars.

"I'm not going anywhere until you tell me what this nonsense is all about!" Ceddars says, standing his ground.

"Eugene Knight came forward this afternoon with some rather condemning testimony. He observed you exiting the run-down cottages opposite the police station soon after the murder of William Eriksen."

"Eugene Knight? That lying little oik? You can't believe anything that boy says!"

"He was instrumental in giving accurate evidence regarding the person that turned out to be Sheng's brother. In my book, that makes him a reliable witness."

"Why didn't he come forward earlier?"

"He was terrified of retribution. Until you threatened him with an iron pipe, that is. He came to the station straight afterwards."

"That's not what bally happened. The boy is a liar!"

"Even so, inspector," I say. "That's just his word against a respectable doctor's. And I was there, Ceddars didn't threaten anybody."

"His statement isn't the only evidence. A crossbow and a set of poisoned bolts were found after a subsequent search of the doctor's residence."

"What? That's quite preposterous! How the bally hell did they get there?"

"We can discuss that at the station. Now doctor, are you coming easily or not?"

"This is not right, inspector, not right at all."

"Do you want me to instruct Jakes to take out his truncheon?"

"Please don't make me do that, sir," Jakes says, with a surprising amount of threat. "I 'ave been known to break an arm or two in the past, unintentionally of course, but I wouldn't risk it if I were you."

Ceddars gives Jakes a wounded look and nods in defeat.

I grab Troughton's arm. "But inspector, what is his motive?"

"You mean you don't know?" Troughton says with nasal triumph. "The vicar was blackmailing your friend here. It turns out Wilson-Smallsey was somewhat of an unsavoury character. He knew of the doctor's many indiscretions, including an illicit relationship with a certain secretary of Mr William Erikson. He extorted hundreds of pounds from him. Isn't that true doctor?"

Ceddars says nothing, but his eyes drop to the floor.

I stare pointedly at the inspector. "My guess is that the vicar was blackmailing a lot of people in the village."

Troughton shrugs his shoulders. "Maybe he was, Miss Crookshanks, but not all of them have murder weapons in their possession. And I would be careful about what you say publicly about the Reverend Wilson-Smallsey. The bishop contacted me directly about this matter. We need to keep this hush hush, understand?"

"What the bishop or anyone else thinks is unimportant, inspector. You should know that. You may have evidence but what is the doctor's motive for murdering William Eriksen?"

"I'm not one-hundred percent sure. But those two did not

like one another. If I were to hazard a guess, I'd say Francesca Feltham was the root cause. A pretty girl like that and two healthy men? It's not an uncommon story."

"Franny has nothing to do with it!" Ceddars grumbles through gritted teeth.

"And now, Miss Crookshanks, I'll be off. As I told you before. Murder is always a straightforward, ugly business. Always."

Jakes pushes Ceddars into the back of the police car, and Troughton gets into the front seat. The engine chatters into life and they drive away.

I knew that Ceddars was paying the vicar a lot of money. I saw that from what I glimpsed of those papers hidden under Eriksen's bed. Either Sheng took that evidence to Troughton, or the inspector got access to the vicar's desk—where I suspect he kept his dirty dealings. One thing is for sure, the Reverend Wilson-Smallsey was not who many thought him to be. The man wasn't just a womaniser and a gambler, he was also extorting money by blackmail. Despite the bishop's efforts to avoid gossip, I wonder how Little Pucklewick will respond to such a scandal.

But can Ceddars really be the murderer?

I take a deep breath and go over what I've discovered about him. He had opportunity for both murders, that was for sure. I can't forget how soon he turned up at my house just after Wilson-Smallsey was shot. A fact that has been weighing on my mind somewhat. And he was gone a long time to pick up the Bugatti when Eriksen was murdered. But why kill Eriksen? Did Ceddars really believe Fran was seeing him? The other question being… was Ceddars 'seeing' Fran? Maybe, maybe not. There was certainly more to their relationship than simple friendship, something I gleaned when I first saw them together in Eriksen's mansion. Then again, Wilson-Smallsey could've been using the village rumour-mill as an opportunity for blackmail when no indiscretion had taken place. I'd prefer that to be the case, although my romantic interest in the doctor must remain a secondary concern.

What niggles me the most is why the doctor didn't mention the poison on the darts after the vicar's murder. Was that a mistake or an intentional attempt to put me off the scent? The murder weapon was also found at Ceddars' house. He was with me all day, meaning that if he had killed Wilson-Smallsey and Eriksen, then the crossbow must've been in his possession all the time I was with him. Very probably hidden in his doctor's bag, as I surmised. The only chance he could've had to unload it was when we returned to his house to change his clothes—where it was found by the police. It all adds up, but not completely. I don't believe Fran was the reason behind Eriksen's murder. And if it wasn't her, what motive could the doctor have?

The evidence points to Ceddars, but I cannot find it in me to believe he is a murderer. And not because we shared a kiss. It's my gut, plain and simple. If I'm right and Ceddars is not guilty then the only other conclusion is that he was framed. But by who?

I decide to go back to the doctor's house to do some snooping. Perhaps I'll find some evidence that exonerates him. If someone planted the crossbow in his house, they may have left a clue.

I leave Simmons' cottage and make my way northwards past the church and onto the road where my cottage sits, stopping by the gate. I want to go inside. To sit down and have a think. And to perhaps look at those paper clippings again. But I'm reminded of Molly and her hysterics and carry on walking. The road takes me past the threatening presence of Dooleys Wood. Its thick, twisted boughs rustling and creaking even though there is no breeze. The dark history of the place appears to have imprinted itself on them. I ignore the shudder that passes involuntarily down my spine and continue walking. I'm a person of logic, but the trees seem menacing. Shadows lie within. Shadows and dank places. I remember the heavy tree branch that fell on Ceddars and myself. At the time it seemed like an accident, but now I'm not so sure. Was the wood trying to kill me? I shake my head to rid my mind of such silly thoughts, but they do not quite go away. I realise I'm missing Ceddars' reassuring presence. Like an essential part of my being has been removed. Which is odd, because I'm independent minded, resourceful and not to be messed with. Or at least that's what I believe. The truth of the matter is that I'm still trying to work out who I am. My life began this morning when I was awoken by Molly. There is nothing beyond that. Nothing that I can remember. And yet that oddly doesn't concern me. I'm so focused on the mystery of these murders that nothing else matters.

Ceddars' house is thankfully a short way away and I get there as quick as I can, quelling an irrational desire to run. A police car pulls up and Constable Jakes emerges and goes to stand guard outside the front door, a bored look on his face. I wait till the car drives away and slip unseen down the side of the house to the kitchen door.

It's locked, but not for long, and I slide inside, closing the door behind me. I decide to begin upstairs and find myself in Ceddars' bedroom. It's functional, decorated with little fuss, although it's a mess. The place has been recently searched. Probably by Inspector Troughton or Jakes. The bed linen has been tossed aside and the drawers to his bedside tables and dressers are open, the contents spilled onto the floor. I go through the drawers anyway, feeling guilty—not an emotion I'm too familiar with. I suppose, somewhere deep down, I'd hoped to have been spending some time in this room on a more fun pursuit. Then again, if the doctor had been entertaining the lovely Fran Feltham, I wouldn't want to play second best...

I find nothing of interest upstairs and tiptoe down to

the ground floor, the sound of a telephone ringing making me jump. It's coming from behind a door. I open it to find a small alcove containing a telephone table and a stool. I'm in two minds as to what to do but answer it anyway.

"Doctor Robert's residence," I reply.

"Hello. May I please speak with Doctor Roberts?" The voice is posh and self-assured.

"I'm afraid he's popped out for a moment. Can I take a message?"

"That's a shame. I'm very busy and this is a courtesy call. Can you tell him Doctor Enwright phoned. From Harley Street. Although I'm not sure when a good time would be to phone me back. I have a stacked afternoon."

"Oh, Doctor Enwright, of course. Doctor Roberts has been expecting your call. Is it about Mrs Gladys Willoughby?" Ceddars told me he had been chasing up Mrs Willoughby's cough that was worrying him, it appears he was telling me the truth.

"Yes, yes it is. But how would you know that?"

"I'm sorry. Let me introduce myself. I'm Miss Crookshanks, Doctor Roberts' secretary and nurse. The Doctor shares sensitive information with me in our work together. You can safely give me the message and I will pass it on in confidence."

A long pause. *"Well, I don't normally do this, patient confidentiality and all that, but as he is the local GP, I think he will need to know that Mrs Willoughby has lung cancer. Inoperable I'm afraid. She has a matter of months to live. If that. She wanted treatment but it is too advanced. ...Are you still there?"*

"Yes, thank you doctor. I will pass that on. Good day."

I replace the receiver.

Mrs Gladys Willoughby is dying. This knowledge adds a new dimension to the mystery. A dying person has nothing to lose. Nothing at all. She could've killed the vicar over his gambling debts, over all her money he had wasted. But what was her motive for killing Eriksen? Did she just dislike him? It's unlikely. A terminal illness doesn't normally turn regular people into murderers, otherwise it would be happening all the time. However, I can't discount that possibility.

My eye is drawn to an item of jewellery lying on the blue carpet of the telephone room. I pick it up, recognising it at once. A pearl drop earring mounted in silver. One of the same earrings Fran Feltham was wearing earlier. She was in possession of both earrings this morning when I met her in Eriksen's mansion. She was also wearing them when she turned up at the police station with Eriksen, driving his red van, which means the girl visited the doctor's house sometime afterwards. Did she also plant the murder weapon that implicated Ceddars? She was on her bike and was adamant in not wanting a lift. A bike with a large basket big enough for a crossbow. I surmise that she had planned to go to the doctor's house alone. But why here... in the telephone room? The answer is a simple one. Fran must've made a phone call. I lift the receiver and dial for the operator.

"Hello caller," a female voice says at the end of the line, her voice quizzical. I guess she's wondering why an unknown woman is calling from the doctor's house.

"Hello Ethel. I'm Emily Crookshanks and—"

A sharp intake of breath.

"Is there a problem?"

"No, no. Of course not. What number do you require?" Her voice is full of restrained excitement, then again, today must be one of the most exciting days of Ethel's gossip-obsessed life.

"No number. I just wondered if anyone had made a local call from this phone earlier today."

"Nothing came through the exchange from this number."

"I see. I suppose you've heard that Doctor Roberts has been arrested?"

A long pause. *"Do you want a number, caller?"*

"Know this, Ethel… Ceddars is innocent. I'm sure of it." I replace the receiver and stand up. Why did I say that? I can't be certain Ceddars is innocent. Perhaps I'm hoping he will be for my own ends.

A minute or two later I open the front door to a startled Constable Jakes who doesn't quite know what to say or do. I ignore his bumblings and stride over to the parked Bugatti, sliding into the driver's seat. Can I drive? There's only one way to find out. I locate the ignition button and the car jumps into eight-cylinder life.

I push it into gear and roar away. Constable Jakes shouting incoherently under the sound of the powerful engine.

I love driving this machine, I realise. It suits me somehow. Smaller and lighter than Eriksen's Mercedes, it packs a lot of power under its bonnet. Ceddars chose well when he bought the Bugatti.

I arrive at the junction to Little Pucklewick and pause, the engine turning over in expectation. Right will take me into the village, left… who knows where? I'm suffering from two distinct and competing feelings. One to leave this place and to never come back, the other to continue my quest to find the murderer of the Reverend Wilson-Smallsey and William Eriksen.

But I must escape!

The words leap forcefully into my mind, accompanied by a sensation of entrapment and imminent danger. I glance around, worried that some attacker may have snuck up on me, but the road is empty. I try to force myself to turn left, but it's no use. I'll never be able to leave Little Pucklewick until I've solved its mysteries. To do anything different is impossible. But I promise myself that when this is done, I will leave here and never come back.

Ten minutes later, I park outside the Green Dragon public house. A small country pub on the edge of the village with a large beer garden. I walk inside, turning heads—women rarely visit pubs in this day and age. And never unaccompanied. I give the startled looks no concern and stride up to the bar. "Miss Fran Feltham," I announce. "I need to see her urgently, where is her room?"

"Outside, around the back. First set of steps by the cellar doors but…"

"But what?"

"She packed up and left just over an hour ago."

Photographs & Franny

I **ORDER** a G&T from the landlord, and he serves me the drink with a disturbed look on his face. I'm not sure if he disapproves of me drinking alone or drinking at all. Perhaps he disapproves of women altogether, but it doesn't stop him taking my money.

I adjust my hat, tipping it back a little, take a sip of the restorative gin, and turn to stare at the faces pointing my way. "What's a matter? You've never seen a woman having a drink on her own before?"

The men look aghast, before returning to their beers, chuntering to one another.

I turn back to the bar, raising my glass to the landlord before taking another sip, my mind flashing back to Eriksen's mansion and the photo I found in Fran's desk. I take it out and give it another look. A youthful Reverend Wilson-Smallsey standing next to a beautiful young woman. There's nothing extra I can glean from it, although I'm sure I'm missing the obvious. The house behind the handsome couple is indistinct but appears to be in a built-up area. London? Or another city? It could be anywhere. I show it to the landlord. "You know this person?"

"Pretty lass, but I ain't seen her before. Looks like an old photograph. That vicar did very well for himself though, didn't he? Not that I want to speak ill of the dead, but..." he shrugs.

"You mean he was a ladies' man?"

He nods, lowering his voice. "He might've had half the village fooled with that holier-than-thou act of his, but he never fooled me."

"Can you think of anyone who would want him dead?"

"Other than the doctor you mean?"

"You've heard?"

"Who hasn't?"

"You think he's guilty?"

Another shrug. "Not for the likes of me to say. We all came back from the war as changed men, but…"

"But what?"

"Well, I've had to take the doctor home on several occasions after he'd drank too much. But more than that…" his voice drops even lower. "…He gets dreadful maudlin like. And angry. Very angry. And… and he mentioned how much he hated Wilson-Smallsey."

"Ceddars was a regular customer?"

"Yeah. But he stopped coming soon after that Feltham girl moved in."

"You think those two things were connected?"

He shrugs.

"And Miss Feltham?"

He shakes his head. "I didn't see much of her. Kept herself to herself. I liked her, but then again," he winks, "there wasn't much of her not to like."

"I don't suppose you saw her earlier today at around ten-thirty?"

Another shake of his head. "She'd be out working for that poor Mr Eriksen, at his mansion. I quite liked the fellow. It was a shame what happened to him."

"Could Fran have come back here without you seeing her?"

"Not a chance. We had our weekly beer delivery this morning at ten. If she'd come back at ten-thirty, I would've noticed. I was out the back for a good two hours."

I reel at the news. Fran was lying about her whereabouts this morning. And if she didn't come back to her lodgings, where did she go? To murder the reverend perhaps? She could've overheard Billy telling William Eriksen about his visit to my cottage and decided to act. She was also in the vicinity of the police station at the time of Eriksen's murder, and there was also evidence she had visited the doctor's house. "Did Miss Feltham leave a forwarding address?"

"Nah. She was in a hurry. Paid her bill and that was that."

I finish my G&T, suddenly remembering the letter of recommendation from Fran's employer. I remove it from my inside pocket and unfold it on the bar. "Where's the nearest telephone?"

"I have one in the back, why?"

"I need to use it."

The landlord is flustered to have a woman in the private area behind his bar, but dutifully points out the phone. "This to do with the murders?"

I give him a laconic smile. "Everything about today has been about those murders." I dial the London number and a few moments later I'm talking to a Mrs Winterbottom. The phone call is most instructive. I learn all about the secretarial agency and modern career girls, before I mention my interest in one of her employees.

"Francesca Feltham? I'm afraid there is no one of that name working at this agency. Are you sure the letter of recommendation came from myself?"

"I'm holding it now."

"Oh dear, that is disturbing. The whole premise of this agency is that these young women are trustworthy. I always perform a series of strong vetting procedures for my gals."

"Do any of your ladies live in Feltham?"

"…Why do you ask?"

"It's important."

"Actually, one of my best gals lives there, although I've not heard from her in a while…" Mrs Winterbottom leaves the end of the sentence open, and I get her meaning at once.

Obviously, some of her ladies going missing is not an unusual occurrence. I imagine these girls disappeared either due to romantic entanglement or even—oh no!—pregnancy.

"Do you have a name and any contact details, or a phone number for her?"

"Actually, I do..."

I end the phone call a few minutes later and look at the photograph again. Fran Feltham has jumped into number one place in my list of possible suspects. I try not to get too excited, like I did when I accused William Eriksen, but the pieces are falling together very nicely. Very nicely indeed.

I leave the bar and get back into the Bugatti. Troughton needs to hear about what I have found.

Ten minutes later, I march into the station to find him sitting at his desk and typing. Ceddars sits bowed opposite him, his hands manacled. The inspector's face drops. "What do you want, Miss Crookshanks?"

Ceddars lifts his head and looks at me hopefully. "What ho, old girl. Seems like I'm properly in the soup this time. You've hopefully come to get me off? Using that tip top noggin of yours, what?"

"You're in luck, doctor. I do indeed have some new evidence that throws doubt on your guilt."

"You do? That's absolutely splendid! I knew you'd help me out. I knew it!"

"And don't call me *old girl.*"

"Sorry Em'."

Troughton's thin moustache twitches with irritation. "I don't want to ruin your little reunion, but..." He sighs. "... You mentioned *new evidence?*"

I take out the pearl earring.

Ceddars' eyebrows raise at the sight. "I say, doesn't that belong to Franny?"

I nod, turning my attention on the inspector. "I found this in the doctor's house."

It's Troughton's turn to raise his eyebrows. "I see."

"Now, now, Troughton," Ceddars blurts, his face a turning a quick shade of red. "Don't read anything into that."

"No, inspector, you misunderstand. I'm not suggesting Fran Feltham was there for an assignation with the doctor. I saw Fran wearing this earring, one of a pair, this morning at Eriksen's mansion, and again when we met her outside the police station. The doctor was with me all day until you arrested him, meaning that Fran visited the doctor's residence alone soon after the murder of William Eriksen. I believe it was then that she lost the earring."

Troughton nods. "What exactly are you suggesting?"

"Let me first show you this." I take out the photograph I found in Fran's desk and hand it to him.

The inspector examines it closely. "A photograph of the young vicar and a very beautiful woman, what of it?"

"The photograph belongs to Fran Feltham, although I found out that isn't her real name."

Ceddars sits up. "I say, what?"

"Look at the woman. Does she remind you of anyone?"

Troughton examines the photograph very carefully, his eyes suddenly widening.

"You've noticed it as well. I missed it at first, but I believe this is a picture of Fran Feltham's mother and father, although her real name is actually *Francesca Wilson*."

"You can't be serious, Em'… can you?" Ceddars splutters. "Wilson?"

"I have every reason to believe she is the illegitimate daughter of the dead vicar. We must assume Wilson-Smallsey abandoned Fran's mother once she became with child… leading to the possibility that Fran killed her own father out of revenge."

"That is quite an accusation," Troughton says.

"Fran has also packed up and left her room at the Green Dragon, but obviously not before visiting the doctor's house."

Troughton sits back in his chair, his eyes focused on mine. "You're suggesting that Fran Feltham planted the murder weapon?"

"That's exactly what I'm suggesting."

"What?" Ceddars blurts. "You can't be serious… can you? You're accusing poor Franny? That's quite ridiculous. You were also convinced Eriksen was the bad apple, and you got that wrong. Very wrong. Remember?"

I ignore Ceddars' outburst. "Her behaviour is suspicious and should be investigated. And there's more. She told me that at the time of the vicar's murder, she was back at her room at the Green Dragon, looking for her glasses, but the landlord disagrees. He was outside at the time with a delivery, and she never appeared. Fran Feltham lied, meaning she has no alibi for the first murder. And remember, Fran was seen outside the police station shortly before the murder of William Eriksen."

Ceddars jumps to his feet, his handcuffs rattling as he tries to wave his arms. "No! No way. You've gone too far this time Emily! Too far indeed."

"Sit down, doctor!" Troughton orders and Ceddars demurs, throwing himself back onto his chair and throwing me a face of disgust.

Ceddars' gallant streak will be his undoing, that's for sure.

Inspector Troughton picks up a sheet of typed paper. "You're forgetting one thing, Miss Crookshanks. Eugene Knight's statement. *I saw Doctor Roberts running from the run-down cottages opposite the police station soon after the murder of William Eriksen.*"

Well, here's my statement, inspector. "I entered those cottages moments after the shooting, as you witnessed. I didn't see Ceddars or Eugene. Or anyone in fact."

Troughton shrugs. "The boy has no reason to lie. He gave accurate evidence regarding Mr Sheng's brother. In my eyes, he's more than a credible witness."

"Can I see his statement in full?"

Troughton passes it to me, and I quickly scan through, noticing some information—or the lack of it—that the inspector missed, the thrill of discovery flowing through me. "Eugene doesn't mention that Ceddars was carrying the crossbow."

"What?" Troughton reads the statement again.

"If Ceddars disposed of the weapon at the scene, where was it?"

"He obviously hid it somewhere," the inspector replies.

"If that's the case, when did he have the chance to retrieve it? The doctor was with me all the time from the shooting of William Eriksen until you arrested him."

"You're saying the doctor had no chance to drop off the weapon at his house afterwards?"

I shake my head. "The doctor went home to get changed, and I accompanied him."

Inspector Troughton raises his eyebrows.

"I remained downstairs. But don't you see, inspector? If Ceddars shot William Eriksen, he must've been carrying the crossbow when Eugene saw him. If not, he must be innocent. You need to talk to the boy again."

This news doesn't appear to shake the inspector in the slightest. "A minor detail, Miss Crookshanks. And, I must say, you are very much clutching at straws here, but I do need to re-interview the boy, obviously."

"It's not about whether I was carrying a bally crossbow or not." Ceddars protests. "I wasn't there! Eugene's story is total rot. He's lying."

"And Francesca Feltham?"

"Leave Franny out of it!" Ceddars blurts. "I can vouch for the girl! She is not involved!"

Inspector Troughton raises his hands and Ceddars stops speaking. "As far as I'm concerned, the evidence against Doctor Roberts is more than enough to keep him under arrest. I'll re-interview Eugene Knight at the earliest opportunity."

"And Fran Feltham, nee Wilson?"

"It's not against the law to use a fake name."

"Don't you think you should at least talk to her?"

"Franny has got nothing to do with this, you hear me!"

"If you don't pipe down, doctor, I will put you in the cells. It was only courtesy that stopped that happening earlier. So don't push me." The inspector grabs my arm and roughly escorts me outside. "I told you not to interfere in my investigation, or don't you remember?"

"I'm a private citizen and can do as I please."

"Not when you're interfering with an active police investigation. The higher ups are very interested in this case. This is cut and dried as far as I'm concerned. We have got the right man, and I don't want you walking around saying otherwise. Good day."

Witnesses & Widows

I LEAVE the police station, my mind trying to understand Fan Feltham's motives. I can see why she might kill her father, the vicar, but have no idea why she would kill her boss, Eriksen. But there will be a reason. I'm sure of it. Perhaps the young woman was completely off her trolley and on some protracted murder spree?

I catch myself. I won't make the same mistake again. I so easily ran away with my notion that Eriksen was the murderer, only to be proved totally and unequivocally wrong. Sure, Fran Feltham is looking guilty, very guilty, but I must force myself to keep on investigating. It's a mental wrench, but I put Fran to one side and consider the other suspects.

Curate Simmons, for instance. The evidence so far points to him being the source of those rumours posted around the village. Maybe he was in cahoots with the person we disturbed in the church vaults? Although I have an incomplete theory about that as well. My only problem? Poison pen writers are a different type of person to murderers. Preferring to keep themselves hidden, whilst remotely enjoying the results of their rumourmongering. And if he didn't print those posters—my incomplete theory again—what would be his motive to kill both men?

And then there is the vicar's wife. Ceddars believes Mary Wilson-Smallsey is too ill to be considered as a suspect. There is no doubt that she is a very attractive woman, and attractive women are able to turn the most intelligent and serious-thinking men's heads. Mary may not be as infirm as she appears to be, and she certainly had motive to kill her husband. The man was a philanderer and a blackmailer. And I can't forget those athletic and archery trophies I saw in her room. But, like Fran Feltham, what possible motive could she have to kill the explorer, William Eriksen? If anything, he was a thorn in her husband's side, and in that respect, somewhat of an ally.

The late arrival to the Monday Morning get-together, confirmed to me by Charlotte, the vicarage maid, made possible suspects out of both Mrs Willoughby and Dorothy Knight. I must admit, I have no idea why Mrs Willoughby would want to kill the vicar, but her terminal disease meant she would have nothing to lose if her mind had turned to murder. She is a very proud woman… would she sully her name and reputation in such a way? It's unlikely. And if Dorothy Knight was the murderer, why kill the man she was in love with and sure she was to marry?

William Eriksen again. His murder is the most confusing of all. A death that I can make no sense of. What I need is more evidence. I stare at the run-down cottages across the road from the station. It occurs to me that in the heat of the shooting and death of William Eriksen, I neglected to do a proper search of the place where the shooter likely fired from. I decide to correct that oversight right now.

I head to the cottages, over the wall and back through the open doorway towards the missing staircase. This time, I fully climb onto the upper storey taking note of how easy it is for me. I'm still young and limber, but that is not true of the other suspects. I've learnt to never make assumptions about people based on their physical attributes or supposed illnesses and afflictions, or their age. Killers often hide behind our mistaken assumptions. For example, would Mrs Willoughby struggle? She is a big woman, but that doesn't mean she wasn't able to do this. The same for Mary Smallsey, the vicar's wife who may not be infirm. The other suspects, Curate Simmons, Fran, Ceddars and Dorothy Knight and her son, could all get up here without much trouble.

The upstairs is gloomy, the internal walls all missing, the only light coming from the boarded-up window, with its one panel pulled partly aside. The exposed nails are shiny, meaning it was done recently. Probably by the person who shot Eriksen.

I go over to the window and stare out of the jagged opening, imagining I'm carrying a crossbow. There is little room for manoeuvre through the tight gap, meaning anybody firing from this position couldn't be sure of hitting their intended target. Then again, all they had to do was scratch Eriksen and the deed would be done—which they did. It would be a difficult shot, but not impossible. I think back to earlier in the day. Eriksen was walking with Sheng at his side and Troughton behind him. Could the intended target have been Sheng or Troughton, and the shooter missed? Possible, but unlikely.

I climb down and retrace my route into the overgrown back garden and literally bump into Eugene Knight. This time, I grab his jacket tightly. The youth has fled too many times for me to let him get away again.

"Hey, get off me!"

"It's time you answered some questions, young man."

"I don't have to talk to you. You're no policeman!"

"Maybe not, but I know a liar when I see one. Why did you lie about Ceddars?" I ask him, my face close to his, deciding to try and scare the boy into talking. "Is it because you're the murderer? Did you shoot Eriksen and kill the vicar?"

"What?" His face is incredulous. "Don't be stupid. Why would I do that?"

"You must be lying for a reason… *what is it?* Why do you hate him so much? What exactly did he do?"

Eugene goes suddenly limp. "Ask him. Ask the doctor."

"I did, he has no idea why."

Eugene scoffs. "Now who's lying?"

"You're saying Ceddars knows why you hate him?"

"I saw him, didn't I? Saw what he was up to." Eugene's face twists with disgust.

"Saw what? Why won't you tell me?"

"I've told you… ask the doctor, ask him what he's been doing behind everyone's back!"

The boy is an angry brick wall. "If you won't tell me, perhaps you'll tell the police. Inspector Troughton wants to talk to you again about your statement. He's not completely convinced you were telling the truth." I'm lying just to see the boy's reaction. His eyes widen and the blood drains from his cheeks. "When the true murderer is brought to justice, your lies will be exposed. If I were you, I'd come clean to the inspector now."

"You don't frighten me."

"I'm sure I don't, but Inspector Troughton can and will put you behind bars."

Eugene jerks back into abrupt life, kicking me sharply in the shin and I lose my grip on him, forced to double up in pain.

"Everyone lies in this village!" he shouts at me before running away. "Everyone!"

I stumble towards the Bugatti, rubbing at my shin, annoyed that I let Eugene get away yet again. He is one messed up kid. What is it about the doctor that has him all riled up? Still his words have inspired me to act. He told me *everyone lies*.

I fire up the Bugatti and drive to the vicarage. This time I go directly to the kitchen door, and go inside, surprising Charlotte the maid.

"You again? Get out before I—"

"Tell me," I say, interrupting her as she gears up for what I'm guessing will be quite a tirade. Breaking into the vicar's study didn't go down well with her. "Did you have any deliveries to the kitchen this morning?"

"I beg your pardon!"

"Do you want to find out who killed the vicar?"

"But it's all over the village—it was the doctor that done it."

"You don't really believe that do you?"

Charlotte's anger leaves her. "He's always been kind to me and me mum. And only charges the bare minimum. I was shocked to hear he'd been arrested when Ethel told me. I couldn't quite believe it. And besides, that Inspector Troughton, well, I shouldn't be speaking ill of the police, but everyone knows he ain't up to much. He was one of those who was promoted due to the war. He couldn't serve, because of his feet or some other ailment and well, he was just a copper when the war started out and now look at him. He's all jumped up. No mistakin'"

I nod, concurring with Charlotte's description of the man. "I believe Ceddars is innocent, that's why I need you to help me, to help him. Now answer my question. Did you have any deliveries this morning? It's important."

"There were only poor Billy who popped by. Early on like. He picked up a note from the vicar to take to your house, miss. I invited him in and gave him a cup of tea and some cake."

I remember Molly telling me the same. Billy had quite a good thing going on. "And no one else?"

Charlotte shakes her head.

"You're sure? It's been a difficult day…"

"Of course, I'm sure."

"Did you leave Billy on his own at any time?"

"I took him to the vicar's study. I didn't see the poor lad after that. He probably made his own way out."

"Thank you." I push past her and head into the house.

"Where do you think you're goin'?"

"To see the lady of the house." I find the stairs taking

two steps at a time, before opening Mary's room and striding inside, Charlotte loudly complaining behind me.

"Good afternoon, Mary," I say to the startled widow. "We need to talk."

Charlotte follows on my heels. "I told you, she's not to be bothered!"

I ignore her and sit down.

Mary waves the maid away with a flick of her hand. "It's alright Charlotte."

"But she can't come bargin' into your rooms like this! She's already been caught trespassin' in the vicar's study!"

"Please go."

Charlotte, still not convinced, sighs very loudly, and closes the door behind her.

I decide to ignore the pleasantries and to get right to it. "Now Mrs Wilson-Smallsey, will you tell me why you lied this morning?"

Sherry & Ceddars

"I DON'T quite know what you mean?"

"Oh, I think you do…"

"Perhaps Charlotte was right, she should call the constable."

I notice a slight slur to her voice. A quick glance around the room reveals a sherry decanter and a single empty glass, half-hidden on her small table. She's been drinking. "But you won't do that."

Mary turns away from me to stare out of the window. "What do you want, Miss Crookshanks?"

"You told the doctor and I that you saw nothing out of the ordinary this morning while you were performing your usual habit of watching the comings and goings of the village folk."

"Yes, that's right."

She doesn't say anything about the doctor's arrest, which I'm sure she must've heard about. That, more than anything, makes me suspicious of her. "That's interesting, because two women were late to the Monday morning vicarage get-together. And if you were at your window as you said you were, you would've noticed."

She shrugs. "Is that it? Ceddars would tell you that I'm prone to bouts of sleep, sometimes I'm not even aware I'm doing it. I think that's what must have happened."

"How convenient."

"I'm not a well woman, Miss Crookshanks."

"You were not aware that Mrs Gladys Willoughby and Mrs Dorothy Knight did not arrive on time?

Mary shrugs.

"Both lack convincing alibis as to where they were, meaning either one of them could've murdered your husband."

"Surely that's a moot point? Ceddars has been arrested for the crime. It's a sad story, but it is what it is."

"I'm not so sure. If I am correct in my belief in Ceddars' innocence, then the whereabouts of one or both of these women could be very important."

She scoffs. "You believe he didn't do it?"

"Don't you?"

"I put my trust in the police. If Ceddars is guilty of Albert's murder, he must hang. For good or for bad."

Mary is far colder than I realised. "I see."

"I was shocked when I learnt he also killed poor Mr Eriksen, although I knew Ceddars couldn't stand the chap. But… it was well known that the doctor wasn't quite right in the head. The war. It sent many a good man doolally."

"He seemed perfectly fine to me."

"Even so, he had a motive for both murders… didn't he? And before you tell me, I've already heard the rumours… that Albert was blackmailing Ceddars over that Francesca woman and God knows what else. My guess is that the good doctor finally cracked."

"Aren't you concerned that your late husband, a respected member of the clergy, was capable of blackmail? That the whole village must be going into meltdown over the news?"

Mary shrugs again.

"No. It doesn't concern you does it, Mary? Because you knew already what he was like, the man he really was under that cloak of fake piety."

"Albert was… *complicated*. But do you really believe one of those two warring ladies from the Monday morning get-together could have anything to do with his death? Really? That sounds very far-fetched."

I find myself agreeing with her, although I keep my face neutral.

"Ceddars had motive and opportunity," Mary continues. "Didn't he turn up at the scene of both murders moments after the deeds were committed?"

"He did. However, when it comes to investigating a murder or murders, everything must be considered. Every suspect. Every clue…"

A smile widens Mary's cheeks. "Now I see it. You like Ceddars, don't you? More than like him."

"My personal feelings about the doctor are not what is at stake here, Mary. I'm a seeker of truth and nothing else."

"Doesn't it bother you that he was seeing that Feltham girl? That his interests were elsewhere?"

"We all have pasts and I only met Ceddars this morning. And besides, if I believed him to be a murderer, what I think about him, good or bad, would not interfere with my investigation. I do not believe he is guilty and with that in mind I am compelled to discover the real killer. I'm more interested in the other suspects. First… tell me about Mrs Willoughby."

Mary takes a long time before answering, her eyes locked onto mine. A slow intake of breath and she finally replies. "Albert's right-hand woman? I've discovered a few things about her…"

I lean further forward in my chair. "Go on."

Mary reaches for the sherry decanter and refills her glass, taking a large gulp. "She loved him, did you know that?" Mary obviously believes this is quite a revelation and delivers it with more than a sneer. "She's been in love with Albert for years, ever since the sudden death of her husband in fact."

"When was that?"

"Over thirty years ago."

"And what did her husband die of?"

Mary laughs. "You think that old battle axe killed him?

Maybe she did. She inherited a tidy sum of money, that's for sure. More than tidy. And after his death, she followed Albert to this parish and set up home here."

"Didn't that bother you?"

"Mrs Willoughby?" She snorts. "The deluded woman is not Albert's type at all. No, he liked them young and fresh, I doubt Mrs Willoughby has ever been either." She drains her sherry glass and refills it, looking at me unashamedly.

"It's true then? Your husband was an adulterer?"

"You know it's true, so why ask me? He was still my husband, and he was still murdered. And I'm still a grieving widow."

"You're saying he and Mrs Willoughby never had an assignation?"

"I doubt it very much. But why does it matter now that he's gone?"

"May I say that you seem particularly unconcerned about his adultery."

Mary scoffs again. "I've had a lifetime to deal with it. To deal with him."

"And apart from Mrs Willoughby, who you believed to be in love with him, there were others… is that correct? Those young and fresh women you mentioned?"

Mary's face darkens, her eyebrows furrowing in my direction, and for a moment all the beauty is drained from her face. "Is that why you're here? To humiliate me? Well, Miss Emily Crookshanks, my whole marriage has been one humiliation. Albert's interest in me didn't last very long. But you can guess that." Her words are bitter and heartfelt.

"You were in love with him?"

"I thought so. Naive as I was. I was the youngest daughter in my family, with a very small dowry. But Albert was more interested in my name. The Smallseys are a well-regarded family with connections to royalty. I thought it romantic that he wanted to have both our surnames conjoined. I soon realised it was for his own ambitious ends. And he was ambitious in those early days. He could have gone a lot further than Little Pucklewick. He could've been a bishop. But he was fatally flawed. His love of drink, of women and of horses brought him down. He may have Smallsey in his name, but at heart he's always been a Wilson. Is that what you wanted to hear? Or do you require that I am more humiliated?"

"You must be aware of the gossip that now surrounds your husband. I'm afraid my questions will be nothing compared to all the wagging tongues."

"It's him at fault not me."

"But that's not how it works. You'll be irretrievably tainted."

"I'm the infirm wife stuck at home in bed. I think people may be more forgiving than you realise."

"Possibly."

"I'm a weak, bedridden, wronged woman."

"And what about his other misdemeanours? The accusations contained in those printed rumours? That kind of scandal will follow you around wherever you go unless you go abroad, won't it?"

"Whoever pinned them up knew a lot about him, that's for sure."

"All those rumours were true?"

Mary shrugs. "What if they are? I will pretend to everyone that I know nothing about them. That I am as shocked as everyone else. Don't you see? I will also become a victim of his. I think everyone will pity me."

I wonder if she is right. Mary is the type of person who may be able to turn nasty gossip around, that much is for sure. Her demure looks do not hinder her. "If that is the case, why are you telling me this?"

"Do I have a choice? You're a force of nature, Miss Crookshanks. I don't like you, not one little bit, but that doesn't mean I don't trust your discretion. You are a woman after all… or so I'm led to believe. And women stick together."

I digest her words for a few moments. "You're right to trust me. But if I think you are involved in any of this, that you've lied to me about anything that is needed to get to the bottom of these murders, I shall not hesitate to reveal everything."

"I wonder who they will believe? Me, the wronged wife, or you the… eccentric investigator with the hots for the philandering and murderous Ceddars?"

I ignore her jibe. "I just need to know everything you know."

"If you want a complete list of my horrible husband's conquests, all his wronged lovers, then you're barking up the wrong tree. I simply do not have one."

"No, I do not require that. I'm only interested in his recent dealings, which brings me onto Dorothy Knight. She's older and has put on weight, but in her day, she must've been quite the siren."

"What if she was?"

"Did Dorothy Knight have any hold over your husband?"

"Why don't you ask her? See how she reacts to your horrible questions?"

"I *have* talked to her. And I fully intend to talk to her again, although the death of William Eriksen has hit her hard. Very hard. But that aside, my guess is that Dorothy Knight and your deceased husband were more than acquaintances… did they know each other from before the war?"

"I have no idea, although Albert was annoyed about her arrival in Little Pucklewick."

"Annoyed?"

"He was a complicated man." Mary's face creases in sorrow. I'm so eager to hear what she has to say that I'm forgetting she is a recent widow. She may not have loved her philandering husband, but that doesn't mean she is not grief-stricken… unless she killed him that is. My eyes glance again at her display of acting medals and the bust of Shakespeare. This could be another performance. If so, it's a good one.

"I only know my husband. The man he was, the things he was capable of. With that said, it's very possible he and Dorothy Knight may have known each other. I imagine that she was once an attractive woman."

"She still is."

A dark smile breaks through her creased face. "But she's no longer young."

"If they had an assignation, it must've been some time ago?"

Mary shrugs. "Possibly. She certainly had a hold over my husband after she came here to live."

Mary is holding back. I'm sure of it. "Why do you think that?"

"Mrs Willoughby, that's why. Albert allowed Dorothy Knight to push her way into the women's group and to take over some of Mrs Willoughby's duties. She was not pleased."

"Why should your husband care what Mrs Willoughby thought?"

The dark smile returns to Mary's face. "Money of course. She doted on Albert. She was always giving donations to his church fund and for other *charities*. Money that went straight into his pocket."

"But wouldn't upsetting Mrs Willoughby risk cutting off one of his cash streams?"

Mary nods.

"Those rumours posted around the village… Do any of them relate to Mrs Willoughby or Dorothy Knight or perhaps Fran Feltham or anyone else?"

"Fran Feltham? Are you hoping she has something to do with this? Do you want to rid yourself of the competition?"

"I have no interest in her other than as a possible suspect."

"Not because she may be the doctor's lover?"

I ignore her attempt to get a rise from me, but I find the thought an irksome one. "Ceddars told me otherwise, that she rebuffed him."

"And of course, men never lie, do they? Especially where the reputation of a young woman is at stake or, more importantly, *their own reputation...*"

Mary's words make sense. And Ceddars has been irritatingly gallant where Fran is concerned. "You seem to know a lot about her?"

"I've seen Fran Feltham cycling around like butter wouldn't melt," she sneers.

"You don't like her?"

A shake of the head.

"Why is that?"

"Do *you* like her, Miss Crookshanks?"

The question takes me by surprise. "She told me that your husband, the Reverend, tried it on with her."

Mary grimaces but doesn't look surprised. "She didn't let him... I hope?"

"She is very much in control of herself. I sense she is quite the force of nature."

"I'm sure *she* thinks she is." She lets out a guffaw. "The men of the village certainly think so. That kid Eugene is quite taken with her, that's for sure."

"He is?"

"I see him creeping around, following her."

"He's interested in Fran Feltham?"

She gives me a sideways look. "You know what young men are like. Although he's nothing more than a boy. Where Fran goes, Eugene is soon to follow."

I wonder if Eugene had followed Fran this morning after she left Eriksen's to supposedly go back to her lodgings at the Green Dragon to retrieve her spectacles? It's possible Eugene knows where she actually went. The angry shin-kicker may hold vital clues. I curse myself for letting him get away yet again. Hopefully Inspector Troughton will catch up with him and get to the bottom of things. However, where the inspector is involved, I'm less than confident.

I take a deep breath and fix Mary with my eyes. "Fran Feltham was the vicar's illicit daughter."

My statement shocks Mary. It's obvious she had no idea of the connection between them, I'm sure of that. I also sense her shock isn't that her husband had fathered an illicit child, but that Fran was one of them… that there were others… She knows what I only suspect, what the poster stated…

Has fathered many bastards

I only met the vicar for a few minutes before his dive into Mollie's sponge cake, but I took note of his features. And, of course, I have the photograph of him as a young man. He was handsome with a thick flock of black hair and eyebrows. Features that he passed down to his offspring. "How many other bastards are there out there that you have heard of, Mary?"

"My husband was a busy man… it wouldn't surprise me if half the village children were his offspring. You must've noticed Billy? His thick black hair and good looks? I often chatted to the boy. He seemed a good sort. I used to give him treats." Tears appear in her eyes. "It was quite horrible what happened to him."

Mary has mentioned something I only suspected. "You believe he was the vicar's illegitimate son?"

She nods.

"And that didn't bother you?"

"Of course, it bothered me! Despite my weak condition, I'm fully capable of bearing children, but Albert wasn't interested. I've always wanted a family. Billy was the closest I could come to being a mother."

"I'm sorry to hear that."

She dabs at her eyes with a handkerchief.

I decide to change the subject. "Let's go back to Dorothy Knight. The last time we spoke, I asked you if you knew what she and your husband were arguing about before he was murdered, is there anything more you can tell me about that?"

Mary shakes her head. "You will need to ask her."

"I did, she told me the reverend was dead set against her marrying William Eriksen. Forbade it in fact."

"Did he? Yes, I can see that. Albert liked to control people's lives. But you can't think Dorothy Knight is the murderer, can you? Why would she kill William Eriksen? She was dotty over him. Quite embarrassing, by all accounts."

"All accounts? Who told you this?"

"That awful man, Simmons. He loved gossip."

"Do you know anything about the printing press I found in the church vaults?"

"In the vaults? You mean… it was Simmons who made those dreadful posters?" She takes a slurp of sherry and looks me in the eye. "I certainly wouldn't put it past him."

"You wouldn't?"

"Like I said. He loved to gossip. I often thought he should get together with Ethel. They were made for each other. The vaults are the curate's responsibility. He has the keys, meaning he can come and go as and when he pleases. Also, Albert told me the man was always hanging around, eavesdropping onto his conversations, and sticking his nose into his private business. He'd been onto the bishop to get Simmons replaced. It's not a great stretch to believe the curate is behind those dreadful accusations."

"Accusations that we now know are all true."

Mary shrugs. "Like I told you… ask Simmons."

"I was down in the vaults with Ceddars earlier and disturbed someone. It definitely wasn't the curate."

"Well, of course not. There's no way Simmons could've

put up those posters himself. Have you seen him? He's over six foot and unmistakable. What if he'd been caught? No, he probably had an accomplice… probably the person who attacked you… the stranger I spotted roaming around the village."

"Mrs Willoughby told me she'd also seen the same man putting up the posters this morning, and I agree, I believe it was the same person we caught dismantling the printing press down in the vaults."

"Well, there you have it!" she barks in triumph, finishing her sherry.

"Have you seen the curate since his visit this morning?"

A quick shake of her head. "He's probably at church, lording it up now that Albert has gone."

"I was there earlier. Simmons was conspicuous by his absence."

"Was he? That doesn't sound like him."

"I also thought that odd."

"Perhaps you should go and find him." She closes her eyes and sags in her chair somewhat theatrically.

"Mary?" I go over to her and rock her shoulders, but she's either passed out or is pretending to have done. I try to wake her a few more times, but she appears to be out like a light.

I make my way downstairs, finding a white-faced Charlotte sitting on a chair, more tears streaming down her face. "I never wanted to believe it, miss. I thought it was that Troughton, acting all grand an' mighty, but…"

"But what?"

"That was Ethel on the phone. He confessed, miss. He's confessed to the murders. To everythin'."

"Who has?"

"The doctor. I can hardly believe it. He's admitted it all."

Tea & Ice

"**WHAT** on earth?" I reel inside. Why would Ceddars admit to the murders? Unless… was it him, was it really him who did it?

"I just can't believe it, miss. He was always so kind to me. And funny. To think he had a black heart all this time. I wonder what else he's been up to?"

The news hits me like a blow to the head. I'm stunned, disorientated, and find it hard to breathe.

"You alright, miss? You want some water? Or some tea?"

I'm vaguely aware of Charlotte taking me to the kitchen before something warm is thrust into my hand, and my hand pushed to my lips. I take a drink, warm, milky tea filling my mouth and spilling into my throat. I forget to swallow, spluttering and coughing.

"Miss! Oh my!"

Her voice becomes distant, echoed and abruptly… she's gone, and I find myself encased in a cold, stark darkness. Shivering, my teeth chattering. I stand up, coming back to myself, astounded to find the kitchen covered in ice, frost clinging to every surface, white and glistening. The floor and walls are brittle with rime, windows coated with a slick icy film, curtains limp and frozen. Icicles hang as glistening crossbow darts from shelves, cupboards, sinks and tables. Everything is still and silent, as if time has stopped.

The kitchen has transformed into an icy, numbing tomb. I shiver again, shuddering at the sharp, chill air that bites at my exposed skin, seeps into my bones, and makes it hard to breathe. Another shiver, but this is a shudder of fear. A nameless dread hunts me.

I can feel it.

A terrifying, heinous creature from a different world. I stumble over to the windows and scrub away the ice to stare outside, shocked at what meets my eyes. Writhing tentacles covered in oily black scales encase the vicarage, coiling and tightening…

> *…And in that moment, I know what it is and where I am. I'm trapped in a petty murder story, the bloodseeker searching for me, and desperate to penetrate my majiks.*

> *The monster found me in Little Pucklewick, and in the eccentric sleuth, Emily Crookshanks. Her papery thoughts intertwining feverishly with my own. As if somehow my unfinished spell has commingled us, has made us one and the same. I sense Emily's keen mind, her vast intellect, and her petty lusts. But her skills at deduction and catching murderers, and her flaw of falling for them, cannot help me now.*

> *No. I must stand and fight alone. I push Emily down within myself, the knowledge of who and what I am growing inside of me like a powerful, intense, underground fire. My wand thrums, warm and pulsating within my fist—and I squeeze it tightly, incanting words of power, their sound low, guttural, and terrifying to my ears.*

> *A red cinder bursts from the end of my wand, followed by more, a torrent of them, showering the kitchen in crimson sparks. I grunt and stagger at the effort—ice melting with a cascade of dripping*

water. The impatient inferno that waits eagerly inside of me is ready to explode—and it won't be denied.

I fling open the outside door and raise my wand, unleashing the power that dwells within all witchweavers—raw, dangerous, unstoppable. I shout incantations like curse words, my body shuddering with the effort. Releasing more scorching cinders in a second, more powerful spurt of crimson. This time the motes burst into flaming stars, creating a raging wildfire that incinerates everything it touches.

The now burning bloodseeker tightens its coils, wrapping itself ever tighter, bricks and mortar crumbling around me. But I stand firm, reaching further inside of myself, touching the wand to my chest to become living flame, a flame that blazes red then white hot.

I fling myself at the monster, the bloodseeker screeching in pain at my touch, my fingers blasting tendrils of lava down its sinews and nerves, incinerating muscles and bone. I let the broiling heat rise within me to a shuddering crescendo and, with a mighty blast of light, I explode into a supernova.

I come to, dazed, my eyes quickly checking my hands and clothes, consumed with a memory of threat, of intense cold and burning, of constriction and entrapment. Of a terrific explosion. But all I find is myself, Emily Crookshanks, amateur sleuth and detective, sitting down in the chair I was in moments ago.

"Miss! Are you alright?"

I stand up onto shaky legs, those intensely strange and terrifying memories, turning into nothing more than a vague mist and disappearing.

"Miss, you should be sittin' down. You've had a shock. It's the doctor. What he's done. It's shocked us all."

The doctor. Ceddars. His confession. "I was positive he was innocent, sure of it. I felt it in my gut. He can't be..." My voice dries. What can I say? I was wrong again.

"If you excuse me for talkin' out of turn for a moment... you liked him, didn't you, miss?"

I nod. In place of my now forgotten memories, I see a flood of images and sounds. Of a smiling joking Ceddars, forever at my side making light of everything. Was he purposely trying to confuse me? "I think I've been rather naive. I was convinced he wasn't the murderer and yet the clues were all there. Perhaps I didn't want to see them. Perhaps, I was fooling myself."

"But from what I've heard, miss. You ain't been very well. You can't go blamin' yourself. It's not your fault the doctor took advantage."

Her simple, heartfelt words are meant to soothe, but they scythe into me. I've been made a fool of. Kissed and used. But most of all, I'm embarrassed. "I'm heading back home."

Charlotte's thick eyebrows furrow. "You sure, miss? You've obviously had quite a shock. It's hit you hard, miss. Very hard."

I straighten my hat, ignoring Charlotte's fussing, and head to the front door. "Molly will look after me. Thank you."

"Goodbye, miss. You take care."

I emerge into the sunlight of the afternoon. The air is invigorating, but I'm still light-headed. I need to go home. To lie down. To rest... I'm incredibly tired. I exit the vicarage garden through the north gate in the high wall and come face to face with the unsettling presence of Ceddars' Bugatti.

I avert my eyes and walk quickly past it into my garden. The windows of my cottage are thankfully shut. Molly has had a change of heart since the events of this morning. Perhaps now she'll always keep the windows closed. I open the door and walk inside, feeling at once safe and protected.

Molly's red, rounded, friendly face pokes out from the kitchen, her russet curls framing a concerned expression. "That you, miss?" Her smile has a tinge of sadness to it. "So it were the doctor all along. Who would've thunk it?"

"You've heard?"

"Ethel has been workin' overtime. The most shockin' day Little Pucklewick has seen in many a long year." Her rounded body joins her head, and she emerges into the hallway, giving me a concerned look. "Ooh, miss, you do look beat."

"It's been a long day."

"It has been that… and then some."

"I'm going to my room."

"You do that, miss. Have a nice lie down, and I'll bring you up a lovely pot of tea."

My feet are heavy as I walk up the stairs, my legs aching. But finally, I reach the landing and my bedroom. My bed is soft and welcoming, but I ignore it. Instead, I enter my walk-in wardrobe and find the hatbox with the paper cuttings I discovered earlier. I empty them out, looking for the one cutting I failed to read this morning.

Emily Crookshanks—the scandal that shook South Africa

The full story of the downfall of South Africa's once pre-eminent sleuth, Emily Crookshanks, aka, The Headmistress.

The story is folded a few times and attached to it are

other clippings. I return to my bedroom and lay them all out on the bed…

> *Miss Crookshanks first came to prominence in the mystery of the Pretoria Pearl. Her deductive reasoning solved the perplexing mystery of its whereabouts after it was supposedly stolen by thieves.*

> *It was a case that delighted the nation, especially as the thief turned out to be none other than the Pearl's owner…*

I scan the story, which relates the details of my early career and some of the astonishing sleuthing that brought me success and fame. I would be very pleased, if it wasn't for the daunting headline.

This is the story of my downfall.

I read on, a sense of foreboding growing inside of me. It appears that after my successes on a few high-profile cases, I became the darling of not only the press, but of the glitterati and polite society. I was wined, dined, and feted. I was even asked to join the government. A request I politely refused.

Everything was going very well for me until *The Case of the Murdered Mine Owner.*

The name sends a shudder through me, despite my amnesia. At this time, there were two rival gold mining companies. One owned by the charismatic Willem Van Der Oosthuizen, who came from old money and the other, owned by the so-called 'upstart', Piet Schalk. The two men had been at loggerheads for years, mostly fighting over land and mining rights. Land and rights often won by the wilier Schalk. The men hated each other. Piet Schalk was progressive and charismatic. He was popular with politicians and his men alike, as well as being somewhat of a society darling.

When Piet Schalk was found brutally murdered, suspicion fell on his rival. This was when the Headmistress entered the picture. Brought in to investigate the murder, hoping to succeed where the police had failed. It was widely believed the police had been bribed as part of a larger conspiracy and cover up. Apparently, I performed my investigations and found nothing that incriminated Van Der Oosthuizen and publicly announced my findings in a widely reported press conference. However, during my investigations, rumours arose of a possible romance between myself and Willem. Rumours that were perpetuated by Piet Schalk's family who owned one of the main South African tabloids.

Indeed, after my findings, they used the paper to harass the man they thought responsible, and myself, the woman who had exonerated him. But they did more than this, they invested in their own detectives who over the next few months of intense media interest ultimately unearthed the true story. Willem Van Der Oosthuizen was guilty. He hadn't committed the act himself but had paid for the killing and the cover-up. Van Der Oosthuizen took his own life soon after.

I can only read what the article is telling me, but it appears I was distraught, and unable to believe my lover had lied to me. That my love for this man had made me blind to the truth. That it was very likely Willem Van Der Oosthuizen had played me for a fool, which was to put it lightly.

The gutter press saw it very differently. In their eyes, I was at worst complicit in the cover up and at best, a deluded, love and money-struck woman. I was forced to leave South Africa. The reason why I've found myself here in England, in Little Pucklewick.

I put down the clipping and sit back, aware of the parallels between what I've just read and the present investigation. Is that it then? I'm a great detective who suffers from a single, yet fatal, flaw? A silly woman who can't see through the men she has a love interest in, or who show interest in me?

I can't help but wonder if Ceddars made a deliberate attempt to skew my investigation from the start. After all, he spent the whole day with me, didn't he? Was that so he could keep an eye on me, to keep me at bay and put me off course? I think back to the kiss and redden. It appears so. I knew very little about him. But his plans went astray. Eugene saw him escaping after he killed Eriksen. Throughout my investigations, the youth was convinced of his guilt, and I never believed him. Instead, I was trying my best to convince myself of his innocence. Is that what happened with Willem Van Der Oosthuizen? Did I fall for him and become blind to the real man he was? A murderer?

I lie back down on my bed, my head sinking into my pillows. I want to close my eyes and go to sleep. To perhaps awake again with amnesia,, with no memory of today's events.

The bedroom door bangs open and in walks Molly with a tray containing a teapot, two cups, milk and four slices of cake. "Hope you don't mind, but I took the liberty of adding an extra cup. I thought I'd keep you company." She slams the tray down on the table next to my bed and begins to pour. "There you go, miss. This'll sort you out. Heaven knows how we all coped before tea. It doesn't bear thinking about, does it, miss?"

I take the cup off her and cradle it in my hands.

She also fills a cup and takes a long, loud slurp. "Pardon my manners, miss. But I were gaspin'. It's been a sad day, no mistakin'. I've been quite popular. People wantin' me to tell 'em what I know. The poor vicar gettin' shot like that. And now the doctor's the one that did it. It's always the ones you least expect, ain't it? But then again, accordin' to gossip, the vicar had it comin'. There's been a lot of posters found around the village containin' such horrible rumours about him, but… it appears some of it were true! Who can believe it? It's a shocker, that's for sure."

I let Mollie prattle on, taking a sip of tea and feeling instantly rejuvenated. I take another sip and swirl it round my mouth. It tastes just like tea, and yet, it somehow has powerful restorative powers.

"And then there's poor Billy. I shed a few tears for him, that's for sure. It broke my heart to hear what had happened to him. And so young." She slurps again at her tea, this time without an apology.

Billy.

The name spins in my mind.

"Run over in the prime of life."

And then it hits me. Billy! Who ran him over? It wasn't Ceddars, because he was with me all day. And after examining William Eriksen's car, it certainly couldn't have been his white Mercedes. I sit up, energised by the tea and by this oversight. I'd been so upset that Ceddars had confessed that I totally forgot about the murder of Billy. And it was a murder, I'm sure of it.

"You alright, miss? You look all peculiar."

"I'm fine Molly." I take a slice of cake and stuff it all into my mouth, swilling it down with a large gulp of tea. "I may have messed up with Ceddars, but someone needs to discover who killed Billy Brown."

"You mean, it wasn't Ceddars who done it?"

"That's exactly what I mean."

"But Ethel has been saying it was him."

"You can't believe everything that woman says." I take another large bite out of one of the remaining slices of cake, wipe my hands and get off the bed. "I've got a job to do and I will do it."

I jog downstairs and outside, heading for the Bugatti, stirring the engine into life and tearing off down the road.

Photos & Fanaticism

I DRIVE towards the scene of Billy's accident. I want to go over things again to see if there is anything I missed, excited by the opportunity of redeeming myself. I catch my thoughts. Just who am I redeeming myself for? The answer is a simple one…

Emily Crookshanks.

Ceddars made a fool of me, just like Willum Van Der Oosthuizen. But it's time to put that all behind me. I have an opportunity to do some simple sleuthing, to get to the bottom of who killed Billy and why. He may be a kid, but his death is just as important as the vicar's.

Just before the bottom of the hill where the accident occurred, I spot a semi-circular glint in the hedgerow and reverse the car, pulling to a stop and jumping out. It's the back mudguard off Billy's bike. It's twisted and snapped. Again, I see traces of white paint, but there is also a smudge of green. *Green!*

I examine the road. There is a skid mark that looks like it was made by the back tyre of Billy's bike—and he had no brakes. A vehicle must've hit him from behind, that much is for sure.

I drop the mudguard into the Bugatti and slowly continue down the hill to the bend, keeping my eye out for any other evidence. I park again and immediately spot another skid mark and scratches in the tarmac—where Billy was run over. I get down on my hands and knees and examine them with my magnifying glass. There are more flecks of green paint. Two colours? The answer is obvious. The vehicle that hit Billy has been repainted. It was originally white, but the later layer of thin green paint was mostly scuffed off in the accident, leaving the white behind.

I've heard of only one green vehicle in the village. The vicarage van that Ceddars described to me. Mostly driven by Simmons and held together by rust, according to the doctor, and parked in a garage opposite Simmons' cottage. I need to take a look at it. And to find Curate Simmons, wherever he has gotten to. His disappearance is yet another mystery I ignored.

Ten minutes later, I park the Bugatti outside Simmons' house, and go over to the garage opposite. The doors are unlocked, and I creep inside. A dark green van squats in the gloom. I spot the damage even in the dark… the front of the van is freshly bent and twisted, white paint visible where it's been scratched. I open the drivers' door and discover the keys hanging in the transmission. I was hoping to find them missing, to be instead nestling in the pocket of the person who hit Billy. Who ran him over in cold blood. Finding them in the van means anyone could've been driving. Still, at least I now know what vehicle was involved in Billy's death. That's half the battle.

I close the garage doors, cross over the road to Curate Simmons' cottage and knock on the door again—not expecting an answer, and don't get one. The house remains silent. I saunter around the terrace end and enter its garden through a small side gate. There's another gate at the far end of the garden leading to open fields. From here, I can see the church, the vicarage and my cottage perched next to Dooleys Wood that covers the hill like a dark stain. I turn my attention back to the house and stare through its windows into a small, sparse sitting room and a kitchen. There is a door here. I twist the knob and find it unlocked, stealing inside.

"Hello! Is anyone here? Curate Simmons?"

No reply. The sitting room has a single chair in front of

a fireplace and a cross on each wall. An open door on the far wall indicates a staircase to the first floor while another door leads to the front of the house. I call out again. No reply. I head to the front room and come to a cellar door. It's locked with a new and impressive padlock. I'll come back to this later. The front room is also sparse, apart from more crosses. Lots of them. I suppose Simmons is a curate, but it does seem like overkill.

I call Simmons' name again, but I'm convinced the house is empty. I go back past the cellar and up steep stairs until I come to a small landing, off which are two doors. One leads to Simmons' bedroom. Again, the room is sparse. There is a single wooden bed covered in a thin, rough sheet and crosses on every wall. The second room is empty apart from a single wooden chair sitting at its centre, in front of which is the largest cross so far.

Creepy.

I go back down to the locked cellar door and smile. Padlocks and I have an understanding. I take out my hairpins and, moments later, the lock snaps open, the door swinging inwards to reveal stone stairs sinking into a murky darkness, the lock jiggling in my fingers to fall clattering into the gloom. I cringe and hold my breath. The house stays silent, despite all my blundering about.

As my eyes adjust to the dark, I become aware of flickering lights below. I take a deep breath and descend, one step at a time, the air growing warmer. At the bottom, the steps twist to the left, revealing a low-ceilinged room, the walls painted black. Candles, lots of them, splutter on the far wall, surrounding a shrine of some sort. But this is no devotion to a saint or similar, it is entirely different. In its centre is a photograph of the Reverend Wilson-Smallsey.

There are other photographs of him and clippings from newspapers, pages taken from ledgers, and receipts including betting slips. There are also photographs of Fran Feltham,

Eugene and Dorothy Knight, William Eriksen and Sheng, Gladys Willoughby and... Billy. All taken surreptitiously. As well as many photographs of the church spire. A bench on the far wall has two large photographic baths, and printing equipment. It appears Simmons' was an amateur photographer. Something that didn't come out about the man during my investigations. There is one more thing, all the photographs are scrawled with words written and smeared in blood.

Sinners! Sluts! Bastards! Gamblers! Adulterers!

Drunkards! Fornicators! Thieves! Whores!

The camera never lies!

And the number 666 written repeatedly. Simmons is unhinged, that much is obvious. I get closer to the photograph of Billy. It's taken at an odd angle, the shadows on his face making him look almost evil. Scrawled underneath are the words: *The Antichrist Revealed!*

Was that it then? Did Simmons see the vicar as a centre of evil and his offspring, Billy, as the antichrist? As ridiculous as it sounds, it would seem so. Simmons is not a well man. Scrawled on the other walls and on the floors are prayers and religious avocations. The man wasn't only unhinged, he was deranged. I examine the photographs, realising that one person is missing... the vicar's wife.

Mary...

I hear a noise behind me. A push to my back catapults me onto the floor where I smack my head heavily, the weight of someone jumping on top of me. I try to roll over, but they bash my head on the hard stone and with a flash of blinding light, I lose consciousness.

Spoons & Smoke

IWAKE with a thumping head and a stiff neck, my legs cramping. I pull them up to my chest, becoming aware that my feet are tied together, my hands also tied behind my back. Dazed, I roll over onto my side and force open my eyes.

Blackness.

Did the hits to my head blind me? But as my eyes adjust to the dark, I notice a glimmer of light. I push myself across the floor until I reach a step—the bottom of the stairs. I thread my feet through my arms and sit down. The light is coming from a small crack in the now closed cellar door. I push myself up, one stair at a time. The effort winding me. At the top I use my shoulder to try and open the door, knowing that it will be locked but I push at it all the same. It's hard and unyielding.

"Let me out!" I shout, my voice sounding weak. I try again, but my words are stifled by the thick masonry walls.

Now what?

I sit back against the door and test my bonds. Whoever tied me up knew what they were doing. Thick rope tightly encircles my wrists and ankles. The knots are simple, but well tied. My fingers are not strong enough to unpick them. I need a tool of some kind. I think of my fountain pen nestled in one of my many pockets, but it would break easily. I need something stronger, or a flame to burn the rope. I remember the candles that drew me down here and decide to search the cellar as best I can in the hope of finding a box of matches or a tool to help me escape this predicament. I slide back down the stairs and enter the blackness of the cellar room. All I can do is shuffle and roll along the floor, which I do methodically. I find the candles by the far wall, pushing myself up to stand, but they are all extinguished. And no matches.

I remember the photographic baths and printing equipment and gingerly feel my way around the wall, hopping towards that side of the room and bump into the table. I hear the slosh of chemicals and a smell akin to vinegar. What I understand of photography tells me that these chemicals are not strong enough to burn my bonds. I'm glad, I'd hate to be forced to use acid. I might burn off my bonds but what other damage would that do? I search around the tabletop and my fingers brush against cold object. A spoon!

It's not the best tool, but it will have to do. I struggle back to the steps and sit down, aware of sounds coming from above.

"Who's up there! Let me out!"

Someone is moving around, banging and dragging things.

"Curate Simmons? Is that you? Let me out of here!"

Silence.

I wonder if they heard me at all. I bend the end of the spoon back and forth until the bowl falls off, leaving a sharp, ragged edge that I busily plunge into the ropes surrounding my feet. But I'm also aware I now have a weapon, should I need to use it.

I use the broken spoon to lever the knots, stretching the rope, and cutting and slicing. I have small feet. All I have to do is get one heel out and I'll be free. Well, free to walk, not that I can go anywhere. Then I can at least work on the ropes surrounding my hands. But it's tiring work. I'm scrunched over, my back muscles screaming at me, my fingers sore from the effort. I'm concentrating so hard on freeing myself that I don't notice the smell of smoke, well not at first, and now it's the only thing I can think about.

Smoke!

Which means burning. A fire. I've got to get out of here!

I frantically stab at and stretch the ropes around my feet, the threat of being burned alive, giving me renewed energy, the pain in my back and hands disappearing as I concentrate only on freeing myself.

The smell of smoke becomes stronger, accompanied by sounds of burning above, and a growing heat. How the hell will I get out of here? I swallow hard, panicking won't help, Instead, I focus my energies on freeing myself, until I slide my feet triumphantly out of the rope. I run up the stairs, banging on the cellar door again, aware of a strong heat coming from behind it, an orange glow visible through the single crack. I need to find another way out of here.

I go back down into the cellar, frantically examining the walls, but they are all solid granite. My fingers find… is it a light switch? I flick it downwards and the cellar is at once bathed in red light. Of course, Simmons would need a safe light while he was working? Why didn't I find it before?

There's no time for recriminations. I quickly scan the room for anything that might help break the cellar door down, and its then that I notice black cloth pinned over… could it be a window? I jump up onto the table and pull at the fabric that is only held in place by a series of drawing pins. It reveals a small window through which I can see plant plots. A cellar window! It's small, but I'm petite. I can get through, with a push.

Creaking from above and flame erupts along the far side of the ceiling. The cellar filling with choking black smoke. I fumble the window latch open and push, but it obviously hasn't been opened in many years. It won't budge. I use the spoon as a lever and push with my other hand. It bursts open, but my relief is short-lived. I'm hit by a whoosh of air that knocks me off the table, while fire erupts into a frenzy around me.

My eyes fall on a burning newspaper clipping lying on the floor. A headline and photograph. I grasp at it with a quick hand, but it turns into embers in my fingers. Another clue! But what are clues if I'm burnt alive? I pull away from the leaping, worrying flames, and climb back onto the table, gasping for air. I push my hands out of the window, trying to find purchase. Anything I can grab to pull myself out while my feet scrabble at the wall. The heat at my back burning me through my clothes.

And then, someone grabs my hands and I'm hauled upwards and outwards into the refreshing air.

"I say, old girl! What on the bally earth were you doing down there?"

Rescue & Refreshments

CEDDARS pulls me away from the burning cottage and I stumble after him, confused.

"Aren't you supposed to be under arrest?"

Ceddars reddens. "Absolutely, old girl, but I'm also the chief of the village fire voluntary force don't you know? That Troughton fellow gave me special dispensation, seeing that the fire was in danger of taking out the entire row of houses. I have to say Em', I was mightily surprised to find you in the cellar, somewhat singed and in mortal danger."

I say nothing, my eyes staring deeply into his. "Did you really do it, Ceddars? Did you murder the vicar and Eriksen?"

His face flicks away from mine. "Yes, I suppose I bally did."

"But I was convinced of your innocence. You lied to my face? You kissed me and lied? Look at me!"

Ceddars' face creases, the redness deepening. "Sometimes a chap has to do what a chap has to do and bugger the consequences. Sounds a tad harsh, now that I'm saying it out loud but… oh blast it! I'm just a bad sort Em'. A bounder and a cad. I'm very sorry old girl. Very sorry. I would've liked to have got to know you better but…" He shakes his head. "I really have to go and help out." He gives me a sad smile and rushes over to the other volunteer fireman.

Forty minutes later and I find myself sitting in the back of an ambulance opposite Curate Simmons' smoking cottage. The flames are now gone, the fire extinguished. Ceddars and the other volunteer village fireman, including Constable Jakes, Mr Shufflebottom the undertaker, and the landlord of the Green Dragon, busy themselves with the aftermath. But they do not work alone. The entire village has turned up, either helping or watching from the side-lines, including Mrs Willoughby and a still-grieving Dorothy Knight who both stand a more than respectful distance away from one another. I also glimpsed Grantham and his mates lending their youthful energy to battle the fire—everyone helping out as best they could. Molly is here too, working with the other servants and maids serving water, tea, and sandwiches—most of which are consumed by the onlookers rather than the working men.

I'm also aware of a lot of askance glances and gossiping. I've only been out and about in Little Pucklewick for a single day, but it appears I've made quite a splash.

Inspector Troughton has been directing the effort or trying to. From what I've seen of the man, he's been more of a hindrance than a help. Although throughout, he's been keeping his beady eyes on Ceddars who is still his prisoner. He talked to me earlier, telling me in no uncertain terms to stay put.

After another half an hour the men all pull back, their faces blackened, their clothes streaked with ash, and make their way to the refreshments table. Ceddars has been too busy to talk to me since he pulled me from the burning cellar. I'm thankfully uninjured, although my hair is slightly singed and my wrists sore from the rope. I'm mostly upset about my hat that was lost to the blaze and more than thankful to be alive.

Troughton finally comes over to me. "I can't say I'm surprised you were pulled out of the fire. What were you doing in the cellar of Simmons' cottage anyway? Snooping again?" I draw breath to speak, but Troughton raises a thin finger to his thin moustache and shakes his head. "Tell me how the blaze started?"

I rub at my sore wrists and explain what happened.

Searching the curate's house and finding his wall of madness—the photographs, the scrawled insults, and admonitions in dried blood. And then being hit on the head, before waking up bound in thick ropes and nearly burned alive.

"Someone knocked you out?" he asks with irritation. "Curate Simmons?"

"I said I didn't see who hit me. It could've been anybody."

"But how could it be anyone else? He sounds like he's gone completely off his rocker. It happens to a lot of men who came back from the war. You don't read about it in the papers, but the jails and hospitals are full of them. Now is there anything else you want to tell me? I've first-hand experience of how you like to hold back information."

"I was snooping around in the garage where the vicarage van is kept." I point to the open doors standing ajar not far away. "A detailed inspection of the van will reveal that the green and white paint found on Billy's bike and on the road is an exact match."

"It was Simmons who ran the lad over? That makes sense. Especially as he thought Billy was the Antichrist. Is that what you said?"

"Yes, but—"

"But what? It's all falling into place. You discovered the van. He spotted you, knocked you out, tied you up and set fire to his own house to put us off the scent. The classic actions of a lunatic, I'd say."

"We can't be sure of that. The keys were left in the van ignition. Anyone could've been driving it at the time of the collision."

"But it had to be Simmons? Surely? It was his house, and he was the person who regularly drove the van. And haven't you noticed? Simmons is conspicuous by his absence. No bodies were found in the fire, which makes it obvious he was the one who did this. Now that we have this damn blaze under control, I'll put my men on the lookout for him. It's a shame that evidence was burned, but it does suggest that Simmons was demented. You will give a witness statement to that affect?"

"Of course. What I saw were the ramblings of an insane man. He regarded the vicar as an evil force in the village. He knew of the Reverend Wilson-Smallsey's embezzlement, gambling, and womanising. And more."

"Now, now, Miss Crookshanks, please remember that the bishop is keen to limit the damage to the clergy over this affair—that information will not be needed in your statement."

I open my mouth to protest, but Troughton puts his finger to his lips again. "And no talking to the press about this. The bishop and I will deal with that." He drops his voice to a whisper. "However, considering what you have told me, it does seem likely Simmons was responsible for those awful rumours posted around the village. At least we can agree on that?"

I shrug. "Maybe."

"There's no maybe about it." Troughton pulls himself up to his full height and takes a deep breath. "I won't pretend it hasn't been a difficult day, but I now have a hard suspect for the killing of young Billy and the vicar's murderer in custody with a full written confession. Talking of Doctor Roberts, I need to escort him back to the station. Goodbye, Miss Crookshanks. Please, try and stay out of any further trouble. And remember… keep schtum."

Troughton strides away like he's won some kind of argument. And I can't help but be irritated. I've made a mess of this entire investigation and was nearly burned alive for my trouble. I don't like Troughton's simple reasoning regarding who hit me over the head, but the curate is the best suspect for the attack, that can't be ignored. As for his motive… I'm not so sure. The man was deluded and quite possibly made insane by the war and what he discovered about his boss, the vicar. Unlike the inspector, I shouldn't jump to easy conclusions. Evidence and fact is what is needed. Not supposition.

I listen to my thoughts. It's like I'm unable to stop investigating. To keep moving forward in this way is a compulsion, I realise. A character flaw. An arrogant inability to accept that I've been wrong. That I've misread the clues and the people around me. And yet, I won't give up, even if it's obvious that's exactly what I should do. To go back home and leave be. I think of my small cottage perched beside Dooleys Wood. It's a haven, I realise. A place I can hide away in. A place I want to hide inside, and yet, that's impossible.

I sigh, wondering what other dangers I may blunder into. What other things will I get wrong?

I'm distracted from my inner reveries by a lull in the general conversation. All eyes have fallen on the Inspector as he goes over to Ceddars. The doctor offers up his hands and Constable Jakes handcuffs him again.

I was convinced that Ceddars was innocent. And, I suppose, deep down inside, I still am. But he admitted it. To my face. The thought that Troughton might be the better investigator pops into my mind. Can that really be true? The man is jumped up and arrogant, a small-minded—my thoughts stop dead in their tracks. I've spotted a familiar face at the back of the crowd. A face I wasn't expecting to see.

I jump out of the ambulance and stride over towards Fran Feltham.

Confessions & Consternation

FRAN Feltham sees me coming. I expect her to react, to perhaps run away, but she remains perfectly calm, her attention switching between me and the handcuffing of Ceddars. Then again, she doesn't know what I've found out about her, that Fran Feltham isn't her real name. That she is a *Wilson* and the illegitimate child of the Reverend Wilson-Smallsey. She wears a smart coat, gloves and is carrying a handbag and suitcase.

Before I can get to her, she walks towards Inspector Troughton and taps him on the shoulder.

"Inspector, I need a word," she says loudly.

Troughton turns around, a startled look on his face, but not as startled as Ceddars' expression.

"Miss Feltham?" Troughton says.

"I'm afraid you have the wrong man, Inspector." Again, her voice is loud enough for everyone to hear, especially in the sudden silence.

"I'm sorry, I don't quite understand what you mean."

"Don't do it, Fran," Ceddars pleads, his moustache twitching in frustration. "Don't!"

"I have to, I'm afraid. This is quite, quite ridiculous. I won't see an innocent man hang for something he didn't do. No matter what the personal cost."

"Don't listen to her!" Ceddars barks. "I told you, I did it. I murdered the vicar and Eriksen."

Fran carries on, unabashed. "The doctor couldn't have killed the vicar because at the time of his murder he was… with me. In his house… *In his bedroom.*"

Sounds of shock and consternation follow Fran's announcement.

"She's lying, Inspector," Ceddars says. "She doesn't know what she's saying. The poor girl is in love with me."

"I'm certainly not in love with the doctor," Fran scoffs, carrying on in a matter-of-fact voice. "Although I do believe the opposite is true. The doctor is quite besotted with me. As to why he would want to admit to a murder he couldn't have committed is beyond me. But I was at the station ready to get on the London train when I heard what he'd done. And, as I said, I couldn't let an innocent man hang."

"But… but he's confessed," Troughton stutters.

"I'm willing to give a full statement at the police station. Please, why don't we go there now? This is embarrassing enough without all these onlookers."

"I'm sorry, Miss Feltham, but you are a known deceiver. A liar. I have discovered Fran Feltham isn't your real name."

For the first time in the exchange, Fran Feltham's composure is shaken. She clutches her handbag more tightly. "That is true. I did come to Little Pucklewick under an assumed name. There's no law against what I did, Inspector. I checked."

More consternation, and I find myself also *consternated*. What Fran is doing, if true, is committing social suicide. Then again, she is young, hard-headed, and very much in control of herself.

"I'm sorry, Miss Feltham, or whatever you wish to call yourself. I have a written confession. I have no idea why you are doing this, but that is the evidence that will convict Doctor Roberts. Not… this sordid nonsense."

"But there is a witness."

Troughton is taken aback. "A witness? Who?"

Fran points a gloved finger. "Eugene Knight. He's standing over there in front of his mother. Ask him."

All attention focuses on the teenager, and his cheeks

glow red, the crimson highlighted by his white-blond hair.

"Tell them, Eugene," Fran says. "I saw you lurking outside the doctor's house when we left it this morning—at the time of the vicar's murder. You were spying on me again, like you always do."

"You and that doctor… it's disgusting!" Eugene shouts. "It wasn't the first time I've seen them together. They've been at it for weeks!"

The consternation now reaches unprecedented levels.

"What he says, is quite true, Inspector," Fran continues. "And…" she turns her face towards the crowd, "…I am not ashamed."

"If that is right, Eugene," Troughton says, "why didn't you come forward earlier?"

"The answer is simple, inspector. The boy is infatuated with me."

"She's a slut and a whore!" Eugene shouts.

Dorothy Knight puts her hands on Eugene's shoulders and pulls him protectively towards her.

"Why are you doing this, Fran?" Ceddars says. "Why?"

"I could ask you why you signed a confession that was an outright lie. What on earth were *you* thinking?"

Ceddars shrinks, his head slumping. "I was protecting you. Your reputation. Miss Crookshanks had worked out who you really are. She came to the police station and informed the inspector. I wanted to prevent you any… shame."

Fran smiles, her face becoming a picture of strident beauty. "Oh Ceddars. Gallant to the last."

"And what of Eriksen?" Troughton says turning on Ceddars. "You admitted to killing him. Was that a lie as well?"

"I'm afraid so, old chap. In for a penny, in for a pound, what?"

Troughton turns to Eugene. "And your statement that you saw the doctor leaving the broken-down cottages after the shooting of William Eriksen, that was a lie?"

Eugene nods. "I… I just wanted him to be punished."

Inspector Troughton shakes his head in disgust. "The boy needs to be reprimanded, Mrs Knight. Lying to the police is not the behaviour you should be fostering in a young man."

Dorothy Knight bristles, clutching Eugene protectively, and ignoring the look of pleasure on Mrs Willoughby's face.

"And you doctor… I should arrest you for wasting police time. But with these revelations… well, you're finished in this village. And when the news of this scandal gets out, I doubt you'll find a practice anywhere in the British Isles that will have you. Uncuff him, Constable. He's free to go."

"Oh!" I exclaim.

All faces turn to me. I didn't mean to make a noise, but I couldn't help myself. *I now know who did it.* Or at least I think I do. With what I found in Simmons' cellar, everything has come together. Everything has made sense. I've doubted myself for too long. But the clues were there from the beginning.

I breathe a sigh of relief and start coughing. I inhaled rather a lot of smoke in the fire. But it matters not. Solving this annoying mystery means everything to me.

Everything.

"Do you have something to say, Miss Crookshanks?" Troughton says, turning towards me, an irritated expression on his face.

I shake my head, but inside my heart is pounding. Now is not the time to reveal what I know.

"Good, I want every man and woman on the lookout for Curate Simmons. I now believe that he is the man responsible for the murders and for the recent attack on Miss Emily Crookshanks. But do not approach him. The man is unhinged and very dangerous."

"Inspector?" Sheng stands on the outskirts of the crowd.

I wonder what Eriksen's companion is doing here.

Troughton's face shows even more irritation. Sheng is yet another reminder of his incompetence in this investigation. "Now, now, sir. It has just been proved that Doctor Roberts was innocent of the murder of your... erm... friend, Mr Eriksen. We don't want any bother. And besides, we've had a major breakthrough in the case."

Sheng bows. "You looking for Curate Simmons?" he says calmly in his slightly broken English.

Troughton nods.

"I found him."

Friendship & Foolishness

A **PLEASED** looking Inspector Troughton, accompanied by Constable Jakes and Sheng get into a police car and drive off towards Dooleys Wood a few moments later, after giving everyone strict instructions to 'go home and lock your doors until further notice'. A directive that many of the sheep-like inhabitants of Little Pucklewick follow without question.

Dorothy Knight frogmarches Eugene back to her shop, a look of thunder etched across her normally warm face. Gladys Willoughby also goes, loudly whispering the word 'sinners' as she passes Ceddars and Fran Feltham. I watch Ceddars and his erstwhile lover having a heated discussion. A discussion that ends abruptly when Fran purposely picks up her suitcase and stomps away, leaving Ceddars somewhat shell-shocked in her wake.

"Oh, hi Em'… erm, Emily… Miss Crookshanks." Ceddars says nervously when he sees me. "Looks like I made a right old mess of things here in Little Pucklewick, what? I hope you're not too brassed off with me?"

I say nothing.

"Will you forgive me? I was only bally doing what a gentleman would do. Protecting the little woman, what?"

"Is that what you call it?"

His lips widen to give a somewhat toothy grin, his face blackened with soot. "I suppose the opposite is true, the old girl protected me, rather. I've been a bit of a dumb Dora, haven't I?"

"Fran was using an assumed name. It made no difference

what she admitted to, here in Little Pucklewick. No shame will follow that girl once she steps on that train, and she knows it. I'm not up to date on the morals of middle England, but yes, you have rather blown it, haven't you? This is very serious for you, personally, isn't it?"

"It is, rather."

"But worse than that, you were really willing to hang for *her*? The girl who just left you? The girl who I'm guessing doesn't want anything more to do with you?

"I suppose I was. Fran was rather annoyed with me actually. Tore a strip right off. Told me I was a fool to my face. I'm a bit hopeless when it comes to the fairer sex."

"From where I'm sitting, you seem the opposite of helpless. Nevertheless, your predilection for the ladies has brought you down."

"My brother Johnnie always told me women would be my downfall. The old bugger was bally right, of course. If he was here, he'd disown me. But I'd still prefer to have him back. And now, well I suppose there's nothing left for me but to pack my things, get my affairs in order and leave for foreign climes. I'll be lucky to not be struck off once this gets out."

"There are a lot of places outside of England where I'm sure you'll fare very well."

"Like South Africa?"

I still have no memory of the country I supposedly travelled from. And the closest thing I've come to any memories of living there are from those newspaper clippings. "Maybe."

"I do still like you though, Em'. I thought we made quite a good team, what? And investigating is so much more fun than lancing boils and listening to tales of aches and pains and whatnot."

"And I like you, Ceddars."

"You do, even though I'm a bit of a hopeless romancer?

And after my very public assignation with Fran Feltham? Kissing you on the same day me and Fran were…"

"Because of it."

"Because of it? Oh Em', you really are one of a kind."

"Maybe, maybe not. But I'm not easily fooled. That's quite a skill you have, for deceiving people."

"I think it's more that I'm adept at deceiving myself. Like I said to Troughton, I'm the in for a penny, in for a pound kind of chap. Like in the war, I didn't want any of it, to be honest, but once I was up in my kite, I was more than ready to give the Hun hell!"

Ceddars' eyes sparkle. He's a far more complicated individual than I ever imagined. For someone who has had his reputation thoroughly taken to the cleaners, he is quite chipper. Then again, he was facing a death sentence.

"And what about you, Em'? You'll never live down the vicar dying in your sitting room if you stay here. Will you be moving on? Isn't that what you detectives always do. Solve a murder and then go off to some other exotic location?"

Exotic location? Is that what he thinks Little Pucklewick is? Then again, I suppose, in its quintessential way, he's right. "As to what I will do after this mystery is solved, I'm not sure."

"But you heard it from Troughton. It was Curate Simmons all along."

I shake my head.

"It's not Simmons? Then who?"

I stare at Ceddars' expectant face for a long time. "That is for me to reveal when I think the time is right."

"But Em', it's all over. Surely? Me and Fran are off the hook, even if she did put the kibosh on my life here in good, old Blighty. And didn't you tell me poor Simmons was off his rocker? That he was the one who also killed Billy and tried to burn you alive?"

"Let's get in the Bugatti and follow Troughton.

Apparently, Sheng has found the curate."

"You want to be there when the old chap confesses?"

"Simmons won't be confessing anything."

Ceddars moustache wrinkles in irritation. "What is it with you, Em'? I don't get it. Every time there is a bone fide suspect, you disagree! And isn't the chap supposed to be a lunatic? It all adds up in my book."

"What I meant, dear doctor, is that Simmons won't be doing much of anything. He's dead."

Knots & Notes

"**B**UT how can you possibly know that?"

"I'm an investigator, Ceddars. And I'm tiring of having to explain this simple fact to you."

"You mean… Simmons has also been murdered?"

I don't reply.

"You're not going to tell me?"

"My dear Ceddars, I sometimes wonder that I tell you too much." We reach the Bugatti. "Either you are driving me or I'm heading there on my own, which is it?"

Ceddars shakes his head and gets into the driving seat. "You are incorrigible!"

I sit next to him. "Yes, you've already told me that… remember?"

Five minutes later, we find the police car parked on the road opposite Dooleys Wood between mine and Ceddars' residences. Ceddars guides the Bugatti to a stop, and we jump out.

It's now late evening and the sun is soon to set. Dooleys Wood has an eerie presence at the best of times, but in the darkening hues of the approaching evening it is especially menacing.

Ceddars winks at me. "We'd better watch out for any more falling branches, what?"

I say nothing. Ceddars saved me once today. Perhaps he will come to regret it.

We soon catch up with Troughton, Sheng, and a breathless Constable Jakes, staying at a reasonable distance. Troughton can't force us to leave—this is a public area after all—but I've had too many confrontations with the man today and hanging back is the best option.

The small group enters a small glade and I hear Constable Jakes gasp in shock. I rush forward to see Curate Simmons lying prone on the ground under a tree branch with a cut rope hanging from it. The other end is tied in a crude knot around his neck that is bent at an odd angle. The same rope used to tie me up in the man's cellar. Simmons' face is red and puffy, his tongue, which protrudes from his mouth, black and swollen. A stool lies on the ground next to him.

"I say! The silly bugger took his own life!" Ceddars blurts.

With our cover broken, I stride forward. Troughton eyes me, shaking his head, but leaves me be.

"Went for walk to clear my head. Found him hanging," Sheng says quietly. "Cut him down. But he dead."

I go over to the body and give it a once over. He's wearing the same cassock I saw him in earlier. I examine the rope around his neck and its crude knot, remembering that the ropes that bound me in Simmons' cellar were tied more expertly. I sniff the fabric of his cassock, getting a raised eyebrow from Troughton who is content to let me continue. Next, I touch the exposed skin. Simmons is cold. He's been here for a while. I uncover his feet. The blood has already pooled there, staining the skin dark red, confirming my hypothesis. I lift Simmons' hands, checking them one after the other. His callouses tell me that the man was left-handed. I rub the bump on the back of my head. It's on the right side of my skull. I know from a study of cranial injuries that on average, a left-handed person will strike from the left, a right-handed person from the right.

"Well," Troughton says finally. "He killed himself, yes? This wasn't foul play?"

I nod. "I'd say there is a very good likelihood he took his own life."

Troughton beams. "And you, doctor? Do you concur with

Little Pucklewick's self-proclaimed sleuth? Although I'm not sure your opinion will count for anything anymore."

Ceddars performs the same examinations. "Yes, absolutely. There appears to be no bruising that I can see, apart from around the neck and no lacerations to the throat. A man with free hands would scrabble at the rope around his neck. It looks like he did this awful thing to himself."

"Good," Troughton says. "Of course, we will get Doctor Fellows from Upper Cockshoot to verify these findings, but I think this wraps everything up very nicely. Very nicely indeed."

Ceddars assists me in rolling the body over and I notice folded paper protruding from Simmons' pocket. I grab it before Troughton can stop me. I recognise the same jagged writing style I witnessed on the cellar wall in Simmons' house. I quickly read the words and feel incredibly sorry for the dead curate.

"Give it here!" Troughton commands, snatching it from me.

"It's the suicide note. The reason why he killed himself."

Troughton gives it the once-over. "Jesus Christ! No wonder he did what he did." He takes a steadying breath. "Inspector Jakes, can you please call the undertaker, again. And stay with the body. I need to make a few phone calls. Mr Sheng, I will also need you to accompany me to the police station. I will need a statement."

"What did the note say?" Ceddars asks.

"Simmons knew the real Wilson-Smallsey," I reply. "His extortion and blackmail, his drinking and gambling and his adultery. But his madness pushed that knowledge to extremity. He saw the vicar as an evil force working for the Devil himself. And within his delusion, he came to believe Billy Brown was the Antichrist. The Devil's son born on earth."

"Billy? But he was just a normal lad."

"I'm not sure if Simmons was following the boy, or came upon him by chance, but when the moment came, Simmons deliberately ran him over. You remember that the field had been trampled around Billy's body when we found him? That was Simmons. Apparently, the collision didn't kill him instantly. Billy screamed and cried, wanting Simmons to help him, wanting God to help him. And in that moment, Simmons realised he had murdered an innocent. As to the next events? We can only guess. Simmons left the scene and parked the van back in its garage. At some point, he decided to take his own life and made his way into Dooleys Wood."

"Golly. That's quite a story. Are you still sure he didn't kill the vicar and Eriksen?"

"I'm positive that he didn't."

"I'm wondering if perhaps you are also not quite well. You're recovering from a serious illness and now a blow to the head."

"And therein lies the biggest clue of them all."

"It does?"

"You examined the body as I did?"

Ceddars nods. "Did I miss something?"

"You tell me."

The doctor frowns, his moustache twitching with irritation. "Confound it woman! Are you trying to confuse and befuddle me? What in tarnation are you talking about?"

I grab Ceddars' hand and give it a squeeze. "You want answers, then I suggest you be dressed and ready early tomorrow morning. I want you to come and pick me up. I have a few errands to run."

"But Em', I—"

I put my finger to his hairy lip. "I'm very tired, Ceddars. And my head is thumping. I need a change of clothes, some food, and some sleep. I suggest you go home and do the same. I will see you at nine tomorrow morning."

Toast & Motives

"**MISS!** I'm sorry to wake you, but that Doctor Roberts is downstairs! I don't know why he's here, miss. He shouldn't be out at all, never mind making house calls, especially after we found out what he were up to with that Fran Feltham. An' him also lying to the police! I told him he had to go to the back door. That's where he is now. I'm not letting' him in, miss. Not after what he's done. I have my morals, miss, and that ain't right. It just ain't."

I open my eyes to find Molly staring down at me. She is flustered, her russet curls bouncing around her rounded, reddened face. Another fire roars in a fireplace on the far wall facing me whilst a draft of air blows inside from flung open windows. Molly is a peculiar character, that much is for sure. Nevertheless, the combination of warmth and an early morning breeze refreshes me. I'm reminded of being woken almost exactly the same way… *was it yesterday?*

I push myself up into a sitting position. "What time is it?"

"Nine in the mornin', miss. I know you said eight on the dot, and were very insistent, but after the day you had yesterday with the vicar dyin' and then that poor Simmons fellow knockin' you over the head and tryin' to burn you alive, I thought… well, I thought it best to let you sleep in, miss. But now that doctor fellow is here an' he's sayin' that you were supposed to be meetin' him. That can't be right can it, miss?"

"Let the man in and give him some tea and whatever else he wants. I'm late and need to get dressed." I push myself out of bed and make my way over to the toilet.

"Let him in? I don't think I can, miss. Not with the way he's been carryin' on of late. I was hopin' you'd be wantin' me to shoo him away. Or even call the police!"

"The police?" I remember Troughton and his single-handed attempt to scupper his own investigation. "The police would be a very bad idea, although I will be talking to the inspector later. Now, do as you're told and let Ceddars in."

Molly stands up straight, planting her hands firmly on her rotund hips. "Well, I'm afraid I can't do that, miss. It'd be against all good grace."

I stifle a yawn. "You work for me, Molly, and I suppose that means you do what I tell you, right?"

"You might not care about your reputation, miss, but I've still got mine to worry about. I won't do it miss. And if you don't send him away now, I'll have to hand in my cards. And I don't want to do that, miss. I really don't."

"From what I've been told, Molly, you were lucky to get work here in the first place. Would you really throw it away over something as unimportant as a simple assignation?"

Molly crosses her arms. "You don't understand, miss. I live in the village and that kind of behaviour, well, it taints everyone who comes into contact with it."

"I suppose it's a warm morning. Tell Ceddars I'll meet him outside in the lane. Will that suffice?"

Molly bursts into tears. "Oh, miss. Thank you! I thought I were going to have to go! And only after working here a few days. You made the right decision, miss. And I don't know what you've got planned today, but you can't be seen with the likes of him no more. You can't." She wipes her eyes and takes a steadying breath. "I'll tell him now, miss. And I'll make you a nice full English. Bacon, sausages, eggs, beans, mushrooms and my special friedy bread."

"Friday bread? But today's Tuesday."

"Not *Friday*, miss, fried bread in lard. *Friedy bread!*"

"Lard? Ew. Just a slice of toast will do."

"Just toast? You sure? I can add drippin' to it if you'd like?"

I have no idea what *drippin'* is, but it sounds quite disgusting. "Just buttered toast. I'll be down in a few minutes."

She bustles out of the room, shaking her head, and I quickly get ready. My plan was to kick things off earlier, but I'm thankful for the extra rest. At least my headache has disappeared and the bump on the back of my head has gone down a little. I perform my early morning ablutions and get dressed. Having a uniform of sorts means I can get ready a lot quicker than most women. I pull on my black trousers and coat, and only slow down to choose a hat, ending up with a bright blue, furry fez with a faux ruby pinned to the side. I need to look my best when I expose Little Pucklewick's murderer.

Nice.

The toast that Mollie has lovingly prepared is two great slabs of scorched bread smothered in butter. I baulk when she offers me the plate, but find I'm ravenous, and wolf it down very much to Molly's satisfaction. "And this is for later," she says, handing me a warm package wrapped in grease proof paper. "A freshly made bacon and egg sandwich."

I take it off her and drop it into one of my many pockets.

"Are you sure bein' seen with that Doctor Roberts is a good idea?"

"Absolutely. We are off to visit Mary Wilson-Smallsey at the vicarage."

"What? The vicar's poor widow? And you're takin' Ceddars? I mean, Doctor Roberts with you! There's no way she'll let him in."

"She will, I'm absolutely sure about that."

"Well, she'll be makin' a terrible mistake if she did. And you shouldn't be seen with him at all. You don't know what he might try and do. A man like that, well—"

"I'm afraid men are all like that, as are quite a few women.

Now, stop your blathering, it's small-minded and tedious. And, I'm very serious about this, do not tell anyone where I'm going this morning. Understand? Or I *will* fire you."

"I'm just lookin' out for you, miss, is all."

"And I appreciate it. But from now on, you will remember that I am a detective. That it is my job to mix with those many may see as undesirable. If you cannot deal with that, then you will have to leave my employ. Do you understand?"

"But things are not that simple in Little Pucklewick, they're just not."

I catch Molly with my eyes and give her a hard stare. "I will not be stopping in Little Pucklewick. After today, I will be making plans to leave for London. If you want to come with me, then your attitudes will need to be amended."

"London, miss? You're movin' to London? An' you want me to move with you?" She sits down with a thump on a kitchen stool. "London? That's always been my dream, miss. But…"

"But what?"

"I've only ever lived here, miss. In Little Pucklewick. Nowheres else."

"You'll have a few days to think it over. Now, I need a pair of scissors."

"Scissors? In the draw by the stove, miss. What d'ya want them for?"

"I'll bring them back later today." I take a large gulp of tea and head for the door. "And remember… do not speak one word of where I'm going to anybody, understand? Especially Ethel."

"I won't, miss."

"I want you to promise me."

"Cross my heart and hope to die." She makes a dramatic cross on her chest with her hands and curtsies.

"Good. I'm relying on you, Molly. You're part of my team now. You understand what that means?"

"Yes, miss. I do."

I walk outside into the warm morning, as surprised as Molly with my decision to move to London. But it makes sense. I'm not sure why I came here in the first place…

"What ho!" Ceddars says mutedly as I walk up to him, cutting a lonely figure standing on the opposite side of the road and leaning on the vicarage wall. "I've had quite the experience with your maid. Wouldn't let me in the house and shooed me out of your garden with a large broom, what? Then again, I suppose I'm person non-grata number one in the village right now. You'd think it was me who killed the vicar and those other poor souls. Now, what is this all about? I'm feeling, well, not tip-top. Rather the opposite as it happens. The scandal with Fran Feltham has quite ruined me, and I'm at somewhat of a low ebb. I'm only here because you asked me, Em'. To be honest, I didn't want to leave the old HQ at all."

"We're off to see Mary."

"Mary? What? No, no, no. Why on earth would you want to do that? No! There's no way I should be showing my face at the vicarage or anywhere else in the village. Not now, not ever."

"Curate Simmons didn't murder the Reverend Wilson-Smallsey, nor William Eriksen. Today, I will reveal the true murderer, and I want you there with me."

"Are you sure it's not Simmons? The man was short of a tent peg or three. A total loon."

"Is that your considered medical opinion, doctor?"

"What is wrong with you, Em'? It's like you don't want to believe anything that's put in front of you. But let's slow down a moment and have a think about what you are doing. You upset a lot of people yesterday and I'm worried you will make it bally well worse for yourself?"

"Enough for one of them to try and burn me alive?"

"That was obviously Simmons!"

I shake my head. "The curate was responsible for Billy's death and took his own life because of it. He only confessed to running Billy over. Not the other murders. And he certainly didn't attack me yesterday."

"But confound it, Em'! It has to be him. Who else could've done it and why?"

"Everyone has got motives, Ceddars."

"Everyone?"

"Very much so. Today, we will examine all of the suspects and all their motives—*and all of their lies*—before I reveal the murderer."

"And to do that we have to visit the vicarage, and Mary?"

"I have a plan, a plan you will help me with."

"I see… hang on, is that bacon I can smell?"

Falsehoods & Fingernails

"**Y**OU again! And the doctor!" Charlotte says as she opens the Vicarage front door. "What do you think you're playing at?"

"I've had enough hysterics from maids this morning, Charlotte. Can you please just tell the lady of the house that we want to see her."

"I will certainly not. That man ain't setting foot inside here. No way." Charlotte looks over my shoulder and shrugs. "I'm sorry, doctor, but you understand. But then again, you should have more sense than to be making house visits. You just should have."

"This isn't my idea, old girl," Ceddars says, brushing breadcrumbs from the bacon sandwich out of his moustache. "Miss Crookshanks has a plan and well, who am I to dare go against that."

I raise my hand. "Go and tell Mary that we want to see her. That it's very urgent."

"Both of you?"

"Yes, me and the good doctor."

"Alright, but you're not comin' in to wait. There's no point. I know what she'll say." She closes the door with a thump.

"I told you Em', there's no way Mary will invite us inside, especially me. Are you sure that bump on the head didn't do you any harm?"

"Stay here."

"I say, what? Where in tarnation do you think you're going?"

"You'll soon see."

"You can't leave me here, Em'? I've told you. I'm persona non grata."

"Charlotte will let you in shortly."

"What?

"Do you trust me?"

"I'm not exactly sure that I do."

"See you in a minute or two."

I leave a perplexed and irritated-looking Ceddars and head around to the back of the vicarage, to the wall of ivy underneath the small east-facing window I viewed inside Mary's rooms. Mary loved her trophies and trinkets and yet the ledge in front of this window was curiously uncluttered. The reason was obvious to me. I quickly climb up, using a wooden lattice that acts like a ladder, until I'm level with Mary's windows. I watch as Mary dismisses Charlotte before I open the window and clamber inside.

Mary starts when she sees me, and then stares at me dumbfounded.

"Yes," I say, straightening my trousers, and jacket, and repositioning my blue fez to sit at its preferred jaunty angle. "I know how you've been secretly getting in and out of the vicarage. And if you don't get Charlotte to admit Ceddars at once, I'll announce this fact on the telephone. I'm sure Ethel will love to discover that your supposed infirmity is a complete sham."

"Wh-what?"

"You heard me, Mary. And please don't pretend to swoon or pass out again. It won't work. Now get Ceddars up here, otherwise it won't just be your feigned illness I will talk about, believe me. I take out the folded poster that Mrs Willoughby gave to me yesterday, and put it on her table.

A few minutes later a bewildered looking Ceddars is shown into the room by Charlotte. The maid draws breath to speak, but Mary silences her with a raised hand. "Go now and tell no one about this. And if you think I don't know about your habit of listening at my door, you're very much mistaken."

After Charlotte has departed, Mary sits down at her table, her eyes staring into the distance.

"How the bally hell did you get in here?" Ceddars blurts, pointing at me.

"I'll tell you later."

"I'm very sorry, Mary," Ceddars continues. "This is entirely Emily's idea, I had no—"

I raise my hand. "Mary," I begin, with no prelude. "I want you to do something for me with no questions asked. You understand?"

Mary turns towards me, her face suddenly stern. "No questions asked? Don't be ridiculous."

"I'm being perfectly serious."

"And what if I refuse?"

I reach over to the folded poster. "When I talked to you yesterday, you were very keen to throw suspicion on Curate Simmons. You wanted me to believe it was him operating the printing press and arranging for these posters to be put up around the village. But it wasn't Simmons who was responsible, was it? It was you, Mary."

"I say! Have you gone quite insane, Em'? Mary is in no physical state to do such a thing."

"In that regard, doctor, you are very much mistaken. Have you fully examined her? Have you any evidence other than what you've been told by the vicar's wife?"

"Well, no… but why would Mary lie? Even Wilson-Smallsey explained she was infirm."

"Why would I lie?" Mary replies angrily, giving Ceddars a shock. "It was because I despised my husband! I made a bad marriage. It was obvious from the start. I married for love, he married for my name. I soon came to realise what kind of man he was. And as for my role as the vicar's wife? I had no stomach for it. I wanted nothing to do with those obsequious women he surrounded himself with, so I made a deal with him. I'd leave him to live his life if he left me to live mine. Hence… my illness. I thought I'd won a victory, that I'd found a way to be independent, but I soon realised that illness or no, I was trapped in this room, and in this damn house."

Ceddars gasps. "Oh, Mary, I'm so sorry."

"Don't be too sorry, Ceddars. Mary was attempting to bring her husband down, isn't that correct?"

"His drinking was getting out of hand," Mary continues, a sense of relief in her voice. I guess she is pleased to speak the truth for a change. "As was his gambling and womanising. I'd had enough of this life. Of being stuck in this room. I thought if I started enough rumours, he might come tumbling down. It would give me a reason to divorce him. Of course, I'd never be able to get married again, but I'm sure polite society would've forgiven me for his sins."

"So it really was you, Mary," Ceddars says. "You paid someone to put up those posters?"

"Not quite," I reply.

Mary turns to me. "But how did you find out?"

"Amongst many other things, I am an expert on the human form. On size, shape, and height." I look at Ceddars. "Remember when we found those drawing pins in the village oak and you asked me about the two clues I'd found? Firstly, I noticed that all the posters were pinned at a certain height. Your height, Mary. And the indentations around the pins told me they were pushed in by someone with long fingernails. A female. I noticed your fingernails the first time we met." I nod towards her youthful trophies. "You also have awards for acting. And as you were at an all-girls school, it makes sense that some girls played the male roles. You must have had experience as dressing as a man. In disguising yourself. It was then easy for me to conclude that the stranger seen around town by Mrs Willoughby and Constable Jakes, was in fact you."

"No way!" Ceddars shouts. "But… but didn't you attack me and Emily in the church vaults?"

"She did indeed, Ceddars. Why else was I so keen to return to the vicarage afterwards? I wanted to catch her. Mary must've climbed into her rooms the way I did just now, through the small window to the east."

"So that's how you bally well got inside."

I nod. "The windowsill is slightly scuffed with leather from a pair of brown boots. And the last time I was here, I noticed that it's impossible to lock this window. Meaning that I could let myself in the way Mary has done possibly countless times. The tree outside provides excellent cover. It was obvious to me that someone had been climbing in and out of your rooms. And that someone was you, Mary."

"You think yourself so very clever, Miss Crookshanks."

"That's because I am so very clever, Mary Smallsey. And it was also you who gave Billy that pound note to spread rumours about Curate Simmons, wasn't it? A rumour about seeing him coming out of the vaults. I was suspicious as soon as Billy told me that information. He was too eager."

"You appear to know everything."

"I do. And as I said, I want you to do something for me, otherwise I will reveal all."

"I see."

"I want you to invite the following people for a Tuesday morning get-together at eleven o'clock this morning." I take out a list of names I prepared last night and pass it to her.

"But I'm in mourning and my husband has been revealed as a philandering blackmailer and gambler. People will think this odd behaviour."

"You are *still* very much respected in this village. If you ask, they will all come."

"And what is this get-together for? What is it about?"

"I will reveal who murdered your husband."

"You don't think it was the curate?"

I shake my head emphatically.

Mary glances at the list. "And that's why you want Inspector Troughton and Constable Jakes to also be in attendance?"

"Very much so."

"And you even want me to invite Ethel, from the exchange. That horrible rumour-monger? Are you absolutely sure?"

"Everyone on that list."

"And what of myself? You don't expect me to be at this get-together of yours… do you? You may have discovered my secret, but to everyone else, I'm still infirm."

"Let's say you are having one of your *good* days."

"I'll send these damn invites, but I won't attend."

"It's your choice, you can either be ready downstairs in the sitting room at eleven o'clock this morning to receive your visitors, or you can climb out of your window and disappear. Of course, if you do not show up, I will have to make a phone call to Inspector Troughton… and even if he's not interested in who was putting up those posters, I'm sure Ethel will be thrilled."

"I suppose I have no choice in this matter."

"You don't. "Now, we'll leave you to write your invitations. I will return at just before eleven. Good morning."

Outside, Ceddars moustache twitches in consternation. "I can't believe Mary pulled the wool over my eyes like that. And for so long. How could I have been so dim?"

"My dear doctor, it may not have escaped your notice that Mary is an attractive woman. A very attractive woman. A state of being that I'm afraid you, and a lot of other men, are somewhat susceptible to. I wouldn't blame yourself. You're not alone."

"Even so, Em', I'm supposed to be a professional."

"You may have spent years learning your profession and

taken the Hippocratic Oath, but's quite obvious to me that your heart just isn't in the medical profession."

"You know what, Em'? Sometimes you are so high-handed that… well… it can quite put a chap off, what?"

"But I'm right."

"Are you?"

I give him an emphatic nod of the head. "Doctoring is for more serious men."

Ceddars gives me a hurt look. "Oh…"

"Don't get yourself down about it. When I say serious, I mean of course, very dry, dull, and quite boring. Attributes you simply do not possess. You, my dear Ceddars, are a far more complex and interesting individual."

"Crikey, that sounds like you are actually giving me a compliment for once."

"Possibly."

"What next?"

"I want you to drive me to Upper Cockshoot library."

"The library? It's a very dry, dull, and quite boring place. I'm not sure you'll like it very much."

"Libraries are never boring, and rarely dull, Ceddars. And this one is of particular interest to me. I believe it holds an archive of the national papers. Most larger libraries do, and there is a particular article that I'm interested in finding."

Ceddars appears worried. "I see… and you need this article for what reason?"

"Proof."

"You're not telling me why?"

"And spoil the surprise? We'll need the Bugatti. Let's make our way back to your house." I stroll off, followed by an agitated Ceddars.

"I'm not sure this is a good idea, old girl… I mean, Em'…Emily. Just being seen with me is enough to ruin your reputation. To go to my house where… well, where that unfortunate assignation occurred with Fran…" His voice dries.

"Ceddars. There is one thing you need to understand about me."

"And what's that?"

"I don't give a wet sock what these jumped up, small-minded, hypocritical folk think of me. I am an expert on human nature. So-called morals are only a hindrance to that study. Humans are messy. They steal, murder, and blackmail. They are driven in many differing ways. And yes, Ceddars, they have sex. They want and need it. A desire that I believe is part of the healthy functioning of the human mind and body."

"I say, that's a very modern outlook. To be honest, I've been thinking much the same myself."

"People know the fundamental truths around their own bodies, and their desires. They may pretend to hide behind their so-called morals, but the animal always lurks within—squatting underneath all the crinoline and lace, the fancy clothes, the perfumes, the finery, and the gilded religious books. And it is with this animal that I concern myself. Understanding its desires are fundamental when it comes to solving mysteries, and I exist only for the mystery. Everything else is secondary to me."

"That's a very bleak outlook. What about romance?"

"That has a part to play, of course. Love is motivation enough for any crime you may care to mention."

"You misunderstand me, Em'. I mean, what about you? Do you ever succumb to it? To the fluttering heart and the heaving bosom and all that?"

"I'm just as human as the next person. And just because you think my outlook is bleak, doesn't mean that I'm not susceptible to the same human weaknesses. Apparently, the reason I was forced to leave South Africa was because of them." I give Ceddars a pointed look. "And humans are apt to repeat the same mistakes."

"You see romance as a weakness?"

"If it interferes with my investigations, very much so. If not, I'm all for it. Now, enough of this idle chatter. I have a murderer to expose."

"Are you absolutely sure you've got it right this time? Because the last time you sounded this confident, well, you kind of made a bit of a hash of it."

He's right, I realise. I've gotten things wrong and made quite a few missteps along the way, and yet, now I know who killed the Vicar and Eriksen, and how those two murders are connected, I'm filled with expectation. I'm very close to the revelation, a moment I live for. "All will be explained back at the vicarage."

"Troughton won't be pleased, that much is for sure. You've certainly put the old chap's back up. He's absolutely convinced Simmons is his guy. And, well, I still can't see who else could've done it, or why?"

"Like I said, all will be revealed later."

Ceddars strokes at his moustache in irritation. "I suppose I will be forced to indulge you. But even after all your fine words about moral hypocrisy, I'm still rather unhappy that your reputation will be tainted by your association with me. I really shouldn't be out and about, and certainly not in the company of respectable ladies."

"Ceddars, I am not respectable, nor am I a lady. I am an investigator first and foremost. My reputation is not your concern, nor the concern of any man… or woman for that matter. If you do not wish to drive me to Upper Cockshoot, then lend me your car."

"Well, that's easily decided. I was quite put out you were driving around in my old jalopy while I was resting behind bars. The Bugatti is a machine that needs expert handling."

"Good," I reply as we arrive at Ceddars' house. "Now let's get on."

Twenty minutes later, we pull up at the Upper Cockshoot

library in Ceddars' Bugatti. The doctor is keen to find out what I'm here for, but I make him stay outside. Luckily, I remember the date of the article I'm searching for. And after a short search, I find it, surreptitiously cutting it out of the binding book with Molly's scissors and slipping it into one of my many pockets.

"Well?" Ceddars asks when I return. "Did you get what you came for?"

I ignore his question. "Let's go back to Little Pucklewick and the vicarage, and take the scenic route, we have the time."

"You're not going to show me?"

"Fire up the Bugatti, Ceddars, all will be revealed in time."

Ceddars, still worried about my reputation, guides the Bugatti to the vicarage via the road outside my cottage after a long, invigorating drive. "We're here." He looks at his watch. "And ten minutes early. Good luck."

"I'm sorry, Ceddars, but you're coming in with me."

"What? Go inside again? No way, Em'! No way! It was bad enough that I accompanied you earlier when we talked to Mary. I can't be part of this. It will be wrong for me to be there."

"Do you remember kissing me?"

Ceddars is shocked. "Well, of course I do. A chap wouldn't forget that. I shouldn't have done so, of course I shouldn't, seeing that I'd been with Fran earlier. But in the moment, with the rain and whatnot, and you in that rather fetching outfit and all our banter, I kind of got carried away."

"You took advantage of me."

He hangs his head in shame. "I did. I'm so sorry, Em'. I was a cad. It was a cad thing to do."

"I must admit to rather enjoying it. But I didn't know about you and the Fran girl. You should've told me before sticking your tongue down my throat."

"Oh Em', don't be so gross. You make it sound so ugly."

"I will forgive you."

He raises his head, his eyes full of hope. "You will?"

"On one condition."

"You mean…?"

"Yes, I want you at the meeting with me. You've been my right-hand man all the way through this. It's only right that you should be with me at the end. And besides, I don't want you out of my sight."

"But what about Mary and those women?"

"Mary won't be a problem. As for anyone else, let me deal with them. Now, are you coming?"

"I suppose I don't have a choice."

"No, my good doctor, you do not."

Death & Denouement

I'M surprised to find Mary up, dressed all in black, and waiting for our arrival in the vicarage sitting room.

I smile at her. "I see you took my advice."

"If you are sure Simmons wasn't responsible for the death of my husband, then I want to find out who, even if only to satisfy my curiosity."

I say nothing. Whatever reasons she may pretend to be giving, she is here for one reason and one reason only... *I gave her no choice.* Mary might just survive the social fallout from the murder of her philandering husband, but if it ever came to light that she was responsible for posting those nasty rumours about him and paid Billy to implicate Curate Simmons, she'd never live it down. Her name would be synonymous with her husband.

"And you have brought the doctor again. Do you think that is wise, considering the recent revelations about his disgusting and vile behaviour?"

"It wasn't my idea to be here, old girl, I mean, Mary... Mrs Wilson-Smallsey. I wanted to be back home at the old HQ. But Em', Miss Crookshanks, had other ideas."

"Yes, she is quite the force of nature." Mary turns to me. "Why did you bring him?"

I do not give her the courtesy of an answer. "We will wait in the boot room by the front door until everyone is here."

The doorbell rings a short time later followed by the sound of hushed voices. I can see the entrance hallway via a crack in the door. Mrs Willoughby, Dorothy Knight, and her son Eugene have seemingly arrived together, although the two women are studiously ignoring one another. There are also the regulars from the vicarage Monday morning get-togethers, and a petite older woman with a pinched face, her hair in a tight grey bun, whom I'm guessing is the famous Ethel from the telephone exchange. It appears no one wanted to be late for Mary's little get-together. I suppose it's quite unprecedented. Widows usually disappear into mourning, especially those whose philandering husbands were murdered for their sins, so this meeting is a 'must-attend'. I also hear the thin, whiny tones of Inspector Troughton asking why Constable Jakes is here.

"I were invited, sir. By the vicar's wife herself." He holds up a handwritten note.

"Let me see that… This is all very odd, don't you think, constable? Very odd indeed."

"That's what my wife said, sir. But I couldn't not come, could I, sir?"

The doorbell rings a second time, and the door is opened to reveal Sheng looking respectful in a Chinese-style black jacket and trousers. Charlotte, the maid, baulks when she sees him but lets him in without comment. I assume that Mary has had very strong words with her this morning. At least she hasn't handed in her cards like Molly threatened to do.

The voices disappear into the sitting room, and we follow them, hanging outside.

"I say, Em'," Ceddars whispers. "I'm a tad nervous, what? You really want me to go in there… with all those people. The shame of it."

"You are very much a part of this, and besides, someone in this house is a murderer. I'm sure your presence will become a secondary concern once they are revealed."

"One can only hope so… what?"

"It's so good to see you up and about, Mary," I overhear Mrs Gladys Willoughby saying. "Especially after yesterday's awful events." She, like everyone else, is wondering what this occasion is all about, and cannot hide her curiosity at Mary's sudden recovery.

"Thank you, Mrs Willoughby," Mary replies. "I'm very pleased you could all make it this morning, and so promptly. But I'm afraid it wasn't my idea to invite you all here."

"It wasn't?" Inspector Troughton says. "I don't understand."

I grab Ceddars by the arm and drag him into the sitting room, a rather large and somewhat bleak room with a wooden floor, worn carpets and ancient looking curtains. I close the door behind us and stand in front of it. "I asked Mary to invite you all," I say, "and she kindly acquiesced."

"You?" Inspector Troughton says, his voice almost shouting, his eyes flicking between myself and Mary.

The man is unsure how to act, but he, like everyone else cannot do anything. They were invited here by the dead vicar's wife, and their misplaced sense of decency means they will not be leaving anytime soon, even if I have somewhat hijacked proceedings. "Yes, inspector, me. Miss Emily Crookshanks."

"What is she doing here?" Dorothy Knight says. "And the disgraced doctor? His presence is demeaning us all."

"And that dreadful Sheng fellow?" Mrs Willoughby adds, from between coughs, a black lace handkerchief covering her mouth. "It's disgusting."

Mary gives both ladies a sweet smile. She is trying her best to hide her dislike for these women, her acting skills again coming to the fore. "I will leave that to Miss Crookshanks to explain."

"Thank you, Mary." My use of her first name startles the others, but I carry on. "I am here to reveal the murderer of the Reverend Wilson-Smallsey and the explorer, William Eriksen."

Dorothy Knight sits back in shock. "I beg your pardon? Wasn't it the Curate? Didn't he confess, inspector?"

"No, not for the vicar and Mr Eriksen," Troughton answers from a clenched jaw. "His suicide note only mentioned poor Billy Brown. But I have very good reasons to believe he was the culprit. Evidence Miss Crookshanks herself found in the curate's cellar showed the man was deranged. That he had an unhealthy interest in the vicar's..." The inspector gives Mary an apologetic look, "...in the vicar's wrongdoings. He knew all about them. I'm sorry, Mrs Smallsey, but Simmons thought your husband was the devil himself. Isn't that correct Miss Crookshanks?"

"It is, inspector and—"

"And isn't it true that Simmons found you in his cellar snooping around, like you have a habit of doing, and that he hit you over the head and tried to burn you alive?"

"No, inspector, that wasn't Simmons."

"Troughton scoffs. "It wasn't?"

I turn to Ceddars. "Doctor, what is your professional opinion on the time of Curate Simmons' death?"

Ceddars flushes red. "The time of his death. Crikey!"

Mrs Willoughby jumps to her feet, dressed in a rather absurdly over-the-top black outfit, her black handkerchief ready to stifle her coughing which I've noticed is getting markedly worse. "Really, you are going to let this awful man speak? After what he admitted to, after what was done with that Fran Feltham harlot? I'm sorry Mary, but this is too much." She bustles towards me.

I stand my ground, blocking the door. "The doctor will say his piece and you will listen. Mary has asked us all here to find out the truth and no one will be leaving until that truth has been exposed." I glance over to the vicar's widow for support, and she begrudgingly complies.

"My husband was murdered," Mary says, her voice a lot louder than the gentle sing-song I've been used to, "and I have invited Miss Crookshanks here to tell us what she has found out. For good or bad. The sooner you let her, and the doctor, speak, the sooner this will all be over. Now please, Mrs Willoughby, *Gladys*, sit down."

Mrs Willoughby grumbles but acquiesces.

"Continue Ceddars, Doctor Roberts."

Ceddars takes a deep breath, preening his moustache nervously. "Um well. Let me think back. When I examined Simmons in Dooleys Wood, soon after the fire was put out at his cottage, I found the man's skin was ashen, showing a certain degree of lividity. Rigor had begun to set in and, um, the pooling of blood in his legs from the hanging suggested, that um… he'd been dead for, I'd say three to four hours. Oh my!" Ceddars grasps his lower jaw. "There's no way he could have attacked you, Em'. He was already dead! I'm such an idiot. Why didn't I connect that before? You must think me such an awful doofus."

"In your professional opinion, doctor, you believe Curate Simmons hung himself long before I was attacked. Is that correct?"

"Yes, unmistakably."

"He looked fresh enough to me," Troughton says. "And the coroner from Upper Cockshoot agrees."

Ceddars raises his eyebrows. "Does he now? But you must know that Doctor Fellows is a dreadful lush. You can't trust his opinion."

"And we are to believe yours?" Troughton says, waving his Homburg. "The man who yesterday lied to me about murdering the victims, who was having an out-of-wedlock assignation with a girl half his age. Not only are you a liar, doctor, you are disgusting."

A chorus of consternation follows the exchange. I hold up my hand until the voices die down. "May I ask, inspector, did the coroner, Doctor Fellows, inspect the body?"

Troughton shuffles in his chair. "Well, no, he didn't actually. He was unable to come over in person. I talked to him on the phone. He was happy enough with my description to agree with me that Simmons was recently deceased and was alive at the time of the attack on yourself."

I turn to Ethel, who is standing at the back of the long room behind the others, a startled look on her face when she realises I'm about to talk to her. "Did you overhear the exchange between Doctor Fellows, the coroner, and Inspector Troughton?"

"I… I'm sure I don't know, miss."

"Isn't it your usual habit to listen in on phone conversations and then to share the contents of those conversations around the village?"

Ethel turns a pale shade of grey. "No, miss, no. I would never do that."

I hear Mary scoffing behind me. "But you did overhear the conversation I'm referring to?"

Ethel looks terrified and she's a right to be. I'm being at my most intimidating.

"I might've overheard part of the conversation…"

"Then tell us what you heard."

"You don't have to say anything you don't want to, Ethel," Troughton says, "this isn't a trial."

"Shush, inspector," Mary says, "I want to hear Ethel's answer. Go on and tell us the truth."

"Well," Ethel begins nervously, "it's as Doctor Roberts says, the coroner sounded very much worse the wear for drink, to me. He wasn't sober." Her voice gains more confidence. "It's why he couldn't come over and look at the body. And I've heard the rumours about him too. It's well known he's a drunk. Famous for it."

"And the inspector would've noticed this?"

Ethel glances at Troughton and at her eager audience. "I'm very sorry, Inspector, but yes, yes, he would. He did."

I smile. "Do you think the coroner was sober enough to give a medical opinion?"

Ethel shakes her head emphatically. "Oh no, miss. He

wasn't. He was quite puddled."

"Thank you, Ethel." I turn back to the upturned faces, ignoring the thunderous expression on Inspector Troughton's face. "Doctor Roberts may have revealed that he possesses a lack of morals and decency normally associated with the doctoring profession, and it is indeed likely he will be struck off for his recent actions, but he is still a medically trained practitioner, and his opinion is one I agree with. I'm also a student of physiology, of death and its many causes and the effects of death on the body. There is no way Curate Simmons knocked me over the head and set fire to his cottage. He can't have. I was also struck by a right-handed person and Simmons was left-handed. No. My assailant attacked me to throw blame onto the curate, not knowing that he was dead at the time."

Troughton huffs and puffs. "That well may be, Miss Crookshanks, but he was certainly alive for the murders of the vicar and William Eriksen, for which I have posthumously charged him."

"I do wonder, inspector, if you have any interest in solving these murders at all, seeing that you have put obstacle after obstacle in way of this investigation."

Troughton sneers. "Have I now? Perhaps I should've listened when you came to the station with your outlandish theories about William Eriksen and his manservant, or shall I call him, his *special friend?* Were you or were you not convinced he was the murderer?" He looks around the gathering somewhat triumphantly.

"What ho, he's got you there, Em'," Ceddars whispers to me.

I ignore him, turning my attention to Sheng. "Yes, you are correct. I did think it was the explorer who was responsible for the murder of the not so Reverend Wilson-Smallsey, but that is simply because that is where the evidence led me. And, I also admit, I did get carried away with it. But a good investigator will sometimes travel the wrong path. However, all paths are part of the process if they lead to finding the guilty party… or parties. With that in mind, I must apologise for entering William's private quarters. It was wrong to do so, but the evidence I found was essential in unlocking the true character of the vicar. And knowing everything about the victim is vital in solving a murder." Sheng gives me a curt bow and I nod back respectfully. He is just as keen to find out who murdered his secret lover as Troughton is seemingly keen to blame the wrong man.

The inspector preens his moustache in victory. "You heard it from her in black and white. You got it wrong, didn't you Miss Crookshanks? Very wrong."

"And didn't you get it wrong by arresting Sheng, and then Ceddars?"

"There was compelling evidence to arrest both of those men!"

"Exactly. But, my dear inspector, the art of deduction is a stiletto, not a lump hammer."

Troughton scoffs again. "Alright then, Miss Crookshanks, if you think you know who the murderer is, why not tell everyone. I do not have all day to sit around listening to your nonsense, but if it will end this charade, I'm more than happy to let you get this out of your system so that we can all move on, especially Mrs Smallsey, who must be finding this quite galling."

"I will come to that forthwith, inspector. First, let us go through the sequence of events…. The explorer William Eriksen held a talk at the village hall two nights ago. A talk that was attended by almost everyone. Indeed, the vicar himself and Mrs Willoughby were there, although they were not as welcome as the others. They were successful in disrupting his talk and, in the commotion, a Chinese crossbow and a series of bolts were stolen. The murder weapon.

"Yesterday morning, the Reverend Wilson-Smallsey

rose at his normal hour and, as was his habit, wrote a series of letters and communications as well as reading his mail. Indeed, he wrote a note to myself, inviting himself for tea and cakes at my cottage at eleven in the morning. A letter delivered by the unfortunate Billy Brown. Billy then travelled to the Eriksen mansion where he let slip about the vicar's visit, meaning that Sheng, William Eriksen and his secretary Fran Feltham all knew where the vicar would be at the time he was murdered.

"Meanwhile, that same morning, the vicar received a note from Mrs Dorothy Knight. A note he read and burned in his fireplace, leaving one single scorched word, 'marriage'. This note was delivered by Eugene Knight, her son." I turn to the youth. "Isn't that right?"

He looks at his mother who gives her approval for him to answer. "Yes, yes I did."

"And what was in that note, Mrs Knight?"

The woman gives me a cold stare from puffy eyes, she is still grief-stricken about the death of William Eriksen, the man she was sure would marry her. "I told you all about that. Albert… I mean the vicar, forbade me and William to marry. I… I was very angry with him about it. I wrote him that note and told him to meet me at the church at ten that morning to discuss it."

"And what was the nature of the vicar's objection?"

"He said Eriksen was *ungodly*, a *heathen*."

"But surely he couldn't stop you, if that was your intention?" I flick a look at Sheng who appears to be confused by Mrs Knight's words. I believe a marriage is news to him.

Dorothy Knight's expression is one of pure sadness and loss. "But you know what Albert was like? He had a lot of power here. It's not easy to cross such a man. But it wasn't my marriage he was against, he was threatening to ruin William's career."

"He had been writing to the Royal Academy, is that

correct?”

She nods.

I give Mrs Knight a compassionate smile. “And, as awful as it is for Mary to hear, the vicar was a blackmailer. Did he have any hold over you to prevent this marriage?”

She shakes her head emphatically. “He wished. But I only recently arrived in the village, and I've always lived my life to the highest of virtues.”

“After you had your heated discussion with the vicar, where did you go?”

“I went home, as I told you before. I was very upset and needed to look my best for the Monday morning get-together.”

“And on your way home did you see any of these posters?” I hold up the poster I took from Mrs Willoughby.

“What? I don't understand,” Dorothy replies. “That's not what you showed me yesterday.”

I turn the poster around, realising it's Fran Feltham's fake letter of recommendation from *The Lady's Secretarial Agency*. I apologise and take out the actual poster and unfold it. “Did you see any of these? They were posted all over the village.”

“I was in too a tearful state to notice anything. Please put it away. I don't want to read those dreadful things again.”

“I see.” I fold up the poster and return it to my pocket. “As everyone is aware, after the conversation with Mrs Knight, the vicar then came to my cottage. On the way there, he fell into an argument with a gentleman who Eugene Knight assumed was Sheng, but who, it turned out, was Sheng's brother. It was at this point in my investigation, that I became convinced William Eriksen and Sheng had been working together to murder the vicar.”

“And you were quite wrong,” Troughton says.

I ignore the inspector and continue. “We have heard from Mrs Knight that Wilson-Smallsey was determined to destroy William Eriksen's career, and it came to my attention that the vicar was in possession of some rather explosive information regarding the explorer. Information that would indeed end his career. As to what that information was, I will not reveal, but—"

"We were together..." Sheng says, speaking for the first time, his English tinged with a thick Chinese accent.

"Together?" Mrs Knight intones.

Sheng bows, a look of pride running across his features. "Yes. Together."

"I was not going to reveal the nature of the information the vicar held over Eriksen's head, but this was indeed the scandal. Eriksen was a homosexual. And the reason why Sheng's brother came to Little Pucklewick—to convince him to leave his lover. And why he was disowned."

"No!" Mrs Knight shouts, standing up. "No, this cannot be! We were to be married! He loved me, not this vile foreigner... how dare you say such a disgusting thing!"

"Please sit down, Dorothy. What I will be revealing will be hard for everyone, but do not forget you are here at the invitation of Mary Smallsey."

Dorothy Knight sits down and frowns, and I see a million thoughts cross behind her eyes as she digests the information.

"It seemed entirely plausible that Eriksen and Sheng had used the arrival of Sheng's brother to plan a very clever murder. They knew where the vicar would be at eleven, they hid Fran Feltham's glasses, so she was forced to return home to look for them, and while Sheng was with his brother, Eriksen killed the vicar, knowing full well that Sheng would be the main suspect, but that he would be let free once his brother came forward. He even added to the evidence against Sheng himself, or so it seemed. I had discovered motive, opportunity, and a clever plan for murder. But it was too perfect. And I was proven to be... *sadly mistaken.*"

Troughton scoffs again, this time more loudly.

"And that mistake led to the death of William Eriksen. As to how, I will explain later. But first, let me get back to the sequence of events. The vicar visited my cottage at the proscribed hour of eleven o'clock and was shot through my open windows with the bolt fired from the crossbow stolen from Eriksen the night before. The bolt pierced his heart killing him instantly, convincing me that the person who shot the vicar must've been a marksman. And it was upon this premise that I based my original investigation."

"Soon after the killing, Doctor Roberts turned up, supposedly alerted to the murder by the screams and shouts of Molly that he heard through my cottage's open windows. I have wondered quite a lot about this. The shock of the vicar's killing meant I couldn't be absolutely sure when he arrived. Was it moments or minutes? And if minutes… how many? It certainly made him one of the chief suspects and it was for this reason that I decided to keep the doctor close.

"But I'm innocent," Ceddars says. "Everyone knows that… and *the rest*."

"Possibly."

"Just what are you getting at, Em'?"

"I'm saying you had more than enough motive to kill the vicar. The death in poverty of the postmaster's daughter and being blackmailed by the vicar about your affair with Fran Feltham were two strong reasons for murder.

"I say, Em', this is bang out of order!"

I stop him speaking with a raised hand. "As I mentioned earlier, Fran Feltham went back to her lodgings to supposedly look for her glasses. This was a convenient lie. We found out that she didn't go back to the Green Dragon, as the landlord was taking a delivery at the time, and he didn't see her. No, she was somewhere else. If her evidence yesterday is to believed, she was at the Doctor's house for a pre-planned assignation. However, the timings were never that precise. As you have heard, the doctor arrived at my house minutes after the murder, meaning their assignation must've been over, giving them time to get dressed and for the doctor to walk the short distance to my cottage. And if the doctor could be at my house close to the time of the murder... so could Fran."

"But Fran wouldn't kill anyone!" Ceddars blurts. "And besides, I saw her cycle off to Eriksen's before I made my way to poor Mrs Bates. Fran couldn't have done it!"

"Of course, she could."

"I don't understand, Em'. What on earth are you getting at?"

"I'm saying that you both had motive to murder the vicar. Fran Feltham's real name is *Francesca Wilson*. She is the vicar's illegitimate daughter."

"But we were seen!" Ceddars protests over the consternation and intakes of breath. "By that oily little tick, Eugene. He was spying on us."

"I don't doubt he did spy on you. I also don't doubt that your assignation took place. I'm left wondering what happened next. There was nothing stopping Fran cycling into Dooleys Woods once she left you. Nor running ahead to pick up the stashed weapon and kill the vicar. She could've done it alone or you could've planned it together."

"That's tosh!" Ceddars shouts. "She'd never do such a thing!"

"But isn't Fran, shall we say, rather hard-hearted?"

"I don't get it, Em', are you really accusing her? Us?"

I pause, aware of the upturned faces, before shaking my head. "No, I'm not accusing anybody just yet. I'm just taking you through the sequence of events and considering what may or may not have happened. What was possible and what wasn't. Mrs Willoughby. You were over twenty minutes late for the eleven o'clock Monday morning meeting, were you not?"

She jumps. "I beg your pardon?"

I repeat my question.

"I was busy taking down those vile posters that had been put up all over the village."

"Vile posters that were proved to contain the truth," Mary says.

The blood drains from Mrs Willoughby's face. "Yes, I still can't quite believe it."

"You were very close to the vicar, Mrs Willoughby. Is that true?" I ask her.

She nods. "All those nasty rumours…"

"You loved him, didn't you?"

Mrs Willoughby doesn't answer, but it's obvious from her expression she was very much in love with the man. "I would've done anything for him. Anything."

"And you did, didn't you? You've already told me how many thousands of pounds you squandered on him—money given to his different charitable causes and for the church roof. Money that went straight into his pocket. But you knew that, didn't you?"

Mrs Willoughby sags. "He promised he'd stop the gambling and the drinking, but it only got worse."

"You knew about him?" Dorothy Knight says with spite. "You knew what he was like, and you still gave him your money? You must've loved him."

"I thought he loved me back," Mrs Willoughby replies, her voice nothing more than a whisper. "He told me we could never be together. Me as a widow and he as an unhappily married man whose wife was too unwell to fulfil her… *wifely duties*. I never pushed him. We never did anything untoward. But I thought we had an understanding. A special love. But when I found out about his philandering…?"

"You murdered him?"

"No. I didn't kill him… I loved him, I…" her words are consumed by a long coughing fit.

I wait until she regains her composure to ask her a very

delicate question. "Mrs Willoughby, isn't it true that your cough is more than a simple summer cold?"

"It is."

"Tell me, how long do you have left to live?"

"I say," Ceddars interjects, "that's private information. You can't go sharing that kind of thing in public like this, and besides, how did you find out? I didn't even know that."

I wave Ceddars outburst away with a single hand. "How long, Mrs Willoughby?"

The large woman shrugs. "I won't last the summer... I gave the best years of my life to that man and for what? For him to run around with a host of other woman, rearing god knows what unfortunates in his wake!"

Inspector Troughton sits up, suddenly interested. "I beg your pardon, are you admitting to killing him, to killing the vicar?"

Mrs Willoughby recovers her composure and stares daggers at the inspector. "And curse my immortal soul? No! I did not kill him. I loved him, for better or for worse. I've kept it secret for so long, but now, as I reach my end... what does it matter?"

"Did the vicar know of this? That you were dying?"

"I didn't tell him. But he knew. He always could see right through me."

"But the fact remains, you are a wronged woman, are you not, Mrs Willoughby?" I ask her.

The large woman doesn't answer.

"You gave the vicar thousands of pounds, and he betrayed you. And instead of giving you the comfort you thought you deserved after so many years of devotion, he side-lined you, did he not?"

Mrs Willoughby's face creases with anger. "Yes, he did. In preference to her, to Mrs Knight. She had a hold on him, I'm sure of it. Why else would he insult me by taking away my village responsibilities. She's just a lackey. A factory worker who came into money. She's got no class. Nothing!"

"And with nothing to live for, you lost your temper, and murdered the vicar. Am I right? Is that why you were late for the meeting?"

She shakes her head vehemently, tears running down her face to pool at her jowls. "No. I loved him. I'd never hurt him."

"I don't understand," Troughton says to me. "What are you doing here? I thought you were revealing the murderer. So far it seems like you have no idea and are trying your best to get a confession."

"I'm taking you all through the sequence of events and suspects that cropped up along the way. Which means… you're next."

"Me? What on earth are you on about woman? I'm an inspector in his majesty's police force. You cannot possibly suspect me."

"Why not? You also arrived suspiciously quickly after the murder and studiously refused to examine either the body or the crime scene. You've made snap decisions based on very little evidence, giving me the impression you are somewhat of a clod."

Constable Jakes chuckles and immediately covers his mouth.

"How dare you!" Troughton shouts. "Mrs Smallsey, you can't let her speak to me this way. Please may I be excused?"

Mary shakes her head. "Let's hear what she has to say."

Troughton sits back, his face a mask of thunder.

"But you're not a clod," I begin. "It's your social station that is the issue here. Which is why I talked to Ethel, who was most informative on the matter. Isn't that right?"

Ethel nods.

"She was privy to a few conversations you've had with your superintendent in London. He wanted this case closed and closed quickly. The reason, the Reverend Wilson-Smallsey was an embarrassment to the clergy. More pointedly to the bishop who is the brother of the superintendent. They promised you a promotion if you solved the case quickly, and you are so very ambitious."

Troughton gives Ethel an evil stare. "I will make it my personal duty to get you removed from the exchange as soon as possible. This is outrageous!"

"But you're not saying it's untrue, are you, inspector?"

He begrudgingly shakes his head.

"And I believe Ethel has already handed in her cards. She won't be eavesdropping on any more conversations anytime soon. I made sure of that."

Ethel hangs her head in shame.

"I was perplexed by you, inspector. For a time, I was wondering if the vicar was blackmailing you as well. You were also one of my suspects. But at least we can cross you off."

I turn my attention back to the group of gripped faces. "After Sheng was released from jail, Eriksen himself was shot and killed by the same crossbow. And this is where the mystery deepened. Eriksen was only grazed by the bolt, but he died anyway. The reason? The crossbow bolts were tipped with deadly poison. My assumption that the killer was a marksman was incorrect. Instead, I came to believe that the death of the vicar by a shot to the heart was a lucky mischance and that instead, the murderer was relying on the poisoned bolts to kill their victims. It put me off the real culprit for quite a while because no real skill was needed to murder in this way. Quite simply, I was stumped. It could've been anybody.

"Also, this second murder made no sense to me. There were plenty of motives for the murder of Wilson-Smallsey, but none that I could see for William Eriksen. Why was he killed? Unless... *he wasn't supposed to die.*"

"What on earth are you on about, Em'?" Ceddars says.

"Eriksen was murdered, wasn't he? There's no two ways about it."

"But consider this, my dear Ceddars. What if the murderer didn't know the crossbow bolts were poisoned?"

Troughton chuckles. "I'm sorry to agree with the doctor. Miss Crookshanks. But you're talking nonsense. This has gone on long enough."

"You're both missing the point. If the killer wasn't aware the crossbow bolts were poisoned, then, both shots must've been taken by a marksman. One shot through the heart to kill the vicar, the other to graze William Eriksen's leg, to remove any suspicion from him."

Troughton shakes his head. "Will this be another one of your far-fetched theories?"

"Let me backtrack. In this room we have three excellent marksmen. Ceddars, from his piloting days, Mary, who won many awards for archery, and Mrs Dorothy Knight who tested sniper rifles during the war."

"Hey, I may have been a whizz in a dogfight," Ceddars says, "but, as I told you, I never used my pistol. And you simply can't accuse Mary! That's bang out of order."

"Oh, I think I can. She was always very high on my list of suspects."

Mary's face turns to one of alarm. "What? You promised that—"

"I won't reveal your secrets. I gave you my word, and I will keep it, but I won't pretend to those assembled here that you are nothing but a very healthy woman. You knew what your husband was from early on and chose a life of supposed infirmity to keep you away from him and his associates. No one will blame you for that. But it does also mean you had the motive and the ability to kill your husband."

Mary's pinched face speaks volumes. "I've not picked up a bow and arrow in over twenty years. This is nonsense."

"I agree," Dorothy Knight says. "I'm also no marksman.

I told Miss Crookshanks that. I never fired those rifles. They were all tested by men. They wouldn't let us women near them."

I take a deep breath and address Dorothy Knight who sits clutching her son, Eugene protectively. "And that is the one lie that this case rests upon." I produce the folded sheet of newspaper that I snipped from the library and walk over to her, holding it out. "Do you recognise this?"

She pushes herself to the edge of her chair, takes out her pince nez and squints at the newspaper through the thick lenses, a chubby hand abruptly snatching at it, but I pull it away.

I turn to the many expectant faces. "This is a newspaper clipping, the duplicate of which, I found in Curate Simmons' cellar. Unfortunately, it burned before I could rescue it, but fortunately, I remembered the date. It wasn't hard to track this down."

"I say, Em'?" Ceddars says. "Is that what you wouldn't show me earlier?"

I go back to the doorway and hand it to him. "Why don't you read it out?"

Ceddars obliges. "It's dated august 1917. *Southend Sharpshooters Helping Our Boys Win The War!*"

With sons and husbands all away fighting for King and Country, the women snipers of Southend are doing their bit to help us win the war, from stock and barrel manufacture to sight calibration and yes, even sharpshooting! And what crack shots some of them have turned out to be. And they need to be to get those rifles tip top and ready for our boys to use in action. Hats off to the ladies! There's a photograph captioned with, *Mrs Dorothy Knight and her girls on the firing range.*" Ceddars holds up the clipping for everyone to see.

I turn to Dorothy. "You lied to me twice about this."

She shrugs. "What if I did? I'm a lady now. Testing sniper rifles? Such a thing is below my new station here in Little

Pucklewick. I was embarrassed about it. And why shouldn't a lady lie to protect her reputation. There's nothing wrong in that. I can't see how this is remotely important."

"You can't? Earlier in my investigation I told my misplaced theory about Eriksen to only two people. Doctor Roberts and Inspector Troughton. I explained my theory about William Eriksen directly to Ceddars, directly under the open window of your shop and you must've been listening. And in an attempt to prove Eriksen's innocence, you shot him with a glancing blow. Nothing more than a scrape. The shot of a marksman. I can't imagine what you must've gone through after you realised your mistake. You were so very upset at his subsequent death, as evidenced by your breakdown in the police station when you discovered what you had done. There was no doubt your grief was real and heartfelt. You, like the doctor, missed one simple piece of information about the stolen crossbow bolts. They were coated with deadly poison. In an attempt to exonerate the man you loved, you inadvertently killed him.

"But this isn't supposition. I went back to those abandoned cottages opposite the police station and examined where you fired from. The shot was particularly difficult, requiring timing and accuracy."

Dorothy shakes her head and takes out her pince nez. "Have you not seen these? I can hardly see anything in front of my face, never mind fire a crossbow."

"You are short-sighted, as are many people. But, you could see well enough to follow me into the curate's house and hit me over the head. As for your long sight, you proved to me that it was excellent the first time I met you here, in the vicarage yesterday."

"I certainly did not!"

"You said to me, *I heard Charlotte let Mrs Willoughby in and poked my head out of the sitting room door. I noticed the clock. It was twenty past the hour.* Even I had difficulty telling the time from that distance. I checked again this morning on my arrival. It would take someone with excellent distance vision to read that clockface."

"Poppycock!"

"But that is not my only evidence. If you remember, a short while ago, I supposedly showed you one of the posters that had been put up around the village. You noticed, straightaway it was not the poster, but something else. There is nothing wrong with your long vision. Nothing at all. As witnessed by everyone in this room."

All faces stare at Dorothy Knight. "You think you are so very clever, Miss Crookshanks," she spits, "but you are missing one important thing… I had no motive to kill the vicar. None at all."

"That is where you are sadly wrong, *Mrs Knight*, although that's not quite correct is it?"

"What do you mean?"

"I mean your name isn't Mrs Knight. I have no idea what your maiden name was and still is, but you were never married."

An audible gasp passes through the room.

"I won't sit here and be talked to like this. Of course, I was married. To Mr Knight. I loved him. Everybody knows that."

I shake my head. "You had Eugene out of wedlock. He is the illegitimate son of the Reverend Wilson-Smallsey. You were blackmailing the vicar, were you not? After you tracked him down to Little Pucklewick. The sum of money you say you 'came into', actually came from him didn't it? Most likely via Mrs Willoughby. In fact, I believe he was regularly paying you money given to him from that source."

"Albert was giving this vile woman… my money?" Mrs Willoughby shouts, descending into a fit of coughing.

"I'm afraid so. And when Dorothy Knight told him her intention of marrying his enemy, William Eriksen, he forbade it. Threatening to expose you for what you are… an *unmarried mother*."

Dorothy Knight stands to her feet, her face red with anger. "How dare you call my son a bastard! How very dare you! He looks nothing like Albert!"

I turn to Eugene. "I'm sorry, young man. None of this is your fault, but you deserve to know the truth."

"This is nonsense, supposition! You can't prove any of it!"

"But I do have the proof. And for that, I have Ceddars to thank. Without him, I would never have found your motive. In that respect, he helped me greatly."

"I did, old girl? I mean Em', Miss Crookshanks."

"You asked Dorothy Knight about her husband, Thomas, did you not? When we met in her shop. I remember thinking your question was an irrelevance. But she told you that she and her young husband eloped to Gretna Green. As you are all no doubt aware, Gretna Green is a small parish on the border between Scotland and England. The Scottish laws allow those who are under twenty-one to marry. It is a tiny parish, and all marriages, no matter how informal, are recorded. There is no such record of a Mr Thomas Knight's nuptials between seventeen and eighteen years ago. The vicar knew this because he was the father of your child. He gave you money, and a house and very possibly paid for you to set up your business, but he wouldn't let you marry William Eriksen. A man upon which all your hopes for the future rested. That is your motive for murdering him."

"And you can prove all this?" Troughton says.

"Yes, inspector."

"Constable Jakes, arrest Mrs Knight at once!"

Before the overweight constable can react, Dorothy reaches into her handbag and pulls out a poisoned bolt and runs towards me. "It was all your fault, you bitch! You're will die for making me kill William!"

There's no way I can dodge her, but at the last moment,

the slippered foot of Sheng whips past my ear, kicking Dorothy in the face, knocking her off her feet.

And it's then that I see the crossbow bolt sticking in her hand.

Scoundrels & Swans

AFTER the consternation caused by the unmasking of Dorothy Knight as the twin murderer, and her subsequent accidental death at her own hands, a very pleased Inspector Troughton took quick control, ushering everyone from the vicarage sitting room. The murder was solved to his satisfaction and his promotion seemingly in the bag. Ceddars was still persona non grata, but at least the wagging tongues of Little Pucklewick would be talking about something other than his indiscretions for the weeks to come…

We leave the vicarage through the north garden gate and on to the road that goes past my cottage. Ceddars is uncharacteristically quiet and I too, feel deflated. I was living for the mystery and now it is solved there is an emptiness. An emptiness I'm very keen to fill.

Ceddars turns to face me, his moustache twitching. "I don't get it Em'. Why put me and everyone else through the wringer like that if you knew all along that Dorothy Knight was guilty? It wasn't very pleasant, old girl, not pleasant at all. You had me believing Fran had bally done it at one point. I was even doubting myself…"

"My dear Ceddars, my job as a sleuth is not to just solve the mystery, it is to also entertain. To get everyone on the edge of their seats. To get them suspecting each other."

"Well, that certainly worked. But I'm not happy about it. Not at all. You bally well insisted I stand at your side, and for what? To confuse and humiliate me? I suppose I deserve it. I've acted like a bally fool."

"Of course not, Ceddars. I needed you to corroborate Simmons' time of death. And besides, you were crucial in solving the mystery, were you not?"

"I suppose I was, what? But may I ask, when did you have the time to go through the marriage records of Gretna Green? Did you get someone else to do it for you?"

"That? Oh, I was bluffing."

"You were? Bloody hell!"

"Dorothy Knight, or whoever she really was, lied about her marksmanship at every opportunity in an attempt to throw me off course. Once I realised that the murderer was indeed a sharpshooter, she became my prime suspect. Everything fell into place except her motive. Why would Dorothy Knight kill the vicar? Because he had something on her. It was then that I looked more closely at Eugene."

"The poor blighter has been put through the wringer in the last two days, that for sure. Although I was pleased to hear that Mary is taking the lad in. I was surprised to find out he was another of the vicar's illegitimate children. Very surprised."

"Yes. He will be very handsome when he grows up some, but he's nothing like his father. His blond hair for instance and his striking similarity to his mother. It wasn't obvious that he was the vicar's son. But hereditary doesn't always work like that. So... *I gambled.* I have absolutely no idea what records they keep in Gretna Green. They can't be that extensive, especially as even the local blacksmiths can apparently marry a couple by simply striking a hammer against an anvil. I gambled Dorothy Knight would be fooled into making an admission, which she did. Somewhat dramatically."

"You didn't gamble, Em', you *lied.*"

"It worked, didn't it?"

"My God, Em'! This sleuthing business is dreadfully complicated and somewhat cut-throat, what? I have a new respect for you folk, that's for sure."

"As I told you before… it takes someone to think and act like a murderer, to catch a murderer."

"Indeed. At least, I was of some help, even if for most of the time I was pretty damn useless."

"I wouldn't say that. You were instrumental in solving the mystery. And I liked having you around."

"You did? Even though I've been proved to be somewhat of a thoroughly rum cove, a cad, and a liar—a scoundrel who creeps in and out of ladies' beds? I think you're better off without me. And besides, I'm leaving. Probably abroad. I'll never live this affair down, that's for sure. Which means, well, this is goodbye." He steps back and formally offers me his hand.

"But you still have time for one more trip in the Bugatti, surely?"

"I do? Where to?"

"The Black Swan."

"I'm sorry… what?"

"I've had time to think things through, Ceddars, and I've come to conclusion that I fundamentally disagree with you about something. Something very important."

Ceddars looks crestfallen. "You do? About what?"

I lift up my eyes and stare deeply into his. "Remember the Barrington-Stewarts?"

"Yes, of course. What are you getting at?"

"I believe they are just the kind of couple who get up to hanky-panky. Shall we go and find out?"

Ceddars beams, his moustache twitching magnificently. "Oh, Em'!"

I pull him towards me, and we kiss for long, delicious moments."

"I say!"

The *END*…

…I clutch Ceddars closely to me, abruptly aware that he's becoming insubstantial. Falling apart, falling away. I pull back in alarm. He's nothing more than a rapidly collapsing pile of blackened cinders. He slips through my fingers, his ashes disintegrating into nothingness on a suddenly dead air. Everything is collapsing around me. The road and walls. The church and vicarage. My cottage and its once green garden. Even the trees of Dooleys Wood and the sky above.

"I look down at myself. My clothes are also fragmenting, dropping away from me, revealing blue…

My jeans!

And then it all comes back to me.

I'm not Emily Crookshanks, I'm a witchweaver on the run. Forced to hide myself from my enemies and their dreaded bloodseeker. Searching for any hiding place. Weaving a desperate spell that put me in Little Pucklewick… inside Emily's story.

And yet the bloodseeker still found me! The monster chased me down into the mystery to attack me, using the residue of my majiks, of my weavery, like a beacon. I wasn't fast enough.

By all rights, I should be dead. Bloodseekers are summoned from the dark dimensions. They are indestructible and unstoppable. And yet, I was able to not only defend myself, but to destroy it.

But how?

The weird unpredictability of my weaving, of my spell, I guess. And Emily, the hero of the story. The protagonist. She must endure to the end. That's how stories work. Emily must overcome all obstacles to reveal the bad guys. It was this that helped me destroy the monster, I know it. She gave me the extra strength I needed. We did it together! Emily and I! Commingled. And I can still sense her, somewhere at the back of my mind.

I'm elated, yet I'm still in danger. The Land Rover is outside. I need to escape the spell and fast. I reached the story's end, so the spell should release me… shouldn't it? But where am I? I'm not exactly surrounded by blackness, but by an 'emptiness'. By a 'nothing'. I may have weaved my spell in haste, but all spells must have an endpoint, otherwise they cannot be created.

Then, far in the distance, I see what appear to be a series of words. They slowly become larger as I watch, until I can read them…

Oh no!

If you enjoyed the adventures
of Emily Crookshanks. Then read
on and enjoy the second book of
this series' compilation.

Epilogue: The Steamship Anubus

"**E**M'! Emily, you sleepy head, time to wake up. We were very busy last night. Did I tire you out, what?"

I open my eyes to find myself lying in a cramped bed in a small hot room. The air is full of heat and heavy with moisture. Portholes tell me I'm on a cabin on a ship of some sort. Ceddars leans over me, a smile on his face. "There she is. It's almost time for breakfast and we don't want to be late."

"Where… where am I?"

"What, my darling? We're on our honeymoon of course. A cruise down the Nile. You so wanted to visit Egypt and here we are. And I have to say, it's bally hot, what?"

I jump naked out of the bed, and stare through the portal at a shoreline dominated by vast pyramids rising into a bright, blue, sun-filled sky, my head swimming with half-remembered memories of wanting to escape, of fleeing.

"You alright, Em'?"

"I think I must've had a bad dream."

He grabs me from behind, his large rough hands encircling my waist, pulling me towards him and spinning me around. "I can certainly take your mind off that!"

I look into his handsome eyes and hear a pop.

"Sounds like they've opened the champagne early, what?" Ceddars says, his moustache twitching.

"No, Ceddars, that's not a champagne cork, that's unmistakably a Smith and Western Colt revolver."

"Crikey! Oh Em', you certainly are the real beans. Shall we go and investigate, what?"

Reviews

If you enjoyed reading *Tea, Cake & Murder!*, can I ask you to please give it a star rating and, if you have the time, to write a review? It really makes a difference, and I always value a good honest critique.

I will retweet links to reviews to my social media followers - and possibly include them as quotes in publicity releases.

Over to you…

Many thanks in advance!

Kev

Acknowledgements

Thanks for the red pen, scribbling and 'telling me off in no uncertain terms' talents of my lovely editor:

Suzanne Heritage

And my beta readers:

Deanne Charlton
Stuart Morgan

Links - Get to know me!

Linktree

All my latest social links (Threads, Mastodon, Insta, Twitter/X, etc.), my online store homepages & my up-to-date book list, all in one easy place.
https://linktr.ee/kjheritage

Join K.J.Heritage's Newsletter

Sign up and get a free novel of my short stories: *The Lady in the Glass* and an inside track on all future releases, access to early reading copies (ARCs), sneak previews, and more.
http://kjheritage.com/join

K.J.Heritage Facebook Group: *Mostly Readers*

Fun chat and posts about reading… mostly (well not at all to be honest. Just mostly a lot of daft stuff). Request to join and myself or a moderator will approve you.
https://www.facebook.com/groups/mostlyreaders

Website

http://kjheritage.co.uk/

Email:

Want to get in touch? Well here's your chance
contact@kjheritage.com.

Also by *K.J.Heritage*

Paranormal Mystery

The Peculiar Case of the Missing Mondrian
Tea, Cake & MURDER!

Mystery Sci-fi

Shattered Helix *(Vatic #1)*
Shattered Web *(Vatic #2)*
Blue Into The Rip
Quick-Kill & The Galactic Secret Service
The Lady In The Glass - 12 Tales Of Death & Dying

Sci-Fi Compilations

Once Upon A Time In Gravity City
Chronicle Worlds: Legacy Fleet
From The Indie Side

Contemporary mystery

Dying Is Easy

Fantasy

The Scowl
The Iron Savant *(writing as Heritage Adams)*

Non-Fiction

All About Editing: *55 Easy edits to improve your writing skills forever*
All About Character Flaws: *Making your characters miserable & rewarding your readers forever!*
3000 Writing & Plot Prompts A-C: *Supercharge Your Creativity & Improve Your Writing Forever!*

Online stores

Find all ebooks, paperbacks, hardbacks & audiobooks
by *K.J.Heritage* at the following stores:

Amazon & Audible, Apple, KOBO, Barnes & Noble/
Nook, Google, Smashwords & more.

About *K.J.Heritage*

"K.J.Heritage's uncanny sense of pacing and story puts him at the forefront of today's speculative fiction writers."
Samuel Peralta, Amazon bestselling author and creator of The Future Chronicles

When K.J.Heritage isn't penning third-person descriptions about himself, he's an international bestselling author writing the books he likes to read. From military/action science fiction and adventure to contemporary mysteries, crime thrillers, comedy, and paranormal fantasy. He should really stick to one genre, but he's not that kind of writer... or reader.

His first short story, *Escaping the Cradle* was runner-up in the 2005 Clarke-Bradbury International Science Fiction Competition. His other short stories have appeared in several anthologies with such self-publishing sci-fi luminaries as Hugh Howey and Samuel Peralta.

K.J.Heritage's short story, *Churchill's Rock*, part of the *Chronicle Worlds: Legacy Fleet anthology*, will be aboard the Astrobotic's Peregrine Lunar Lander set for launch on the United Launch Alliance's Vulcan Centaur rocket platform bound for the surface of the moon in 2024.

K.J.Heritage has worked all the requisite 'writer jobs' such as driver's mate, factory gateman, barman, labourer, telesales operative, sales assistant, warehouseman, IT contractor, Student Union President, university IT helpdesk guy, British Rail signal software designer, Premiership football website designer, gigging musician, company director, graphic designer, stand-up comedian, sound engineer, improv artist, magazine editor and web journo... Although he doesn't like to talk about it. *Mostly... Maybe a little bit.*

He was born in the UK in one of the more interesting previous centuries. Originally from Derbyshire, he now lives in the seaside town of Brighton. He is a tea drinker, avid Twitterer, and neurodiverse (ASD) human being.

All the very best,

K.J.Heritage